ALSO BY PATIENCE GRIFFIN

∽

Sweet Home, Alaska Series

One Snowy Night
Once Upon a Cabin

Kilts and Quilts Series

To Scotland with Love
Meet Me in Scotland
Some Like It Scottish
The Accidental Scot
The Trouble with Scotland
It Happened in Scotland
The Laird and I
Blame It on Scotland
Kilt in Scotland

Happily Ever Alaska

Patience Griffin

BERKLEY ROMANCE
New York

BERKLEY ROMANCE
Published by Berkley
An imprint of Penguin Random House LLC
penguinrandomhouse.com

Copyright © 2023 by Patience Jackson
Excerpt from *One Snowy Night* copyright © 2021 by Patience Jackson
Penguin Random House supports copyright. Copyright fuels creativity, encourages
diverse voices, promotes free speech, and creates a vibrant culture. Thank you for buying
an authorized edition of this book and for complying with copyright laws by not
reproducing, scanning, or distributing any part of it in any form without permission.
You are supporting writers and allowing Penguin Random House to continue to
publish books for every reader.

BERKLEY and the BERKLEY & B colophon are
registered trademarks of Penguin Random House LLC.

ISBN: 9780593101513

First Edition: December 2023

Printed in the United States of America
1 3 5 7 9 10 8 6 4 2

Book design by Alison Cnockaert

For DRNCL,

part of our found family. *Thanks for taking care of us.*

Chapter 1

LOLLY CROCKER STEPPED outside to get her mail, glad for the warmer days of July and to be free of a jacket. A group of her home ec students would arrive any minute at her humble abode on the cheap side of Sweet Home, Alaska, population 573. Over summer break, Lolly was giving baking lessons based on *The Great British Baking Show*, a favorite binge for both her and the girls, who were in her class at Sweet Home High. Today's bake was macarons, a treat that Lolly loved. Which was perfect—it was her thirty-fourth birthday. She'd returned to her hometown around this time last year to take a position teaching family and consumer science, but since the end of school, she'd basically been holding her breath. Rumor had it that noncore subjects like hers might be cut from the curriculum in the fall. But as each day passed and the new school year drew nearer, she felt more confident. No teachers had been laid off, according to the grapevine, which was more accurate than the *Nightly News*. And yet, Lolly couldn't breathe easy until the district sent her a new contract. Hers must've fallen through the cracks. On Monday, she planned to call and find out what the holdup was. The first day of school was in one month and four days. Surely her missing contract was just an oversight.

As she reached for the mailbox handle, a blue Ford pickup pulled in beside her. Newlyweds Jesse and Tori Montana grinned at her as they disembarked.

"Hey, Lolly." Tori gave her a hug with a gift bag in hand.

"How is your *staycay*-honeymoon going?" But Lolly needn't have asked. They both seemed to be floating on air.

"We've made progress on our new home," Jesse said, "and when Shaun gets back, it'll go much quicker." But as soon as he said it, he seemed to regret bringing up his brother.

Probably because he'd seen Lolly blanch.

Shaun Montana was Lolly's one regret in a long line of breakups. She had quite the record of dating good guys and then cutting them loose. A couple of times—*okay, three*—she'd even been engaged: Howard from Missouri, whom she'd met her senior year of college; Ted the history teacher, who taught at the same high school in Oregon as she had; and Frank, who owned three dry cleaners, all three men whom she'd met when she lived outside of Alaska. Each time, after she got engaged, when her stomach started hurting, she knew without a doubt that Mr. Right This Time hadn't really been right after all, and she broke it off. Her only consolation was that all three of her ex-fiancés had married soon afterward, started families, and had their happily-ever-afters, in spite of her.

But the story of Shaun had gone differently. They'd never been engaged, but Lolly had been convinced that they'd had a love for the ages.

Lolly looked up into Jesse's face and realized the air surrounding them was fraught with awkwardness. "Sorry? What did you say?"

Looking embarrassed, Tori held out the gift bag. "No worries. I brought you a present."

Lolly accepted the bag, though she wasn't sure what was going on. "Present?" What she really wanted to ask was

When is Shaun going to be back in town? Lolly had seen him at their wedding but only from a distance, as if he was trying to stay away from her on purpose. And then suddenly, he'd been gone. No one had said when he was coming back.

Jesse came around from his side of the truck with their labradoodle, Scout, following him. "You did an amazing job on our wedding cake. You really made the log cabin come to life, not to mention the miniature of Scout. We wanted to thank you."

Lolly reached down to pet Scout, a good friend and playmate to her own Bichonpoo, Thor, who right now was in her fenced backyard. "No need to thank me. The cake was my present to you." She smiled at the two of them. "Really *I* should be thanking *you*. I love baking but I seldom get the opportunity to use my decorating skills, especially on a cake of that magnitude . . . and McKenna's cake, of course, too." Tori and her sister had had a huge double wedding, with people coming from all over. McKenna and Luke's cake was shaped like the Alaska map, with the town of Sweet Home in 3D on top.

"Go ahead and open your present." Tori seemed excited, so Lolly reached in and pulled out the gift: an adorable reversible apron—one side masculine, in a print of rustic wood and animals, and the other side a pieced, colorful Christmas tree design with forget-me-nots and fireweed making the other colors pop. "Thanks, I love it! You know how crazy I am about flowers."

"It was Jesse's idea to make it reversible."

"Guys like to cook, too, you know," he put in.

"Well, I'm honored that you would gift me with an original Alaska Chic design," Lolly gushed. Tori's new clothing company was all people were talking about in town these days. "Are you going to make a whole line of kitchen products, like potholders, dish towels, and coasters?"

"I never even thought about it," Tori said, "but I'm sure if McKenna got wind of your idea, she'd say, *'Absolutely!'*"

Lolly held the apron to her chest as if to model it. "I'll treasure this forever." What a nice, unexpected birthday gift.

"Oh, before I forget," Tori added, "Piney said to tell you that we're all supposed to meet at the lodge at seven for an impromptu meeting of the Sisterhood of the Quilt."

Lolly shot her a suspicious look. Their quilting group had a standing date to sew together the first Saturday of every month. Yes, they gathered at other times, usually to make a comfort quilt, and sometimes for celebrations, but . . . "What's the reason for tonight's meeting?"

Tori winked at her. "No reason. No reason at all. But Piney did want you to whip up one of your special cakes and bring it with you. You know, the one with the three layers—yellow, pistachio, and chocolate?"

Lolly shook her head. So Piney wanted Lolly to make her *own* birthday cake for the surprise party they might or might not be throwing for her. "Sure. I have all the ingredients." She'd been planning to make a small version for herself anyway. "Is there anything else that Piney needs me to bring?"

"Do you have extra birthday candles? Piney said she didn't have enough at the store."

Lolly laughed. "I'll see what I can dig up."

Jesse laughed, too. "Don't you just love living in Sweet Home?"

"I wouldn't want to be anywhere else," Lolly answered honestly.

Tori gave her another hug. "See you tonight."

"See you tonight." Lolly waved as they pulled away. She'd nearly forgotten why she was standing by the road, but now she opened the mailbox and pulled everything out. The first envelope held a birthday card from her best friend, Paige, who was in Denver teaching a series of workshops for various quilt guilds. The second bore the return address of the school district. *Finally*, she thought. But it seemed too thin to be her contract.

She slipped her finger under the flap, tore open the top, and pulled out the letter and read:

We regret to inform you that we will not be renewing your contract for the upcoming school year.

Lolly looked around as though someone might be watching and know her shame. The school she loved so much didn't love her back enough to have her for a second year. She read the note again, this time to the end. Budget cuts, nothing to do with her, blah blah blah. But still . . .

What was she going to do? The Sisterhood of the Quilt would tell her to take her problems to God; He could fix anything. But the truth was that Lolly had coasted by on her own, not bothering Him with any requests for a long, long time. It felt rude to come rushing back to the Big Guy Upstairs for help now. Maybe she should've done a better job of checking in with Him while things had been going well.

She wanted to call Paige and grumble about her bad luck, but Lolly's students were going to be here any minute.

She frowned at the cottage she shared with her sister. Jilly, a traveling nurse, was gone most of the time and had been thrilled when Lolly moved home to do all the cooking and split the rent. But how could Lolly do her part when she wouldn't have a paycheck come August first?

"So much for being excited about being back home," Lolly muttered to herself. It was very late—*in fact, too late*—to find a job for this school year, but she'd have to try anyway.

Then reality set in.

She'd have to move.

She'd have to come up with first and last month's rent and a pet deposit for Thor.

She'd have to leave Sweet Home, when she'd only just gotten back a year ago.

As she started to head inside, sixteen-year-old Ella Stone

pulled up right on time in her dark blue Subaru Outback filled with her friends—Lacy, Uki, Ruthie, and Annette. They scrambled out of the vehicle with loads of enthusiasm, but then Ella stopped short.

"Is everything all right, Ms. Crocker?"

Lolly dug deep and produced a smile. "Yes, all good. Thor has been waiting for you. He's in the back. Do you mind letting him in and taking off his protective jacket? I'll be just a minute."

"No problem." The girls laughed and hurried inside, leaving Lolly a moment to pull herself together. She wished she had time to think things through, but the girls and macarons were waiting. Lolly tamped down the sadness and disappointment and went to her front door, feeling like she'd mastered her emotions. Then she reached for the doorknob, and—

Oh, crud. I have to face the Sisterhood of the Quilt tonight. Maybe between now and then, she could pull herself together. Actually, she'd need to brace herself for the advice they surely would bombard her with.

In the kitchen, Uki, Annette, and Ruthie were busy digging through the cabinets and setting out bowls and measuring cups while Ella and Lacy sat in the window seat. Ella had Thor in her lap and Lacy held the recipe card, but she wasn't reading off the ingredients. Instead, Lacy wrapped an arm around her best friend's shoulders while Ella complained.

"I can't believe Mom wants to have a baby!" she whined. "At her age!"

Her comment struck a chord with Lolly, who was a year younger than Ella's mother, Hope. Lolly always assumed she'd have a husband and kids by now. If only she'd been able to follow through with at least one of the engagements, then maybe she'd have a couple of kiddos to call her own.

Lacy squeezed Ella. "C'mon. She's not pregnant, is she?"

"No. I just heard her talking to Dad about having a baby."

"If they do," Lacy said, "they won't forget you."

Ella hung her head, which told Lolly that Lacy had pinpointed the problem. Lolly knew this feeling all too well. She'd felt the same way when her little sister, Jilly, was born, when Lolly was ten. Ella was going on seventeen, a rough age. Happily for Lolly, she and Jilly were always good friends despite having opposite personalities. And though Lolly occasionally nagged her wild-child sister, they were super close now that they were adults.

But Lolly would hold off giving advice. She knew it was important, as the adult in charge, to be invisible and let the girls talk this over among themselves.

"Having a little sister or brother is cool," Uki piped in. "They look up to you and think you know everything. I bet you'll like it."

"Except when it's time to change poopy diapers." Ruthie screwed up her face as if she'd had experience with little ones.

"The crying all night can be annoying, too." Annette had a nephew who was two or so. She glanced over as if just noticing Lolly was in the kitchen. "What should we do first?"

"It looks like you've made a good start. The ingredients are in the pantry, as you know. I thought we might cowork in the space today. While you work on the macarons, I need to make a cake for the Sisterhood of the Quilt."

Uki smiled broadly. "Yeah, we heard about the cake you need to bake today. Happy birthday, Ms. Crocker." The other girls joined in with their best wishes, too.

Their sweetness really lifted Lolly's spirits. As did the sweets they were making. Somehow, sifting flour, mixing batter, and pulling baked goods from the oven was the best therapy, always making life more enjoyable. And in this case, perhaps, bearable. Once again Lolly wondered what her life might've looked like right now if she'd gone against her mother's wishes and opened a bakery after graduation, one of several dreams she'd let go of long ago.

"What would you like for your birthday?" Ella asked.

To have my job back. But of course Lolly kept that sentiment to herself. "How about some help chopping up the pistachios that are in the freezer? And to be honest, eating the yummy macarons you're baking will make my birthday brighter."

"We're on it." Ruthie went to the freezer.

They spent the next couple of hours chopping, stirring, and beating. Baking seemed to make even Ella forget her troubles and helped Lolly ignore her uncertain future and lack of employment . . . well, mostly.

As the last batch of macarons came out of the oven, her cell phone rang. "Hey, Piney. What's up?"

"Do you have any of those chocolate chip oatmeal wonders in your freezer that you could share with the store?" Piney asked. "I forgot to turn on the oven again and my cookies won't be ready for the lunch crowd."

"I have several dozen." Lolly was beginning to wonder if Piney was being forgetful on purpose. This was the fourth time this month she'd asked at the last minute for baked goods for her Hungry Bear diner and grocery store.

"Can you run them up to me? I'm all alone at the store and can't get away."

Lolly glanced at the teenagers. "Sure. I'll be right there."

"You're a lifesaver," Piney said.

Lolly hung up and turned to her students. "Piney needs me to bring cookies to the Hungry Bear. Do you mind if I'm gone for a few minutes?"

"We've got it under control, Ms. C," Ruthie said, always so full of confidence.

"I know you do." Lolly went to the freezer and pulled out the containers that held three dozen of her favorite cookies—actually, one of many favorites. She didn't shove them in her Hungry Bear upcycled grocery bags right away but opened a container and pulled out a pancake-sized cookie for herself. *Delivery tax*, she thought. She'd worry about the calories later. The extra pounds she'd put on this last year were a nuisance, but she chalked them up to starting a new job. Still, she'd have to start paying attention soon. She couldn't eat anything and everything the way she had in her twenties. Today, though, this cookie was more than a craving; it was medicine. She needed it to help counteract the lousy news that had come in the mail. "Can you keep an eye on Thor? I should be back in about ten minutes."

Ella smiled at her and nodded. "Will do."

"Don't worry," Annette said. "We're on it."

Lolly hurried out the door with the bag looped over her shoulder. Normally, a good brisk walk to the Hungry Bear was rejuvenating. But this walk only gave her mind time to dwell on what she'd lost . . . her livelihood, and possibly her hometown, since she'd more than likely be forced to move. Not worrying if she cracked a tooth, she broke off a bite of the frozen cookie and hurried on to rescue Piney.

AS SHAUN MONTANA drove from the airport in Anchorage to Sweet Home, he kept checking his rearview mirror, as if his past were hot on his trail. He had been scheduled to leave Houston tomorrow, but when he got the chance to get out sooner, he took it. Too many bad memories in Texas.

He laughed to himself. *Yeah, like Sweet Home holds no bad memories at all.*

Well, in thirty more miles, he'd be home. Thirty more miles until he could put the last four years behind him.

Yes, he'd briefly returned for his brother's wedding, driving the forty-two hundred miles in his Jeep Cherokee, loaded down with all his worldly goods so he could get a jump on moving home. He'd had to immediately fly back to Houston to train yet another new person before leaving for good. After the training and handing off the final project yesterday, he caught an earlier flight back to Alaska and picked up his vehicle from long-term parking.

He told himself that leaving Houston early had nothing to do with hearing about Tanya's engagement to her ex-boyfriend. He didn't understand how he'd been so naïve. It had taken her *two years* to say yes to Shaun's proposal, then another year of dragging her feet. When he finally pushed to set a date, she said they were in two different places and she wanted to take a break. Now all of a sudden she was *marrying her ex*? Shaun usually only saw the good in people, but all signs pointed to the fact that Tanya had stepped out on him.

Maybe now you'll change your ways, huh? For someone who was supposedly smart—he was a software developer for the petroleum industry—he sure was dumb when it came to relationships. Shaun had fallen in love too many times. He'd just never done the casual thing, for which he blamed his parents; they'd had a real, lasting love until the day his father died. Shaun always assumed he'd have that, too: a partner to share everything with. His parents made it look easy. Yet the women he dated never seemed to want the same things he did—a home, family, and roots. The result? His heart had been trampled again and again.

The way he saw it, he could either sign up to become a monk or learn how *not* to get so attached to the opposite sex. He was still on the fence about which way to go.

In the meantime, he had plenty to do to keep him busy. He needed to get up to speed on what had to be done on Mom's homestead before Jesse and Tori left town to film the first season of HGTV's *Homestead Recovery*, for which Jesse was the show's host and homestead expert. Plus, Jesse needed help finishing his cabin, which should be a fun project for Shaun. This was all good. Shaun would be too busy to go into town often. He'd make sure of that. Town was where he might see Lolly Crocker, the first person to stomp on his heart. The last thing he needed was to run into her day in and day out. It was bad enough seeing her at Jesse's wedding.

Shaun hadn't been able to do anything but gawk at Lolly in her pew as he made his way down the aisle. She looked even more beautiful than when they dated in high school, and he'd had to work hard to keep from staring at her. But remembering how she'd coldheartedly broken up with him made it easier. Back then, Shaun had thought the two of them would be together forever. That he'd follow her to Oregon to go to college the next year after he graduated. That they were strong in their love. But, boy, was he wrong. After dumping him, she'd left him standing on her front porch while she went inside without a backward glance and turned off the porch light.

If only he'd been able to turn off his feelings for her as easily. And seeing her at the wedding made all those old emotions come flooding back. The anger, the feeling of betrayal . . . how stupid he felt for loving her more than she loved him.

Of course, in the end, Shaun really should be thanking Lolly. He didn't follow her to Oregon but instead went to far-off Texas for school. There, he found a new life, one without her. Only once had he asked his mom about Lolly, shortly after he graduated from college.

"She got her teaching certificate in Oregon and took a job there. She wasn't right for you, Shaun. It's for the best."

Once again, Shaun wondered why his mother hadn't warned him before the wedding that Lolly was back in Sweet Home. Or Jesse—although his older brother had already left home when the whole thing with Lolly went down and Jesse didn't really know how badly she had skewered Shaun's heart.

Shaun had given Lolly a wide berth at the wedding reception, which might have been a mistake. Maybe he should've walked right up to her and shown her that she meant nothing to him now but ancient history. That he never thought about her. That he never asked himself, *What if?*

But he hadn't, so he'd have to continue to keep his distance from her. Lolly was where it all started. She was where he'd gotten off track and the reason he kept repeating the same mistake in relationships over and over. Falling for the same type of woman—*heartless*. It was past time to learn from his mistakes. Stay away from Lolly-type women and from Lolly herself. This would be the only way he could move on and not repeat the past.

The population sign for Sweet Home appeared, along with the speed limit. He decelerated and pulled into town. Out of the corner of his eye, he caught movement as someone stepped into the road from between two SUVs. Shaun threw on the brakes and came to a screeching halt before hitting the woman, who wore an apron and hugged a grocery bag to her chest, the kind of grocery bag that was given out at the Hungry Bear. Was the woman holding a cookie in her other hand?

Without thinking, he jammed the SUV into park and jumped out. "Are you crazy? You could've been killed!"

"Sorry. Distracted." She bit her lip and brought her blueberry eyes up to meet his. That's when it registered whom he'd almost run over.

"It's good to see you, Shaun."

Chapter 2

LOLLY CRINGED AS the proverbial daggers shot from Shaun's eyes. The anger emanating from him surprised her. Shouldn't he have gotten over what she'd done to him long ago? All of her other old boyfriends had moved on to successful relationships. Why hadn't he? Of course, she would never forgive herself for *all* the breakups, especially the one with Shaun.

The decision to break up had been a complicated one, steeped in Lolly trying to do the right thing, plus trying to learn from her mother's mistakes. Since the day Lolly's dad abandoned them when Lolly was ten and Jilly was a newborn, how many times had Mom complained that there was no one to share the load? Then as the cherry on top, Mom added, "I went from helping my own mother with my brothers and sisters to having a family of my own. I saw my friends having fun, but I never did. I expect you and Jilly to do better than me. Your dad was my first boyfriend, and you see how that worked out. I should've known he wasn't the type to *stick*. I'm telling you now, Lolly. Date a lot; date them all. Just promise me that you'll live it up before you settle down."

For Lolly's whole life, these had been opposing forces.

On the one hand, she felt this sense of urgency to find some-one to *share the load*, and at the same time, she knew she was supposed to *have fun* before she married. When Lolly and Shaun had started dating in high school, she knew that she'd found him too soon. Her first boyfriend, her first love. Ending things with him had been hard, the hardest thing she'd ever done.

And now that Lolly was in her thirties, another of her mother's complaints haunted her. "It's too late for me to find someone new," Mom had said when Lolly turned thir-teen. "I'm too old and all the good men are gone." Well, that meant the clock had certainly run out for Lolly, as her mother was only thirty-one at the time . . . and Lolly was thirty-four today!

It wasn't that Candy Crocker hadn't liked Shaun—she'd loved him. "But you're too young to be so serious, Lolly," Mom had said. "Play the field. *Have fun.* You'll never get this chance again. If Shaun's the right one, he'll be there for you when you're ready."

But Lolly never really had all that much fun. And Shaun hadn't been waiting for her when she stopped by his house after coming home from college for the summer. He'd left for Texas and hadn't answered her many letters or phone calls.

It took a long time for Lolly to start dating again. But when she did, she was resolved to get over Shaun. Though she was determined to find someone, she never ended up feeling as serious about the boy as he felt toward her. Mom had also told Lolly to *Trust your gut*, and invariably, Lolly's stomach would start hurting when the guy decided that he wanted a permanent relationship. She'd ignored her upset stomach the three times she'd said yes to proposals. But inevitably, her stomach would win, and she would break it off with her latest beau. She wondered if it was retribution for ending things with Shaun so badly. It was funny, though, that when she'd been with Shaun, Lolly's stomach never ached at all, like it did with the others after him. It had nearly killed her to tell him that she had to break up with him before she headed off to college. A memory that would haunt her forever.

"Forget the niceties, Lolly," Shaun said, bringing her out of the past and back to his hard gaze. "I'm not interested in small talk. We're not going to be friends."

It felt like he'd slammed a door in her face. A double whammy. First, she'd lost her job, and now she couldn't help but feel the pain of losing Shaun all over again. Finding out so blatantly he hadn't forgiven her was almost unbearable. Their time together had been the best of her life, and being with him had been the most wonderful thing to ever happen to her. She had always wondered if they might get back together . . . ?

Seeing the anger in his eyes, the answer was clear. An emphatic *No!*

He wasn't the Shaun she'd dated back in the day. Of course, he wasn't a boy anymore but a man. He dressed like a man, too, in a crisp polo, dark jeans, and new cowboy boots, too. His features were hardened, his life chiseled into his face. No smile for her like he'd had in high school. Actually, it looked as if he hadn't smiled in a long time, making Lolly wonder if she was to blame for this stony version of Shaun. Seeing him now, she wished the old Shaun was here instead of this ticked-off one. She missed her Shaun terribly. Heck, she'd missed him since the moment she broke up with him. He used to look at her as if she were a rock star and he was her groupie. She suspected, because she was a year older, she'd been able to manipulate him the way teenage girls could, and maybe that's why he'd been so crazy about her. She'd been crazy about him, too. And a girl just didn't get over her first love, especially when that first love was Shaun Montana. She just didn't.

"Yes, you're right. Not friends." She took another bite of her cookie, for fortification, but it had lost its magical powers.

He gave her a nod, as if they'd gotten that straightened out. "Next time, look before you step into the street."

She idly wondered if that was a threat. But she knew him. Shaun would never hurt a soul. Not even her. Whom apparently he couldn't forgive. "It was good to see you," she couldn't help but say.

For a second, it looked as if he was going to set her straight again, but instead, he turned and stomped back to his Jeep.

She awkwardly hollered at him, "It was good to see you, but not in a *friendly way*!" She watched as he peeled out and drove away.

Piney called to her from across the street. "Are you bringing those cookies in here or are you going to stand in the road and direct traffic all day?"

"I'm coming." Lolly glanced both ways before hurrying to the other side, wishing all the while she'd been better prepared for her first real encounter with Shaun and she wondered how she was supposed to act when they ran into each other in the future. He wanted them to be strangers, but she wanted . . .

Well, she didn't know.

Piney held the door wide as Lolly rushed inside. "Can you take the cookies into the diner and put them in the case?"

"Sure."

But Piney hadn't waited for her answer and was already back at the cash register checking out the next customer.

It wasn't just any customer either.

"Oh, hi," Lolly said to Shaun's mom.

"Was that my son you were talking to?" Normally Patricia Montana was as sweet as they come, but everyone knew she had a protective streak when it came to her boys, Shaun and Jesse. And even Luke, Jesse's best friend.

"Yes, we just . . . ran into each other," Lolly answered honestly.

Patricia came closer and guided her away from Piney. "I need to speak with you."

"About?" Lolly said, trying to calm her already frazzled nerves.

Patricia shook her head as if what she was about to say was unpleasant. "Listen, Lolly, I don't normally get involved in my sons' lives"—*completely untrue! Patricia had always appointed herself referee when Shaun and I were in the middle of one of our teenage squabbles*—"but I'm warning you . . . stay away from my son." That was strike two for today—*another Montana, another threat.* One more strike, and Lolly would be out.

Patricia continued. "You know how fond I am of you, Lolly"—*maybe at one time*—"but after breaking Shaun's heart . . ." She let her trailing words speak for how she was feeling toward Lolly now. "Anyway, it's nothing personal. It's just that he's been through enough heartache already, don't you think? And you know good and well it's better that I speak with *you* about this. If I'd gone to Shaun and told him to keep his distance from you—you know how stubborn he is—then we both know what would've happened."

No, Lolly didn't know. And for some weird reason, she was disappointed that Patricia hadn't expounded on the subject.

"Can you do this one favor for me?" Patricia asked earnestly.

Lolly wondered if it would have been better if Shaun hadn't hit the brakes but plowed right over her; anything to keep from being run down by Patricia now. Certainly, roadkill felt livelier than Lolly did at the moment.

Patricia waited patiently until Lolly finally acquiesced. "Sure."

"Okay, then." Patricia left her and returned to the cash register, where Piney was waiting.

It hadn't always been difficult between herself and Shaun's mom. At one time, Lolly and Patricia had been tight—a comfortable, easy relationship. Better than friends. Lolly had looked on Patricia like she was a second mother. In fact, they had the kind of relationship that Lolly only dreamed of having with her own mother. Yes, Patricia had been upset when she broke up with Shaun, but when Lolly returned last year, Patricia had seemed to mellow somewhat. But she'd also been gravely ill at the time. Lolly regularly made chicken and wild rice soup and sourdough bread, plus Patricia's favorite desserts, then took them out to the homestead, sometimes sitting with her, encouraging her to eat. Mostly, they chatted about the comings and goings of Sweet Home. Sometimes, they sat in silence. But one time, when things were looking particularly bad, Patricia had opened up and confided in Lolly about her illness.

Patricia had been gazing out the window, something she did often then. "I feel desperate and regretful."

Lolly had taken the chair across from her. "What do you feel desperate about?"

Patricia sighed forlornly. "I meant to have things more settled, you know, in case the worst happens. When Dale died suddenly, I was so heartbroken. I know the boys were, too. I had this overwhelming feeling that I needed to get things in order. The number one thing to get done were the Montana Family Quilts for each of the boys and their future wives. Of course, that includes Luke, since he's like my adopted son."

It still hurt that Lolly hadn't been able to come back for Mr. Montana's funeral six years ago. Strep throat had been going around at her school, and she'd caught it right before she was to fly home to Sweet Home. It was awful for her not to be there for Patricia and for Shaun and to grieve with the town. But now she knew the strep throat had been a godsend. If she'd been there, it would've been extremely awkward for the Montana family, and the last thing Lolly wanted was to make things worse.

She glanced over at Patricia, whose head was bent. "What would the Montana Family Quilts look like? Like a Photo quilt?"

Patricia turned her gaze toward Lolly and shook her head. "No. I've saved Dale's work shirts and jeans. And some of the boys' favorite jerseys from when they played football and basketball. Luke had a favorite pair of cargo pants that I wanted to cut into blocks for his quilt. I still have Shaun's baby blanket that he dragged through the house until he was almost five. Each quilt would be personalized, you see. Nothing fancy. Maybe just a patchwork quilt. King-sized, for them to use when they got married."

At that time, Jesse and Tori weren't seeing each other yet, nor were Luke and McKenna. Shaun, however, was engaged, and it always felt like a sucker punch when someone from Sweet Home mentioned his upcoming nuptials.

"I'm just kicking myself that I haven't started on their quilts. Something to leave behind, you know?" Patricia had said sadly.

Lolly had heard the fear—and the words she'd left unspoken: *I'll never get to them now.*

Patricia had straightened then and shot Lolly a look that said that she just realized who she was talking to. "Oh, don't mind me. I'm just rambling. Can you do me a favor and get me another cup of hot tea? While you're in there, can you cut me a small piece of the sticky toffee pudding? You really do make the best I've ever had. I think I might be able to eat a bite or two, while I look out the window at the homestead."

At that moment, Jesse walked in and helped Lolly fix a tray for his mom. Many times since that day, Lolly thought about Patricia and how it had felt a little like old times between them. But that was then.

Patricia wasn't keen on Lolly now, though Lolly couldn't imagine that Patricia would go so far as to hate anyone. But she certainly blamed Lolly for all of Shaun's heartache. Lolly thought maybe his recent ex should take some of the blame, too.

She went to the door to exit the Hungry Bear but stopped when Piney called out. "Hold up, Lollipop." Jilly had given her that ridiculous nickname when she was little. The rest of the town, Piney included, had latched onto it and it had stuck, even though Lolly had been gone from Sweet Home for years.

Patricia gave Lolly a sad smile as she passed on her way out.

"What's up?" Lolly asked.

"Did you get the message about bringing a cake for tonight?"

"Yes. But I don't feel much like celebrating," Lolly said. "Can I just deliver it and leave?"

"Who said anything about a celebration?" Piney said haughtily. Then she eyed her closely. "Is something going on with you? Is it because Shaun Montana is back in town?"

"No, of course not." But their little altercation out in the road hadn't helped Lolly's mood. "I'm fine. It's just been a long day."

"It's only quarter past noon!" Piney exclaimed.

"Oh. Well. It feels later than that," Lolly said. "Listen, I gotta run. My students"—actually, not her students anymore—"are at the cottage, baking."

"Yes, go on. But don't forget to bring the cake tonight."

PINEY WATCHED AS Lolly—and her upended aura—hurried from the Hungry Bear. When Piney could find a moment, she'd fix a cup of tea and sit with her tarot cards to get clarity on what was going on with Lolly.

But finding that time today was wishful thinking. The lunch rush was on and she had no help in the store today. Two nights ago, Rick had cornered Piney and asked if she would give her blessing for him to marry Sparkle. Piney hadn't liked Rick from the get-go—he reminded her of all the smooth talkers who came through Sweet Home, just looking for a good time. *Like Sparkle's father.* Who never hung around long enough to even know that Piney was pregnant.

But Rick had stayed and seemed devoted to Sparkle.

And Sparkle had really come out of her shell since she and Rick had started dating. With some reservation, Piney finally consented to their marriage. Now that she'd given her blessing, she knew she would have to quit giving Rick such a hard time and stop waiting for the other shoe to drop. Maybe, perhaps, Rick was one of the good guys.

The rest of the day flew by and Piney never found that moment to pull out her tarot cards or to stare into her crystal ball. But she really didn't need to consult with Mother Universe to know that Lolly's imbalance had to do with Shaun and whatever had happened earlier in the middle of the road.

Right before closing, three out-of-town fishermen came into the Hungry Bear and then took their time picking out groceries. No amount of hinting from Piney that she needed to close shop to get to her quilting group made them move any faster. At least the trio spent enough money to make it worth being late to tonight's Sisterhood of the Quilt meeting.

As she locked up the store, she thought about Lolly. The quilters had agreed to gather thirty minutes early to put streamers up for Lolly's surprise birthday party. Piney didn't feel bad that Lolly had to bake her own cake. "No one in town has her talent when it comes to baking sweets and savories," Piney said to herself as she got into her VW Beetle. "I sure hope she was in the right frame of mind and did a good job of it."

Piney made it out to Home Sweet Home Lodge just ten minutes before Lolly was to arrive. She hurried down the hall, ready to take charge of tonight's event. But when she stepped into the sewing studio, all the decorating was finished and a lively conversation was in progress with Miss Lisa, standing at the front of the room, talking a mile a minute.

"What's going on here?" Piney asked.

Hope rolled her eyes. "You're just in time. They're taking a vote."

"A vote for what?" Piney asked.

Hope sighed heavily. "Whose side they're going to support."

"Who's feuding this time?" Piney asked as she set her large sewing bag on a table.

Miss Lisa took a step toward her. "Not feuding, per say. We were discussing who we should stand behind—Lolly or Shaun."

Aberdeen jumped in. "We decided it was a good time to discuss it, since Patricia isn't coming tonight; she wanted to stay home for Shaun's first real night back in Alaska. And with Lolly coming later, Miss Lisa called for a vote."

Lisa always did love parliamentary procedure. Piney scanned the room. "Where's Ella and the other girls?"

"In the kitchen," Hope said, "pulling out plates, forks, and napkins for eating cake. I told them to set up the dining room table to keep the food out of here."

"And to keep them out of this?" Piney asked.

"Yes."

Aberdeen pointed to the whiteboard and did the recap. "Shaun got his heart broke recently—"

"Don't forget," Miss Lisa interjected, "that Lolly broke Shaun's heart in the past."

Hope leaned into Piney. "You know, Shaun and Lolly would not appreciate their lives being put up for debate like this."

Aberdeen continued. "You know Lolly's nickname— Love 'em and Leave 'em Lolly."

Miss Lisa put her hand up as if testifying in court. "She's certainly earned that reputation."

Piney knew why Aberdeen might be siding with Shaun, as she knew what it felt like to be in his position; she'd had her heart broken many times, starting with her ex-husband abandoning her and her daughter when Lacy was a little bit of a thing, not even out of diapers yet.

"Yes," Miss Lisa said, "Lolly has been known to be a runaway bride. Look what she did to that poor boy from

Missouri. All that money he put into their destination wedding in Hawaii." She shook her head. "Dating Lolly certainly didn't work out well for him."

"Yes," Bobbi Jo Nightingale agreed. "My poor nephew Jimmy was really upset when Lolly broke up with him in college."

Many of the middle-aged mamas nodded, concurring.

"But she can really bake," said Ella from the doorway. All the other high school girls were behind her. "And isn't it romantic that Ms. Crocker might have a second chance at love with her high school boyfriend?" The teenagers agreed enthusiastically.

Hope gestured to her daughter. "Ella, we should stay out of it, don't you think?"

"That's not what you were saying to Dad last night," Ella argued. The girls crowded into the room.

Hope opened her mouth but Miss Lisa rushed over to the girls while glancing nervously at the doorway. "We better hurry. Lolly will be here any minute. Let's put it to a vote now. All those in favor of standing behind Shaun, raise your hand." Miss Lisa put her hand up as if to show them how it was done.

"Wait." Hope looked at Piney. "Say something, Piney. This is preposterous. Shaun and Lolly are part of the community, and we're all friends with both of them."

Miss Lisa waved her hand. "Yes, yes. I see what you're getting at."

"Good. Then we'll stop this discussion—" But Hope was cut off by Miss Lisa.

"I move that the Sisterhood of the Quilt does everything in its power to keep Shaun and Lolly apart."

Before Piney could open her mouth and tell them that the universe wanted it the other way, Aberdeen said, "I second it."

"All in favor?" Miss Lisa raised her hand again. So did Aberdeen, Bobbi Jo, and the other mamas who had sons.

If only they knew about the premonition Piney'd had last

week when she'd gripped Lolly's arm. They could try to keep Shaun and Lolly apart, but it would be a fruitless endeavor. Mistress Universe would always get her way. At that moment, Courtney Wolf caught Piney's attention. Courtney was absolutely beaming, and Piney had an inkling what was up with her. Sweet Home's prettiest and most eligible bachelorette planned to take advantage of the situation and have a go at Shaun for herself. Piney had a choice: either tell Courtney to keep her mitts off Shaun, as ultimately, he belonged to Lolly; or subtly help nature's course and trip her up. She smiled to herself, thinking the latter would be more fun.

"Hold on!" Hope took a stance in front of Miss Lisa. "I'm putting a stop to this. No one is going to interfere with Lolly and Shaun, one way or the other. Leave them alone or I'll . . . I'll cut all the power cords on your sewing machines *and* lock up the sewing studio for good! Is that understood?"

Piney was proud of Hope. She certainly had a backbone, which was important for all women, but especially for women in Alaska.

Hope continued. "There isn't a person in this room who hasn't made a mistake or two. Myself included." A pained look crossed her face, and Piney, along with the others, understood that Hope's sorrow had to do with her tragic past. "Whatever grudges you believe you have toward Lolly because someone might've broken up with you or a loved one, I beg you to set your feelings aside. What do you say?" There were murmurs around the room, with all of them finally saying, "Okay." It didn't sound convincing to Piney. But she trusted the universe would fix things, as Lolly and Shaun belonged together.

Lacy grabbed Ella's arm and whispered loudly, "Ms. Crocker's here!" Everyone hurried to their stations and took an awkward stance.

A moment later, Lolly walked in with Donovan's dog, Boomer, on her heels; no doubt he smelled the cake within the plastic-covered carrier that Lolly was clutching.

"I'll take that," Ella said.

Lolly handed over the cake with a smile that looked as if she'd plastered it there with her frosting knife. But to Piney, it mostly looked like a grimace. Piney wondered if she'd misread Lolly's aura earlier. The look she had right now had nothing to do with Shaun Montana being back in Sweet Home. "Lollipop, what's wrong?"

"Nothing. Everything's fine." Lolly looked around the room in desperation and seemed relieved when the decorations registered. "What a nice surprise. The studio looks great. For my birthday?"

Piney put her arm around her. "You can tell us what's going on. We're your family."

Lolly sighed and hung her head. "I might as well tell you all. You'll know soon enough. I might have to leave Sweet Home—thanks to budget cuts. The district has decided to remove family and consumer science from the curriculum."

The high school girls gathered around Lolly, but it was Ella who spoke. "They can't do that, Ms. Crocker. We won't let them. You're the best teacher we've ever had."

The other girls joined in her protest. "Yeah, we won't let them."

Lolly mustered a real smile, though it was sad. "It's okay. It's a done deal."

For the first time in a long time, Piney was worried the universe had gotten it wrong. Lolly had to stay in Sweet Home—*had to!*—to fulfill her destiny with Shaun.

Or maybe this time *Piney* had gotten her wires crossed and misread the signs. She'd heard of this happening to other intuitives, but never to her.

But being wrong wasn't something Piney could accept. She might just have to help make sure everything turned out as it should. But it wasn't going to be easy. Piney had heard Patricia warning Lolly off her son, and Courtney seemed determined to have Shaun for herself. Shaun might be a problem, too, if Piney had read Lolly's disappointment correctly after their encounter in the road.

So many obstacles to overcome, but Piney liked a good challenge. First, she had to realign the Sisterhood of the Quilt to be fully behind Lolly and the idea of getting her and Shaun back together. "All right, ladies, let's get Lolly's birthday party started, then we can get to sewing."

Chapter 3

SHAUN GRABBED THE other end of the log to help his brother, Jesse, move it into place. They'd started early this morning and progress on Jesse's cabin was being made. Hope's husband, Donovan Stone; his business manager, Rick Miller; and Luke McAvoy were all helping. Shaun expected more of Sweet Home would show up soon, too, as Jesse had given many of the local folks help in building their homes and barns, plus miscellaneous homesteading assistance in general.

Helping today was about more than brotherly love for Shaun, though. He was grateful for a legitimate reason to put some distance between him and his mother. Yes, his mom was great, and he loved her, but last night, she'd hounded and nagged him so much about staying away from Lolly that he was tempted to head back to Houston on the first flight out of Alaska.

"What's going on with you today?" Jesse asked. "You look like you ate a bushel of rotten tomatoes."

"*Mom*," Shaun said by way of explanation, then added an eye roll. "Lecturing me last night."

"About what?"

"Lolly Crocker. She told me to stay away from her."

Jesse looked shocked. "She told me that she wasn't going to say anything to you about Lolly. Especially since you were likely to do the opposite of whatever she told you."

"Yeah, she mentioned that. I could tell she was kicking herself for telling me to stay away from her. But still . . ."

"But still, what?"

"I'm afraid that Mom is going to drive me crazy. Maybe I can live in your cabin while you and Tori are gone?" He put it to his brother as a question. "Mom wouldn't listen when I told her that I'm not in the least tempted to make another play for Lolly. *Once* was enough." At the same time and as weird as it was, Shaun was glad Lolly was in Sweet Home. She would be just the reminder he needed that he was done with serious relationships. Like electric shock therapy or the old rubber-band snap to the wrist. Because every time he thought about Lolly Crocker, it was like taking a knife to his chest.

"Do you want my opinion?" Jesse asked.

"That's rhetorical, right? I assume you're going to give it to me whether I want it or not."

Jesse nodded as if it was a given. "You need to stay away from Lolly, at least until you know that you can be civil to her. You seem volatile right now. And come to think of it, at the wedding, you looked like a ticking time bomb. I hope you'll be nice to her when you do finally run into her."

"I already did. *Run into her*, that is. In fact, I almost ran over her with my vehicle," Shaun said.

Jesse's jaw dropped in disbelief. "When did you have time to do that? I thought you came straight to the homestead."

"It happened when I rolled into town yesterday."

"Did you play it cool?" Jesse asked, not with curiosity, but as if he already knew the answer.

"It didn't go well. She tried to be all, 'It's good to see you, Shaun.'" He mimicked Lolly in a girly voice.

"And you said?" Jesse prompted with a frown.

"I told her straight up to forget it. That we're not going

to be friends." Shaun might have related the encounter with complete confidence, but in his heart, he knew he'd bungled it.

"Don't you think it's time that you let this go? It was a long time ago, and you were in high school." Jesse spoke as if he were the much older and wiser brother, but the truth was that Shaun was only two years younger, and in his opinion, they were on equal footing when it came to wits.

Shaun raised an eyebrow. "You don't know what you're talking about and should mind your own business." He wished he could be this frank with his mom, but he couldn't. He stalked away to the woodpile to select the next log.

Jesse followed. "Well, you should try to pull it together anyway and not take your current heartache out on Lolly. What Tanya did to you was crappy, but Lolly doesn't deserve your attitude."

Shaun turned around and faced him. "You have no idea what went on between Lolly and me. You were long gone." And Shaun still resented that his brother left right after high school. No, it wasn't rational, but he'd liked having his brother around. Luke had been living with them at the time, too, until suddenly, both of them were gone. Jesse for a job and Luke to college. The cabin had turned lonely. But these were things he'd never admit to his brother. Finally Shaun said, "Let's drop it, okay?" He was done talking about Lolly and that time in his life.

"Rick?" Donovan hollered. "Can you give me a hand?"

Shaun glanced over to see Rick sitting on a log. His head was hung low as he stared intently at his phone.

Donovan left his place at the portable sawmill and headed to Rick. "What's going on with you?"

Rick glanced up as if he'd seen a ghost. Something had rattled him.

"Is everything okay?" Donovan asked.

Shaun, Jesse, and Luke walked over to Rick, too.

"It's this email I got," Rick said. "It's from a woman who claims to be raising my daughter."

"What?" Donovan said. "You don't have a kid. It's gotta be a hoax."

"I don't know. She gave me all her information and some pictures of the girl. She's three years old." He held up his phone for Donovan to see. Shaun got a glimpse of a cute kid in a Sunday-best dress and shiny black slippers.

"I looked up the woman. She's a professor at Stanford and says she's the girl's aunt . . . that her sister used a sperm bank." Rick groaned. "Oh my gosh . . ."

"What?" Donovan asked, seeming alarmed now.

"Right before I graduated from college . . ." Rick made another guttural sound, as if in physical pain.

"What about it?"

"There was one of those recruiting-type things at school, you know, where they set up the tables. This particular table was looking for men to donate to a sperm bank." Rick shrugged. "I didn't ever plan on getting serious about any-one ever, let alone getting married and having a family. I needed some quick cash, so I thought, *what the heck*."

"But that was, what? Thirteen years ago?" Donovan asked.

Rick took back his phone, did another search, and then handed his phone back to Donovan.

"It says here that sperm, when frozen, can be viable for up to fifty years," Donovan read. "But how did this woman find you?"

"Look at the email . . . 23andMe. Sparkle and I did 23andMe just for fun, remember? I wanted to learn more about where my family came from, and, well, Sparkle . . ." He trailed off, but it didn't take a rocket scientist to figure out how that sentence would end. Sparkle was probably try-ing to find out something about her dad or his family, since she didn't know who her father was. "I thought the notifica-tion I got from 23andMe was a mistake."

"What notification?" Jesse asked.

"They said I had a daughter." He glanced down at his

phone. "But I thought it was a mistake, and I didn't believe it."

"You said the aunt contacted you," Shaun said. "Where's the mother?"

"She died a couple of months ago. Car accident. The email says she was single. The aunt is going to start her third round of chemo next week. She says her prognosis isn't good. She wants me to take the girl . . . *my daughter.* Apparently, she has an aggressive type of cancer and there is no other family."

Luke moved closer. "You should look into this. Make sure it's all on the up-and-up. Maybe hire a private detective."

Rick stood. "I don't think there's time. I need to get to California right now and see about the girl."

"What's the girl's name?" Donovan asked.

Rick looked over at Donovan, his eyes wide. "Ava."

"I don't believe it." Donovan looked dumbfounded, too.

"What's going on?" Luke asked but didn't get an immediate answer.

"Do you think it's a sign?" Rick asked Donovan.

"What? What sign?" Jesse asked.

Finally Donovan turned to the others. "Ava was Rick's mom's name. She died when he was a kid."

"It sounds a little fishy to me," Luke said. "If you're not ready to dig into it yourself, do you mind if I have someone look into this aunt and find out what is really going on?"

"Yeah. Sure." Rick stood and dusted off his pants. "But in the meantime, I have to talk to Sparkle. And book a flight."

"Do you want me to come with you to California?" Donovan asked.

"Yes, but no. You're needed here. You're in the throes of high season for the lodge. And Hope and Ella need you here, too." Rick gave him a sad look.

Shaun nodded but he was feeling like Luke . . . *suspicious.*

He could easily see Rick's problem for what it was . . . just another example of how women could put men through the wringer.

LOLLY ROLLED OVER, lifted one eye open, and glanced at her phone, not for the time, but for the date. For over two weeks, she'd been too tired to get out of bed, except to feed Thor, take him out, and grab a cookie or a peanut butter sandwich for herself. In those moments, while she was up, she had good intentions of applying for teaching positions, but instead, she would shuffle back to her room and crawl under the covers. Thank goodness Thor was a good dog, content to keep her company and cuddle while she slept. Sometime over the last couple of weeks, she'd decided she must be truly sick to be this tired. One clear thought stayed with her; she was grateful Jilly had been gone for work and Lolly hadn't been forced out of bed. She'd just needed to sleep. But Jilly would be home today, and everything around their cottage was a wreck . . . including Lolly. The cottage needed to be picked up and she needed a shower.

Instead of rolling out of bed right then, though, she pulled Thor closer, ignored the missed calls and text notifications on her screen, set her phone back on the nightstand, and fell back to sleep.

She woke when Thor started barking wildly, which only meant someone was here. A moment later Jilly was shaking her awake. "Get up, Lollipop. I'm home now and you have to help me get moved back in."

Lolly pulled the pillow over her face. "Why? Mom won't be here until next week."

"Change of plans. You would know that if you had read your texts or answered your phone in the last couple weeks. Which we'll discuss in a moment. Mom said she'll probably be here tomorrow or the next day. She wants to do some shopping in Anchorage first before returning to Sweet Home."

Candy Crocker had left two years ago for the warmer climate of Phoenix. Each summer since, she returned for an extended stay back in Alaska, which was the reason Lolly and Jilly would be sharing a room again. Just like they had while growing up in this cottage.

Jilly yanked the pillow off Lolly's head. "Just so you know, I'm not cleaning up your mess. And the clock is ticking. You need to get everything done before we head over to Home Sweet Home Lodge tonight. The Sisterhood of the Quilt is meeting."

"I'll pass." Lolly couldn't go; she was too embarrassed. If she'd kept quiet about the layoff and hadn't blurted that she was *basically getting fired* to the Sisterhood of the Quilt, as if she had no self-control, then maybe she would have had time to process the news without all the pitying glances the ladies had given her. Heaven knew that there were more pitying looks to come, and she just couldn't endure it. *Shaun must know about it, too,* she thought, which was so strange, and random, that it made her inhale sharply.

"What's wrong?" Jilly looked up from her phone. "Did you just get the text from Mom, too?"

"No. What about Mom? Is she okay?"

"Yeah, she's fine, except she's decided to come in tonight instead."

"Okay. I'll get up." Lolly loved her mom, but seeing her was always a mixed bag. Not a mixed assortment of chocolate bars like at Halloween, or like the yummy mixed nuts at Christmas either. This mixed bag was full to bursting with emotions, always propelling Lolly back to childhood, when she wasn't in control of her own life and she had the undying need to please her mom. Lolly was certain that Candy Crocker would have plenty to say about her layoff, and Lolly would feel three feet tall again.

Jilly pulled Lolly to her feet and then brushed her hair away from her face. "I love you but you stink. Go take a shower."

For a moment, Lolly felt like they'd slipped into an

alternate universe where she and Jilly had reversed roles. As the older sister, Lolly had always been responsible for Jilly, making sure she did the right things at the right time—or at least trying to—but ultimately just trying to keep Jilly on the right path. Lolly prided herself on choosing the correct lane and then remaining between the lines. Jilly, on the other hand, was the wild child—always running full speed ahead, venturing this way and that, making everyone worry what collision course she was on this time. The only calculated thing Jilly ever did was set her sights on becoming a nurse.

In a snarky way, Jilly gave Mom all the credit, because Mom had said many times how Jilly would never do anything sensible and would probably end up in jail or tending bar her whole life. But Jilly showed Mom, plus surprised everyone in Sweet Home . . . at least regarding her profession. She was still a wild child on her days off but a responsible healthcare professional when she was on the road, tending to patients like some kind of saint. And now, shockingly, Sweet Home High's Most Likely to Succeed, Lolly, was the mess in the family . . . with no job at all. She plopped on the bed and covered her face again with the pillow. "I'm sick."

The mattress dipped as Jilly sat next to her. She pulled the pillow away. "Yeah, I know . . . sick. Hope told me what happened with your job. You should've picked up when I called. I was worried."

"My phone's on silent."

"I figured. It's the reason I sent Piney over to make sure you still had a pulse."

"I thought I dreamed that." But Lolly knew Piney had been here—probably used the key from under the bear figurine on the porch. "She held a mirror to my mouth to see if I was breathing, and she tried to get me out of bed by taking my quilt away."

Yes, it was great being back in Sweet Home, but it had taken a while for Lolly to adjust to Sweet Home's ways.

Sweet Home citizens took care of each other. Most of the time, their care felt like a warm and cozy quilt; at other times, it felt like being smothered. When she'd had a scratchy throat last fall, she'd been shocked when she'd found three different chicken soups in her refrigerator after she'd gotten home from school. At the time, their actions made her feel loved, cherished. And even the thought of their kindness now brought back a nice memory. But the flip side to a close community was that when Lolly wanted to be left alone—like she had for the last two weeks—people either knocked on her door or came on in to see her wallowing in despair. Miss Lisa had even tapped on Lolly's window one afternoon until she got up and yanked the curtains closed . . . *tight*.

Jilly laid a hand on her arm. "Piney was just trying to get you out of bed. When you failed to get up, she called me and said she and the Sisterhood of the Quilt were either going to drag you from your bed or camp out here until you got up. I told her to leave you be. But I know they've been taking turns calling you . . . because then they called me to tell me that you never picked up! So what the hell, Lolly? I was trying to work but I had to keep answering the phone. Not to mention that I was concerned about you. I need you back to normal, so they'll leave me alone and I can get back to it."

"Oh, so this is really about you? And not my midlife crisis?"

Jilly scoffed. "Hardly a midlife crisis. Just a little hiccup. Now it's time to shake it off."

Lolly didn't like how Jilly sounded so nonchalant about Lolly's life being in a tailspin, or how Jilly was acting like the sage old wisewoman. "You don't know what this feels like. You still have a job." Lolly rolled away from her.

"And you have options!" Jilly threw the pillow at her head. "Need I point out that you won't find another job by staying in bed all the time? Besides, Piney said the Hungry Bear is out of your cookies, and Hope called to tell me that you canceled the rest of the cooking lessons for your high school girls via text. You love doing your *Great British Baking Show* thing with them. What's up with that?"

Lolly huffed as she sat up. "Don't you see? I'm no longer their teacher."

"No one ever said you couldn't continue their lessons. I think you owe them an apology . . . and *me* something good to eat for putting up with all the interruptions these last couple of weeks. Come on, I'm hungry. And it's part of our agreement that you feed me, remember?"

Lolly rolled her eyes. "Yeah, so is paying half the rent."

"Don't worry about that right now. You know I can cover it. The more pressing matter is that if you don't whip something up in the kitchen soon, my stomach will be rumbling so loud that you'll become too distracted to make anything."

"I'll make you French toast, but I'm not going out to the lodge tonight."

"Yeah, you are. Even if I have to drag you there, kicking and screaming. Better me than Piney and the whole Sisterhood, right?"

Lolly stood with a huff and handed Thor to Jilly. "Can you take him for a quick walk? As you said, I need a shower." She grabbed Thor's new predator-proof vest with the spikes and bright neon pink bristles on the back and handed it to Jilly, too. "Be sure to put this on him."

Jilly looked horrified. "Where did you get that? Bikers "R" Us? And pink, really, Lolly?"

"Thor thought the pink looked nice and would surely scare away the big bullies more effectively than green or orange."

Jilly nuzzled Thor's neck while speaking to him. "If any predators see you in this contraption, they're going to laugh at you. I mean it, Thor. Full-on-belly-rolling-on-the-ground laughs. And it'll be all your fault, because you're tolerating this nonsense from your human."

Lolly patted Thor's head. "Better laughed at than becoming some eagle's afternoon snack."

"Fine. But I'm not paying for Thor's therapy. Poor little guy looks like he should be in a carnival act." Jilly gave Thor a kiss on the top of his white fluffy head. "It's bad enough that he has a backyard that looks like the circus for the tortured and demented—between his dog run being covered in bird-proof netting, the bird spikes in the trees, and the scarecrow owls posted all over the place, it's a wonder Thor isn't traumatized by all the countermeasures you've taken to protect him."

"Hey, at least I took down the bird balloons." The beach-ball-sized balloons with the large yellow eyes had frightened even her.

"Yeah, those things wigged me out. Thor was terrified of them, too. I'm glad you finally saw reason and realized that they did nothing to deter flying predators." Jilly smiled, then left with Thor, speaking to him in an encouraging tone as she slipped his new spiky jacket on him. Most people thought Lolly was the more motherly of the two, but when Jilly knew no one was looking, she could certainly be a mother hen, too.

By the time Lolly was done in the shower, Jilly was back, Thor was out of his vest, and she was brushing out his fur.

"Thanks for doing that," Lolly said. "I haven't felt up to grooming." *Him or me.*

"Well, you both are getting a little spa treatment today," Jilly replied. "The world thanks you for showering. Can you do something with your wet hair, though?"

Lolly flicked a bread crumb at Jilly and then got back to making French toast. When Lolly took the first piece out of the pan, she didn't plate it but took a bite. Nothing had ever tasted better.

Jilly rushed over and complained, "Hey, I usually get the first piece."

"Not today. *French toast tax*," she explained. "Besides, I'm malnourished from my *illness*."

"I'm glad you're out of bed. I'm going to start the laundry." But Jilly did more than that. She picked up the kitchen, rinsed off dishes and loaded them into the dishwasher, pulled the sheets from Lolly's bed, and Swiffered the living room and hallway.

"Thanks," Lolly said as she set a heaping plate of French toast on the table, along with cut-up fruit and some of her homemade salmonberry syrup. "Do you want coffee or tea?"

"Tea," Jilly said, taking her seat. "You better have some, too. We should enjoy the calm before the storm."

"Yeah, I know." Things would be hectic when Mom came to stay. She had a vibrant energy that many people were drawn to, but it was draining to those who were around her for long periods of time, especially now that Jilly and Lolly had fallen into a casual rhythm while living together.

"What are you going to work on tonight at the Sisterhood of the Quilt meeting?" Jilly asked. "Piney told me to bring a UFO." An *unfinished object*.

Lolly just raised an eyebrow. "I told you already that I'm not going."

"Yeah, you say that now, but I know you won't make waves. You never have. It's the reason I do. Besides, you owe it to the quilters to make an appearance, to show them you still have a pulse and are breathing. But mostly to let them know that you're going to be okay. Do I need to remind you that we're Alaska-born?" Jilly asked with one superior eyebrow raised. "We're tough women, and we don't let a little layoff throw us off our game." Jilly stopped. "Wait a minute. Stay right here." She pushed back her chair and rushed from the room.

Lolly rolled her eyes and said in a raised voice, "I already told you that *staying right here* is what I intend to do."

Jilly returned with a binder—the notebook that Lolly

had decorated in middle school with her favorite fabrics, ribbons, and buttons. She'd written and added to the binder until she was a junior in high school, when she finally gave up her dream and did what her mother wanted.

"What are you doing with that? I distinctly remember throwing it out." Where all old, impossible dreams should go: to the trash.

"About that, it got saved from the burn barrel before a match was lit to it. I hid it in the top of the hall closet. I couldn't bear to see you let go of something you put so much time into making." Jilly set the binder in front of Lolly and flipped it open to the first page. "There it is. Your bakery."

Lolly didn't have to look down to know every detail. The crudely drawn building with two large windows. Above the door was the name: Happily Ever Baking. She'd been romantic back then, in both her reading and her baking . . . *and with Shaun*. But since she'd thrown her binder away, she'd only been reading textbooks and writing syllabuses, relegating her childhood dreams to the past, where they belonged . . . along with her Easy Bake Oven and her training bra.

Shaun was another story. She'd done her best to forget about him. But, well . . . She put those thoughts aside. She didn't have the energy to examine what she'd done with the memories of Shaun.

"What do you expect me to do with this old bakery binder?" Lolly was truly puzzled by what Jilly wanted.

"You have to see this layoff as an opportunity to try something new. I think it's time to revisit your first love and make it your profession. You have a chance at a do-over. You should take it."

"That's ridiculous. I can't make a living by baking. Especially in Sweet Home." A population of 573 wasn't enough to support such a venture. Yes, Piney said the tourist season had been better this year, with the quirky hardware store newly reopened as an attraction and the Home

Sweet Home Lodge back to full capacity, but the tourist season was short. What about the other nine months of the year?

Jilly flipped to the next page, which was a drawing of a display case with all the different treats that Lolly had planned to serve—sweet rolls, Danishes, coffee cakes, muffins, and doughnuts. Though Lolly still liked the basics, now her tastes were more sophisticated. *The Great British Baking Show* had certainly fanned that fire, too. She was slowly working her way through every signature bake, technical challenge, and showstopper of the show, and she'd made some good headway on that bucket list. Her high school girls had been a great help and had fun helping Lolly achieve that goal. They enjoyed eating and sharing each bake, too!

Lolly pulled the notebook over to get a closer look and spied her imaginary future dog—Cupcake, a Yorkie—sitting near the cash register as a mascot so all the patrons could easily see him while they ate their goodies. She couldn't help but smile. She looked over at Thor, knowing he would love to stand in as the bakery mascot. Not for the treats, but because he was always looking for his next owner. She'd gotten him from the rescue in Anchorage—the cuddliest dog in the world. But he was constantly buttering up everyone he met, seemingly in case he found a better pet parent. Which she knew he never would. She loved him to pieces!

"What's on the next page?" Jilly asked, which broke Lolly's reverie.

Lolly turned the page, though she already knew what she'd see. "The menu. Prices and daily specials." She flipped again to the next set of sketches, which had the layout of the kitchen with the appliances labeled. She'd certainly been thorough.

"What do you say? Is it time to make your dream a reality?"

Lolly slammed the binder shut. "Of course not. I'm a

family and consumer science teacher. Not an entrepreneur. Period." Besides, her meager savings account couldn't afford the ingredients, let alone the professional appliances, to get it up and running. Professional kitchens cost a fortune. Speaking of, Lolly now wished that she hadn't bought a set of specialty pans last month, along with Silpat mats, a nonstick rolling pin with rings to adjust the crust thickness, a steamed-pudding mold, and new blind-bake beads. Her high school girls had certainly been excited about the new baking tools. But Lolly was going to need that money to live on until another teaching position opened up.

Jilly put her hand on her shoulder. "Piney would say that the universe shut the door on that one. It's time to look around for where it's thrown open a window. I believe the answer is sitting right there in front of you."

Lolly shrugged off Jilly's hand and stood. "Thanks, Dear Abby, but I don't need any advice."

"Suit yourself." Jilly went back to her laundry and Lolly cleaned the bathroom. She only wished she could shirk the idea that Jilly had put into her head—*a bakery of her own!*—as easily as she'd shrugged Jilly's hand from her shoulder.

Chapter 4

WHEN LOLLY AND Jilly walked into Home Sweet Home Lodge's sewing studio, they saw that Sparkle was being bombarded with questions by the Sisterhood of the Quilt. Poor Sparkle. She seemed nervous as she looked around at the women who crowded her, and she dropped her head, letting her hair curtain her eyes. And here Lolly thought she would be the most uncomfortable person in the quilting studio tonight.

"What's going on?" Jilly asked Piney, who was standing on the outskirts with her arms crossed and a frown on her face.

Piney rolled her eyes. "Apparently, the apple doesn't fall far from the tree. Sparkle is as gullible as I was. Rick's story about a *sperm bank* sounds as outlandish as something that Sparkle's *sperm donor* might've fed me back in the day . . . a bunch of bull-hockey!"

Hope gently elbowed Piney. "You know Rick isn't making this up. I told you that Donovan saw the emails from both the girl's aunt and from 23andMe."

Lolly had no idea what they were talking about. She felt out of the loop, which was strange for a tiny place like Sweet Home. How long had she been holed up in her cottage?

"Here's the deal," Hope started. "Rick donated to a sperm bank when he graduated from college . . ." She told Lolly and Jilly everything and then ended with "The results of the paternity test came back and the girl is definitely his."

Lolly glanced over to see how Sparkle was taking it and saw that the engagement ring was still on Sparkle's hand. So at least they were still together, but when she glanced up, the furrow between Sparkle's eyebrows didn't bode well for a happily-ever-after.

"Where's Rick now? Still in California?" Lolly asked.

"He's headed home tonight," Piney spat.

"And his daughter?" Jilly asked.

Piney glared at Jilly, but Hope was the one who answered.

"He's bringing her here. I offered to move his things out of the cabin and into the lodge so they could have easy access to the washer and dryer. Plus Donovan, Ella, and I would be there as backup, but Rick wants to stay in the cabin with Ava until the . . ." She was probably going to say *wedding* but Lolly couldn't be sure. Hope continued after glancing at Sparkle with a worried look on her face. "Excuse me. I better put a stop to this." She reached over and grabbed the bell from the windowsill and rang it. "Everyone, get to your sewing machines. I'm sure you have plenty to do." Hope tilted her head toward Piney. "Don't you agree?"

Begrudgingly Piney stepped forward. "Yes, everyone, get to work and give Sparkle room to breathe."

Lolly saw Sparkle give Piney a thank-you-Mom nod. But Lolly worried about Sparkle and Rick . . . and the fact that Piney had always been suspicious of him and his intentions. But she didn't get to ruminate on it, as there was a bustle outside the door and then a loud, familiar female voice sang out, "Hi, honey, I'm home!

It was Mom, arms raised like a TV game show model but with shopping bags in each hand. "Did you miss me?"

The Sisterhood of the Quilt cheered and swarmed her with hugs, while Candy gave air-kisses to each woman.

Mom was bigger than life, though she was only five one. Her platinum-blond hair seemed a shade brighter and her fingernails were painted a trendy coral. Perfect for a beach vacation, but not wise for manual labor in small-town Alaska. For the previous summer visits, she had filled in at the fish-processing plant, but this year, Hope had asked her to help out in the kitchen until the end of tourist season. The lodge was fully booked for the summer, which was a boon for all of Sweet Home's businesses. Lolly wished now that when there were openings at the lodge, she, too, had applied for a position. But she had already planned to bake with the high school girls, give Thor lots of walks, and just enjoy her summer off from teaching.

If she'd only known a few months sooner, she would've found a summer job to help make ends meet in the coming months.

Mom grabbed her and gave her a bear hug. "Sorry about your job," she said into Lolly's hair. "But you know what I always say."

"Unemployment helps you lose weight because there won't be enough money to buy food?"

Mom pulled back and gave her a hard stare. "*Things could always be worse.* You know they could."

"I'm not so sure."

Mom hugged her again. "You could be fifty-something and still be all alone."

"Yeah, well, at the rate I'm going, I'm sure I'll get there. My love-life track record says that I'm a cat lady in the making," Lolly carped.

"Maybe," Mom said good-humoredly, "but you should consider Thor's feelings in this plan of yours."

"It's not a plan . . . it's reality."

Mom acted as if Lolly hadn't responded. "Thor won't be happy about cohabitating with one feline, let alone twenty of them." Her smile faded as she stared over Lolly's shoulder.

Lolly turned to see what was going on and gasped.

Shaun and his mom were standing right behind her. Lolly could be wrong, but it looked as if Aberdeen, Bobbi Jo, Miss Lisa, and a few others went to stand beside Patricia, all of them giving Lolly a we're-snubbing-you look. She wondered what that was about, except for Patricia, who had cause to give Lolly the cold shoulder.

"Why is Bobbi Jo glaring at you?" Candy asked.

"I don't know," Lolly whispered back. "Some of the women seem mad at me about something."

Piney clapped her on the shoulder. "Don't worry about them, Lollipop. I'm going to fix it. Some of the women think you should stay away from Shaun because you broke his heart before—"

Lolly cut her off, hissing back, "Of course I'm going to stay away from Shaun! Should I make an announcement or something when *he* and Patricia aren't around?"

"No, no. Leave it to me. I've been waiting on the universe, but"—Piney nodded—"the universe has probably been counting on me to take action. I'm going to make it my job to remind that crowd of their own mistakes. They've racked up some sins in their day." She tilted her head toward Aberdeen. "Aberdeen's not blameless. She's broken up with her fair share of men over the years." Next she glared at Miss Lisa. "When Lisa gets bored, she's been known to cause trouble around town." Lolly also knew from Patricia that Miss Lisa had taken her under her wing when she came to Sweet Home as a new bride. Miss Lisa had taught her all kinds of quilting techniques back when the Sisterhood of the Quilt was newly formed.

Piney continued her evaluation of those standing with Patricia. "And Bobbi Jo over there seems to forget that her nephew Jimmy isn't still broken up over you, Lollipop. He's married to that sweet girl from Talkeetna, and they have three beautiful daughters together. Yes, I'll have to intervene on behalf of the universe and fix those ladies' attitude."

Lolly noticed Courtney ogling Shaun again. Piney must've seen it, too, because she continued. "Don't worry about Courtney either."

But Lolly knew that no guilt trip would stop Courtney from pursuing Shaun. And really, Lolly shouldn't care one way or the other.

Piney gave Lolly a toothy grin. "I have a plan for her, but it will take a little finagling to fix it."

Lolly stepped aside to make room for Patricia, Shaun, and their entourage to pass. Lolly had every intention of giving Shaun plenty of distance.

She didn't see her own mother push her way through. Lolly should've expected her mom to do something out of the ordinary, but she wasn't prepared for her to grab Shaun by the shoulders. "Look at you! All grown up. And more handsome than ever!" She turned back to Lolly. "Don't you think so, Lollipop?"

"Um . . ." Lolly's less-than-brilliant response had her wishing that lightning would strike her down that very moment. It didn't help that Shaun was staring at her like she was the conductor of the imbecile train.

But, good ol' Candy Crocker went and outdid herself with her next statement. "Oh, I have a great idea. Lolly, you don't have to be alone. Why don't you and Shaun pick up where you left off all those years ago? It makes perfect sense. You're both back in town and you two were so cute together back in the day. And you're both getting to that perfect age, you know!"

"Umm," Lolly replied.

Hope, the lifesaver, horned her way through and latched onto Shaun's arm. "Come on in and say *hi* to everyone. Most of us didn't get a chance to visit with you at Jesse and Tori's wedding. You were out the door before we knew it. How is it being back on the homestead? Donovan said you've made a lot of headway on Jesse's cabin."

Shaun nodded and walked forward stiffly, as if he was facing a firing squad instead of hanging out with old friends.

Lolly just stared after him as if he were a triple-layered lemon raspberry cake with walnut and cream cheese icing. Inwardly, she groaned. But Shaun spun around as if she'd groaned out loud. He stared back at her, looking puzzled, which made her wonder if he could still read her mind and her emotions like he'd done back in high school.

To add insult to injury, Patricia was glowering at her even more than before. She huffed past Lolly and took Shaun's other arm and dragged him over to Miss Lisa.

Lolly couldn't help but hear every word that Patricia said. She gushed over Shaun and his accomplishments. Lolly was impressed with the things he'd done, like how he was the senior programmer at a large oil and gas refinery in Houston and how he'd quickly advanced to be the best in the business. She thought it said a lot about his integrity to leave it all behind to come home and help his mom on the homestead.

Once again, regret filled Lolly. A recurring emotion every time she thought about Shaun. She'd really screwed up when she'd broken up with him. They just didn't make men like him anymore.

Nodding at Patricia show-and-telling Shaun to all the older ladies, Piney whispered to Lolly, "Listen up, Lollipop. You better pull yourself together if you're going to get him to realize that the two of you really do belong together."

"What?" Lolly sputtered. She'd ruined things before with him, and yearning after him now—even a little bit—would surely be a recipe for disaster for the both of them. She swatted away the idea. "We don't belong together," she muttered back.

Piney put her arm around her. "Sure you do. I have the inside track." She waved with her other hand. "Shaun, get over here."

"No!" Lolly said louder and more emphatically than

she'd meant to, which made everyone in the room turn to look at her. She hissed at Piney, "What are you doing?"

Piney ignored her as she pulled Lolly forward to meet Shaun halfway. Patricia rushed after him as if to block the exchange.

"What can I do for you?" Shaun asked Piney politely, though his expression was anything but.

"I thought you might like to say a proper hello to the Crocker girls. Though not really girls anymore, are they?" She elbowed Shaun. "As you can see, they're *women* now, especially this one. Which I'm certain you've noticed." The older woman waggled her eyebrows suggestively, which in turn made her crow's-feet waggle, too.

Lolly wanted to evaporate.

Before Shaun could open his mouth, Patricia butted in. "Come on, Shaun. Miss Lisa wasn't done showing you her large star quilt."

To Lolly's surprise, he didn't budge but stared at her again for a long moment, as if she were a complicated piece of computer code. He gave her no salutation. She didn't have a clue as to what he was thinking, and she wondered—*no, fantasized*—if he was mesmerized by her. *Fat chance*.

Abruptly, he snapped out of it and glanced over to where Jilly stood with Hope. "Hey, Jilly, how's it going?"

Speaking to Jilly instead of her was the perfect snub, and Lolly didn't blame him. Besides, Patricia would've probably grounded him if he'd spoken to her.

"Hey, Shaun," Jilly answered back. "Good to see you."

Lolly wished she could comfortably say hello to Shaun, too, like her sister. She had to admit that on the most basic level, it was good to see Shaun. *Really good*. Just like she was eighteen all over again, she raked her eyes over his body with her insides all aflutter. He had on a crisp white oxford shirt and what looked like another new pair of jeans. He seemed ready to head into the office on casual Friday to knock out some code with that sexy brain of his. Or to write a new app. Or to make the female employees fight over who would get to flirt with him at the water cooler.

How did he look so good after working on Jesse and Tori's cabin all day? At least that's what Jilly had said he'd been doing.

Lolly hated to admit that she was still as crazy about him as she'd always been, but that was just old dreams coming to the surface. *Unrealistic dreams.* The dream of him—of having it all—Shaun, a family of her own, and a happily-ever-after. The same unrealistic fantasy that had popped into Lolly's head when Jilly had pulled out her dream-bakery binder, forcing her to look at her life through her idealistic younger glasses once again. Old dreams should stay dead and buried, or else they'd only remind Lolly of the heartache she'd suffered when she'd let go of Shaun the first time.

"So, Lolly, what's the plan?" Courtney asked, which brought Lolly back to the present and her gaze to the former Miss Alaska second runner-up. "How's the job hunt going?" Courtney glanced down at her perfect fingernails, inspecting them. "I know I said it before, but I'm really sorry you lost your job."

Lolly didn't believe Courtney's sorrowful expression for a second. With the way she'd perked up when Shaun walked in the room, Lolly was surprised Courtney's tentacles hadn't latched onto Shaun the moment he'd pulled into town. Though Lolly didn't want to, she had to agree with everyone else that Courtney was the obvious choice for Shaun. The room seemed to be waiting for Lolly to respond, so she opened her mouth to say something, but only "I'm, I'm—" came out.

But Patricia wasn't at a loss for words. "I'm sure you'll have to look for a teaching position out of state, right?"

Yeah, Patricia sounds all shook up that I have to move away!

"Yes, out of state," Bobbi Jo echoed, seeming satisfied with herself.

Patricia turned to her son looking worried, as if Shaun might be gullible enough to fall for Love 'em and Leave 'em Lolly all over again.

Not likely. Which made Lolly exceedingly sad.

He frowned. Lolly couldn't figure out if it was because he was disappointed in his mom for bringing it up—surely wishful thinking on Lolly's part—or maybe he didn't want Lolly to move away, which was even more delusional! More than likely it was just that Lolly couldn't read Shaun, though he sure seemed to be able to read her.

Piney piped in. "But we're not letting Lolly leave."

Half the room looked unhappy about that statement, including the two Montanas present. Miss Lisa and Aberdeen moved forward and it felt like they were putting themselves between herself and Shaun again.

"We have something in mind for Lolly," Piney announced.

"Like what?" Shaun asked, surprising them all.

Piney grinned and scooted closer to Lolly. "There's plenty of baking for her to do. I have a list here for her." Piney pulled a folded sheet out of her pocket. "There's enough on there for the lodge and around town to keep her busy from now until Christmas."

Probably not, Lolly thought. But if it were true, what would she do for a job after Christmas came and went? Tourist season dwindled in the fall, as if the first snow had the ability to banish the Lower 48 crowd back to the Lower 48. With no tourists in January, February, and March, heck, until June, surely Lolly would be even more desperate for a job than she felt right now. Piney handed over the list and Lolly saw that the page was filled with requests.

Shaun nodded, then shoved his hands in his pockets. "Will you excuse me?"

Lolly watched him stalk from the room and she felt her ridiculous heart trail after him, leaving her in the sewing studio, feeling empty on the inside. Desperate. Not at all like the Lolly who'd tried to get on with her life after she'd tossed Shaun away. But realization hit her squarely when she saw that all the other eyes were on her. Courtney was glaring as if Lolly had been the one to tell him to go away. Piney and some of the others were giving her pitying glances. Patricia, Aberdeen, Miss Lisa, Bobbi Jo, and others seemed happy, as if they were glad that Lolly had no chance with Shaun and that she'd run him off . . . again.

Lolly felt more uncomfortable than ever, which moments ago hadn't seemed possible. And here she'd thought she'd felt uneasy when she'd arrived at the lodge. It was strange what a couple of minutes—*and being in Shaun's presence!*—could do to her mental well-being.

Lolly glanced over at Jilly to see if she was ready to go, but Jilly looked like she was settling in for the evening as she pulled her Mustang car paper-piece project from her bag. Mom was settling in, too, talking to the other mamas from the Sisterhood of the Quilt.

And Lolly, well, she just wanted to curl up in a ball and disappear. But she noticed Miss Lisa was having trouble threading her sewing machine, as she was leaning over, holding a magnifying glass in one hand and thread in the other. Lolly started heading in the older woman's direction to help, but stopped, worried Miss Lisa would tell her to go jump in the river out back. But Lolly went to Miss Lisa's side anyway. "Do you mind if I give it a go?"

Reluctantly, Miss Lisa handed over the thread to Lolly and stood back. Lolly was able to get it threaded in one try. "Thank you," Miss Lisa said.

"While I'm here, what else can I help with?"

A little begrudgingly, Miss Lisa picked up the pattern. "They made the print too small. Can you read off step three for me?"

Lolly took the pattern. "I'm happy to." She stayed by Miss Lisa's side for the rest of the evening, helping the older woman lay out her quilt blocks and even doing some of the stitching for her. Lolly noticed that Piney was making the rounds to all the women who had been guarding Shaun and

Patricia earlier. As Piney spoke to each woman in what seemed like fervent whispers, glances were shot in Lolly's direction. She guessed Piney was doing some *fixing*. Lolly certainly hoped so. She didn't like them looking at her as if she were the enemy.

By the time the evening was over, Miss Lisa had made great headway on her second star quilt with Lolly's help. For her small deeds, Miss Lisa grasped both of her hands. "Thank you, dear, for being my eyes and hands tonight. Come by the house sometime for tea and a chat."

"I'd love to," Lolly answered honestly. She guessed she'd done some *fixing* tonight, too, as Miss Lisa's rebuff from earlier had turned into a lovely, wrinkly, grateful smile in the end.

UP UNTIL NOW, Shaun had successfully dodged the citizens of Sweet Home by working on Jesse's cabin and by staying out on the homestead doing chores. But tonight, his mother had insisted that he take her to the lodge for the Sisterhood of the Quilt meeting. Then she'd twisted his arm until he agreed to come in for a minute, actually guilting him into it by decreeing that she had a right to brag about her son. Apparently, she also must've felt like it was her right to show him off, dragging him from person to person as if he were one of her newly finished quilt tops, fishing for compliments, extolling his accomplishments as if he were the most special boy in the world. *I'm not a boy anymore, Mom; I'm a man.*

But he did appreciate that his mom did her damnedest to keep him from Lolly. Even more, he was glad to get out of the sewing studio, away from their questions and their looks. A little bit of Sweet Home's attention went a long way. He was especially glad to escape the room that Lolly was in.

Without running into anyone else, thank goodness, Shaun made it to the back porch of the lodge. The river was raging, but he didn't get lost while gazing at the rapids like usual. He'd heard about Lolly losing her job, and he felt bad for her, but mostly he felt bad for himself, knowing he might see her around town more often if she wasn't busy teaching at the school. He glanced back at the lodge. Had Piney been serious that Lolly could make a living by baking for the citizens of Sweet Home? But then an idea had hit him. Actually, it was his mom's statement about Lolly finding a job out of state that had gotten his wheels spinning, but now he was unstoppable. He pulled out his phone, selected his boss's number, and waited until his boss picked up. Shaun didn't even get to say hello.

"Hey, Montana. You saved me making a phone call. I was just thinking of giving you a ring," Brian said. "I was wondering if you could do me a favor. Can you take a look at Carl's code? I don't want to push it until I know it won't bring down the whole system. Lucinda is putting out fires elsewhere." Lucinda had replaced Shaun. "We miss you here, son."

Shaun would do anything for Brian. Brian had been his mentor. Taken him under his wing on day one and then continually promoted him. Shaun had spent many holidays having dinner at Brian's house with his wife and kids. He also understood why Shaun had to leave . . . that he had to get home to help his mom. But Shaun hadn't told him it was also to put Tanya behind him. "Sure, Brian. No problem. Go ahead and send it to me." Shaun paused before continuing. "I was calling to ask you a favor, actually a favor for . . . a friend." Saying Lolly was a friend was a stretch, but they had been that and more back in the day.

"Anything," Brian said. "Oh, but first, I wondered if you'd heard that Tanya is getting married. Bob in accounting told me; he's second cousins with Tanya's mom. Then the invitation came in the mail today for Georgia and me."

Sourness returned to Shaun's stomach. Tanya had some gall to invite *his* boss to her wedding. "Yes, I'd heard she was getting married." He could almost hear Brian shaking his head.

"I don't understand it, Montana. You and Tanya were together for a long time. We all thought you two were going to be the ones to get hitched. Weren't you engaged or something?"

"Yeah, *something*." But Shaun really didn't want to talk about it. "Listen, about that favor. I was wondering if your wife might know of any openings for home ec teachers in Houston. Or anywhere in Texas for that matter. I have a friend here in Sweet Home whose home ec program was cut from the curriculum, and she needs a job." Shaun felt like he was out on a limb. His boss's answer held everything in the balance.

Shaun had left Houston to get Tanya off his mind. Now he needed to get rid of Lolly, too. Yes, to Brian, he'd made it sound like it would be a favor for Lolly, but getting Lolly away from Sweet Home would be a huge favor for Shaun—actually, a necessity, anything to help him quit thinking of her. An escape to Texas had been the answer for him to get over Lolly in the first place, and now maybe Texas could be the answer again. But this time, Texas could take *her* away! "She'll move anywhere. Small town, big city. Anywhere."

"Okay," Brian said. "Being superintendent of her ISD in Houston does mean Georgia has connections all over. I'll speak to her and let you know. Sound good?" He didn't give him a chance to answer. "Now, about Carl's code . . ." They spent the next ten minutes talking through the issue.

"I'll work on it tonight and get back to you in the morning," Shaun said.

"Let me know your hours, and I'll make sure you're paid for them," Brian said. "And don't think about telling me that they're on the house. You have been a valued employee. I know I said this before, but I really hate to lose you. Would you think about coming back?"

"My mom needs—"

"I know," Brian said cutting him off. "Family does come first. But I just don't know why your mother couldn't have moved to Houston to be with you. Isn't she tired of snowy winters?"

Shaun smiled at the phone. "You'd have to know my mom. She's an Alaskan woman through and through."

"All right, then," Brian said. "We'll talk in the morning."

Shaun hung up feeling pleased with himself. He went inside and returned to the sewing studio. His mom was speaking with a group of women. They suspiciously stopped talking when they saw him. *Great.* He just loved being the town's source of gossip. And he could guess what it had been about. But if everything went well, Brian's influential wife could dig up something for Lolly, and quickly, too, as Brian always said that his wife had more influence than the governor of Texas when it came to the education system. Shaun was counting on it!

"Mom, I need to head back to the homestead. Brian needs me to take care of something."

His mother's eyebrows rose in question. "Your former boss?"

"He ran into a problem and needs me to take a look at some code. It's no big deal, just a quick favor." Shaun felt like he needed to reassure her that he wasn't leaving her, especially with Jesse heading out on Sunday. "Just give me a call when you're ready to come home. I'll run back over and get you."

Piney waved her hand. "Don't worry about your mama. One of us will give her a ride." The room turned into a sea of bobbing heads. In moments like these, he was grateful for Sweet Home because the town had his mom's back and, more than likely, his back, too. A close community had its advantages . . . and its gossiping downfalls. Such was the yin and yang of small-town life.

Shaun could deal with moving back. He really could. Especially if Brian's wife found Lolly a job. In the meantime, though, he had to keep Lolly Crocker off his mind.

Chapter 5

LOLLY HAD FELT jumpy all morning, probably due to lack of sleep. Who could blame her? Unexpectedly seeing Shaun last night had kept her mind reeling into the wee hours. And the pressure to complete all the baked goods requests felt overwhelming. When was she supposed to find time to look for a job? Finally, at three a.m., she rolled out of bed and started baking. The first items on the list were the ones Piney had assigned her to bake for Jesse and Tori's going-away party this evening. Lolly decided that she wasn't upset; she was grateful for the distraction.

By noon her brain had returned to its one track. She worried about what to wear tonight. She fretted over what she might say to Shaun if she had the chance. Most of all, she wondered if he was going to stare into her soul again and see once more that she was lacking.

Just as Lolly pulled the last tray of brownies from the oven her phone rang. She wiped her hands before answering. "Hello."

"I need you to get to the Montanas' now and decorate the dessert table in the barn," Piney said. Instead of having the party at the lodge or at the Baptist church or at Tori's company on Main Street, Patricia had declared the party would be held in their barn. Just like the parties when Shaun and Lolly were in high school.

Lolly frowned at the phone. "I thought I would decorate the table tonight before the party started. I'll just leave home a couple minutes early. It won't take me long. Besides, setting up the table right before the event will save me a trip, and Jilly said she'd help and she isn't here right now." Jilly had run to A Stone's Throw Hardware & Haberdashery to buy some rickrack for the new kuspuk—a hooded shirt—she wanted to make for herself, and Mom, always up for a shopping trip, went with her.

"I don't have time to explain. I need you out there now. I left a table where I want you to set up." Piney hung up.

Lolly stared at her phone, then laid it on the counter. There was no sense in calling Piney back to argue. When Piney got an idea in her head, it was best to just go along with her.

Lolly left the brownies out to cool but loaded the rest of the newly baked goodies in her ten-year-old Toyota Corolla. This morning, she'd taken out the frozen baked goods that she and her students had made earlier; she loaded them into her car, too.

She scribbled a quick note for her sister and her mom, though she would probably beat them back. Throwing a tablecloth on and laying out a few decorations would take no time at all. Unfortunately, Lolly caught sight of her reflection in the mirror by the front door and stopped short. She looked hideous, but she didn't have time to fix her crazy light brown hair or change into something more appealing than her old gray track pants and jacket with flour dusting the front, especially since Piney seemed hell-bent on Lolly being there ten minutes ago.

As Lolly hurried to the car, she decided she'd be okay if she snuck in and snuck out of the Montanas' homestead at the speed of light. Shaun would undoubtably be working on Jesse's cabin and not be in the barn. Besides, what did she care if she was a mess or not? Shaun certainly didn't care one iota about her now.

She just wished that the muscle memory of her heart were as smart as her rational brain. Just thinking about him, her silly heart beat faster—sometimes pounded like crazy, trying to get out of her chest. Each time that she'd seen him, her lungs had malfunctioned, too, as if the sight of him made her breath catch.

Before she left, she checked one more time to make sure that the baked goods in the back seat were secured, as if she were double-checking that a child was strapped in correctly. Satisfied they wouldn't shift, she set off for Shaun and Patricia's. The first part of the drive went just fine and she was proud of herself for being a mature woman who could handle a chance meeting with her high school boyfriend. But the last two miles had Lolly wanting to make a U-ey and head back home.

"What if he's there?" she asked herself. Her heart was pounding out a *Shaun, Shaun, Shaun!* rhythm all the way up to her ears.

But when she pulled down the Montanas' lane, she didn't see any vehicles near the house or the barn. Her heart rate began to slow and she began to breathe more evenly. At the same time, she felt disappointed, let down, which was absurd.

She pulled her car up to the barn and got out, trying not to look around. Jesse and Tori's cabin was over the hill and out of sight of the house and barn. Lolly had to stop herself from hiking up the hill to look for Shaun's Jeep on the other side . . . or to look for Shaun the man.

Disgusted at herself, she sighed heavily and made the first trip to the barn, loaded down with baked goods. When Lolly got inside, she scanned the room but didn't see the table that Piney had promised would be there. Frowning, she set her load of cupcakes and cookies on the riser along the wall, the same riser that had probably been borrowed from the high school choir room. When she turned to get the next load, she stopped short. Shaun stood in the doorway, a folding table leaning against his body. She had the crazy notion that he'd been standing there watching her for more than a single moment.

She was frozen, caught in his gaze like a deer in headlights. She gazed back, feeling as if they were playing a game of chicken. She had no intention of being the one to look away first.

But the table slipped from its position, breaking the moment, and he caught it before it hit the floor. "Where do I need to put this?" he said gruffly, as if his voice hadn't been used all day.

She pointed to the right of the stage. "Piney wants it over here." *Piney*—the one who'd clearly orchestrated this tête-à-tête!

He frowned at her as if she was the one to blame for them being alone together in the barn.

To defuse the mood, or to keep him from thinking this meet-cute was her idea, Lolly said, "So Piney called you, too?"

"Yeah." He walked the table over to its spot and proceeded to set it up, pulling the legs out.

Self-consciously, Lolly grabbed the baked goods and walked with faked confidence toward the boy she'd once loved . . . who'd turned into a man. A gorgeous man. The man she wished she'd never broken up with. The kind of man she wouldn't mind having in her life now. But she couldn't.

He flipped the table over and turned to her. Then he frowned and took the boxes from her and set them on the table.

"Thanks for setting up the table for me," she said.

"Correction," he said. "I was doing it for Piney. Now . . . where are these decorations that Piney was telling me about?"

"Don't worry about it." Yet, she wasn't in a hurry for him to leave. Even though they couldn't be together, she liked being around him. Which didn't make any sense, especially since it was clear that he was still mad at her for breaking up with him. "I'll take care of it from here."

"Are the decorations still in your car?" he said as he walked toward the barn door.

"Yes, in the trunk." Lolly needed to speak with Piney and tell her to stop interfering. It was just making Shaun like Lolly less . . . if that was even possible.

A minute later, he was back, his arms loaded with boxes, which would have taken her several trips. Lolly had moved everything from the table to the floor, only just remembering after he mentioned the decorations that she'd have to put the tablecloth on first.

"What next?" he asked.

"Really, Shaun, you don't have to help."

"Yeah, I do. We need to get this done before my mom gets back."

His comment rang of old times, when they had been kissing on his couch and his mom and dad were due back any minute from running to the Hungry Bear for provisions. The memory made her smile . . . and then sad. Being Shaun's girlfriend had been the happiest time of her life. Yes, she'd been contented this last year, being home, but with him back in Alaska, she just didn't seem to be able to get him off her mind.

She really should concentrate on getting another job out of state. But she was afraid that now he'd awoken all the old feelings in her, she would never be the same.

They both reached down to pull things out of the same decoration box and their hands grazed one another. To her and her off-the-rails heart, the touch felt like a caress. Shaun pulled away immediately.

"You'll need chairs for the table." He was gone, stalking toward the back of the barn, where chairs on carts were ready to be set out.

She had to say something normal, something to defuse the awkwardness between them. She called out, "Do you recall the last party your parents threw in the barn?" She could remember it clearly. But the look on his face had her wishing she could take it back.

"You weren't at the last party." His voice sounded dead. "The last party was my graduation party. You were long gone by then."

Lolly had been remembering her own graduation celebration. She hadn't been around for his, but Jilly had told her all about it. How Shaun had changed—miserable, never smiling—and was no longer the sweet, happy guy she remembered. And it was all Lolly's fault.

"Yes, you're right. I was thinking of my own party."

He stopped and stared at her. "Purple everywhere—streamers, balloons, paper table coverings."

And Shaun had gotten her a purple carnation wrist corsage. She reached over and rubbed her wrist. That purple flower, now faded, was still pressed within the pages of her grandmother's *Better Homes and Gardens Cook Book*, right next to Shaun's favorite recipe: cinnamon-raisin bars. Which were also a favorite of his mom's. This past year was the first time she'd made them since they had broken up. She looked over at the blue container. Had she made cinnamon-raisin bars for tonight with Shaun in mind?

She reached into the box again, retrieved the sunflower tablecloth, and spread it over the table. Shaun carried the chairs over while she smoothed out the last corner. The sunflowers were cheery; maybe the sunflowers would cheer up the other half of the decoration committee.

But he still frowned. "I figured there'll be two people managing the table so I brought two over."

"It'll probably just be me. But it never hurts to have a second chair."

"Why only you?"

"Since I've been home, I seem to do most of the baking," she explained lamely. She didn't want to tell him how she hadn't dated since she'd been back. How she had no expectations of leaving the table because no one would want to dance with Love 'em and Leave 'em Lolly. Then she tried again. "If I'm at the table, I can tell people what ingredients

I've put into the desserts. In case someone has an allergy or something. Where's your mom?" she asked feebly.

"A doctor's appointment." He glanced at his watch. "She'll be back within the hour, I expect."

But Lolly was staring at the inside of his wrist, where the pi symbol peeked out. *So he hadn't removed it!* She started to lift her own wrist to show him her *matching* tattoo, an image of a pie. *Their inside joke.* He, the math geek, computer scientist, nerd; she, the cooking and baking savant. They'd gotten their tattoos at the beginning of her senior year, his junior, on a trip to Anchorage. Her mom and his parents had been furious with them, but they hadn't cared. They were in love and loved that their pi/pie tattoos tied them together forever. She just couldn't believe he still had his.

For her, it'd never been a question of whether to remove it or not. She liked having him permanently tattooed on her wrist, if not her heart. In the strangest way, Shaun had been her one constant. Even though she'd been engaged to others, her fiancés had oddly felt temporary. Had she gotten engaged to them to get over Shaun?

"Are you okay?" he asked, seeming genuinely concerned.

She snapped out of it and grabbed the paper plates from the box. "Oh, yes, fine. Just fine." *Just stumbling down memory lane.* She pushed her hair behind her ears, wishing she'd taken a moment to brush her mop and put on some lip gloss. She couldn't do anything about the way she looked, but she could do something about how she was acting . . . like a lovesick idiot. "So how is life, now that you're back on the homestead? Have you adjusted to the slower pace?"

He laughed, and seeing that old smile of his did her heart good. "Slower pace? You've got to be kidding me." He chuckled again. "Between working on Jesse's cabin and making sure to keep my mom happy, oh, and apparently, be at Piney's beck and call *and* bend to her will, I haven't had a moment to myself . . . or a moment to reflect." He gave a shrug. "I guess that last part is a good thing."

Lolly knew he'd been engaged but didn't know why it had ended. She also knew she couldn't ask. Eventually she'd hear the truth from someone. Or a version of the truth. *The truth according to Sweet Home.*

The mood seemed lighter as they positioned everything on the table, but they left the food covered for later. Lolly was starting to feel comfortable, but then the barn door opened, and all the good feelings between her and Shaun seemed to exit the building.

Patricia halted. "What's going on in here?"

"Uh," Lolly stammered.

Shaun had better presence of mind. "We were just finishing up, weren't we, Lolly?"

She could only nod, as she was intimidated by this Patricia . . . *Angry Patricia.* Lolly really liked the old Patricia. Lolly couldn't think of one thing that would get her back into Patricia's good graces, except to move away as far as possible. And to have made it happen yesterday!

Patricia stayed at the door, holding it open, as if to show Lolly the way out. Or to make sure that she actually left.

Lolly stacked her empty boxes on the floor with Shaun helping. He was probably trying to rush her out of the barn as well.

"Thanks." She looked up and he was staring at her.

"No problem." But he seemed confused.

She reached to pick up the empty box tower, but he snatched them up.

"I can get them." She glanced over at Patricia, who didn't seem happy that Shaun was being so helpful.

"Don't get the wrong idea." Shaun shrugged again. "I'd do this for anyone."

"Okay." But it didn't stop her heart and mind from getting all kinds of wild notions. Hopeful thoughts really.

Lolly just didn't know how she was going to stop herself from falling in love with him again.

SHAUN IGNORED HIS mother's hard look as he walked past her to Lolly's car with Lolly trailing behind him. He would have to talk to his mom again and remind her that he was too old to be mothered.

"You know," Lolly started, "she means well."

He turned and faced her. "You're defending her? You do understand, don't you, that if she could, she'd ship you off to Siberia on the next boat?"

"I think it's a good sign that she's feeling better. Feisty," Lolly said sheepishly. "A year ago, I don't think she'd have had the strength—"

"To nag me to death?" Shaun said, cutting her off.

She gave him a hard stare, like she was about to lecture him. "Your mother loves you. And she's a good mom!" Lolly's own words seemed to register with her and a weird expression crossed her face.

Yeah, he knew what that was about. Lolly's relationship with her mom had always been odd. Lolly seldom agreed with Candy Crocker, but somehow, Candy always got Lolly to do her bidding. Shaun didn't understand why Lolly never stood up to her mom. Oh, what did he know? Maybe things had changed between her and her mom while he'd been gone.

Things had certainly changed between him and his own mother. Before now, they had always gotten along, but suddenly things were strained between them. Didn't his mom understand that he'd been living his own life, answering to no one but his Maker, since the day he left Sweet Home? He didn't need her to smother him with advice.

Lolly stuck out her chin. "Also, you need to understand that your mom is being bombarded with a lot of life changes right now. Big changes. Jesse getting married, and now he and Tori are headed off for several months to film his TV show. She's going to miss them." She looked down at the ground. "Patricia is fond of Tori."

Which only accentuated the fact that his mom wasn't fond of Lolly. *At least not anymore.* Suddenly, and for reasons he couldn't understand, he wanted to tell his mom to lay off of Lolly, too. He knew his mother meant well . . . but still. The breakup had been a long time ago. She should get over it. He was over it. Wasn't he?

Though it had nothing to do with anything, he appreciated Lolly's discretion. She'd had an opportunity to ask him about his broken engagement, and she hadn't . . . unlike the other residents in Sweet Home. His broken engagement was his business and his business alone.

He glanced over to see Lolly looking lonely and sad. "Is everything all right?" He started to ask if she wanted to talk about it, but it wasn't his place anymore. He'd noticed her rubbing her wrist, where the pie had been inked into her skin, which somehow made him wonder if they were still connected through their tattoos. He wouldn't blame her if she refused to answer him or if she told him that what was going on with her was none of his business.

"Just the same ole, same ole." She gave him a reassuring smile, but it kind of missed the mark. Next, she straightened her shoulders and it felt like she'd switched gears. He knew she was about to say something snarky. "Nice try, though. We're not exactly done talking about you. You can't blame your mom for being out of sorts, you know. I'm sure it must be challenging for her to have to be living with you again." Lolly raised her eyebrow and stared him down for a second longer before flouncing past him to her car. She opened the back door and waited for him to follow as if he were her servant . . . and she was a grand lady.

Which she wasn't!

But dang it, she could still make him smile.

"I'm sure it's no picnic living with you either," he shot back because it was never good to let Lolly have the upper hand. "If I recall correctly, you are the antithesis of a neat freak. Candy and Jilly would back me up on this, don't you think? By the way, what does your kitchen look like right now?"

Lolly blushed—either from embarrassment or in frustration that he still knew her as well as he knew his own reflection.

Lolly smiled then, seeming to challenge his assessment. "For your information, Mr. Smarty-Pants, I have a perfectly good excuse for leaving my kitchen in less-than-perfect order. Piney called and insisted I come out here pronto. I didn't have time to straighten up before I left."

"I can see that." Shamelessly, he gave her the once-over, just to throw her off her high horse. Or at least that's what he was telling himself. But the truth was that he liked looking at her. He always had. And it didn't matter if she was dressed to the nines or wearing jeans and an apron. Yes, he was playing with fire, acting like he was starting something with her, but in reality, he had no intention of getting burned again. Regardless, he cataloged every bit of her. She was rumpled, as if she had wrestled with Thor on the floor between pulling items from the oven. She had a patch of white flour on her cheek that was in the shape of a heart. Her hair was pulled back in a ponytail, but half the curls had escaped, a light brown disarray framing her pretty face. Her gray track suit—possibly the same one she'd worn in high school!—must've been the last clean thing in her dresser because it was tattered and so out of style.

And he couldn't help but think that, somehow, she'd never looked more beautiful.

He cleared his throat. "Yeah, well, I see your point. When Piney called, she demanded I drop everything and get over here quickly. As if it were an emergency." Piney and her meddling! She'd cornered him at Jesse's wedding and read him the riot act, saying that he should get over whatever happened in Houston because there was a certain Crocker girl who was single and would be thrilled to have him back in town.

"Listen," Lolly said, "I'm really sorry about Piney. You know I'm more than capable of moving a folding table from point A to point B." She paused as if gathering her thoughts, or maybe she was trying to summon courage. "I'm sorry that Piney has been doing what she's doing. I know it's uncomfortable for you to be around me."

She didn't mention how she felt about being around him, though.

Today, he thought, hadn't felt all that unpleasant. But he didn't dare say those words aloud, especially when he couldn't quite believe it himself.

He slipped the empty boxes into the back seat.

Lolly leaned toward him and touched his arm. "About your mom . . ." she said quietly.

But he couldn't really concentrate. It had always been this way when Lolly was near. Or just seeing her across a room. Or if he had been thinking about her. Or when she'd been touching him like she was right now. "What about her?" His blasted arm was tingling where her hand rested, as if her touch were an electric current that pulsed through him to the beat of her own heart. If he'd had the strength, he would've pulled away from her, but he wasn't strong enough. He was curious to see if this was an anomaly. Or had he gone absolutely nutty with her so close?

"Cut your mom some slack. She means well." Lolly paused for a moment and then straightened, taking her hand with her . . . leaving his arm feeling cold and lonely. "I think your mom's right about you and me." Lolly looked sad. "And Piney . . . well, she's being Piney. She's misguided in this situation, but you know as well as I do that we can't keep her from butting in where she doesn't belong. I'll tell you what. I'll do my best to keep plenty of distance between us so you can keep the peace with your mom. If luck is on our side, I'll be moving away soon anyway . . ." She frowned, then added, "When I find a job."

He opened his mouth to tell her about the call he'd made to his boss. But he thought better of it. Maybe he should call his boss back and tell him to forget about it. In this moment in time, Shaun didn't want Lolly to move away. He wanted her to stay right here, looking like her wholesome, sweet, one hundred percent Lolly self. And maybe, if he was lucky, she would touch his arm again like she'd done a second ago. And how thoughtful was it that she was taking his mom's feelings into consideration?

It took everything in him not to reach up and brush away the flour on her cheek. Surely, he was experiencing temporary insanity, because what other explanation could there be? What he was feeling for her couldn't be real. Good sense would return at any moment, and he'd remember how deeply Lolly had cut him when she'd rejected him. That pain had made him leave his home vowing he would never come back. She'd taken with her his dream of living the rest of his days with her by his side. But somehow, the pain from the past felt *less* with her nearby. Which made no sense at all.

She gave him another sad smile. "I better get going. I have more desserts to make. Thanks for carrying the boxes." She slid into the front seat but leaned out. "You better hurry back in the barn and make nice with your mom. I suggest that you grab a couple of cinnamon-raisin bars from the blue container for her. They're one of her favorites. That should help smooth things over." She shrugged, once again looking sheepish. "That, plus me being gone."

He nodded but didn't plan on going back in the barn. He waved as she pulled away, thinking Lolly had a kind heart . . . one of the kindest he'd ever known. Maybe not so kind to him, but certainly kind to others. The opposite of Tanya, who'd always thought only of herself.

He wanted to get in his Jeep and drive to Anchorage. Maybe hit a club. Anything to get Lolly off his mind. But tonight, he would have to do his duty and attend the going-away party for Jesse and Tori's sake. And his mother's sake, too. He just wasn't looking forward to another encounter with Lolly. This visit hadn't been disagreeable, and that was the problem. In the next few hours, he'd better get his head screwed on straight . . . or he had the awful feeling that he might just do something really stupid.

He didn't understand it, but for some reason he was having second thoughts about hating Lolly forever.

Chapter 6

LOLLY HOPED TO have time to rest or at least find some peace and quiet to process how she, Lolly Crocker, had spent amicable time with Shaun Montana! She wanted to go over every detail of the encounter, again and again. But there was no peace to be had in the Crocker household, especially with Candy Crocker in residence. In normal fashion, her mother had taken over their cottage since she'd arrived, chatting away, regaling Lolly with her wisdom, and filling the corners of the cottage with her abundant energy.

Lolly just wanted to lie down. Be alone. To think. Or not.

Instead, she did as her mother directed—started a batch of chocolate chip pecan cookies and made chicken salad with grapes and walnuts. Candy binge-watched *The Great British Baking Show* while Lolly whipped up her mom's favorite dessert—Ian's carrot and orange cake, season three.

Lolly didn't know where the afternoon had gone, but it was nearly time to leave and her hair was still a mess.

"You can't go to the party looking like that," Candy observed as she came out of her bedroom, looking fresh and young.

Lolly felt like the old hag in the family.

"Go fix yourself up," Candy said.

The front door opened and Jilly sauntered in, setting her goth handcuff handbag on the end table next to the couch. "What's going on?"

Candy waved at Lolly. "Please help her get ready. Make sure to do something with her hair."

"Well, at least my mother didn't say anything bad about my clothes," Lolly said sardonically.

Mom gave her *the look*, then turned to Jilly. "Make sure your sister looks presentable. I don't want the others to think I didn't teach my eldest daughter how to dress for a party."

Jilly shook her head, laughing. "Mom, stop with the compliments, already. You're going to give Lolly a big head."

"A complex is more like it," Lolly muttered.

Jilly ushered her into their shared bedroom. "I think you should wear my black dress and biker boots."

"That's too . . . *much* for the going-away party," Lolly argued. Though the biker boots would tone down the dress.

Jilly went to the closet and pulled out her little black number, which was a head-turner. "Listen, you need something to boost your spirits and . . ."

"And what?" Lolly didn't like the way her sister was looking at her.

"You were acting weird around Shaun last night. I think if you showed up in a killer outfit, and flirted with a bunch of other men there, you would stand out in a different way than you did last night in the sewing studio."

"For your information, I wasn't acting *weird*—as you put it—because of Shaun. I'm just out of sorts because I'm out of a job." That was only a half-truth. Shaun was definitely affecting her and she didn't know what she was going to do about it. Except what she'd promised him: to keep her distance. Which was hard to do since Sweet Home was a tiny village and he would basically be at every function she was.

Jilly thrust the dress at her. "Here. Put it on."

"What are you going to wear now that I'm wearing your favorite black dress?"

"Nothing from your closet, that's for sure. It looks like a garden of pink and blue flowers exploded in there."

Lolly didn't have to remind Jilly that it was Mom who always said that pink and blue went with Lolly's freckly complexion and deep blue eyes. Jilly, on the other hand, had always dressed the opposite of what Mom wanted. *Wild Child* could get away with being rebellious, but *Lolly-Pollyanna* couldn't.

Lolly washed up and donned Jilly's dress. Both Jilly and Mom had ideas about what to do with Lolly's hair, but in the end, she went with Jilly's idea of a messy bun with tendrils framing her face. She wouldn't let Jilly go full goth on her makeup, but she wasn't prepared for what she saw in the mirror when Jilly was done. Lolly was now a mixture of contradictions: the freckled girl next door was made up as a *badass*, especially when she looked down at the biker boots covering her feet. Jilly's dress was much shorter on Lolly than it was on her. Lolly felt embarrassed and, at the same time, empowered. It was surprising how putting on different clothes could make her feel strong. Dressed like this, she could handle whatever the evening threw at her.

But when she walked out of the bedroom, Candy had to comment on the transformation. "My, my. So you're trying to be Jilly Bean's twin?"

Which was ridiculous, as Lolly had wavy light brown hair, freckles, and plain blue eyes, whereas Jilly was petite with short, spiky black hair, striking green eyes, and creamy white skin. Mom swore they came from the same father, but she and Jilly were both suspicious of that claim.

"I'm ready." Lolly was trying to stop her mom from saying more about her appearance. "We better get going." They followed her out to the car.

When they arrived at the Montanas', Piney was waiting for Lolly at the door. "Head over to your dessert table.

We're going to eat straightaway when the guests of honor arrive."

Lolly nodded and walked toward her table, but she kept an eye out for Shaun. The barn had been transformed from earlier in the day. Streamers and twinkly lights were hanging from the rafters, and tables were lined up in rows at the back of the barn. The Good Time Band had set up on the riser and were quietly rehearsing a Zac Brown song. Lolly was glad she'd come earlier to set up the dessert table, because she definitely didn't want to bend over in this dress and unpack the boxes as she had this morning. She was also glad she and Shaun had gotten a chance to chat, because if not, she would've been more nervous than she felt right now. At home, Jilly's clothes had felt like armor, but now, Lolly might as well be naked, as she was sure everyone could see through the facade. And she was correct.

The Sisterhood of the Quilt descended upon her and didn't hold back when it came to speaking their minds about her edgy look. The group was split down the middle as to whether they liked it or not. But they seemed to agree on one thing—Lolly's change in style was so Shaun would notice her.

Piney nudged her in the ribs. "You took my words to heart. Good for you." She gestured at Lolly's outfit. "That'll make that boy think twice about looking at another woman tonight."

Miss Lisa was next, taking Lolly's hand and patting it gently. "Sweetie, you look different. Are you trying to make that boy want you back?"

"No. Not at all," Lolly protested. "I'm dressed this way because I needed a little pick-me-up. I—"

But Miss Lisa cut her off. "No need to explain. Piney says we all have to stay out of it. So I will. Besides, you're a good girl and I want the best for you." The old woman squeezed her hand, dropped it, and then joined the other quilters.

Piney touched Lolly's arm. "I told you I'd fix it, didn't I?

You and Shaun are meant to be together. It's written in the stars."

Lolly frowned. "Maybe a long time ago, but not now." She'd erased any chance of having Shaun for her own.

"I'll leave you for now. But later, we're going to brainstorm things for you to do to get that boy back."

Before Lolly had a chance to open her mouth and argue with her, Piney was walking away. Lolly decided to let it go for now. She'd been brave and daring to come here tonight dressed as an upscale biker chick and she was going to feel confident regardless of what others thought.

Though Piney was in her sixties, she had no trouble climbing up on the bale of hay. "Quiet down, everyone. Quiet down. The guests of honor should be here any minute." Piney looked at her watch and frowned. "Just fashionably late."

Shaun wasn't the guest of honor, but he hadn't arrived yet either. Patricia, too, wasn't among the early arrivals. Lolly couldn't help but watch from behind the dessert table as others poured in through the barn door with their potluck dinner contributions in hand. Where was Shaun?

As soon as she thought it, he walked in, looking gorgeous, taking her breath away. And with him were his mother, Jesse, and Tori. Tori had brought along her sidekick, Scout the labradoodle, who was heeling beside her. Luke and Tori's sister, McKenna, trailed behind them. Lolly couldn't help but wish she was part of the clan. The Montanas had been a tight-knit family. A warm, loving mother, father, children. But Jesse, Shaun, and Luke weren't children any longer, and Mr. Montana had died. Patricia had been ill but was doing better. A lot of things had changed over the years, but the Montanas were still close.

Suddenly, Shaun's head jerked and he looked her way. It was such an abrupt movement, she wondered if she'd subconsciously called his name aloud. But no one else turned in her direction. He was looking at her, but he wasn't smiling. He seemed confused, as if he wasn't quite sure if it was her. *Yes, perfect.* That was exactly the reaction she wanted—to throw him off a bit, payback for what he was doing to her. Before she could make any kind of gesture—either shrug, or wave, or heaven knew what—Piney was hollering to the crowd.

"Stop the music, please. I thought before we get too carried away with the festivities—eating and dancing—we should raise our glasses and toast Jesse and Tori and wish them all the best before they leave in the morning." She put her hand up to her eyes as if she were zeroing in on them. "Are you two all packed?"

"We're ready to go," Tori said with a big smile. She reached down and patted Scout on the head. "I'm considering taking Scout with me." She gave a sad smile. "I'm having a hard time leaving my best buddy." Jesse put his arm around his wife and squeezed.

Piney tsked. "Don't worry about Scout. Your sister and Luke will do a good job of watching out for him while you're gone. You'll only be away for four months. Just enough time for Shaun to get all the finishing touches put on your cabin." Piney pointed at Shaun and winked before continuing. "And enough time for you to start building a home for your own future family, right?"

Shaun's face turned into an angry blush. He glanced at Lolly as if the suggestion had been hers. Next, he glared at Piney, a more appropriate outlet for his dagger-filled glower. "Jesse and Tori's cabin is the only cabin I intend to build. I have enough to do without worrying about separate accommodations for myself."

Patricia gave a curt nod as if to say, *You tell 'em, son.*

Piney laughed. "Yes, well, we'll see. Now, everyone, get in line to fill your plates." She pointed to Jesse and Tori. "The happy couple goes first, of course."

Jesse and Tori did as they were told, with Patricia and Shaun following them, then Luke and McKenna. Lolly was so engrossed in watching them that she almost missed Courtney making a spectacle of herself as she hustled across the barn to join Shaun in line. He seemed waylaid when she grabbed his arm, but he graciously let her cut the line and stand with him.

Lolly wasn't feeling as generous as Shaun and wanted to appoint herself line monitor and send Courtney to the back. To the back forty. Or even better, to Russia. *No cuts.*

But Lolly wasn't going to cause a scene, so she obediently remained behind the dessert table.

With a helping hand from her partner, Bill Morningstar, Piney climbed down from the bale and walked over to Lolly, smiling like a Cheshire cat. "So, how did you like my nudge? I think Shaun got the memo about what the universe would like him to do."

Bill frowned at her. "You were as subtle as a sledgehammer to that boy's head. I thought you weren't going to meddle."

Apparently, Bill doesn't know Piney at all, Lolly thought.

"I'm not meddling," Piney exclaimed, "just doing what the universe wants me to do."

Bill harrumphed. "I'm getting in line for food." He walked away.

"I agree with Bill," Lolly said, hoping to admonish Piney into stopping her interference. There was no way they were getting back together. "That was embarrassing for me and Shaun. I promised Shaun I would put plenty of distance between us so it would make things easier for him at home with his mom."

"Don't worry about Shaun or Patricia, Lollipop, that boy can handle his mama. You'll see." Piney always acted so mysterious, like she had the inside scoop. But Lolly was pretty sure by now that she was just full of it.

"I'll watch your table while you fill your plate," Piney offered.

"I'm not hungry. I nibbled all day." Which was a common problem for those who loved to cook and bake as much as she did. Besides, she didn't want to leave the table, as she planned to use it as a barrier, a safe place for her to watch what Shaun was up to. Courtney would probably be with him the entire night . . . as she was now, walking with him to the Montanas' table.

Piney was giving Lolly a funny look. "Poor Lollipop. You have it bad, don't you?"

"I do not!" Lolly said, trying to deny the longing glance she'd just given Shaun. "I'm staying here while everyone eats so I can slice the cakes and pies and get them plated." Patricia had stacked dessert plates, the same stoneware that had been used at Shaun's parties in high school. Sweet memories. Fun times.

But no more.

She put her mind back on desserts. Besides brownies and blondies, she had made a Texas sheet cake, her special applesauce cake, and an Oreo surprise that the Sisterhood of the Quilt loved. Others had brought homemade cookies—ginger snaps, madeleines, shortbread—and various quick breads: sour cream banana bread, zucchini bread, and a cream cheese pumpkin roll. Ice cream waited in one of the large freezers over to the side. Lolly had enough to do without worrying herself over what might or might not be going on between Shaun and Courtney.

But a half hour later, when the music started, Courtney—skipping dessert altogether—pulled Shaun onto the dance floor and shook her *thang*. Which made Lolly want to curl up in a ball, this time under the dessert table, less than twenty-four hours since the last time she felt this way.

Jilly sauntered over, holding out a plate. "For you. Mom made me put the broccoli on there, so don't blame me if it's touching your salmon casserole."

"Thanks." Lolly set the plate on the table.

"I know watching them is eating you up," Jilly said, "but you should be more discreet about it."

"I don't know of what you're speaking." Lolly's words were stiff, but she did what her sister suggested and switched her gaze from the dance floor to studying the empty stalls on the other side of the barn. "Besides, you're one to talk. You know nothing about being discreet or practicing proper decorum."

"Yeah, I do. But proper decorum doesn't fit my personality, and since I don't care what others think, some rules don't apply to me." Jilly lifted an eyebrow. She didn't have to spell it out. It was clear that Jilly thought Lolly worried too much about what others thought of her.

Lolly didn't want to argue. She noticed Josh and Nate, two lumberjacks, walking toward them. "You should dance," she whispered. *And leave me alone.*

Josh nodded to them. "Would you two like to dance?"

"You're kind of obligated to, 'cuz there are more guys here than ladies," Nate pointed out with a charming smile.

Lolly shook her head. "I can't, but Jil—"

Jilly cut her off. "Sure. We'd love to." She turned to Lolly. "There's nothing else for you to do here. Let's go have some fun." She practically dragged Lolly onto the dance floor.

But as soon as they got there, the song switched from a fast Keith Urban song to "Bless the Broken Road" by Rascal Flatts. Lolly inwardly groaned. The *broken road* she'd been on had brought her back to the only man she'd ever loved with all her heart. When she'd said yes to those other proposals, she'd tried to convince herself that she loved those men. But it was never like she'd loved Shaun.

Surprising her, Josh pulled her to him, swaying to the song that was killing her. Or maybe what was doing her in was having Shaun and Courtney four feet away with Courtney laughing like Shaun was the star of a romantic comedy and she was his leading lady. Lolly must have stared at them for too long, because Shaun looked over and caught her. Lolly expected to die from embarrassment, but Josh turned them, blocking Shaun.

"You look really sexy tonight, Lolly," Josh said into her ear. Then he leaned down and nuzzled her neck.

She was mortified. But she couldn't pull away . . . or could she?

She did. "I need to cover the food." She rushed away

with her eyes stinging, making her worry she might cry. Which was stupid. She didn't do anything wrong, except agree to dance when her heart wasn't in it. Thankfully, Josh didn't follow her but asked Aberdeen to dance instead.

Back at the table, Lolly watched Shaun and Courtney to her heart's content, as no one was watching her. They were either caught up in the music on the dance floor or caught up in conversation at one of the tables or standing at the punch bowl.

As if she were a clinician, she studied the happy couple. They made a good pair, both of them beautiful to look at. Shaun was cutting loose on the dance floor like they used to do in high school; he'd always loved to dance. Lolly decided to be glad that Shaun had found his equal and that he would be happy with Courtney. But taking the high road hurt. It was pure torture watching them have fun together.

She left the table to find Jilly and found her sister slipping outside with Nate. The two were holding hands. "Hold up. I need the keys to the car."

Jilly pulled the keychain from her wide wrist band and took Lolly's arm. "Are you all right?"

At that moment, Shaun stepped outside, too. He was alone and looked surprised to find the trio. Lolly wanted to ask, *Where's Courtney?* But she didn't.

"Migraine," Lolly lied to her sister. "I need to go home."

Jilly looked up at Nate and frowned. "I better take her."

"No. I'll take her," Shaun said, apparently overhearing them. "That way you and Candy can stay longer."

"But—"

"I'll check in on you when I get home," Jilly said, putting the car keys away and waving as she and Nate walked to the corner of the barn, then disappeared.

Without really giving Lolly a chance to argue, Shaun put his hand to her back and led her across the yard toward his Jeep. "How bad is it, the migraine?"

"What are you doing outside?" Once again, she did a good job of not mentioning Courtney.

"Mom needs a pillow from the house," he said, taking Lolly's arm as if she were feeble or something. "She thought it might make her a bit more comfortable while sitting in the folding chairs."

But Lolly wasn't frail and feeble. If she was being truthful, she really didn't mind his hand cradling her arm. At one time, it had been normal. Now it was an indulgence. No, a fantasy. But she couldn't relish his touch. It was just getting her hopes up, when there really was no hope at all. Lolly dug her heels into the dirt, effectively pulling him to a stop. "You better go get the pillow for your mom." She looked back at the barn. "Or else it'll give her another reason not to . . ." She trailed off. She wasn't going to gripe about Patricia. Patricia had every right not to like Lolly anymore.

"Mom can wait a few more minutes." The air hung with his unspoken *But you can't.* "Listen, I know how bad it was for you in high school when you had a migraine. You shouldn't be driving. And it'll just take a few minutes. I'll be back before anyone knows I'm gone."

She couldn't lie to him any longer. "I'm fine. No migraine. I just wanted to go home."

He dropped his hand from her arm, his disappointment in her evident in his downturned mouth. "Did you even speak with my brother and Tori tonight? Or were you just going to run off?" She could imagine him finishing that sentence: *Just like you ran off to college when you dumped me.*

"Yes, of course I spoke with Jesse and Tori. At the dessert table. I was able to thank Tori again for the lovely quilted apron she made me." Lolly felt herself revving up for an extended ramble. She tried to stop herself but was unable—she deeply missed talking to Shaun. "You should see it. One side of the apron is masculine with animals in the foreground and wood paneling in the background. The other side is multicolored—okay, mostly blue—with a Christmas tree–type design. Tori's a great designer, don't you think?"

He took her arm again. "What's going on with you? And

why are you dressed the way you are? I don't think you've worn a black dress in your life. You like wearing lots of bright colors. Black is kind of Jilly's thing, isn't it?"

Lolly glanced down at the biker boots and the hem of Jilly's dress. These clothes had really let her down. Her outfit hadn't worked as armor after all. If it had been armor, Shaun wouldn't have been able to get under her skin.

"I was just trying out a new style. No big deal." She couldn't tell him that he made her nervous. That she could barely breathe when he was around. Or that she'd never gotten over him or the way the two of them together had been *total magic.*

He stepped closer. She could almost imagine that he was going to slip his arm around her waist and pull her close. "I like the outfit. But I think I like *your* clothes more."

She wasn't quite sure what she was supposed to do with that. "Okaaay."

Time kind of stood still. She couldn't help it when her eyes dropped to his mouth; they were being pulled there as her breathing became shallow. And she knew that mouth so well. At one time, she believed he would be the last person she'd ever kiss. But since then, she'd kissed a lot of guys. Well, not a lot, but some. And she'd broken a heart or two or three or four. Before she did something really stupid— like take the initiative—she moved away from him. She couldn't stand it if she hurt Shaun again. "I promised you that I'd keep my distance."

"Yes. Right." He dug in his pocket, pulled out the keys, and thrust them at her. "Take my vehicle . . . since you're fine. Jesse and I will come by later to pick it up. Leave the keys above the visor."

But Lolly wasn't fine. Not because of a *migraine* but because of a *conflicted heart.* Then she realized that she'd have to drive his vehicle, certain that would be torture, too. The Jeep would smell like him—not exactly like homemade vanilla wafers, but pretty dang close to it and more compelling, for sure.

She sighed into the twilight, feeling certain she was going to end up like her mom—*alone*. But unlike her mom, Lolly was the one who had done the leaving. Another big difference between Lolly and her mom was that at least Candy went after what she wanted, even if it left her hurt. Lolly, on the other hand, wasn't brave at all. Or strong. She was too scared to listen to her heart, and too obedient to go against what others thought she should do. She was trapped in a prison of her own making with no clear way out. Her life would always be filled with loneliness and heartache . . . and no true love to call her own.

Chapter 7

SHAUN WATCHED LOLLY drive away before heading back to the barn. When he reached the door and stretched out his hand to grasp it, he stopped suddenly and about-faced. *Mom sent me to get her pillow from the house, the whole reason I left the party in the first place*, he thought to himself. He marched off toward his mom's cabin, once his cabin, too. "What's wrong with me?"

He knew it had to do with Lolly. And maybe even Tanya. Or Courtney. Heck, all women! He was so off-kilter these days. He wondered when, or if, he was going to get his bearings again.

At home, he retrieved the pillow and hurried back to the barn. Courtney was just leaving.

"Oh, there you are." She took his arm. "I was coming to find you. I'd rather dance with you than any other man here." Lolly had offered to give him space, but Courtney, it seemed, planned to dominate the rest of his night, not giving him any space at all. "We could either boogie for a couple more dances or you can drive me home now."

"Drive you home? What about your car?" he asked.

She glanced over to where a group of women were gathered. "I came with Aberdeen and Lacy. I didn't really make a plan to get home." She had that hopeful look in her eyes, as if Shaun could make all her dreams come true.

Which only confirmed one of his biggest worries. Courtney was okay, but he was getting the feeling that she was gunning for him. And he wasn't available . . . *for any woman.* Plus, Courtney wasn't really his type.

He finally acquiesced. "Yeah, I can take you home." But he would have to borrow his mom's Forester, and he was determined not to lead Courtney on. "Listen, I'm sure you heard about my recent breakup."

She nodded with a slight smile and gave his arm a squeeze. "Poor thing. I was so sorry to hear it."

He didn't believe that for a second.

"Maybe being home will be just the thing to make it all better," she purred, squeezing his arm again and moving closer, wrapping herself around his bicep.

"I'm not really interested in dating right now," he said kindly but firmly. "I'm sure you understand, right?"

She looked up at him with doe eyes. "Give me a chance to change your mind?"

He gently removed her hand from his arm. "Sorry, no."

She pouted as if he'd spoiled her plans.

"You're a great girl," he said feebly, afraid she might cry. "You know there's plenty of men around here that would be thrilled to go out with you." He should've stopped with that but he didn't. "How about Josh or Nate? Or Dewey?"

She pouted even more, shaking her head, making her blond poufy hair sway side to side.

"I'm not in a good place," he said. "I'm not good for anyone right now."

The last bit she seemed to take as a challenge, her eyes heating up. "We can talk about it as you take me home."

But Piney was heading over, calling Shaun's name. "Hold up, there, Shaun. I need you."

He rolled his eyes. He didn't like being in such high demand, which seemed to be a constant problem since he'd come back home. "What can I do for you?"

"I need you to run to Lolly's house and pick up the aluminum foil."

Shaun looked at Piney sideways. He didn't believe for a second that she'd forgotten the aluminum foil and couldn't get it from someone—or somewhere—else. "We probably have some." He handed Piney the pillow. "Can you give this to my mom? I'll run to the cabin to check."

Piney held the pillow to her chest and shook her head adamantly. "No, no. I'm sure you won't have enough. I should've had Lolly bring some from her stash earlier. She has plenty. I called her cell phone, and she has two whole rolls. I told her someone would be by to get it."

"Can't you send someone else?" Courtney said, pouting again. "We were getting ready to leave."

Piney looked struck with an idea, but she didn't enlighten them as to what she was thinking. "Oh, I see," she finally said. "Well, Courtney, you can either wait here, while Shaun runs to Lolly's—"

Courtney cut her off. "No, I'll go with him. I didn't get to say good night to Lolly before she left. I also wanted to tell her about the wonderful almond cheesecake cones I had at a patisserie while I was in Anchorage. I hoped she could make me a batch to put in my freezer . . . before she moves away for her job."

He had to hand it to Courtney, as she was pretty quick on her feet. *Fine*, Shaun thought. He'd take Courtney with him, but he didn't see why Piney seemed so pleased with herself.

Courtney had her hand on his arm again. "Give me a minute, will you? I want to tell Aberdeen you're taking me home," she said before she ran back inside.

Which would only get the gossip mill revved up and speculating about all kinds of unseemly scenarios.

Shaun saw his mom barreling in his direction. He took the pillow away from Piney and held it out to his mom.

Automatically, she took it and shoved it under her arm. "What's going on here?"

"I'll let you two talk," Piney said, smiling broadly as she ambled away.

"Nothing's going on, Mom," he said. "I'm going to borrow your Forester to take Courtney home."

Patricia smiled as if he'd made her the happiest mother in the world. "You and Courtney look so cute together. She's beautiful and she's always had a crush on you."

Yeah, a crush on me and every other guy on the football team.

"Stop frowning," his mom said. "I like you two together. As a couple, you make sense." Mom frowned, looking off in the distance as if seeing Lolly longing after him. Which was ridiculous, as she certainly wasn't. Mom brought her gaze back to him, looking determined. "You and Courtney would certainly make some beautiful babies together."

"Real subtle, Mom. Once and for all, there are no babies in my future. About Courtney, she's okay but she's not my type." Courtney reminded him too much of Tanya—great arm candy, but not enough substance . . . *as opposed to someone like Lolly.* Shaun was shocked at his thought. He couldn't believe he let himself go there and admit it.

Courtney was walking back to him with a wide smile.

"I won't be long," Shaun said to his mom.

"Take your time," his mom said.

Shaun shook his head as his mother walked away.

"I'm ready to go," Courtney announced.

When they got into his mom's Forester, Courtney leaned over and looped her arm around his arm and held on. He started to remind her they weren't dating but decided it would be a waste of his breath. Instead of stopping by Lolly's first, he'd take Courtney home . . . and that would be the end of him and Courtney. He'd make sure of it.

All the way into town, Courtney chatted about her job and the houses she'd listed in the past month. "It's really something how some longtime Alaskan residents are yearning for warmer weather, selling their homes, and moving south, while there's the folks from the Lower 48 who are tired of being cramped, tired of seeing their neighbors, who want space and privacy." Courtney laughed. "I'm not complaining because business is booming and keeping me in nice clothes and spa days whenever I want them. I'm even thinking of buying a second income property out on Cemetery Road." She glanced over at him. "Your mom mentioned that you sold your condo in Houston, but I missed the details. How is the market there? Did it sell quickly or sit for a while?"

"Sold quickly." Though since then, he'd had moments of regret at letting his place go. Having an escape hatch, especially on nights like this when he felt penned in, made him miss the freedom and anonymity that he'd had in a large city. "It sold in eleven days. The real estate agent lined up a stager and I got several offers at the open house." Now his mom wanted Shaun to build on the Montana property like Jesse. But Shaun wanted his own place; he'd let Jesse and Mom have the property. He'd probably end up asking Courtney to find him a house farther away but close enough that he could help Mom out every day.

Courtney took off on a diatribe about how it was hard to find good stagers. Shaun only half listened. When he arrived in town, he turned right on Courtney's street.

"What are you doing?" she asked.

"Taking you home like you wanted," he said.

"I told you I wanted to speak with Lolly." There was a definite whine to her voice.

"I have to hurry back to the homestead right after. Piney needs that aluminum foil."

"That's just an excuse," Courtney said. "She wants you and Lolly back together. You know that, don't you?"

Shaun rolled his eyes before pulling up in front of Courtney's two-story, three-car-garage house with wide arched windows—the nicest property in Sweet Home proper. He had to hand it to her; she certainly lived well, while others were just scraping by. He put the car in park for her to hop out, but before he knew what was happening, Courtney wrapped her arms around his neck and was kissing him.

He pulled away. "Whoa. Stop." He removed her arms from around him. "I don't want to hurt your feelings. You're nice, but as I told you, I'm not interested in a relationship right now."

She shrugged. "Who said I wanted a relationship?" She reached for him again and he grabbed her wrists.

"Come on, Courtney. That's enough."

She sat back in her seat with a sigh. "You can't blame a girl for trying." She gathered her purse and slipped out of the passenger seat. She shut the door but leaned back in the open window. "If you change your mind, you know where to find me." She sashayed up the walkway.

He made sure she was safely inside her house before pulling away from the curb.

Time to head to Lolly's. But he needed to steel himself first. If Lolly was wearing her biker chick outfit, he might ogle her again. Or worse.

When he got to her front door, she opened it immediately, as if she'd been waiting for someone. But she looked confused.

"What are you doing here? Is this Piney's meddling again?" She had the aluminum foil in her hand. She wasn't wearing the black dress and biker boots and her face had gone from goth girl to scrubbed clean. She looked like the old Lolly—barefoot and wearing a baby-blue T-shirt and jeans—and he was relieved . . . and conflicted, too. This was the girl he'd fallen in love with, but she was a woman now. Her comfy clothes, no makeup, looking like the girl next door he knew her to be. Weird, but his heart didn't feel broken right now, as it was pounding out the old familiar rhythm, the one that had him falling in love with her when he was only a kid.

He was glad he'd dropped Courtney off first. Glad he'd come alone.

"What's wrong? Are you all right?" Lolly asked.

What a contrast! Courtney would never ask him how he was doing. She'd never answer her front door barefoot and in jeans either. Courtney Wolf was attractive, but she *wasn't* in the same league as Lolly Crocker!

He did something stupid, really stupid. Maybe it was to counteract how Courtney had come at him. Her kiss had been hard, crass . . . unpleasant.

He took Lolly's hand and pulled her toward him. For a moment, he gazed into her eyes—*her surprised eyes, her familiar eyes, the eyes he'd always gotten lost in*—and then he did the unthinkable. He kissed her. Immediately, he was transported back—the electricity buzzing between them, how she'd always taken his breath away, how natural it was to pull her closer, wanting more.

He jerked away from her. He had no choice. Because kissing Lolly was so very intoxicating, and he was in danger of falling down that slippery slope again. Something he would never let himself do twice.

He mumbled, "Sorry," turned around, and walked toward his mom's vehicle. He stopped short. For the second time tonight, he'd forgotten what he was supposed to do.

Like a man heading to the gallows, he marched back to Lolly. She handed over the aluminum foil, her cheeks blazing red as she refused to meet his eyes. He was glad of it. The last thing he needed was to gaze into her amazing blue eyes again.

Without a word of thanks, he hurried back to the car.

Lolly called out to him. "Good night?"

Her words came off as a question, which had him thinking . . . *had* it been a good night?

He shook his head and started the car. He was not going to analyze it. But that kiss! Lolly's kiss! Had been amazing.

STILL STUNNED, LOLLY watched as Shaun drove away and, ridiculously, wished he'd come back and kiss her again. Just to make sure it had been real. Her lips still tingled, yet it felt like a dream. She pulled out her phone and called Paige. It went directly to voice mail, which meant Paige was still presenting at her Denver workshop. Lolly didn't leave a message. What could she say anyway? *I think I'm falling in love with Shaun Montana all over again.* Or maybe she'd never stopped loving him at all. It was hard to tell.

She stood at the doorway, watching the road for a full five minutes. A moose wandering into her yard had her finally shutting the door and returning to the kitchen to make herself something to eat. She just couldn't figure out what.

Instead, she strode the few feet into the living room and plopped down on the couch. Thor automatically jumped up and settled into her lap, and she scratched him behind the ears. No one was home, but she still looked around before whispering aloud, "Shaun kissed me."

Thor stretched and yawned and snuggled in deeper. She rested her hand on his back. "I don't know why he did it. He spent the whole evening dancing with Courtney, and he looked like he was having a great time with her, too."

But that kiss . . . that kiss! Had been amazing. Lolly couldn't slow her out-of-control, pounding heart. It took her back to the days when she'd taken Shaun's kisses and his love for granted. When she'd been certain she'd be able to kiss him whenever she wanted. Certain that they were going to be together forever.

I ruined it. She'd lived with that mistake ever since.

But why had he kissed her? Hadn't she been clear that she had to keep her distance from him for his mom's sake? What if Patricia found out that they'd kissed on Lolly's front stoop? Would the stress of it be too much for her ailing health?

Lolly decided there was an explanation for Shaun's behavior: human instinct. She had unintentionally set herself up to be a challenge . . . with the help of Patricia, of course. Lolly had become the forbidden fruit, and Adam, or in this case, *Shaun*, wanted her that much more.

"Well, he can't have me," she said to Thor and the empty room. But her pounding heart said otherwise.

She moved Thor off her lap and headed back to the kitchen. She had pulled out all the ingredients to make bread, sure that kneading dough and slapping it against the counter would alleviate some of her frustration, but now she only wanted to make cookies. Something sweet . . . like Shaun's kiss.

She pulled down her favorite cookbook, which her grandmother had handed down to her. Her grandmother had handwritten notes next to various recipes, and Lolly had followed the tradition. At the top of the sugar cookie recipe, which was easy to find because it was tabbed with a Post-it note, her grandmother's scrawl read, *The best!* Lolly agreed.

She put away the bread ingredients and replaced them with the ingredients for the sugar cookies, all the while thinking about Shaun. Her hand hovered over the mixer as she was about to cream the sugar and butter. She stopped, grabbed her pen, and hastily made a note in the margin of the recipe:

Sweeter than sugar.
Made me melt like warmed butter.
Over too soon.

She stood back. "What have I done!" she cried aloud. Why had she critiqued Shaun's surprise kiss in her favorite cookbook? And in pen, too. At least her grandmother's notes were in pencil. Lolly could see where her grandmother had made changes here and there . . . and now Lolly had desecrated the treasure her grandmother had left her. Just like she'd ruined her relationship with Shaun.

She slammed the cookbook shut. "I don't need it anyway.

I know the recipe by heart." Out of desperation, she turned on the radio, hoping to tune out the world, or more importantly, to tune out the voice in her head that called out to Shaun to come back and kiss her again. But when the first notes of "Be Alright" kicked in, she started to change the station—she was certain it wasn't going to *be all right* in the least. Except she didn't turn the dial. She stood there transfixed as the chorus kicked in. "Everything will be alright. The whole world's in His hands."

She'd heard the song many times. But this time, it really spoke to her. She wanted to believe everything was going to be all right, but she was hung up on a guy she shouldn't want again.

She was out of a job and should be putting effort into that disaster instead of baking cookies. The song claimed that everything would be all right and that He had the whole world in His hands. But if that was true, then why was she such a mess?

She forced herself to remember there were worse things happening to others than what she was going through. Like the last few years, when Patricia had been dealing with her illness. Not for all the cheesecake in the world would Lolly tell Shaun how she felt about him and create a fuss, because she wouldn't do anything to jeopardize Patricia slipping back into the hell she'd already been through.

Lolly switched gears, switched recipes, and turned to the page with snickerdoodles. In the last year, she'd made them several times for Patricia, knowing how much she liked them. In the margin of this recipe, she'd written: *Add extra cinnamon.* When all the ingredients were mixed, she rolled the dough into balls and placed them two inches apart on the baking sheet before popping the sheet into the oven.

Next, Lolly went to the shelf above the small desk in the kitchen, pulled out one of the quilt block notecards that she kept for good friends, and wrote:

Dear Patricia,

I'm sorry for the trouble I have caused you and your family. I never meant to hurt you or Shaun.

> *All the best,*
> *Lolly*

When the snickerdoodles were done and cooled, Lolly would package them before dropping them off at the Montana homestead along with the note. She would make sure Shaun wasn't home at the time because this peace offering had nothing to do with him.

And then Lolly would look for a job elsewhere and stop worrying whether Shaun would kiss her again. She would put her heart and soul into the job search. She had to, for Patricia's sake, and for Shaun's sake, too.

Because it was better than the pipe dream that had been floating through her brain. She'd been putting her heart and soul into the wrong thing. The *wrong* someone. And it had to stop now.

Chapter 8

ONCE AGAIN, HIS mom was dragging Shaun someplace he didn't want to go.

He didn't have anything against attending church. He rarely missed a service, either here or in Houston. But today was an exception. He'd made a fool of himself last night by kissing Lolly. When he and Jesse drove into town much later to pick up his Jeep, Shaun had the urge to knock on Lolly's door again. That thought alone made him see that he definitely wasn't in his right mind. Lolly spelled trouble for him! And he couldn't stand it that he would see her here at church this morning. There was no way to hide from her, as the Crockers had always sat behind the Montanas at the Baptist church. Shaun would have to deal with the proximity every week . . . until Lolly found a job and moved elsewhere. Which made him wonder if his old boss had discussed Shaun's request with his influential wife.

Shaun parked his Jeep and followed his mom into the church. He decided not to look around, afraid he might see Lolly, afraid he might have to face her. Afraid he might have to figure out why the hell he'd kissed her, as if she meant something to him. Besides, he already had enough problems without seeing Lolly three days in a row. This morning, his mother had hollered at him, thinking he had something to do with the two dozen cookies that Lolly had left on the front porch for her. For a second there, he thought his mom might try to send him to his room.

As luck would have it, Lolly wasn't in her seat when he stepped into the sanctuary. At least there was that. He hurried down the aisle, leaving his mother at the rear to speak with Miss Lisa and a few others from the Sisterhood of the Quilt. When he got to their pew, he took his seat and pulled out the hymnal, determined to focus on it and not the row behind him.

His mother appeared and sat next to him. "Maybe they aren't coming today."

He didn't need an explanation of whom she meant. "Maybe." But he doubted it. With Candy Crocker back in town, all three of them would be there, even if they were a couple of minutes late.

The music began and the choir started down the aisle. Shaun didn't turn around to watch but kept his eyes on the words in the hymnal, afraid Lolly might have slipped into her pew behind him without him knowing. But surely he would hear her singing, wouldn't he? Lolly had a beautiful voice.

Suddenly, he did hear her. But instead of it being behind his right shoulder as expected, he heard her singing from his left side. He turned to discover her processing in with the rest of the choir. For a moment, she glanced up from her hymnal and smiled. At first he thought the smile was for him, and his chest pounded as if she'd aimed a shot of warmth straight at his heart. Then he realized she was smiling in general—at the song, the beautiful day, being among the church community, or whatever—because when she caught his eye and saw him looking, her eyes snapped back to the music and her cheeks turned red. She even seemed to stumble mid-song. Shaun felt really bad. He'd done that to her by kissing her last night . . . and throwing them both off.

By this time, she was past him, almost to the front, and

he was grateful not to see her embarrassment. He wished he didn't feel it for himself.

The pastor followed along and took his place in front of the altar. But Shaun could only stare at Lolly. He'd stopped singing, too. With his mouth hanging open.

His mother elbowed him and hissed a bit too loudly, "Stop staring." People around them had zeroed in on him. "Sometimes Lolly sings with the choir. It's no big deal."

But it was to him. A little heads-up would've been nice. But he shouldn't be upset with his mom. He wasn't supposed to care what Lolly was up to. She was old news. Or at least she was supposed to be.

He couldn't get over how Lolly just seemed to give and give, and he couldn't help but compare her with Tanya. And Courtney. And every other woman he'd ever known. He thought about the song they used to sing at church camp when they were kids; the first line was "We are made for service." Donovan had told him that "Service" was actually a Catholic praise song. But Shaun didn't care where it had come from. He had always loved the meaning behind the words . . . that it was more important to take care of others than to focus on oneself.

Lolly seemed the embodiment of that song. She really was made for service, and Shaun had always wanted to be like her in that regard. But then there was the other side of Lolly, the way she couldn't commit in a relationship. He'd heard about the other guys whose hearts she'd broken, and wasn't surprised in the least. After all, she'd gotten off to a good start by practicing on him. Her first boyfriend. Her first breakup. He just didn't understand Lolly at all. How could she be all kinds of good and still do what she did to men?

But that kiss! It would take a long time to forget that kiss and how his heart had come back to life again. Even now, he could feel it beating faster just thinking about her.

Lolly drove him crazy, and yet . . . illogically he still wanted her. That little voice in his head had gone off on a tangent again and he needed to straighten it out. Lolly was trouble, plain and simple, plus, he knew the pain and heartache she caused. He wasn't willing to go down that road again. He tamped down the thought of having Lolly in his life once more and shoved it to the back forty of his mind.

He felt someone staring at him and he glanced up at his mother, who was frowning and giving him that look—that look that said Lolly was no good for him. Yes, he agreed, but he really wished his mom would just let him handle his own life and keep her judgments to herself.

"Concentrate on the service," Mom whispered in her lecturing tone.

He rolled his eyes, feeling like a tyke again, getting scolded in church. He wasn't sure he was going to survive moving home to Sweet Home. Survive living with his mother *or* having Lolly in town. He made the decision then and there that when he was done with Jesse and Tori's cabin, he was going to either build a cabin of his own—for *himself*, not a family—or find some other place to live. That property out on Cemetery Road was looking better and better to him each day!

Ignoring his instinct to rebel against her scolding—no man liked having his mother tell him what to do—Shaun concentrated on the service, and from there, a clear message broke through Shaun's thick skull. The preacher spoke of asking forgiveness when you've treated someone poorly.

He'd treated Lolly poorly. He'd used her when he'd kissed her to erase Courtney from his mouth. He shouldn't have done it, and he had to speak with Lolly as soon as possible. Clear the air. Sooner would be better than later, according to Pastor Joe.

Impatiently, he sat through the rest of the service, piecing together in his mind what he was going to say. As soon as the choir recessed from the sanctuary, Shaun headed out to find Lolly.

He saw her slip into the choir room and he waited outside while she presumably hung up her robe. The second she walked out, he latched onto her arm and steered her toward the side entrance, out of earshot of the others.

Lolly pulled away and slammed her hands on her hips. "What are you doing? Jilly and my mom are waiting for me." But at least she stayed put.

"This won't take long." He reached out to pull her closer but stopped himself. He'd brought her here to put a stop to things, but mostly to apologize for what he'd done. But now he couldn't think of the words he'd planned to say, or even where to start.

She stared at him, indignant, but then she dropped her hands, looking concerned. "What is it? What's wrong? Is your mom okay?"

He was blown away by Lolly. Even in this moment, her thoughts were on others besides herself. To be concerned about his mom—who made her dislike for Lolly clear—was astounding.

"Everything's fine." But it wasn't. "Listen," he said, "I'm sorry."

Her eyebrows crashed together. "Sorry for what? You haven't done anything to be sorry for. I'm the one . . ." She trailed off.

Suddenly he wanted answers, thinking if she told him why she broke up with him so long ago, it would probably make it easier on them both.

"Why did you do it, Lolly?" She was a smart cookie. She had to know what he meant.

She looked down at her red shoes below her blue polka-dot dress. A moment later, she raised her head and bravely gazed at him, piercing him with her blueberry eyes. "I thought you knew."

"How could I have known?"

"My letters. I explained everything to you. I wrote you nearly every day my first semester of college. Didn't you get them?" She looked perplexed.

"Oh, yeah. *Those*." He had the decency to feel embarrassed. "I got them. But I didn't read them." He'd chucked them in a burn barrel the second they were delivered and put a match to the paper. Up in smoke. Ashes to ashes, dust to dust. He shrugged as if it was no big deal, but he'd been so angry back then. "Tell me why, Lolly."

Lolly gazed out the window behind him. "I was a coward."

"What's that supposed to mean?" he asked.

"I couldn't stand up to Mom. She thought I was too young to be so serious about you. Plus, she thought I should go to college unattached so I could have fun. I'm so sorry, Shaun."

"She told you to break up with me?" He was in shock. He'd always thought Candy liked him.

"I know it's not a good excuse. I shouldn't have listened to her—"

"It's no excuse at all!" Shaun was livid. At eighteen, he was a full-grown man, living completely on his own, making his own decisions. "You didn't have to do what your mother told you to do."

The second he said it, he was flooded with memories. This had been the primary argument between them back then: Lolly doing what her mom wanted her to do, no matter what. When he'd wanted to take Lolly to an outdoor concert in Anchorage, Lolly had done as her mother wanted and bought the CD instead. When Lolly wanted to cut her hair, her mother told her that Shaun would lose interest in her, even though Shaun insisted he'd love her no matter what her hair looked like. It really irked him that Lolly constantly bent to her mother's will. Back then, he should've been sharp enough to have seen the breakup coming— Candy was constantly harping on Lolly to enjoy her youth, have fun, meet other people, and not settle down too soon.

"So what about the others?" Shaun asked impulsively. "Did your mother tell you to break up with them, also?"

Lolly blanched. "How do you know about them?"

In answer, Shaun cocked an eyebrow.

"*Sweet Home*," Lolly hissed, as if the town's name were

a string of curse words. She composed herself, even haughtily straightening her shoulders. "It's none of your business why I broke up with them."

"Maybe not, but you're going to tell me anyway." Shaun had used that same phrase on her many times before. It was funny how old habits could come back so easily. How they'd fallen into the same old routine. He'd always been bossy with Lolly back in the day . . . even though he was a year younger. She'd never seemed to mind that he told her what to do. Which made him think that Candy and he had something in common, making Lolly bend to their will.

"Fine," she said. She paused for a long moment, as if she were weighing whether to fabricate some clever response or to tell him the truth. Finally, she exhaled with a frown and spilled it. "I didn't love any of the others enough to marry them."

Something about that confession hit him in the chest, almost causing the next question to tumble out. It bounced around his brain like a pinball caught between bumpers. *What about me? Did you love me enough to marry me?* But thank goodness, he stopped those words before he looked like an eager fool. He'd gotten over her. He'd moved on. If only he could stop the question from pounding in his head, looking for the truth. But wasn't it obvious? The truth was that Lolly hadn't loved him enough to marry him either.

She hadn't even given him the chance to ask. He'd planned to wait until he graduated from high school, and he had it all worked out in his head. A beautiful summer day. He'd pack a lunch that they'd have on the picnic quilt they'd used on many occasions. He would get down on one knee to give her the ring he'd been saving up to buy. Back then, he'd known with every fiber in his body that they belonged together. But, in the end, he'd been wrong.

Candy and Jilly appeared at the end of the hallway and Lolly automatically turned to them. Probably because she wanted an escape. She confirmed it a second later. "I gotta go. What was it you wanted to apologize for?"

"Nothing. It's not important now." He certainly wasn't in the mood to say sorry for anything anymore.

"Well . . ." She stood there looking awkward. Her hand reached out as if to touch his arm, but she pulled it back. She didn't meet his eyes before she spoke. "It wasn't anything you did, you know. You were perfect. It was all me." Without so much as a *see you later* she walked away. Back to her family. Away from him. Again.

But this time, he had the crazy urge to run after her. To point the finger at her one more time? He didn't know.

Which made him question if it was all her, or did he hold some blame in what had happened to them? He hadn't thought so, but what if he'd read her letters instead of burning them? Maybe he would've gone after her and things might've been different. Maybe not. Maybe he would've seen the same look in her eyes that he saw now . . . *regret*. Back then, he'd been a pigheaded, prideful teenager. Heck, he was still prideful, and he was a grown adult now.

He looked down the deserted hallway . . . a metaphor for his future. Empty. He would be alone. Sure, he had plenty of people in his life. But no one to walk beside him, a companion for life.

LOLLY WALKED AWAY feeling oddly renewed in her conviction to keep Shaun at a distance.

"What were you and Shaun talking about?" Jilly asked.

"Nothing much," Lolly said. But actually, it was everything. Everything she should've made clear in the first place. She should've made sure he knew the truth sooner, like sixteen years sooner. Instead of leaving Shaun on the porch, when she ran inside the house after breaking up with him, she should've explained everything so he would know that she hadn't wanted them to end.

Why did *I do what Mom wanted?* Jilly would've laughed in Mom's face and not thought twice about telling her, *Like hell I'll break up with the boy I love*. But Lolly had never been rebellious. Or brave. She was ashamed she'd never looked deeply at this part of herself and made changes to who she was sooner. Did that mean she was willing to change now? It was probably too late.

Candy took Lolly's arm. "Get that look off your face. You'll give yourself premature wrinkles."

Like Lolly cared. She was going to be an old maid, and old maids couldn't care less about their appearance.

Lolly glanced over her shoulder, expecting Shaun to be following them, but he wasn't. She wondered if he'd escaped out the side door of the building, wanting to get away from her as fast as he could.

Mom guided Lolly through the front door. "Piney wants us all to gather at the lodge for a while this afternoon to talk about the wedding quilt for Sparkle and Rick."

But Lolly finally had the motivation she needed to look for a job. As soon as she was alone, she was going to put everything she had into getting a job and not get sidetracked with baking or sewing or the hundred other excuses she used to procrastinate. She had to get out of Sweet Home. Get a life. A new one.

Because being near Shaun was too hard on her.

Too hard on everybody. Especially Patricia and Shaun.

Lolly couldn't continue to be the cause of Shaun's pain, the same pain that had shown clearly on his face moments ago. In truth, Lolly couldn't bear to see any of them like that anymore.

But at least they had cleared the air a bit. And he knew the truth now. Or part of the truth. Yes, she really hadn't loved those other men enough to marry them, but it was only saying it out loud that made her realize the deeper truth, which she was loath to admit: a lot of her decision-making was steeped in fear. Fear that she would be rejected or abandoned if she didn't do what others wanted. That kind of fear ran deep . . . maybe it was caused by her father leaving her as a little girl. She didn't know.

Then there was the fear that if she stayed with the men

who had become serious about her, all really nice guys, she'd end up like her mom, an unhappy woman feeling trapped in her marriage. Or worse, she could end up like her dear old dad. What if she went through with one of those weddings, only to walk out and let everyone down? *Yes*, she had assured herself, it had been kinder to end the relationship early, spare the men what she and Jilly had gone through after their father left. Better to strike preemptively than to wait too long, right?

Jilly loudly cleared her throat, as if to bring Lolly back to the church's front door and stop inspecting her past with a microscope. "Piney doesn't seem thrilled with Rick at the moment," her sister said. "Supposedly, he'll be back later today . . . with his new daughter in tow."

Lolly glanced at Jilly. "I think it's great that Rick's stepping up. Some people might not have." Some might ignore their progeny altogether, like their dad. Not a word in twenty-four years. For all Lolly knew, the man who had lived in their house until Jilly was born might be dead. Lolly had few memories of him, especially since he worked for months at a time on a fishing boat on the Bering Sea. Or at least that's what their mom had told them. Lolly used to fantasize about her father coming back one day, bearing gifts like an absentee Santa Claus, offering lots of hugs, apologies, and tears.

"Well, we're all going to the lodge regardless," Candy said definitively.

Lolly started to say okay, but then she asked herself, *Am I just afraid to make waves?* She took a deep breath and pulled her mom to a stop. "I won't make it out to the lodge today." The panic inside her rose incrementally with each word; she felt so uncomfortable going against the grain.

"Why not?" Candy asked.

"I have things to do." *I'm on a mission to make things right with the Montanas by finding a job elsewhere.* But Lolly couldn't say that. However, she was proud of herself for standing up to her mom.

"What things?" Candy said, as if Lolly didn't have a world of problems beyond what quilt to make for Sparkle and Rick's wedding.

"Mom, I'm out of a job and I have to invest time into finding one."

"Haven't you been doing that since you found out the news?"

"No," Jilly answered with an eye roll. "Apparently, Lolly has been hiding under her covers, if Piney is telling it correctly."

"I was processing!" Lolly protested. "You would've done the same thing if you were fired with no warning." But that wasn't necessarily true. Jilly was strong and not afraid of anything. She probably would've demanded that the school board meet again so she could explain why the school system needed a life skills class like family and consumer science.

"Okay. Stay home," Mom said, surprising Lolly. "But you should call and explain it to Piney first. She'll still want your input on the wedding quilt."

Ever helpful, Jilly said, "I should probably hang back, too." She winked at Lolly. "You need help with the job search, right, sis?"

"Good try, but no. I'll be okay on my own." Lolly didn't say that she needed some space from them—actually, from everybody right now.

After a quick lunch at home, Candy rushed Jilly toward the door to meet up with the Sisterhood of the Quilt but stopped before herding her out. "Do your job search for a while," Mom said, "but I expect you to make an appearance. I know Piney wants everyone to be involved with the wedding quilt. You are, after all, a member of the Sisterhood of the Quilt, too."

"Fine," Lolly acquiesced. "I'll make an appearance." Mom frowned at her, then gave her a distracted hug before closing the door behind her.

Lolly cleared the table, taking the dirty dishes to the sink. When every plate and piece of silverware was clean, she picked up Thor, hugged him, and buried her face in his neck, giving him a loving squeeze. "You're a lucky pup, you know. Your only job is to cuddle. And you're really good at it."

She couldn't help but think she was in an impossible situation. Between being unemployed and her horrible track record, she had few options left. She could give up altogether the idea of having a man in her life, or do the two things Pastor Joe suggested this morning at church: first, ask forgiveness from those you've wronged. Lolly could put a small checkmark beside that one. Second, talk to God about your heartaches. Which had to do with Shaun, as well.

There was a real problem with that idea. When it came to religion, Lolly had coasted her whole life. She'd never really prayed, thinking that her measly problems were just that, too small for a God so big. But she wished she'd stayed in better touch, at least kept an open line of communication between her and the Big Guy Upstairs. Because now, well, she didn't know where to start.

She looked around her living room, where there wasn't a pew in sight. Or a kneeler like they had at the Catholic church. Sitting on the sagging couch to pray seemed sacrilegious for some reason. She set Thor on the floor and sat down, cross-legged, beside him. She pressed her palms together and closed her eyes, feeling stupid. She waited for inspiration, but nothing happened, except Thor climbed into her lap and lay down.

"What am I supposed to say?" she said to no one. She waited and finally opened her eyes, only to stare upward. "Here's the deal, God. Father Joe says You see everything, so You know that I'm a mess. I don't have a clue what lies ahead. So here it goes."

She closed her eyes and bowed her head. "I need help. *Your* help, to be specific, because I can't do this on my own.

The path before me looks pretty murky. Father Joe says that we have to be open to Your plan, and I gotta tell You—that scares me. What if I don't like what You have in store for me?" Lolly stopped herself, worried that it sounded as if she were picking a fight with God, which had to be a bad idea.

"Sorry about that. You can see I'm not good at this. But I'll get better." Father Joe said it was best to start the day off with prayer. Practice was supposed to make perfect. "I'm signing off for now." She opened her eyes and felt a little better, like somehow she wasn't carrying the load all by herself anymore.

She moved Thor to the floor before she stood and stretched. She noticed Thor was stretching, too. He followed her to the table, where her laptop sat open. She worked hard to ignore her dream bakery notebook sitting on the counter. Jilly must've pulled it back out after Lolly had put it on the bookshelf in their room.

She decided to start the job search at her old school in Oregon first, wondering if she might be lucky enough to find her old job available. She knew the ropes there, which would make it less stressful than starting at a new school. But a quick scan showed her that the only opening was for a high school math teacher. She wished now that she'd minored in something besides philosophy. Even though she had to swallow her pride, and the whole endeavor might be in vain, she wrote a short note to her old principal, asking him to keep her in mind if an opening did become available.

Next, she searched for jobs throughout the Northwest and applied for three—one in Washington, one in Northern California, and one in Idaho. She wasn't excited about any of them—she wasn't a perfect match—but at least she'd tried. Thor put his front paws on her knee. As she scratched him behind the ears, she said, "Looking for a job sure is demoralizing, buddy. Especially when my skills don't seem to be appreciated the way they once were." Thor hopped down and went to the kitchen for a drink from his dish. Lolly was about to expand her search to include the whole U.S. when a text came in from her mom. When are you going to get here? Lolly took it as a sign that she'd done enough job hunting for one day. Besides, she'd had her fill of disappointment.

Chapter 9

SHAUN DID HIS best to ignore the disgruntled noise his mother made as they passed Lolly's car parked on the road near the entrance to Home Sweet Home Lodge. He had no intention of going in to hang out with the quilters, as he was determined *not* to run into Lolly again today. Talking to her in the hallway at church had turned his mood from apologetic to bitter. He still couldn't believe Lolly broke up with him because her mom told her to. On top of that, the fact that Lolly left those snickerdoodle cookies for his mom was just unforgivable. Could he never get a break from her? Was there no way to get any real distance?

He wondered if he needed to make a second call to his boss in Houston, skip the pleasantries completely, and get his boss's wife on the phone stat. He would beg her to find Lolly a job in her school district, maybe offer to make a sizable donation to their athletic department or the band boosters, any bribe to get Lolly out of Sweet Home and out of his head. Yes, his perspective about Lolly had shifted—he saw the good she did for others, and that kiss they'd shared had knocked him for a loop—but it was so much wiser to relegate Lolly and all datable women to the hands-off zone. He was just too smart to be interested in a relationship after what he'd been through.

Shaun had thought about asking his mom what was in the note that had come with Lolly's cookies, but he held his tongue. Apparently, his mom wanted to keep it private, as she'd taken the missive to her bedroom. He was surprised that she hadn't thrown it in the trash. Only for a brief moment did he consider secretly reading the note while his mom was at her Sisterhood of the Quilt meeting. He shouldn't have let himself even think it. But when it came to anything to do with Lolly, rational thought seemed to escape him.

Shaun pulled around the lodge's circular entrance to drop his mom off.

"Are you coming in to say hi to everyone?" she asked.

"I'll pass," Shaun said. "I need to change your oil and then get back to work on Jesse's cabin." As soon as Rick was back in town, Shaun would help him with the renovations on the three-bedroom bungalow that he'd bought for him and Sparkle . . . and now Rick's three-year-old daughter. Shaun hadn't heard much about the kid but expected the gossip mill would kick into high gear once Sweet Home laid eyes on the girl.

He wondered how Piney was going to deal with having a built-in granddaughter. Or for that matter, how was Sparkle dealing with becoming a stepmother? His mom had said Sparkle was handling it just fine, but Shaun knew from growing up with Sparkle that she was good at hiding her real emotions. Which was the opposite of her mother, Piney.

Shaun waited while his mom unbuckled and gathered her things.

"Don't worry about picking me up," Mom said. "I'll catch a ride home with one of the ladies."

"See you later." He watched as his mom got out, made her way up the steps, and slipped into the lodge. Just then, Rick pulled in behind him and flashed his lights.

Shaun put his mom's Forester in park, killed the engine, and got out.

Rick motioned him over and rolled down his window. "Can you see if Hope is ready for me and Ava?" he said, his voice lowering as he glanced over his shoulder. "She fell asleep, and I'd rather take her straight to the cabin we'll be staying in until our house is ready. If I take Ava in the lodge, she'll wake up . . . you know, with the Sisterhood of the Quilt there and all. She didn't sleep well on the flights."

Shaun peeked in the back seat to see a dark curly-haired angel conked out and strapped in a car seat. "I understand," Shaun said, thinking about how the quilters were going to make such a fuss over the newest addition to Sweet Home. "I'll get the key from Hope."

"Find out which cabin she wants us in."

"Sure." Shaun knew from his mom that there had been a lot of chatter about how Rick and his daughter weren't planning to stay with Sparkle and Piney in their apartment over the Hungry Bear. Which amped up the speculation that the couple would break up. As far as Shaun was concerned, it was nonsense. Everyone knew Piney's apartment was the size of a gnat and couldn't squeeze another person in there, let alone two.

Then a thought occurred to Shaun. "Where's Sparkle? Isn't she inside?"

"No," Rick whispered. A flash of worry crossed his face. "She's home, working on wedding stuff, apparently." He glanced back at his daughter again. "I couldn't stop by because Ava was sleeping."

"Oh. I see." Maybe Shaun had been wrong. There might be trouble in paradise. Rick's demeanor had changed. He used to smile all the time—one carefree dude. Now he was serious, with worry lines etched between his eyebrows—a man whose life had been altered completely. "Right," Shaun said, "I'll run in and see Hope." Yes, Rick had problems, but so did Shaun. Five minutes ago, he'd been certain he wouldn't see any more of Lolly today, and now he was walking into the lion's den.

He trudged up the porch steps and went inside. As he got close to the sewing studio, he could hear Piney talking.

"Besides the wedding cake, Lolly, you'll cater the reception, too. Get that look off your face. You won't have to do it alone. I've assigned a group to help you with cooking and baking and serving."

Shaun stopped in the studio's doorway and Lolly swung around as if she had some kind of radar when it came to him. He wasn't going to take the blame for her shocked expression, though. Surely that look was due to the amount of work that Piney had just assigned her.

The whole room was staring at him, too.

"Yeah, um, Hope? Rick's outside and needs the key to whichever cabin you want him and his daughter in."

The room rushed him, physically and verbally. "Where is she?" "What does she look like?" "Does Rick seem to be adjusting to fatherhood?" "Why doesn't he come in?"

Shaun decided to only answer the last question. "Rick can't come in because the kid's asleep. He just wants to take her to the cabin to put her to bed."

Hope stepped forward, waving off the Sisterhood of the Quilt. "Keep talking about the wedding. I'll get the key to Wandering Moose Cabin and be right back." She might as well have said *Down* to the Sisterhood as if they were a pack of dogs. Surprisingly, the ladies backed off.

Shaun felt sorry for Rick. With the upcoming wedding and his house not nearly ready for occupancy, and now single parenthood to a daughter he'd never known, the town was sure to drive Rick crazy. Idly Shaun wondered why Rick hadn't made a run for it while he had the chance, but it was clear to anyone who had eyes: Rick and Sparkle really loved each other.

Alas, Shaun knew the unfortunate truth. Sometimes love just wasn't enough.

In that moment, he made the decision to put his brother's

new cabin on the back burner and focus solely on getting Rick's house done first. Shaun couldn't have a happy ending, but he could do this for Rick and Sparkle . . . and Ava. Another idea struck Shaun. He should move into Jesse's cabin until he and Tori returned home. That way Shaun could finish up work on their cabin in the evenings or odd hours.

Hope patted him on the arm as she left the room. "Do you mind moving Rick and his daughter in? Donovan's taking inventory at the hardware store or else I'd send him out to help, too."

"Yeah. Sure. I'm happy to." Shaun turned to leave.

When he did, Rick appeared with the girl in his arms. "Ava woke up and needs the bathroom." He held a miniature toilet seat in one of his hands, which seemed so weird for the carefree bachelor Shaun had come to know.

He stepped aside to make room for Rick to pass by. The tearstained face said the girl had been crying before, but now she only looked sorrowful. *Poor thing.* Her mother dead. Her aunt dying. Now adjusting to a father she'd never known.

But as Rick moved past the doorway of the sewing studio, the quilters came pouring out into the hall.

Rick held up the toilet seat. "Bathroom emergency. And Ava's shy. She's had a lot of changes."

Shaun put his arms out as if herding the cattle back into the corral. "Let's give them some breathing room, ladies." That's when he noticed that Piney hadn't rushed out into the hallway to greet the new arrival, which answered Shaun's question about Piney's thoughts on Rick having a daughter.

But then Piney surprised him by barreling toward the door. His arms were no match for a determined Piney. "Out of my way," she said.

Shaun stepped aside and Piney put her hand on Rick's arm. "I'll take the girl, Rick; you look like what the cat dragged in. Go get a refreshment from the kitchen and bring back a juice box for the little lady." She handed a clipboard to Miss Lisa. "Take over for me. We don't have time to waste."

Piney pulled Ava into her arms easily, which was surprising since Piney had just barked at Rick and the quilters. She snatched the toilet ring from his hand, too. Shaun was pretty sure she wasn't taking over for Rick's sake, or even for Ava's sake, as she wasn't smiling. But Ava seemed to understand authority and she didn't fuss as Piney started to march away. Suddenly she stopped and looked back into the studio. "Lolly, you go help Shaun unload the car into their cabin."

Now Rick wasn't the only one standing there looking stunned; Lolly's mouth was gaping, too. Piney had pretty much knocked the wind out of the three of them in sixty seconds flat . . . possibly a new record for her. Lolly's mouth transformed into a straight line. She looked ready to argue with Piney. But Piney shot her such a lethal look that Lolly put her head down and obediently walked toward the door. The rest of the room appeared spellbound, as if they couldn't wait to see what was going to happen next. At the last second, Lolly grabbed Jilly's hand and pulled her out into the hall. "You're coming along, too," Lolly said to her sister. Shaun was grateful for the buffer.

As he began to lead them out, he caught his mom's warning glare. *Great!* Another stay-away-from-Lolly lecture would certainly be on the agenda when his mom got home. Yeah, temporarily moving to Jesse and Tori's cabin was looking more and more like a good idea. His spirits lifted at the thought, and he left, patting Rick's shoulder to move him along, too. "We best do what Piney says, don't you think?" He didn't wait for Lolly and Jilly but stalked down the hall with Rick and the Crocker sisters trailing behind.

Hope caught up to them, holding a key attached to a wooden quilt block by a piece of twine. "Where's your daughter?" she asked.

Rick didn't seem to have energy enough to answer, so

Shaun made a thumbing gesture over his shoulder. "Bathroom. Piney took her. We're going to unload the car while Rick gets Ava a juice box." He'd only mentioned the juice box to help Rick remember what he was supposed to be doing. The man was clearly shell-shocked.

"Oh, right. Food. I bet they're starving." Hope handed Shaun the key. "Shaun, you go on. Rick needs a break." She glanced over at Rick with a worried expression. "Let me fix you a sandwich. Is there anything special I can get for Ava?"

Jilly pulled away from Lolly. "I'll stay here and help Rick find something for them to eat."

Lolly acted as if she wanted to retort that *she* was the one who fed people, not her sister. Instead, she rolled her eyes and hurried for the front door to start carrying a load of bags. On purpose, Shaun dawdled by the entrance. He knew he was being ridiculous. It wasn't like Lolly was going to force him to go steady the moment they were alone together. The truth was he wasn't sure he could trust himself. Yes, it was pretty cowardly of him to make Lolly carry Rick's things from the car to the cabin, but Shaun had to protect himself from her womanly wiles, right? A half second later, honor had Shaun pushing away from the doorframe and heading outside to help.

Lolly was hurriedly loading her arms. When she saw him coming, she grabbed a stuffed giraffe, placed it precariously on top of her load, and headed toward Wandering Moose Cabin at breakneck speed, as if she were being chased.

Shaun grabbed the two biggest suitcases from the back and hurried after her. "Hold up!" She seemed to go faster, but a moment later, he caught up to her, and just in time, too. He caught the toppling giraffe before it hit the dirt. Since he had a relatively free hand, now that he'd dropped a suitcase to catch Mr. Giraffe, he took the largest bag from her and tucked it under his arm.

She snatched the giraffe back. "What are you doing? I had it under control."

"I'm keeping you from getting a hernia is what I'm doing." Because she'd taken the giraffe, he relieved her of a second bag, though he wasn't certain he'd be able to get it all to the cabin in one shot. Regardless, he scooped up the large suitcase he'd dropped and started walking. "Take the key from my back pocket, will you, and open the door."

He stopped and turned around to see her with her hands on her hips.

"Stop telling me what to do," she said. "Or at the very least say *please*." She looked so dang cute that he wanted to kiss that frown right off her face. He knew he could do it, too. Back in high school, he'd been able to settle her ruffled feathers with a charming smile and a scoop-her-up-in-his-arms-and-lay-one-on-her kiss. He wondered if that would work now.

She seemed to be waiting for something because she just stood there with a firm, expectant look on her face.

Oh, he remembered. "Don't you know that *please* was implied?" He sighed for dramatic effect. "But if you must hear it, then . . . *please*."

"Fine." She marched over and yanked the key out of his back pocket. He could've sworn he felt the fire of her mood rolling off her. If nothing else, he got a good whiff of her flowery shampoo.

"Take your time," he teased. "I'm just about to drop everything."

She rolled her eyes and strutted off to the cabin. For a moment, he stood there, watching, until he remembered what he was supposed to be doing. He walked to the cabin, watching her as she inserted the key, jiggled the door handle, and stepped inside.

She flipped the light switch on, and he followed her in. She closed the door. Sure, it was important to keep the bugs out, but it made the cabin feel a tad too close, too cozy.

He felt he should say something about the cookies that Lolly had left for his mom. He doubted his mom would say thank you, so he simply said, "Mom got the snickerdoodles."

He glanced at the window and wondered if they should open it. It might help him to breathe better. Instead, he went on, "Did you know snickerdoodles are one of her favorites?" Of course Lolly knew. She'd always had a sixth sense about which cookies, pastries, and cakes people loved, even if they didn't quite know themselves.

In a strangely compelling motion, Lolly ran her hands through her hair. "I'm glad she liked them."

He didn't have the heart to tell her that his mom hadn't tasted the cookies yet, and that she'd left them on the counter in the kitchen without a backward glance.

"Yeah," he said noncommittally. And with that he was done talking. He'd initiated the minimum amount of small talk to avoid being rude; sociable but not too friendly.

But apparently his mouth was on autopilot. "How's the job hunt going?"

Lolly had gone about setting the smaller suitcase near the dresser, but she whirled around when he asked the question. Shock and something like indignation were plastered all over her face, as though he'd invaded her privacy.

"I know it's none of my business . . ." But he still wanted to know. For his sanity's sake, if nothing else. For about the hundredth time, he wondered if he should tell her about the call he'd made to his old boss. But why say something when it was so doubtful anything would come of it? "I've heard others discussing it. You know how Sweet Home is." His mother, Miss Lisa, Mr. Brewster, Dewey Winkle . . . basically the whole town had been talking about Lolly's prospects. Shaun wished he could take the question back, because honestly, he didn't care how the job hunt was going as long as Lolly was out of the picture soon. He'd been spending far too much time thinking about her . . . thinking all kinds of things. And one area he concentrated on was trying to solve her basic problem of not having a job. He'd decided he wasn't going to beat himself up over it either; solving problems was his forte. Ask anyone. Ask his former boss. The upside of thinking about Lolly all the time was that Tanya felt like a distant memory now. A pop psychologist would probably say he'd transferred his feelings from Tanya to Lolly. But Tanya hadn't broken his heart like Lolly had; she'd merely bruised his pride. He knew now Tanya hadn't been right for him, and he hadn't been right for her either. Her only sin was she'd led him on too long. And his sin was that he should've woken up sooner and seen who she really was. Since coming home to Sweet Home, he'd been tallying up some kind of comparison between Tanya and Lolly. But in truth, it was like trying to compare a roach to a gazelle.

Lolly ran a nervous hand over her cheek before she answered him. "Sorry for looking so shocked. I've been home for a year but I keep forgetting that nothing in Sweet Home stays private."

"Yeah, they keep digging and digging until they know everything, or at least they think they know everything. Sorry for asking. Really. I didn't mean to pry. I was just making polite conversation."

She frowned like she wasn't completely buying what he was selling. But she had the good grace not to say so. "It's okay. Between you and me, the job hunt isn't going well. All the schools on the West Coast already have their teaching staff for the year."

"Have you thought about doing something besides teaching?" he said, kicking himself for continuing the conversation.

"Not really. Piney and the others are being nice, keeping me busy with making cakes and other treats for their special occasions. You know, I've been baking cookies for the Hungry Bear for some time now, even before I . . ." She trailed off. Apparently it was still hard for her to say that she'd lost her job.

He nodded to let her know that he understood her predicament. But answered something different to keep her from feeling embarrassed. "I'm a big fan of those oversized everything cookies—delicious. Everything in them except the kitchen sink, that's how Piney describes them."

"With all the baking I've been doing for the town, I'm running out of space at home to store all the ingredients. And cool all the baked goods. I even thought about building something in the backyard as a staging area."

He opened his mouth to offer to build it for her. Thank goodness he clamped his lips shut in time. He shouldn't be doing her any favors.

She continued, not knowing that he was warring with himself. "Can you imagine how tickled the wildlife would be if I set up a nice outdoor buffet for them?" Lolly gave one of her adorable chuckles and it hit him in the chest like getting whacked with a mallet. Or perhaps a defibrillator, from the jolt of hearing it. After all this time, he still loved her laugh, and it really bothered him. He wished he were stronger. He really should be over her by now.

She pulled a piece of paper from her back pocket. "You should see what Piney wants me to do for the wedding. I don't know where I'm going to house all the food while I prep."

He took the list and scanned it. "This'll keep you busy."

She shook her head and smiled to herself. "I need a second oven, maybe a third, but God knows there's no place to put an extra, let alone two more ovens in our cabin. Even more troubling is that my poor oven probably won't even make it to the wedding . . . especially with the workout it's been getting. *She*—my oven, that is—definitely won't be able to handle what's coming down the pike." Lolly gave a sad little smile. "Out of desperation, I Googled the cost of professional ovens today, only the price tag nearly made me faint." She gave a derisive laugh. "Where's the smelling salts when you need them, right? Well, a professional oven is definitely out of the question because my meager savings wouldn't come close to covering it. Besides, I really need to watch what I'm spending these days; you know, my predicament and all."

It was a catch-22. Shaun's mind immediately went rogue and came up with two or three companies where he could take on contract programming jobs—shoot, Brian probably had work for him to do, too—and then Shaun could allocate what he earned to help out Lolly. Then he had another crazy thought. "Maybe you should look into using one of the boarded-up buildings on Main Street. Better yet, you should open the bakery that you've always wanted. What were you going to call it? 'Happily Ever Baking' or something like that?" Internally, he cringed; his motormouth was certainly running full steam. *Full of something anyway.* Why couldn't he locate the off button to his lips?

Once again, she looked at him as if he'd gone wacky.

He went on the defensive. "Why are you giving me that look? You always said you wanted a bakery."

She guffawed. "Seriously, Shaun, weren't you listening to what I just said? I don't have the spare cash to buy oven mitts, let alone the funds to open a bakery. Besides, my dream of owning a bakery was a lifetime ago. I'm shocked you have any memory of it at all."

"Yeah." But to him, the memories felt fresh . . . sitting at her kitchen table while she went over every detail in that bakery binder of hers. He clamped his mouth shut so he wouldn't admit that he recalled all her hopes and dreams, her every expression, and how just being with her made him feel . . . *invincible.* Somehow she'd built him up. He was sure that they'd be together . . . always. Not some vague dream either. He'd seen it clearly back then. She would make baked goods and he'd be an engineer or a computer-coding rock star. It didn't matter where they lived. They'd be together in their own happy ending. Yes, he remembered everything whether he wanted to or not. Everything down to the last detail, as if it had all been tattooed on his soul. He glanced at the pi symbol on his wrist, then looked long-ingly at the door, wondering if he could outrun his feelings.

"We better get the rest from the car," she said.

Yeah, and he should start spending more time with the

grizzly men of Alaska because he was feeling pretty mushy right now.

Lolly walked out of the cabin saying, "You coming?" without looking over her shoulder. She kept walking as if she knew that he'd follow her anywhere. "Speaking of my bakery pipe dream, Jilly pulled out my old bakery notebook. Do you remember that, too?"

He caught up to her, not admitting anything.

"I was certain I'd tossed that notebook, but apparently Jilly rescued it."

Of course he remembered the notebook. She worked in it all the time. He also remembered when, in frustration, she had pitched it in the garbage can by the back door with tears streaming down her face. He had held her while she cried, trying to tell her she didn't have to do what her mother had said, *Get a safe, steady job, become a teacher. You don't want to end up like me and take menial jobs the rest of your life.* Candy should've known that he would take care of Lolly. Even worse, nothing he could say could convince Lolly that was true. She was defeated. For some weird reason now, he was glad he'd saved the notebook and had given it to Jilly to put somewhere safe.

"Why not open the bakery now?" he repeated, though he should've kept his trap shut. Why would he want Lolly to open a bakery, especially when he'd been working to get her out of town? But still he continued with his nonsense. "You don't have anything better to do, do you?"

"That's what Jilly said."

"I always said your little sister had a good head on her shoulders."

"Yeah, but don't tell her that. She already has a healthy ego without you praising her." Lolly was silent for a few moments. "It's a good idea . . . I mean, to use one of the abandoned buildings as you suggested. Not to open a bakery, but just a place to use temporarily, until I get through the wedding."

As they were gathering the rest of the bags from the

vehicle, Sparkle pulled up behind Rick's car and parked. Shaun wished he wasn't here. He had a feeling there was going to be more drama. Not from Sparkle, but from Piney. He just hoped that Piney watched what she said in front of Ava. The poor girl had been through so much; she didn't need to hear any negative words about her father.

"Hi, Sparkle," Shaun said.

Sparkle gave an obligatory wave before she hurried into the lodge. Shaun took the suitcase that Lolly held. "You go. You might need to mediate."

"Forget it," Lolly said. "I'm not mediating anything. It should be someone else. Like Hope maybe."

"Go on anyway. I'll take care of the rest." He was done walking down memory lane with Lolly. He'd said more than he should've, too. What compelled him to say anything about her opening a bakery? What had happened to his vow of maintaining his distance? Being around her was too much, and he was getting out of there as soon as he dropped this last load off at the cabin.

"Thanks," Lolly said. "And thanks for the idea about using a larger space to bake and cook."

He nodded, foolishly thinking that he was done with the torture for the day. But God help him, because as he drove away from the lodge, he suddenly remembered the new-in-the-box range that sat in the barn, the one he'd bought as a wedding present for Tori and Jesse, ready to be put in their cabin. Shaun decided in that moment he was going to donate it to Lolly's baking endeavors and replace her old oven at home, the one on its last legs. He would buy Jesse and Tori a new one before they returned. The hard part would be installing the range at Lolly's without her knowing it was from him. Maybe this final act would let him be done with her. He could move on. At last.

But instead of turning onto the road leading to their homestead, Shaun kept heading to town. He had no intention of getting further involved with Lolly and her bakery . . . he just wanted to peek in the windows of the abandoned buildings on Main Street to see which one would work best for her shop.

When that idea popped into his head, he should've slammed the brakes on. Clearly, he needed his head examined. But on he drove into town just the same, telling himself that once Lolly got settled, then surely, *surely* he'd be able to get on with his life.

He did pull the car over then. Lolly opening a bakery here was in direct conflict with what he wanted . . . which was space from the woman who had obliterated his heart. He didn't understand himself and he doubted if a hundred therapists could help him figure it out either. Deep down, he guessed, he just wanted Lolly to be happy.

Though the thought of her remaining in Sweet Home made him more miserable than ever.

Chapter 10

PINEY WIPED DOWN Ava's face with a clean washcloth and then held her up to wash her hands under the running water. "Always wash away the germs after using the toilet." She thought back to raising Sparkle, how she'd worked hard not to emulate her own strict mother. She'd found fun ways to teach Sparkle, wanting her to be a free spirit like herself. But Sparkle had turned out to be a shy young woman who didn't want to make waves. Of course, since Rick had come into the picture, Sparkle had stood up for herself more and more. Which was a good thing, Piney thought. Life for a young woman was hard.

"Later we'll brush out your pretty hair," Piney said to Ava, whose little eyes were sad. "But right now, let's go see your father and find you a snack." She took her little hand and steered her out of the bathroom. Piney wasn't particularly interested in being a grandmother. She was too busy to help take care of a child. Taking care of all the folks in Sweet Home had kept her plate full all these years.

Besides, growing up with her single mother on the East Coast, she'd never known either of her grandmothers. But Piney had asked her mother many times about the other women in their family. *Never mind about them. They aren't us*, her mother had said. Which made Piney want to meet them all the more. But back then, there wasn't the Internet. Or DNA tests. Or any number of ways for people to find each other like there were now.

She caught sight of Sparkle walking into the kitchen. "Would you like to meet Sparkle? She's my daughter."

Ava looked at her as if Piney were speaking a foreign language. But Piney wasn't alarmed; sometimes it just took a while for shy ones to get used to others before they opened up. And for the first time, Piney wondered if things did work out with Rick—she wasn't holding her breath on that one, but if they did—might Sparkle be just the right woman to care for Ava? The little girl seemed as shy as Sparkle had been. But Piney wasn't going to count any chickens before they hatched. Whether anyone was going to admit it or not, little Ava here might be the undoing of Rick and Sparkle's engagement.

Piney walked Ava down the hall to the kitchen, where Rick and Sparkle were clearly in deep conversation. Rick stopped immediately when he saw them, rushed over, and picked up Ava, who immediately laid her head on his broad shoulder and hid her face.

"She's all cleaned up," Piney said gruffly.

Hope laid a plate on the table that held a peanut butter sandwich—naturally with the crusts cut off—and a cut-up peach. "Ava's okay with peanut butter?"

"Yes. She loves it," Rick said.

Hope nodded. "What about dirty clothes? Do you have some for me to put in the laundry?"

"Yes, but I'll take care of it," Rick said.

"You're going to need all the help you can get," Piney said. "You might as well accept it now."

"Mom," Sparkle said in warning.

"Fine, fine. Don't mind me and my vast experience. I've been a single parent most of my life, so sue me for trying to help." But she hadn't really been trying to help, only pointing out that raising a child is no picnic on a warm day.

Hope took Piney's arm. "Let's get back to the sewing studio and leave these three in private."

Piney wanted to stay and give them her two cents on the whole situation, but Hope practically pulled her from the kitchen and down the hall.

"We have to let them figure this out on their own," Hope whispered.

Piney wanted to save Sparkle the heartache and tell her to break it off here and now. But then she thought about the sad little girl who'd come right to her without a fuss . . . and wondered if she was right.

THOUGH LOLLY HAD walked calmly away from Shaun— or at least that was the look she was going for—she couldn't catch her breath as she went inside the lodge to find the others. Being around Shaun had that effect on her, making her wonder if she shouldn't make an appointment with a pulmonologist, which was exactly what Jilly would suggest. But, heck, Lolly couldn't afford it anyway, as her health insurance was running out at the end of the month.

She peeked into the kitchen as she passed. Hope and Jilly were no longer in there, but she did get a glimpse of Rick holding his little girl in his arms, her face buried in his shoulder, sound asleep. Sparkle stood on the opposite side of the room, looking stony, her arms crossed over her chest. It was the first time Lolly could believe that sweet and mild Sparkle was actually Piney's daughter.

Lolly headed toward the studio but stopped suddenly, feeling certain that the vibe in the studio wasn't going to be much better than the one in the kitchen. Patricia was certain to give her *the look* for helping Shaun unload the car. As much as Lolly didn't want to face Patricia again, it would be nice if she acknowledged the cookies that Lolly had left for her on the front porch of her cabin. But that was silly. Lolly wasn't trying to buy her love, which was the same way she felt about Shaun. It would be a hopeless endeavor anyway.

Lolly shouldn't have stopped, because from where she stood, she could hear Rick.

"Listen, Sparkle, maybe we should postpone the wedding. Your mom thinks we should and she may be right."

Oh, no! Not them, too. Sparkle and Rick's relationship had been like a fairy tale that made the world a brighter place for the rest of them to live. Even if Lolly couldn't seem to navigate romantic relationships, it was wonderful to see that Sparkle could. Those two made it look easy.

She shook her head, reminding herself that fairy tales weren't real. And for most—especially for her and Shaun— happily-ever-afters were out of reach. She hoped Sparkle and Rick would figure it out and get it right. They deserved to be happy. Lolly didn't. That realization was a surprise to her. She wasn't usually down on herself like this, but facing so many memories recently, Lolly was too aware she'd caused the men in her past a lot of heartache and pain . . . starting with Shaun. There was no way to make up for what she'd done to them. No way to atone.

Lolly hurried away so she wouldn't hear any more of their intimate conversation. At the door to the sewing studio, she took a fortifying breath before crossing the threshold. Immediately she said, "Hey, I'm heading out, if that's okay with everyone." *And even if it isn't.* She pulled out the list Piney had given her and waved it to remind them. "I've got a lot to do. Mom, Jilly, I'll see you both at home." She didn't wait for their response but hurried back down the hallway to escape. She didn't dare stop and listen for more of what was going on in the kitchen either. She kept her head down and didn't look up as she passed the doorway. If her bad luck with relationships had rubbed off on Rick and Sparkle, Lolly surely didn't want to witness the end of them.

She slipped outside and noticed Patricia's SUV was

gone. Not that Lolly was looking for the whereabouts of Shaun or anything. But he must've left for his mom's homestead.

Lolly got in her car and headed home. Thor needed her. But really, she just needed to get away from the others. She also needed to schedule and plan out how to conquer Piney's list for the wedding.

Only there might not be one. It was a sobering thought. She couldn't wait to get home and feel safe.

When she pulled up to her house, it was almost nine thirty p.m. As she opened the door, Thor was jumping up, showing off with a set of twirls. "You want to go for a walk, don't you, little man?" She grabbed his leash and harness from their hook and fastened him in. Thor's tail wagged so fast it looked like a blade in a blender.

Once outside, they headed up the street past Hope's old place. It wasn't that long ago that Hope was having a hard time making ends meet. Now she was living her best life with Donovan, the boy she'd loved her whole life, according to her. *Well, there was proof that love could prevail. Once in a while.*

Lolly and Thor rounded the corner onto Main Street. She looked down the line of buildings, thinking the old butcher shop might be the right size to use for a cooking-baking space like Shaun had suggested. She hadn't planned to check out any vacancies right now, especially this late at night, but in Alaska summer days were long and it was still twilight. Besides, she and Thor were only steps away from peeking inside Dmitri's Butcher Shop.

"Come on, boy." Thor headed straight for the shop as if meat still sat in the long-gone meat case.

Once there, Lolly wiped the window and peered inside but couldn't see much except that it was a narrow space. It might be enough space to store her ingredients, and possibly even install a borrowed oven. Or maybe the Sisterhood of the Quilt could tell her where she could get one at a discount.

"Not big enough." Shaun's voice came from right behind Lolly, making her jump and clutch her chest. Thor finally glanced up from sniffing the door and barked lightly at him.

"What are you doing here?" she asked, still trying to catch her breath. She frowned down at her mutt. "Some guard dog you are. I thought you were supposed to alert me to impending danger."

Shaun leaned down and scooped up her dog, who showed his approval by giving puppy kisses to the man she used to kiss herself. "Thor knows I'm a friend." He rubbed him behind the ears. "Don't you, boy?" Thor leaned into him . . . and Lolly was jealous. Jealous of a dog!

Then his words hit home. "So we're friends now?"

Surprisingly, he didn't hesitate or hedge. "Yes, Thor and I are friends." Shaun frowned. "Oh, what the heck, I guess we can be friends, too. Why not." But he was looking around as if to make sure no one saw the two of them to-gether, which didn't seem like something a friend would do. "In a town this size, we don't really have a choice but to be friendly, do we?"

Friendly wasn't exactly the same as being a friend.

"What are you doing here?" That's when she noticed his mom's SUV was parked near the Hungry Bear. "I thought you went home to work on the homestead or on Jesse's cabin."

"Yeah, me, too. But I expect I'm doing what you're doing."

"Walking your dog? You don't have Checkers with you." Though she knew exactly what he meant.

"I wanted to take a look at the vacant buildings on Main Street to see if one of them would work for you. As I said, the butcher shop is too small. There's no room for café ta-bles and chairs."

"I only need space to prepare and stage the food for the wedding. Nothing for customers."

He and Thor cocked their heads the same way, giving her a look as if she weren't exactly telling the truth. "Lolly, for your bakery," he said in way of chastising. He kissed the top of Thor's head before setting him on his feet. "Come on, you two. Let's go to the other side of the street. That storefront next to Tori's Alaska Chic business I think was Miss Lisa's boutique back in the day?"

"I believe Tori and McKenna's uncle Monty bought that building, too, since it's next to Tori's. Maybe he was thinking that she might need to expand one day; I don't know."

"Well, it looks like it would be just the right size for what you'll need."

"What are you talking about? How could you possibly know what I need?"

He stopped walking and gave her that know-it-all look he'd given her back when they were dating. "Because the drawings in your notebook had nine small round tables. On one side was the row of display cases that held your baked goods. You had a large display window and a bright front door that had all the personality and character you always said your bakery would need. I bet we could even find just the right bell to hang above the door."

Lolly could only gape at him. How could he have remembered all that from so long ago?

He answered as if she'd spoken it aloud. "Your bakery was all you ever talked about . . . until you gave up your dream of owning one." Other words hung in the air between them, unspoken words. He didn't have to say them for her to hear the accusation. *You gave up on us, too.* It wasn't really an accusation but, more accurately, *the truth.*

"Will you ever forgive me?" she asked impulsively. She reached out to touch his arm but didn't get the chance, as he slipped the leash from her hand and walked away with her dog. Thor, the little traitor, pranced beside him as if he were a little prince heeling beside his king.

Lolly just stood there waiting for the answer she wasn't going to get.

Shaun kept walking but, without looking over his shoulder, said, "Come look through the window with me."

Which had nothing to do with the forgiveness she was longing for.

She ran to catch up to him. "Listen, Shaun, I appreciate you putting in the effort, but you have it all wrong. I'm a teacher, looking for a job. I'm just helping out Piney and the others until I can get back to my career."

"Sure. Yeah." He did look at her then. "But just peek inside and tell me if you see what I see."

She did as he said. Once upon a time, Miss Lisa's boutique had racks filled with clothes, long mirrors everywhere, and a dressing room in the back. Lolly remembered her mom bringing her to Miss Lisa's shop to buy a kuspuk for her birthday—fireweed and forget-me-not fabric with dark trim. Mom also got her the matching kuspuk for her doll. Jilly played with that doll, too. It had to be packed away somewhere.

But now Miss Lisa's shop was empty, and like magic, she could see what Shaun was talking about. The shop was the perfect size for the bakery that Lolly had always dreamed of. Without thinking, she leaned up and kissed his cheek. When he looked taken aback, she flushed and said, "Um, thank you for suggesting this place. There will be plenty of room. Not for a bakery, of course, but for the wedding prep and just until a job opens up for me elsewhere." He seemed appeased, so she added, "I really do appreciate it."

She decided she would stop making Shaun uncomfortable by asking for his forgiveness, and for goodness' sake, she wouldn't kiss him innocently on the cheek again either. Just letting her cheek rest against his for a moment after the kiss, breathing him in, soaking him in, being close, had her whole nervous system tingling . . . as if she had swallowed a beehive. A deliciously warm beehive filled with sweet honey.

In that moment, she couldn't help but wonder . . . what would it be like to be with Shaun again?

• • •

SHAUN HADN'T SLEPT well. Lolly kissing his cheek had about done him in—an arrow to his heart, dead-on bull's-eye. Which was ridiculous. She hadn't had this kind of pull on him since he was a boy. Yet, that silly kiss had kept him up all night thinking about her and how nice it would be to have her close again. He knew logically that the kiss wasn't meant as anything more than a thank-you, but he didn't understand what he'd done to deserve it. She probably would've discovered Miss Lisa's old shop on her own. Oh, well, he wouldn't turn back time and prevent her from kissing him on the cheek, even if he could. He hated to admit it, but he'd missed her a lot . . . her touch, her companionship, everything.

The first thing Shaun did in the morning was to move his stuff into Jesse's cabin. Mom didn't seem as upset about the move as he thought she might be. Next he'd start work on Rick's house but first stop by the bank to see McKenna McAvoy. He and McKenna were somewhat related, as she was his sister-in-law's sister.

He loaded his Jeep with tools and headed into town. On the way, he wondered how he could ask questions without McKenna thinking there was something going on between him and Lolly. But then he remembered that McKenna was fairly new to town and hadn't witnessed his big breakup with Lolly. Which would work in his favor.

The bank sat next to the shuttered medical center. It bugged him that for the past year his mom had nowhere to go for simple stuff like a strep test or vaccinations. But apparently, Jilly helped out with health services when she was home, trying to make sure the folks of Sweet Home at least had some home healthcare, erratic as it was. Shaun parked in front of the bank and walked inside.

He was met at the door by Luke McAvoy, his brother's best friend and McKenna's husband. Luke had always been like an older brother to Shaun, as Luke had lived with them on the homestead for a year. Luke was holding out his hand and the two friends shook. "Hey, Shaun, how's it going? McKenna and I plan to come help at Jesse and Tori's cabin this weekend." Shaun always appreciated how nice Luke had been to him when they were growing up. It wasn't always easy when his older brother and his brother's best friend seemed to own the town. Shaun was lucky they sometimes let him tag along.

"I could certainly use an extra set of hands or two. Thanks. I'm headed out to Rick's house today, though. I want to pick up the slack over there since Rick has his daughter to care for now."

Luke patted him on the back. "Good man. Listen, I'll come help you there, too, this afternoon after my appointment out at the Littlejohn homestead. Running water issues." Luke not only worked at the bank, but he was also a consultant of sorts who helped homesteaders in the area solve problems, from cattle rearing or garden placement to homestead safety and protection. "I'll text you when I'm done." Then he looked at Shaun quizzically. "Did you need something from the bank today? Cash a check?"

Shaun tried to sound casual. "I was wondering if I can have a few minutes of McKenna's time." He probably should've called ahead and made an appointment; it just wasn't something he thought of doing since Sweet Home was so small. But now he wished he had. That way he wouldn't have to explain to Luke why he'd stopped by. Especially since Luke was looking at him expectantly. "It's about one of the buildings her uncle owns."

"Are you thinking about setting up shop? Computer services? I know I could use a website." He laughed. "But only the homesteads that have electricity would be able to access it, so maybe I don't need it after all. But I know plenty of people in town could use your services."

"Working on the actual computers isn't exactly what I'm trained to do. I'm more of a software guy, a programmer."

Shaun missed his job in Houston and wondered if he would adjust to using only his hands to work. He liked using his brain, doing what he was trained to do. He wondered if Donovan had the same problem; he had owned his own tech company before selling his app to a large conglomerate.

McKenna came over and rescued him. "What's up, Shaun?"

"Do you have a minute? I was wondering about a building in town that your uncle owns."

"Sure. Come into my office and have a seat. Luke loaded all that info on my computer. Are you looking to buy or to rent?" she said over her shoulder as she led the way.

"I'm, uh, looking for a friend." Here he was calling Lolly his friend again. How on earth had that happened? The kiss on the cheek popped into his mind, then the kiss he'd given her square on her mouth. Neither image was helpful right now.

McKenna sat behind her desk and clicked her mouse a couple of times. "Hold on a second." She left the office and came back with Luke. "Sorry about that. He'll have to find it. We have a difference of opinion when it comes to where we store our files."

"No problem," Shaun said. But he really didn't want Luke to know he was doing Lolly a favor.

"While he's pulling that up, tell me what you need. I mean what your friend needs."

He might as well spill, because it would be out soon enough—though he hadn't yet figured out how to tell Lolly. "The space would be for Lolly Crocker. She's going to open a bakery." From his mouth to God's ears. He certainly had a lot of nerve to make such a claim, especially without Lolly's consent.

"Sure." McKenna didn't seem surprised in the least. "I wondered if that was the next step. I'm sure she could use more space. I know Piney and the others are passing along a lot of baking projects to her. Also, I saw the menu Piney wants her to make for the wedding. Lolly will need room for a whole crew to help, because I'm sure she can't do it all on her own."

"Which property are you thinking?" Luke asked. Shaun was relieved not to see judgment on his face. If it had been practically anyone else in town, they would've either teased him or warned him off Lolly, like his mom was prone to do.

"Miss Lisa's old boutique, next to Tori's building."

"Ah, good choice. Let me pull up the details—square footage, you know, all that jazz."

And because Luke wasn't being critical, Shaun elaborated on his plans. "You know the range I bought Jesse and Tori for a wedding present? I thought we could give it to Lolly and I'll order them a new one."

McKenna had been leaning over Luke's shoulder, monitoring what he was doing on the computer, but she popped up when Shaun mentioned the new range. "No. Lolly doesn't need a residential oven for this. She needs something professional, and I know the perfect place she can get it, along with everything for a professional kitchen setup."

As excited as Shaun was to help Lolly out, he wasn't sure she would be thrilled that others were making plans for her, too. "How much does a professional kitchen cost?" So now he was suddenly thinking of dipping into his savings for Lolly? *Why in the world?*

"Well, I know a restaurant in Anchorage, Tortellini's, that shut down. The owner is looking to offload her kitchen equipment."

"Really?" Shaun was shocked at the serendipity.

Luke laughed. "This is McKenna's forte. She has a way of making things work out for businesses. Back when we were working at the bank in Anchorage, she was always figuring out ways for people to keep their businesses when they were near foreclosure. Since she took over the bank here, she's been very active helping others keep or start up small businesses. It's her gift."

She squeezed his arm. "Thanks, honey." She turned to Shaun. "I can give Lolly a template to build a business plan, and if all goes well, she can borrow from our bank. Uncle Monty will rent the building for a pittance, I'm sure. He'd be excited for a new business to come to town, which would mean more business for the bank. And about the professional kitchen, I believe she'll be able to get it for pennies on the dollar. I'll speak with the former owner of Tortellini's myself to see what we can work out." McKenna was grinning from ear to ear. "This is so exciting!"

But no one had spoken to Lolly about it yet. He pulled a flash drive from his pocket and handed it to McKenna. "Do you mind copying the business plan template for me?" He frowned at the realization that he'd have to talk to Lolly. Why did he ever want to get involved? Something like this never would've happened in Houston. He went months there without talking to his neighbors. Could run into the bank, where no one would even know his name. But he was in Sweet Home now.

"How about I do both? I have a paper copy of the business plan template here." She pulled it out of her drawer, while Luke took the flash drive from him and said, "I can make a copy for her, also. That way she'll have both."

McKenna chatted about strategy and collateral while Luke copied the file. Meanwhile, Shaun was kicking himself. On the bright side, he wouldn't have to haul Jesse and Tori's new stove into town. The bad news was Lolly was going to kill him for butting into her business, where he decidedly didn't belong.

With a pasted-on smile he thanked McKenna and Luke and started for home. He'd driven about a mile out of town when he saw a Subaru Outback at the side of the road with Ella and a bunch of her friends standing beside it. They waved for him to stop.

Shaun rolled down his window. "Can I help?"

"Yes," said Ella. "My car broke down and Dad is coming to get it now. Can you give us a ride? We're running late."

"Sure," Shaun said. "You'll have to squish in. Where can I drop you off?"

Chapter 11

LOLLY STOOD BY her sink, while Sparkle, Rick, and Ava quietly sat at her kitchen table, sampling bits of cake. Lolly had stayed up half the night baking. The cake tasting had been scheduled several weeks ago but postponed for obvious reasons—Rick collecting his new daughter, for one.

The truth was Lolly wouldn't have been able to sleep last night anyway. If only she'd felt this way about the men she'd dated after Shaun. But she never had. Shaun had a way of consuming her thoughts, and last night she'd been grateful for the chance to put her focus on baking instead of him.

But this cake tasting was no picnic. The air wasn't filled with the giddy excitement on the eve of marital bliss that you'd expect with the wedding six weeks away. Tension filled the room. Ava picked at her cake, occasionally looking up at the adults with her. Rick and Sparkle barely spoke. Lolly couldn't stand the silence anymore. She opened her mouth to ask Ava if she would like to go outside to throw the ball to Thor, when suddenly there was a knock at the front door.

"Excuse me," she said to her guests. She assumed it was Piney, who would definitely have an opinion about the cake for her daughter's wedding. Piney had already declared chocolate cake the winner, saying, "Everyone likes chocolate." But Lolly knew Aberdeen was allergic and Miss Lisa was not a chocolate fan, so she was presenting other options, too.

When Lolly opened the door, it was Shaun, and her heart skipped a beat.

"Can we come in?" He stepped to the side and there stood her high school girls. "You have company."

"Hi, Ms. Crocker. I was wondering if I could snap a picture of the recipe for the macarons. I want to make some for Mom," Ella said.

"Sure. Come in, come in," Lolly said. The girls filed in with Shaun holding the door.

"Hi," said the rest of them, beaming at her. "We can't stay long," Lacy said. "My mom said I have to clean my room before I can help Ella make the cookies out at the lodge."

"Head on into the kitchen." Lolly was happy to see the girls; she'd missed them. But seeing Shaun overwhelmed her. Her heart was pounding and she felt nervous having him so near. Finally, he followed the girls, and she followed him.

At the kitchen entry, he stopped suddenly, and she nearly ran into him. "Oh," he said. "I didn't know you were busy." He gestured with a hand that held a stack of papers, the first she'd noticed them.

The girls had crowded into her already small kitchen, making a semicircle around Rick and Sparkle.

Rick stood. "Join us. We could use your help."

Not just with the cake but to cut the tension, Lolly thought.

"You don't mind, do you, Lolly?" Sparkle asked.

"Of course not. There's plenty." Maybe having Shaun and the girls here would help them reach a consensus. But mostly, the extra people would be a good distraction. "Go ahead, grab some samples."

"We've missed you, Ms. Crocker," Ruthie said, hugging

her as she passed by to get a paper plate. The other girls gave her a hug, too, which made happy tears fill Lolly's eyes. She loved these girls but couldn't help thinking how nice it would be if Shaun gave her a squeeze, too.

"I've missed you, too," she replied to her protégées. She handed Ella the macaron recipe. Ella snapped a picture, handed it back, and said, "Thanks."

"We want to talk to you about continuing our *Great British Baking Show* cooking lessons," Annette said.

Lolly thought about all the work Sparkle's wedding would require. "We'll see. We might need to break until after the wedding."

"Oh, that makes sense," Lacy said. "But we're happy to help with the wedding, too."

"We'll all help," Ella said before taking a bite of the white cake with royal icing.

Lolly laughed. "I'll take you all up on that. There will be plenty of cooking and baking to go around."

The girls started chattering to Rick and Sparkle and Ava, advocating for their favorite cake flavors.

"Hey," Shaun said from right behind her, startling Lolly.

"Stop sneaking up on me," she said.

"I have something I want to talk to you about later."

"Shaun?" Uki said. "Did you ask her yet?"

To go steady? Lolly shouldn't have thought it. These days, she had a one-track mind, and her brain had apparently skipped off to La-La Land. She glanced at him shyly.

He frowned at Uki. "Oh, that."

She looked at him as if to ask *What?*

"The girls said you keep cookies and cakes in the freezer for emergencies."

She grinned at him. "You have a cake emergency?"

"Yeah. Sort of. It's Mom's birthday tomorrow."

"I know." It was one of the reasons she'd baked Patricia the snickerdoodles, though she hadn't wanted to make it obvious that she'd remembered Patricia's birthday.

Shaun seemed embarrassed with everyone watching

him. "I thought I could buy one from you for her. I know it would taste better than if I tried to make it from some cake mix."

"Yuck. Don't do that," said Annette as she filled her plate with cake. "Those box mixes don't taste nearly as good as one of Ms. Crocker's cakes."

Ella's phone dinged with a text. "Dad's here. We've got to go, Ms. Crocker." She turned to Lacy. "He said I can help you clean your room and then he'll come pick us up so we can get started on the macarons."

"Take some cake with you." Lolly handed each girl a second paper plate to cover their first plate.

After the girls were gone, Lolly knelt beside Ava. "Would you like to come outside with me and Thor?" She thought Rick and Sparkle could use some breathing room to figure out what cake they wanted. She looked up at Shaun. "You can come, too, and we'll talk about what cake is best for your mom." Lolly patted her knee and Thor came over to convince Ava to slide out of her chair and follow them.

She noticed Shaun had laid the stack of papers on the kitchen desk before he went to the back door. On his way out, he picked up Thor. Good grief, he was always manhandling her dog, like Thor was *his* or something! And even more annoying was that Thor loved it.

Once outside, Shaun took the seat next to Ava on the porch step. He didn't try to engage her, but instead spoke to Thor. "What do you think, little man"—Lolly's pet name for Thor!—"should I try the chocolate chiffon or the lemon curd cake?"

Thor barked, happy to be part of the conversation, but his bark made Ava jump.

"Yes, lemon curd it is." Shaun took a bite and said, "Yummm," which made Ava look over at him with a half smile. "Have you told Ava about your gift?" he asked Lolly. "How you can tell someone's favorite cake or cookie just by looking at them?"

Ava glanced up at her.

"I wouldn't call it a gift," Lolly answered. "I just make a guess, that's all." But she was sure Sparkle would choose the carrot cake with cream cheese icing, if it were up to her, and Rick would choose the coconut cake. Ava, she suspected, was a chocolate chip cookie girl, with no nuts.

Shaun took a bite of chocolate chiffon this time, which Lolly knew was his favorite. She wondered if she'd subconsciously made it for him. He glanced up at her knowingly, as if he were reading her mind. He nodded, then speared another bite of cake, coconut this time. But before he ate it, he said to Ava, "What's your favorite so far?"

Rick and Sparkle appeared at the back door. They both seemed to be trying harder to look happy, but Lolly wasn't sure she was buying it. "Well, my favorite is carrot cake," Sparkle said. "I know it's not traditional for a wedding, but I've always loved it." She looked over at Rick and he gave her a smile back, more genuine than the smile he had before. Things seemed to be going a little better between those two, which pleased Lolly.

"I'm a coconut cake guy." Rick turned to Ava. "Which one do you like best, honey?"

"Hold that thought." Lolly raced back to the kitchen to grab one of her special-recipe chocolate chip cookies from the cookie jar, the ones that had the shaved chocolate in them. In a flash, she was back outside, laying the cookie on Ava's plate. Ava took the cookie and to Lolly's surprise smiled up at her before she took a big bite, sending crumbs everywhere.

Thor jumped on the crumbs and quickly cleaned them up. Lolly kept an eagle eye, making sure he didn't get any chocolate chips.

Shaun pointed his fork at Thor. "Doesn't he have his own cookies or have you stopped making dog treats like you used to?"

"I made him dog biscuits yesterday. I'll get him some." She ran back to the kitchen once again. When she returned, she extended a dog biscuit to Ava. "Would you like to give Thor a treat?"

Ava nodded and shoved the rest of her cookie in her mouth before taking the dog treat from Lolly. Thor barked again, making Ava flinch.

"Calm down, little man," Shaun said. "Show some manners. You don't want to scare Ava. She's going to be your very best friend." He smiled at the girl. "The best way to give a dog a treat is to hold your hand flat." He demonstrated.

Timidly, Ava held her hand flat with the dog biscuit in the middle. Thor seemed to sense that he better be gentle. He carefully took the biscuit from Ava's hand and she looked up at her dad, maybe to see if he was proud of her. Rick nodded reassuringly. "He likes it. Do you want to give him the other treat?"

Lolly transferred a second dog biscuit to Ava. Once again the little girl held it out in her hand and Thor took it, too. As she watched him eat, she hesitantly ran a hand down Thor's curly-haired back. She must have enjoyed it because she sat down next to him and gave him a hug and a kiss, one of the sweetest things Lolly had ever witnessed.

"What's the verdict about the wedding cake?" Lolly asked, trying to sound chipper.

Sparkle shrugged. "It doesn't matter. Make whatever Rick likes."

"I'll take care of it." Lolly nodded, but she had no intention of going along with that suggestion. Yes, she'd make Rick a coconut cake—the groom's cake, while the main wedding cake would be carrot. Of course, there was a whole subsection of the Sweet Home population who wouldn't eat coconut *or* carrot cake. So Lolly decided to make a variety of cakes to satisfy all the different taste buds of Sweet Home. Even a sugar-free cake for those who were sugar-averse.

Rick picked up Ava. "We need to get going."

Shaun had gone inside and returned with the stack of papers.

Rick glanced at what he held. "What do you have there, Shaun? Is it something I can help with?"

"Possibly," Shaun answered. "I have to talk to Lolly about it first."

"Just let me know." Rick opened the door for Sparkle. Shaun and Lolly followed, as did Thor.

Sparkle glanced at the floor for a second. "We'll be in touch, but . . . we might be postponing the wedding for a little while."

Rick gave her a resigned smile. "If we do, it'll only be for a couple of months, until we can get settled."

"Sure. Whatever you need." They did seem a little better than when they first arrived. It had to be the cake. Cake always lifted everyone's spirits.

As soon as they were gone, Lolly pointed to Shaun's papers. "What is it you wanted to talk to me about? Besides a cake for your mom?"

Shaun handed over the papers. "These are for you. A template to follow when writing your business plan, plus a loan application."

"Loan application? Business plan?" she parroted, confused.

"Yes. McKenna has a line on a professional oven; she'll be able to tell you the particulars about that. I'm sure if you need help with the business plan either I can help you, or Rick can. Especially Rick, since he's the one with the MBA from Stanford."

"I don't understand. I'm not opening a business. I just need a bigger space than our small cottage so I can cook. *Temporarily.*"

Shaun put his hands on Lolly's shoulders and bent his knees, gazing into her eyes, apparently to disarm her. It worked. She gazed back, giddy that he had his hands on her, making her almost forget what they were talking about. "You've always wanted a bakery. Carpe diem, Lolly."

"If I'm going to seize anything, it's to give you a good shake," she said, snapping out of it. "I was thrilled earlier when you wanted to help me find a place where I can cook. But honestly, Shaun, don't you think you've overstepped now?"

He didn't even hesitate. "Not at all." But the worried look on his face a moment later had him seeming contrite. "Just promise me you'll think about it."

Lolly looked down at the pages. "Yes, I'll think about it." But if she did move forward in the direction he was pushing her, she wouldn't ask for Shaun's help. He'd done enough. Besides, she was supposed to be keeping her distance from him. Just because he'd remembered her dream of opening a bakery, and he'd taken the initiative to bring these business plan papers to her, she felt like she might be falling in love with him all over again. She didn't think she could stand getting her heart broken once more. If she had any questions about the business plan, she'd talk to Rick. The first question would be what would she do if a teaching position came through at one of the many schools where she'd applied?

Shaun sat down at the table as if he was settling in. "As I mentioned, McKenna knows about an oven for sale. Actually, she has a line on a complete professional kitchen that's available for pennies on the dollar."

"I told you I'd think about it." Lolly untied the apron Tori had given her and slipped it over her head. She had on her *Baking Is My Therapy* T-shirt and the jeans she should've tossed last year for the holes in the knees, or at least patched them. If she'd known he was coming over, she might've worn a nicer ensemble. "What about the cake for your mom? Any ideas?"

"Sticky toffee pudding cake is her favorite."

Yeah, Lolly knew. "I don't have one of those in the freezer, but I do have the perfect recipe. I even have all the ingredients on hand." What was she saying? Why did she love to overbook herself, to people-please regardless of the cost to her well-being? "I won't offer to make it," Lolly started, feeling proud of herself, "but you can use my recipe and make it yourself for your mom. You can even take home my ingredients."

"I'll bungle it. You know I will. Remember the peanut butter cookies you had me bake? Disastrous."

"Well . . . I guess it would be okay if you used my kitchen. Mom and Jilly won't be home for hours." So much for not people-pleasing.

Shaun jerked his head in her direction. "Did I hear you correctly?"

She rolled her eyes. "Yeah, surprising, huh? It'll be a free baking lesson for you, and I'll be able to sit here and oversee while I get all my upcoming baking organized on paper. You can make some time to bake your mom a cake, can't you?" He probably had no idea what it took to bake— the time, the energy . . . the love. She looked at the boy she loved so long ago. The boy had turned into a man now. And he was staring at her as if considering.

"I'll make you a deal. I'll let you let me use your ingredients. I'll even let you teach me how to make Mom's favorite cake. The only thing you have to do is promise to fill out the paperwork for McKenna and the bank." He paused as if he'd had a second brilliant idea. "Yeah, while I make the cake, you do the paperwork. That way we can help each other."

Boy, some deal, she thought sarcastically. "What exactly am I getting out of this?"

He gave her the cocky, boyish grin that he'd given her a thousand times before. "Your dream business. Plus the pleasure of my company." He said it with such confidence that she had to laugh.

She picked up the apron and tossed it at him. "You haven't changed a bit. You're still full of yourself."

He laughed good-naturedly and fumbled with the apron.

"Wear the wildlife side. It's more your style."

He slipped the apron over his head. "You're probably right about me being full of myself." He wrapped the ties around and tried to make a bow, but the ties slipped loose.

"Here, let me." She took the ties and made a neat bow. "Now you look like Mr. Julia Child."

"Just who I always wanted to be. But seriously, what do you say? Take advantage of me while I'm here; I'm happy to help you fill out the paperwork."

Lolly saw a loophole. "Sure. I'll fill out the paperwork." She'd fill it out, but that didn't mean that she would actually turn it in to McKenna.

But then she wondered what would happen if she did take this first step. What if she did try to open Happily Ever Baking? Mom always said that *It's better to try and fail than to regret.* Lolly wondered where that saying was when her mom made her give up Shaun when she was heading off to college. She remembered what Pastor Joe had said at church about how forgiveness is a *process*. Lolly shut her eyes and said a prayer asking for strength to forgive her mother again.

"Are you okay?" Shaun asked, bringing her back to the present.

"Yeah, I'm fine. Let's get started. Help me get all the ingredients together for your mom's cake."

"And you'll fill out the paperwork without any more guff?"

"Yeah."

This morning, Lolly had sat trying to decide whether to start the cake for Patricia or not. She had decided *not*. But it was lucky that she'd pulled out the recipe and didn't have to go looking for it now.

As Lolly took out the ingredients from the cabinet that held the baking supplies, Shaun took them from her and set them on the counter. Next, she pulled out measuring cups, both dry and wet, and gave them to Shaun. Lastly, she retrieved a little saucepan, set it on the stove, and handed over the recipe.

"It says I should chop the dates first." He looked at her quizzically. "How big?"

"Look what it says—finely chopped," she answered, but he didn't seem satisfied.

"Give it to me in inches, or fractions of an inch."

"Hand me the paring knife instead. I'll show you."

While she chopped the first date, Shaun stood looking over her shoulder. Did he have no clue what his closeness did to her? How breathless she felt? How he made her tremble? She was lucky not to slice off a digit.

"There." She laid the knife on the cutting board, glad that her hands executed the knifework without thought. "Do you have it now?"

He gave her a disarming smile. "Yes, Chef."

She rolled her eyes and went to the table to get some distance from him. She sat and picked up the packet of papers he'd brought. "There's nothing here that says how much rent will be for Miss Lisa's old building."

"McKenna said to leave that blank for now. She has to check with her uncle, but she believes you'll be able to get it for a song."

"I'm not a very good singer," she deadpanned.

He smiled, raising his eyebrows, and she added, "Okay, I'm a decent singer. Now, stop looking at me and grease those pans."

After he prepped the pans and got the dates soaking in boiling water, he sat down and helped her with the application. He had interesting ideas on how to build out her business plan, which made her glad he was there. The truth was she probably would've chucked the whole application packet in the trash if he hadn't stayed.

Soon she got up and showed him how to sift flour and the proper way to combine the dry ingredients with the wet ones.

"What about the date mixture?" he asked.

"Don't get ahead of yourself. Just follow the recipe," Lolly replied, thinking absently that it would make a cute saying to embroider onto the next quilt she made—maybe one decorated with spoons, bowls, and canisters, all the things she used in baking. She looked up to see Shaun staring at her.

She wanted to tell him she was feeling it, too, that this was like old times, hanging out in the kitchen while she baked and he talked about his big plans to get a degree in computer science. It was all so cozy and comfortable then, just like it was now.

And just like then, he took her hand and pulled her to him. She didn't even have a chance to be shocked before he kissed her senseless, like he'd done when they'd been in high school.

Except they didn't end up making out on the couch because he pulled his mouth away.

"Why?" was the only word she could form.

"For old times' sake." He kissed her forehead and let her go.

Of course, her heart wanted the kiss to mean something more. But her sanity wanted to take him at his word, and she said back to him with a nod, "For old times' sake." *Those were good times.*

Apparently, she'd said it aloud because he said with a sad shrug, "The best."

He went back to the recipe, scanned it, then picked up the soaked dates and folded them in as if the kiss hadn't been anything more than a kiss. While she wished it had been a promise of more to come.

SHAUN SILENTLY CURSED himself. He was such a bonehead, crossing the line *again*. Why had he kissed her? He hadn't acted this impulsively since he was a teenager. But he just couldn't help himself. All the hours they'd spent in Lolly's kitchen had come rushing back. All the times he'd interrupted her baking to kiss her for no other reason than he wanted to. Just like he'd wanted to five minutes ago. What happened to his resolve to be done with women?

He opened his mouth to say he was sorry, or to say something to get that sad look off her face, but his phone saved him with a text from his mom. Where are you?

He should be at Rick's, working on the house. But instead, he'd been kissing Lolly again. He wondered if his mom had a sixth sense and knew what he'd been up to . . . not the first time in his life his mom had shown that uncanny ability. He actually looked out the window to see if there were any witnesses to him grabbing Lolly and kissing her, but no one was there. Thor had even slept through Shaun's faux pas, curled up in his bed in the corner.

Finally, Shaun texted his mom back a partial truth. I'm taking care of your birthday present. Hopefully, that would keep her curiosity at bay.

Lolly jumped up and turned on the oven. "I totally forgot to have you preheat."

Which meant he would have to be here that much longer. "While we wait for the oven to come up to temp, do you and Jilly have any odd jobs for me to do?" That way he would hopefully be in another room or outside, away from Lolly. Because apparently, he couldn't trust himself to keep his lips off her. *No self-control at all!*

"Sit and talk to me," she said. Which was the last thing he wanted to do. Lolly always had to get to the bottom of things like this. When they'd been together, she'd made him stretch his emotional depth, made him examine his own inner workings. He expected she now wanted to know why he'd done what he'd done—in other words, she would want to know if he had lost his *ever-lovin' mind*! He was pretty sure he had. Reason dictated he wasn't supposed to want her the way he did.

He had to derail her. "If you're not going to give me any chores to do, then let's finish up your paperwork." There. That should put a lid on her figuring out that he'd lost it.

"Okay." She picked up one of the papers and handed it to him. "There's an obvious major problem. I don't have any collateral. The only thing I own is my sewing machine and my ten-year-old car."

He smiled at her. "Yeah, in Houston that wouldn't even get you in the bank's front door."

She pushed the rest of the papers away from her. "So why go to all this trouble, if it'll never work?"

"You forget we're in Sweet Home. McKenna and I talked about collateral, and she says it isn't going to be a problem." That wasn't exactly the extent of the conversation. After he'd sworn Luke and McKenna to secrecy, he offered his share of the Montana homestead as collateral for Lolly's bakery.

He'd swear on a stack of Bibles that it had been a rational decision. He knew Lolly's bakery would do well. No emotion was involved, not even a little bit. He wasn't sweet on her. To his way of thinking, if she couldn't make the payments, he had the money saved up to outright pay off her debt anyway, so there was no chance he would lose his property. He just couldn't let Lolly know what he'd done.

Shaun couldn't let his mom know either. God help them all if she did! She'd probably do more than blow a gasket. Surely, she'd try to ground him for life.

Lolly touched his arm. "Really? No collateral?"

"McKenna said her uncle Monty is backing loans for new small businesses to boost the economy of Sweet Home." This was the story McKenna swore she would tell Lolly if she was questioned. And since her uncle Monty backed Tori's business, it wasn't a complete lie. "It's the reason the business plan is so important. She wants you to put everything down on paper, so it'll get approved ASAP." In the meantime, he'd see about buying the professional kitchen McKenna had mentioned and get reimbursed for it when Lolly's loan went through.

"But who says Sweet Home can support a bakery?" Lolly said, looking downcast.

He tapped the application. "That's what we've got to figure out, the plan." There he was again, acting like they were a team. He ignored that little voice that was telling him that he shouldn't be helping Lolly to stay in Sweet Home.

"What about Piney? She serves food at the Hungry Bear's diner. I don't want to compete with her." Lolly frowned. "But the truth is I've been providing most of her baked goods lately."

"That settles it, then." The oven beeped. He picked up the cake pan. "You get back to work on the business plan while I put this in the oven."

Before he could, though, Lolly's phone began pinging over and over. She picked up her phone and stared at the screen, her face turning a bright red.

"What is it?" Shaun asked.

"Texts. Lots of them. From nearly every member of the Sisterhood of the Quilt. I never should've joined their group text."

"What are they saying?"

"All the texts are for me." She wrinkled her forehead as she continued to read. "Shaun," she bit out, *what did you do?*"

"I didn't do anything. Honest." He felt as bewildered as she was angry. "Tell me what they want. What's wrong?"

"Oh, nothing's wrong," she said sarcastically, "they're just excited and want to help."

"With what?"

She frowned at him. "My new bakery."

Chapter 12

NEWS HAD TRAVELED faster than the speed of light. Though Lolly was peeved, she wasn't all that surprised to find that the huge uptick in texts came from a combination of McKenna blabbing to the Sisterhood of the Quilt about Shaun's visit and Jilly jumping in to spill the beans about Lolly's incriminating bakery notebook.

Which reminded Lolly. Without telling Shaun where she was going, she begrudgingly snuck out of the kitchen to retrieve the bakery binder. What she gleaned from the texts was that the subset of quilters who had stood against Lolly for breaking Shaun's heart had apparently come around and were excited about the bakery because it was good for the town. So Piney really had fixed things with them, or at least she'd laid the groundwork for this turnaround. All of them except Patricia. But Patricia wasn't on the group text, as she'd only recently been well enough to return to the Sisterhood of the Quilt meetings. Lolly couldn't help but worry about Patricia's reaction when she found out about the possibility of a bakery. The truth was that Lolly wasn't completely on board for a variety of reasons either—her meager savings, the financial outlay, her financial stability in the long run, and of course, her promise to stay as far away from Shaun as possible. But she couldn't worry about all that now.

She picked up the bakery binder and held it to her chest as she headed back to the kitchen. If she was forced to fill out the paperwork, she might as well use the plans she'd laid out long ago. No sense in reinventing the wheel, right?

Once again in the kitchen, she sat at the table, where Shaun approached her and nodded toward her binder. "Returning to the scene of the crime?"

"You're the one who put this in motion," she reminded him.

"I don't think so, Lolls." He pointed at the binder. "You're holding the evidence that proves you're the one who put this in motion . . . how many years ago?" He stopped and watched her. "What are you doing now?"

"Turning off my phone. We'll never get this paperwork done if they keep bugging me."

He gave her a self-satisfied smile.

"What's that look for?" she asked.

"I'm glad you're finally on board."

She didn't tell him that she wasn't quite there yet, but while his mom's cake baked, she'd play along. What could it hurt?

But as they went through her binder, she couldn't help but feel more and more excited. It wasn't just the thought of the bakery that was driving her enthusiasm, though that should have been enough. It was the pleasure of working on this with Shaun. Bouncing ideas off each other. Being close to him. She couldn't help but wonder if her future might be changing. Well, if she was really going through with the bakery, her future *was* changing . . . until a teaching position opened up, of course.

Twenty minutes later, a knock at the door startled Lolly, so engrossed was she in the planning. Or engrossed because Shaun was sitting so near, helping her. She hurried to the door and was surprised to see Hope and Donovan standing

on the porch. "This is unexpected. I thought the Sisterhood
of the Quilt is meeting at the lodge."

"Oh, they are," Hope said as Lolly stepped back for them
to step inside. "I accidentally left two bolts of fabric at the
shop that I meant to bring home, so we came to town to pick
them up." That didn't explain why they were *here*. Now, if
she'd said Piney wanted Hope to pick up some cookies or
something . . . *that* Lolly would believe.

"What can I do for you?"

"Hey, Don. Hope." Shaun was leaning in the kitchen
doorway, wearing her apron, as casual as could be. As if he
lived here!

Lolly felt her cheeks burning. The oven buzzer went off,
reminding her that Shaun wasn't here on a date, though she
was sure that was how it looked to Hope and Donovan
Stone.

"I better get that." Shaun went back to the kitchen.

"Shaun's making Patricia a cake for her birthday," she
explained, as if it wasn't weird at all that he was here in her
house.

Donovan chuckled as if the whole situation were funny,
while Hope took Lolly's arm and whispered, "I won't tell
Patricia what you two are up to." In other words, *up to no
good*.

Donovan sauntered to the cake and leaned over it. "It
smells amazing."

"Thanks," Shaun said. Didn't they realize that the whole
situation was surreal?

Lolly surreptitiously stacked papers on top of the bakery
binder to hide it. "Did you need something? Baked goods
for the Sisterhood?" Lolly asked Hope. She wanted to rush
them out the door as quickly as possible. Having witnesses
to her drooling over Shaun was so embarrassing.

"Do you mind if I get myself some water?" Donovan
asked. He was already opening cabinets as if to look for a
glass.

"Sure. Help yourself," Lolly said.

Hope pulled Lolly closer before retrieving an envelope from her quilted cross-body purse, a design that most of the Sisterhood of the Quilt had made this past year in varying color schemes. She put the envelope in Lolly's hand. "This is a little something that I owe you for teaching the girls how to bake this summer. I meant to give it to you earlier." Hope was lying through her teeth and didn't seem at all uncomfortable about it.

Lolly thrust the envelope back at her. "I don't want this. I taught the girls because we share an obsession with *The Great British Baking Show*. It was just for fun." Or it was until Lolly got canned by the school district. "I didn't do it for the money. I can't take it."

Hope backed away from Lolly's outstretched arm, and she turned for the door. "Donovan, we have to go, or else Piney is going to send a search party out for us."

Lolly followed, still holding the envelope out in front of her. "Hope, I mean it. I don't want this."

Hope pretended not to hear her. "Donovan, I really do have to get back."

As Donovan walked past Lolly, he pressed the envelope back toward her and said softly, "You have to keep it. Look how pleased Hope is to finally have the means to repay you for all you've done."

"But—"

"Besides, we all know new brides have to get their way. Right?" He shot her a smile so bright he looked like the man who had invented wedded bliss. He followed his wife out the door but turned back for just a moment and called, "Shaun, see you later, bro. Remember, don't do anything I wouldn't do."

Lolly's mouth fell open. She started to chase after Donovan to explain that nothing was going on between her and Shaun, but the door closed behind him.

"Well," Shaun said, standing in the kitchen doorway again, looking better than any man had the right to look, "I think Don and Hope won that one."

Lolly glanced down at the envelope in her hand and then back up at the man who made her heart go all aflutter. She couldn't quite wrap her head around how she'd gotten herself into such a tangle. "Leave the cake here to cool. I can decorate it for you and you can pick it up tomorrow."

"No way. First of all, we still have paperwork to get through." He paused for a long moment.

"And?" she said, because the suspense was killing her.

"And I always finish what I start," he said.

The words hung between them, weighed down with subtext. She had the feeling they weren't talking about cake anymore and her insides went all warm in a way she hadn't felt in years.

Only Shaun could make her feel this way, and she'd promised herself she wouldn't fall in love with him again. But perhaps it was too late. Or maybe she'd never really fallen *out* of love with him at all.

Patricia's warning to stay away from Shaun popped into Lolly's mind then, along with her dreadful romantic history, all the men whose hearts she'd broken. The last thing Lolly wanted to do was hurt Shaun again. But she was bound to, wasn't she? It was in her DNA, after all. Love 'em and Leave 'em Lolly took after her dad. He had set the example by leaving her mom. But instead of trying to be the opposite of her father—being someone who saw relationships through—Lolly wondered if she took his leaving as some kind of permission to be a heartbreaker, too. Or so she worried. She just couldn't trust herself to make the right decisions when it came to men. As case in point, with each of her breakups, Lolly felt like she was doing the right thing for the men she was breaking up with. *With the exception of Shaun.* She wondered now if her dad had felt the same way, too, like he was doing the right thing. But she'd never know. The only solution she could think of now was to do the opposite of what she truly felt.

She reined her emotions in and said, "Fine." She would

stick to the subject of cake. "Tomorrow morning, or whatever time works for you, come back and ice it."

This way she could get Shaun out of the house now. Ease the tension that had been building ever since he showed up at her door.

"What about the application?" he countered. "Shouldn't we get that done?"

There was no *we* about it. "I promise to finish it before you come by tomorrow." Hopefully while her mom and Jilly were out.

"Okay. If that's how you want it."

That's how it had to be. But she didn't say that. "Seriously, I'll get it done."

He gave her a peeved look, the one that said he was about to start an argument. She knew him so well. But he surprised her by shoving his hands in his pockets and looking at her without saying a word.

"See you tomorrow," she said, with enough emphasis that she was sure he heard, *Don't let the door hit your butt on the way out.*

It was causing her physical pain to erect this wall between them. But she *had* to set Shaun free . . . if only in her mind. It was safer this way. Because doing anything else would only cause a heap of trouble for everyone involved.

DURING THE WEE hours, unable to sleep, Lolly shuffled into the kitchen intent on making a recipe she'd developed for Sleepytime Cookies. As she pulled the flour down from the cabinet, an envelope she'd never seen before careened to the floor. When she leaned over to pick it up, she read the message on the front: *FOR YOUR NEW BAKERY.* Inside the envelope was a stack of twenties!

"For the love of . . ." She pulled out her phone, not caring a lick if it was the middle of the night. He deserved to get woken up. She punched Shaun's name on the screen, ready to let him have it. Sleepytime Cookies were no good to her now. She was more awake than when she'd lain staring at the ceiling, because now she was rip-roaring mad.

He answered on the fourth ring. "H'lo." He sounded nearly unconscious but she didn't care.

"How dare you leave your dirty cash in my kitchen!"

"Lolly?"

"Yes, it's me, you Neanderthal."

"What time is it?"

"Two thirty."

"Why are you calling me?" She heard the bed creak, his throat clear. "Is everything all right? Do I need to come over?" He sounded less like the sandman and more like himself . . . a worried Shaun. Which gave her pause.

Her heart might've even sighed a little. But she pulled herself away from that kind of thinking.

"Yes, I'm fine. But *you're* not going to be once I give you an earful." She straightened her shoulders, though he wasn't there to see it. "I'm a proud woman, Shaun Montana. I don't need your stinking money."

"What money?" he asked with not a trace of sarcasm or teasing in his voice.

"The money you left under the flour sack in the cabinet."

"I didn't . . . *oh.*"

"Oh, what? What did you just remember? That you wanted to make me feel two inches tall by trying to rescue the damsel in distress?"

"Lolly, calm down. Go to the kitchen and eat a cookie or something."

"I'm already in the kitchen." As if she couldn't help but do as he said, she cracked open the lid to a large Tupperware container on the counter and removed one of the Monster Cookies she'd made yesterday because they were her mom's favorites. She took a big bite. "Tell me what's going on." Yes, she was talking with her mouth full, but this wasn't the time for Miss Manners.

"Listen to me," Shaun said. "Don't you think it was weird that Donovan was looking through your cabinets?"

"He was looking to get a drink of water. I'm pretty sure I saw the glass he pulled out."

"Well, I noticed that he never filled it up," Shaun said. "Hope announced it was time to go immediately afterward."

She looked at the countertop, and sure enough, there sat Donovan's glass, with no sign it had ever been even slightly damp. "Oh."

"Don't you have something you want to say to me?" Shaun said with mock sternness.

"Want a cookie?" she asked meekly. She was only kidding, of course.

"Sure," he said immediately. "I'm wide awake and I might as well ice Mom's cake while I'm up."

"You can't really come over. Mom and Jilly are asleep," Lolly hissed.

"I'll be quiet."

"Well, I was just going back to bed."

"Don't bakers get up around this time anyway?"

"I haven't been asleep yet."

"Why not?"

She wasn't going to tell him *that*.

"Lolly, are you still there?"

She could hear him rustling around. Was he putting his clothes on while he had her on the phone? "I'm here," she finally said. "But I'm not dressed" was the excuse that popped into her mind.

"Now, no more arguments. Get dressed," he said. "You're the one who woke me up, so I'm coming over to finish the cake."

She couldn't help it; he made her smile. His bossiness still drove her crazy and at the same time made her whole body come alive, just like in the old days.

"You'll have to be quiet when you get here," she acquiesced. How much trouble could she get into with her mom and Jilly here? Besides, her defenses were down. Probably due to lack of sleep.

"I'm surprised your mom and Jilly didn't wake up when you were yelling at me before."

She opened her mouth to argue, but he continued.

"When I get there, I expect my apology before we do anything else." He hung up.

She stared at the phone but then remembered she had to change into something more appropriate than her *Live, Laugh, Bake* nightshirt.

Ten minutes later, she was standing on the porch holding Thor. He was sure to give a yip or two when he saw Shaun, and she hoped the house would muffle the sound and keep her mother and sister from waking up. She certainly didn't want them to stumble into the kitchen to catch Shaun there in a late-night tête-à-tête.

A few minutes later, Shaun pulled up in his Jeep and got out, looking a bit rumpled but beautiful to her starved-for-him eyes. Which was ridiculous; she had seen him less than twelve hours ago.

As predicted, Thor gave two sharp barks. But when Shaun got close, the dog quieted. Shaun leaned in toward Lolly and her stomach did three back somersaults and her breath caught. Certain he meant to kiss her, she closed her eyes and leaned in, going up on tiptoe to meet him halfway. But the only thing her lips grazed was his T-shirt, as he took Thor in his arms and, chuckling, walked past her into the house. Apparently, Thor was man's best friend! And the man had the gall to laugh at her.

"Hustle it up, Lollipop. I've got to get this cake iced for my mother."

"Mama's boy," she muttered under her breath.

"Oh, I'm my own man."

The way he said it made it sound like a warning . . . or maybe it was a promise. She should be mad that he'd insisted on coming over. Mad that he'd tricked her into thinking he was going to kiss her. Instead, she felt deliciously warm and exceedingly glad.

• • •

SHAUN BLAMED LACK of sleep for the poor decisions that had led him to coming to Lolly's house in the middle of the night. First, he shouldn't have answered the phone when Lolly called. Second, he shouldn't have provoked her. Third, he shouldn't have jumped at the chance to come. He knew her offer of a cookie was only a tongue-in-cheek peace offering, and not an actual invitation. But here he was just the same.

He'd admit—only to himself—that he had almost kissed her when he arrived. Leaning in to kiss her felt right and natural, just like old times, and it took everything in him to dodge what he wanted to do most. *Playing with fire* was how his dad would've put it. But the more time he spent with Lolly, the more the old barriers were coming down, making him want to pick up where they'd left off. Even more disconcerting, he kept finding more reasons—*or were they excuses?*—to spend time with her. Once again, he blamed his lack of sleep.

Tonight wasn't the only night he'd had trouble getting shut-eye. Lolly consumed his thoughts. When he did sleep, Lolly visited his dreams. Nice dreams, too. It wasn't some ethereal Lolly, but the same Lolly he'd known all his life. The one he'd fallen in love with. She was better than anything his mind could invent.

He looked up at her now and she was staring back. Man, he was in trouble.

He set Thor on his feet. "Go lie down, little bud." Thor toddled off to the small dog bed in the corner of the kitchen, turned around in a circle, then curled up into a C before closing his eyes. Shaun glanced over at Lolly and shrugged. "At least one of us will get some rest tonight." He gazed at her for a long moment, then asked, "What ingredients do I need for the icing?"

"It's not exactly icing. It's a sauce. Get the whipped cream and butter from the refrigerator. The unsalted butter," she clarified. "I'll pull the other ingredients from the cabinet."

He watched from the fridge as she easily dug out the brown sugar but then seemed to struggle with getting something from the top shelf. Even on her tiptoes, she couldn't reach it.

He decided to come to the rescue and stepped behind her. At that same moment, she turned around, reaching for the step stool. Her mouth was opened as if to say something, but apparently, she'd lost her train of thought. He knew exactly how she felt because he had been having that problem a lot lately, too, when he was around her.

He watched as her face turned all kinds of red. It felt like heat was rolling off her. Or maybe the heat was coming from himself. But then he worried that maybe she felt trapped because all he needed to do was to place his hands on the counter on either side of her and she wouldn't be going anywhere. For a moment, he was in a tug-of-war with himself about doing just that. He wanted to kiss her so badly that he could taste it. He couldn't tell if the thump, thump, thump he was hearing was her beating heart or his own.

Apparently, she wasn't as rattled as he was because she reached past him, latched onto the step stool, pulled it over, and climbed up. As she reached for the top shelf, she bobbled and teetered and started to fall. He caught her in time, holding her, gazing into her eyes. Hadn't he seen this exact scene in a rom-com recently, or in an *I Love Lucy* episode? He should let her go, as she felt steady now, but then she did the unthinkable; she relaxed into him and automatically, his arms tightened around her. His chest tightened, too. Warmth spread through him. He realized he was holding his breath.

"What do you need?" he asked hoarsely.

She seemed lost for words. She kept staring at him, her eyes on his eyes one moment and on his lips the next.

He willed her to make the first move, to close her eyes

the way she had on the porch, and lean up to kiss him. That would make up for the missed opportunity from before.

"Your mom," she said, which didn't make any sense to him. But then it did. He set Lolly to her feet. His mom would hate them being together right now.

"I know," he said, feeling ashamed he'd goaded Lolly once again, but this time seriously . . . because he really did want to kiss her. He repeated, "What do you need?"

She laughed, looking away, which somewhat broke the tension. "Oh, Shaun, what I need is too long a list, even for you. You know I need at least two more ovens to do all the cooking and baking Piney has ordered. Actually, what I really need is a new teaching job." Then her eyes came back up, earnest this time as they landed on him. "But mostly I need a man like you." She turned red, but it was with frustration this time. "Stop looking at me like that. I didn't say I wanted *you*. It's just that I've always liked you. You see, you're the original. You've been the standard I've compared other men to." Frowning, she rolled her eyes, looking more frustrated than before. "Ignore me. I'm saying this all wrong. What I mean is I want someone *like* you, not *you*, specifically. I'll have to keep looking. You know, for Mr. Right."

Good thing his mom wasn't here to witness this! She would hate it if he and Lolly got back together. Honestly, even though it might be nice to have Lolly in his life, it wouldn't be worth the endless lectures about how she would only break his heart again. "Yeah, I know," he finally said. "No worries."

She looked how he felt . . . *defeated*. Finally, she said, "Pecans. Behind the sugar." Her words were choppy, staccato, like she might tear up at any moment.

"Yes, I'll get them," he said. He was glad for the opportunity to turn around, to get a reprieve from facing her any longer. Those few moments helped him gather his wits. But he knew her words, *I need a man like you*, would echo through his mind for a long time to come. He liked being her standard. Actually, he felt rather smug about it. *Damn straight, I'm the standard!* He wanted to howl at the moon, pound his chest. Mostly, he wanted to kiss her silly.

"Listen," she said with a sigh, "you better go." She must've been reading his mind. "I'm too tired to do this right now." He wasn't sure if she was speaking of making the sauce for his mom's cake or handling the tension— romantic or otherwise—that was between them now.

"Yeah. Sure. I'm tired, too."

"I'll work on the sauce first thing when I get up. Probably in a couple of hours. I'll text you to let you know when you can stop by to get the cake." She chewed her lip for a moment. "Best not to mention to your mom that I helped you, okay?"

He wasn't sure what he was going to tell his mom about the cake—where he'd baked it and with whom. He probably should've thought about that before going down this path, as now it seemed like a far-fetched plan, and with each passing moment it was seeming less and less like a good idea.

"Yeah, I better go."

Thor woke, stood, and stretched as if he were planning to go with him.

"Stay, little man." Shaun reached down and rubbed his fluffy head. "'Night, Lolly."

"'Night, Shaun."

He didn't dare look at her as he left the kitchen, because he was feeling weak. It wouldn't take much for him to give her a kiss good-bye. Which would only make him want to stay longer.

This nonsense had to stop. Seriously. He'd been wasting his time by hanging around Lolly. He needed to work on Rick's place, finish Jesse's cabin, and start carving out a life for himself. He came back to Alaska to help his mom on the homestead and relish his newfound freedom; and oh, how he had been looking forward to savoring his time alone. Now he wondered if maybe he should take a page from Lolly's book and think about dating someone new.

Any way he looked at it, Lolly had derailed him. Being here tonight was evidence of just how far off track he'd gone. But no more! Shaun was determined to pull it together and get back on the right path. If that meant he had to ignore Lolly, except for helping with her bakery plans, then so be it.

But that was a pretty big exception!

Chapter 13

THE FOLLOWING TWO weeks were crazy-busy. Lolly had no choice but to throw herself into baking, running between houses like a madwoman, using Aberdeen's oven, Bill Morningstar's oven, and her own to get things done. In moments when she wasn't frantic, she wondered how her loan application was going at the bank, sometimes kicking herself for turning in the packet in the first place. She wondered about Shaun also, because she hadn't seen or heard from him since that night—he'd even picked up the cake the next day when she wasn't home. Not that it had kept her from thinking about him—only a couple thousand times a day!

Every day, one or two Sweet Home folks—mostly Sisterhood of the Quilt members—would knock at her door and insist that they needed a baked dessert in the next month and could they get put on her baking schedule? Yes, she'd sold baked goods to neighbors before, but it was like the town had suddenly become addicted to sweets and she was their dealer. At this rate, tooth decay and denture sales would be on the rise for Sweet Home.

Other weird things were happening, too. Aberdeen called one evening to give Lolly a heads-up. "I'm emailing you pastry orders from shops in five other towns. If sales go well, then they want to make it a weekly thing."

"How did this come about?" Lolly asked.

"Oh," Aberdeen said nonchalantly, "I dropped by each of the stores, trying to build up demand before your bakery opens."

Lolly had rolled her eyes. "First of all, I don't have a bakery yet, and I'm not even sure whether my loan will be approved. And secondly, did Piney put you up to this?"

"I gotta run," Aberdeen said immediately. "Lacy needs me to take her out to the lodge to see Ella." She hung up.

The next day, Miss Lisa tried to slip a five into Lolly's hand when she was at the Hungry Bear picking up a bottle of vanilla and more powdered sugar. When Lolly called Miss Lisa on it, the old woman insisted that Lolly had dropped the five between the green beans and the chicken noodle soup. Lolly hadn't even gone down that aisle. The following day, a check arrived in the mail from Tori. In the memo line was printed *FOR PAST COOKING LESSONS, FIRST INSTALLMENT.*

That was the last straw. None too happy, Lolly marched to the bank with the cockamamie check and slapped it down on McKenna's desk. "I'm giving this back to you for you to give to Tori. Tell your sister I don't take charity." She was beginning to feel like a broken record.

But McKenna was unsympathetic. Instead of acknowledging that Lolly was upset, she passed a packet across her desk. Very businesslike. Yellow tabs hung from the margins. "I'm glad you stopped by. Initial and sign where I marked," McKenna said.

"What is this?" Lolly flipped through the packet. "Why do you want me to open a new account?" But she knew.

"Your business needs somewhere for all the money to go. Now, sign."

"McKenna, you're jumping the gun. I don't have a business yet." Business loans took time, which was the reason

Lolly hadn't inquired whether the loan had been approved or not.

McKenna tapped the papers. "Sign."

"Piney must've given you all lessons on how to be bossy." Lolly harrumphed as she signed where instructed. "Just because I'm signing the papers doesn't mean I'm going to use the account."

McKenna took the signed documents and walked toward the door with Tori's check in her hand, too. "I'm taking this to Luke. He'll finish up with this account and deposit Tori's check for you. Don't go anywhere; I'll be right back."

Lolly frowned at her. "You can't deposit the check. I didn't sign it." Which meant that Lolly had won this round.

"No worries," McKenna said flippantly. "We don't need your signature if you're not requesting cash back."

So much for getting the upper hand.

SHAUN RAN INTO the Hungry Bear to pick up dog food for Checkers and to get Mom some herbal tea, the kind Piney had prescribed for her. But as soon as the bell over the door jingled to announce his entrance, Piney hollered to him.

"Shaun! Come sit with us a minute."

Shaun turned in to the dining area of the Hungry Bear and saw not only Piney but Hope and McKenna, too.

"I need you to do something for me," Piney said, which probably didn't bode well for him. She had that look in her eyes, the one that meant she was meddling again. "You know the new school year starts tomorrow."

"No. I didn't." Maybe he'd heard something around town about it, but mostly he'd been keeping to himself the last couple of weeks, working on Rick's place and Jesse's cabin and generally trying not to be seen. He wished now he hadn't come into the Hungry Bear today.

"So you'll help out?" Piney looked at him expectantly,

as if she wanted him to agree to whatever nonsense she was about to ask him to do without hearing the particulars first. It probably meant more torture for him.

"And that would be doing what?" he asked. Better to rip the bandage off quickly than to stand here all day.

Hope took over. "We figure tomorrow will be hard on Lolly, you know, school starting without her there."

McKenna stepped in. "So we thought you should take Lolly to Anchorage to look at the professional kitchen equipment at Tortellini's. I've already spoken with Olive Nightbranch, and she's excited to show Lolly the equipment."

"So, the loan came through?" he asked.

"Not yet. But it would be a good excuse to get Lolly out of town and keep her mind off the first day of school."

He asked the obvious question. "Why me? Surely there's any number of folks who would love to take a trip to Anchorage to support Lolly."

Hope gave Shaun a stern look, and he wondered if she'd learned it from Piney when she'd worked at the Hungry Bear for all those years. "We know you're already going to Anchorage tomorrow. Rick said you offered to pick up the sound system for his house."

Piney sat there looking smug, as if she enjoyed watching others do her dirty work for her. The whole danged town were her minions.

He was starting to feel like one of her minions, too—a reluctant minion. But he wasn't as reluctant as he should be. "What if she won't go?" He didn't add *with me* to the end of the question. But even more importantly, what about his resolve to keep his distance from Lolly Crocker? He was proud of himself for staying away from her the last couple of weeks. Yet he wanted to continue to help with the bakery. Why? He didn't know. He was a living, breathing bundle of internal conflict. Even though it wasn't a good idea, he wouldn't mind taking Lolly to Anchorage to check out the kitchen equipment. What in the world was wrong with him?

McKenna had her phone out, texting. "We'll know in a couple of minutes, either way."

Shaun stood there, dumbstruck that McKenna had turned into a major meddler, too. Finally, he came to his senses and spoke to Piney. "Where can I find Mom's herbal tea?"

"I put it on the checkout counter. I had a feeling she was running out."

He didn't stay a second longer to hear Lolly's reply but went after the dog food to keep himself busy. He found Checkers's food and some doggy toothpaste. On his way to check out, the bell over the door jingled and in came Lolly. Seeing her, especially when he wasn't expecting to, felt like getting blasted with all the rays of the sun. The last time he was with her was during the cozy, middle-of-the-night incident in her kitchen. She'd looked great to him then . . . but even better now. She always had this effect on him. She lit up his day in ways that made no sense at all. He stood there frozen, staring at her . . . the same way she was staring back at him.

Hope cleared her throat, but it was Piney who spoke. "We were just talking about you, Lollipop."

Lolly looked at McKenna. "What's the emergency?"

"Oh, it wasn't an emergency exactly. I just had some news for you."

"About the loan? Do you need some additional paperwork or something?"

"Oh. No, no. I wanted to let you know I've arranged a ride for you to go to Anchorage tomorrow to check out Tortellini's professional kitchen. You know, the equipment for sale? You can see what Olive has available that you might need for the bakery."

"Arranging to see the professional kitchen? Isn't that jumping the gun? Tempting fate?" Lolly said, seeming more than a little nonplussed. "Besides, I have a lot to do." She glanced over at Shaun, and he nodded in agreement with her, though he wasn't sure why.

McKenna tsked. "You can't put this off. From what I understand, there are others who are interested in Tortellini's equipment. Better to check it out now, so when the loan comes through, you'll only need to make a phone call to let her know you'll take it. I'll be able to guarantee the money at that point."

Shaun opened his mouth to say that if Lolly really wanted it, he could put a down payment on the kitchen stuff while they were there. That way she wouldn't have to chance missing out on the equipment. But he clamped his mouth shut.

Lolly turned to him and said, "Why are you here? To convince me to go to Anchorage, too?"

"Not exactly," he said.

"Then what exactly?" she spouted back.

"I'm your ride?" he said weakly.

She rolled her eyes. He was in agreement. Piney and her meddling! But if he really thought about it, he might be just as concerned about Lolly being sad tomorrow as the others were. A brilliant idea came to him. He started to share it but decided to let the three women talk her into Anchorage without his help.

He cleared his throat. "The truth is I'm heading to Anchorage tomorrow to pick up Rick's sound system." After he installed it, he could get back to work on Jesse's cabin. And after that, get started on finding his own place.

She turned back to Piney. "What about the cookies you wanted the day after tomorrow?"

Piney laughed. "There's still plenty of time left today to get those done."

Hope pulled out her phone, too. "I'll send Ella and the girls over to help. You know they love baking with you."

"Yeah, me, too," Lolly said with a sigh. "They're great kids." She hesitated before continuing. "About Anchorage, it seems like a wasted day if I don't have the loan yet."

She turned back to Shaun. "Do you really have plans to go to Anchorage, or is this something else that Piney cooked up?" She gave Piney an eyebrow raise, one that said she had Piney's number.

He held up his hand. "Scout's honor."

Scout, Tori's dog and McKenna's charge while Tori was gone, lifted his head from where he lay at McKenna's feet. He waited for a second before putting his head back down, disappointed no one wanted to go outside.

"It's settled, then," Piney said. "You'll have to stay overnight, though. McKenna, is your apartment still available?"

"Sure." McKenna winked at him. "Come by the bank and pick up the key."

"No need to stay overnight. We'll just come straight back to Sweet Home," Shaun said, though he knew that wouldn't really give Lolly much time to look at the equipment. Plus, it wouldn't give them much time for the treat he'd been formulating for her since he heard she was tagging along to Anchorage.

Lolly seemed dumbstruck, but she pulled herself together. "While I'm here, I need a sack of sugar." She walked away toward the grocery side of the store.

"Piney, I need someone to check out my things." He couldn't wait to get out of there. He had so much to do, so much planning, before he and Lolly left in the morning.

Piney rose but didn't go to the cash register. She pulled Shaun over to one side. "This is a good thing that you're doing for Lolly. We all appreciate it."

Shaun watched out of the corner of his eye as Hope went to the cash register and waited on Lolly. "It's no big deal. As McKenna said, I was going anyway."

Piney removed one of the necklaces she wore and slipped it over his head. He looked down at the crystal dangling from the chunky chain and felt like a dork. "For good luck," she said.

"Thanks." He didn't stick around—afraid Piney might pull out her tarot cards next—but went to Hope's now-empty checkout lane.

"Nice necklace," Hope said with a grin.

"Do you think she's trying to put a spell on me? Or a curse?" he whispered as he removed the necklace and stuck it in the fabric grocery bag.

"Don't be silly. She's not a witch. She's just Piney," Hope said defensively, while she rang him up.

He paid and left the store, wondering what excuse he was going to give his mom for taking Lolly to Anchorage tomorrow. He should've told Piney she had to break it to his mom, but he didn't want any more people digging into his business than already had.

Lolly was waiting for him at the Jeep. "Listen, Shaun, don't worry about tomorrow. I'll just drive myself. No one has to know that we went separately. That way it'll make all parties happy."

Surprisingly, her solution wasn't making him happy in the least. He started grasping at straws. "What about the key to the apartment?"

"Go get the key from McKenna, but I'm not staying there. You've got to know there're a million reasons for us not to travel together."

He ignored her logic. "You'll want me there to inspect the kitchen equipment with you. Right?"

"Maybe. But your mother wouldn't like us spending so much time together," she said, holding on to her original thread.

He decided to try a little logic of his own. "It makes no sense for us to take two vehicles, especially with the price of gas these days." By her instant frown, he knew he'd hit the right note to make her see reason. "Let's economize and save the planet."

"Let me think about it," she said.

But he was pretty sure he had her. "Text me in the next hour. Can you get Jilly to watch Thor, or should we take him with us?"

"Thor will be happy to stay with Jilly. He misses her when she's gone and he's been following her around ever since she got home."

"Well, I think we're all set, then," he said.

"I'll let you know my decision in the next *couple* of hours."

He didn't quibble. He was sure she was going to come along with him. Just as he was sure that at some point while they were away together, he was going to make the most of it and kiss her again. It wasn't smart, but he wasn't going to let the opportunity afforded by being alone together pass him by.

He watched Lolly walk away before he got into the Jeep. But as he pulled away from the Hungry Bear, he realized he still had no idea what he was going to tell his mom.

Chapter 14

THE NEXT MORNING Lolly was up early. She wasn't bright-eyed and bushy-tailed; more like buzzing with anxiety, and maybe some excitement. When it came to Shaun, her emotions were unpredictable and all mixed up. Not unlike the flavors in her famous fruitcake, where you never knew from one bite to the next what you were going to experience. A perfect metaphor for her emotions when she was around Shaun. She looked at the clock. She could either stay in bed and fret about it or get going. She crawled out of bed.

Going to Anchorage with Shaun brought back so many fun memories of the time they snuck off to Anchorage for twelve hours, each telling their parents they were sleeping over at a friend's house. That evening, they'd gotten their pie/pi tattoos, cuddled at the movie theater, had burgers and fries at McDonald's at one a.m., and then drove through the night to be back in the morning, hoping their parents were none the wiser. To hide the tattoo from her mom, Lolly had made a wide fabric wristlet to cover the bandage. It had worked for a while, but eventually her mom found out.

But it had been a magical day, which only begged the question, What would today bring? She couldn't expect to share the closeness they'd felt then. The connection. *The love*. But the butterflies in her stomach wouldn't listen to reason and fluttered away in giddy anticipation.

She stood in front of the bathroom mirror and frowned at her reflection. "Stop it. Today is about business only."

Twenty minutes later, she heard Shaun pull up out front. Lolly opened the door and peered down the road, half expecting Patricia to come peeling around the corner in hot pursuit to block the trip. But the road was empty. Surely, Patricia knew what was going on, because gossip normally zipped through town with lightning speed. And Piney wouldn't have been able to keep it a secret because she didn't know the meaning of discretion. Still, no one was on Shaun's tail. She waved to him when he got out of the Jeep, and put her finger to her lips.

When she'd shut the bedroom door, Thor was in bed with Jilly, cuddled up to her belly, sound asleep. She prayed they both stayed that way because she didn't want an audience as she and Shaun pulled away together. The only thing Lolly had told her mother and sister was that she was headed to Anchorage to look at kitchen equipment. Not a word about who was driving her. Hopefully, Shaun was going to explain why he was doing this favor for her. Real reasons, and not some platitude about saving gas money or the planet.

Shaun was halfway to the house.

"Stay there," she whispered. "I'll grab our coffees and my bag and be right out."

But he kept on coming. "I'll help."

What she needed help with was catching her breath. He looked great this morning. He had on a sage-colored oxford shirt with jeans, like a computer jockey heading into the office instead of driving her through the wilds of Alaska. She turned and hustled inside to get her things.

When she returned, he took the coffees from her. "What else can I get?"

"Nothing," she said, knowing she sounded breathless.

She'd probably need an oxygen tank to survive this cozy trip.

"I thought you might want to bring your bakery binder. In case you want to compare ideas."

She smiled and patted her bag. "I've got it right here." Apparently great minds thought alike.

As she walked with him out to the Jeep, her mom hollered from the door, and Thor, who was in her arms, barked. "Have fun, you two." Thor wiggled and jumped out of her arms, running full out for Shaun.

Shaun laughed and caught Thor in his arms. "You're a good boy, but you can't come with us to Anchorage." Thor licked his face. "Maybe next time, okay, buddy?"

Thor laid his ear to Shaun's chest as if listening for his heartbeat.

Lolly was a little jealous of how brazenly her dog could cuddle Shaun.

Shaun walked over to Lolly's mom and handed the dog back to her.

She said, "Bring my daughter home safely to me," exactly what she used to say back when they were dating.

"I will, promise," Shaun said.

It was feeling like old times, which made Lolly's heart beat even harder. She wondered if Shaun would let her lay her head on his chest to gauge his excitement over the trip. But that was ridiculous.

She hurried to the Jeep with her bag and slipped into the passenger seat. She wished Thor was going with them so she'd have him as a buffer. A second later, Shaun got in the vehicle, too. He didn't start it right away but handed her a plastic-covered folder that looked like a book report to her.

"What's this?"

"Our itinerary." He grinned as if the folder was lined with hundred-dollar bills.

"Why do we have an itinerary? Have you always been this nerdy?"

"For a long time now."

She glanced over, for only a moment, and could honestly say that *nerdy* certainly looked good on him. *Oh, so good*.

To change the subject, she flipped to the first page of the itinerary, which had a picture of a tiny house—actually, a small rustic cabin on wheels. The tiny cabin had a sign plastered on one side: GONE TINY BAKERY. In small letters underneath, it read, WE'RE SMALL, BUT WE HAVE GREAT TASTE.

She looked over at Shaun. "This is cute and clever."

"It's getting good reviews, too; the reason we're going there." He seemed pretty proud of himself.

"We're going there?"

"Yes, indeed." He'd added reviews and ratings, address, hours, and time of year it was open. There was a blank section labeled *Notes*. "I left you room to add your thoughts about what you like or dislike about the place."

"When did you have time to do this?" She glanced over to see his cheeks tinge red.

He stared straight ahead as if he hadn't heard her. She decided not to press him on it or ask *why* he'd done it. She didn't want to embarrass him further.

"Do we really have time to make a stop?" she asked instead. "Aren't we in a hurry to get to Anchorage to meet up with the owner of Tortellini's? What about picking up the sound system for Rick and Sparkle's house?"

"Gone Tiny is just a little out of the way. Flip to the next page."

The next page had the details about a bakery in Anchorage. She quickly flipped through the rest of the itinerary. "Are we going on a bakery shop hop?"

"Most of the shops are in small towns. Actually, all of them, except for the one in Anchorage." He smiled but didn't grace her by looking her way. "Small-town shops are the focus, but I thought you should taste the highest-rated bakery in Anchorage as a comparison. Though they probably won't hold a candle to some of your baked goods."

It was her turn to be flattered and embarrassed. "Thank you."

"It's true." He did glance at her then, and his sparkling gray eyes made the butterflies in her stomach come alive with joy, making her look forward to what might lie ahead.

Calm it down, Lolly. Don't get carried away by his pretty face, she told herself.

"If you check your itinerary, you'll see that we will stay one night at McKenna's Anchorage apartment, and the second night at the B and B in Hero's Pass."

"But I didn't plan for two nights—"

"Don't worry. Piney will let your mom know—"

"But what about *your* mom?" Lolly was seriously more worried about Patricia than her mom, Jilly, and Thor put together.

"Mom'll be fine. I made arrangements for Dewey Winkle to help out at the homestead."

"You know that's not what I'm talking about. Is your mom okay with you running off with *me*?" The second she spoke, she wanted to snatch the words back. She'd made it sound like they were eloping, for goodness' sake!

"I left her a note telling her I'd be gone two nights."

"Oh, Shaun, you need to call her right away." It didn't sound like he'd said anything about her—the woman who'd broken his heart and infuriated his mother.

"Don't worry about my mom. She'll be fine." He glanced over and gave Lolly a look, the kind of look that was telling her to stay out of it.

Which was something she couldn't do. "Well, if you won't call her, then I will." She reached for her phone.

"Don't."

His command felt like a dare, but this was no game to Lolly. She held up her phone with her finger over the screen, threateningly. "It's going to be either you or me. You decide."

When Shaun signaled and pulled over to the side of the road, Lolly knew she'd won. *But not really.* Patricia would not be happy, and Lolly desperately wanted her to be happy. She'd do anything to stop Shaun's mother from hating her.

Shaun looked uneasy as he pulled out his phone. Lolly wondered why she'd agreed to go with Shaun in the first place. Yes, there were the practical reasons, but didn't people's feelings mean more than practicality? Especially when it came to someone she cared about; actually, the two Montanas who meant so much to her. "Mom. Hey." He paused. "Yeah, that's why I'm calling. Yes, I'm on my way to Anchorage . . ." He sighed heavily. "But I'm not alone."

Lolly turned to stare out her side window, wishing she could give him more privacy.

"Yes, I'm with Lolly. I'm going to help her look at some professional kitchen equipment." Another long pause, which signaled that Patricia was letting him have it. "Maybe someone else could've taken her, but I'm the one who suggested she open a bakery."

From the phone came "Why would you do that?" Clear as day.

"Look, it is what it is and there's nothing I can do about it."

Lolly wondered why that made her feel deflated. Did she really think he'd say something like . . . he was developing feelings for her again?

Like those feelings she was having for him. Not because he'd kissed her. Or because he was so darn good-looking. It was just that he was the best man she'd ever known. Exhibit A—the trip's itinerary—was lying on the seat next to her.

He hung up and set his phone in the cubbyhole between them.

"Well?" Lolly said. "Was she pleased as punch?"

"Yeah, sure. Let's go with that." But his face was looking pretty grim as he pulled the car back on the road.

She had the urge to reach over and squeeze his hand. Or tell him that everything was going to be all right. But she wasn't in the mood for rejection.

She was glad for the distraction when he turned on the radio. "Be Alright" had just started. As the song filled the vehicle, she calmed down. Shaun began singing along, which raised her spirits—enough so that she dared to sing along, too, but more under her breath. When they were teenagers in love, they'd sung all the songs on the radio together, sometimes gazing into each other's eyes. Corny but heartfelt. She missed those days so very much.

"It's my favorite," Shaun said after the last note. "'Be Alright' has gotten me through some tough times, especially when I felt like it had all gone to Hades."

"Me, too," she agreed.

Once again, she felt the equilibrium settle between them. Everything was going to be all right. They would survive this trip. They would even deal with whatever fallout might come from them going off together. And the future . . . she just didn't know. She was content to just be with Shaun as he turned off the highway to the first stop on their small-town bakery expedition.

She was smiling to herself when she got a glimpse of the tiny bakery sitting in a parking lot on the outskirts of a town the size of Sweet Home. Cars packed the lot. Four picnic tables were full of people eating their treats. Two lines were queued up at the open window.

"Are you hungry?"

"Oh, yes." She took one more look at the details of Gone Tiny. "They're only open from June to Labor Day weekend?"

"Yes. Gone Tiny picks up and makes her way down south for the winter, staying in different small towns along the way. Apparently, they have quite a following on social media, and people drive from miles around to come see them."

She grabbed her purse. "Let's go."

"Do you have a pen or something to write with?"

"Yes. But thanks for the reminder." She was amazed and thrilled by how considerate it was of Shaun to come up with this tour of treats. "Do you think they'll mind if I take pictures?"

"We'll ask when we get up there," Shaun said. "I bet they'd be fine with it as long as you promise to post them on social media."

She frowned. She used to keep in touch with her students through Instagram, Pinterest, and Facebook by posting her bakes and crafts so they could get excited about what they were going to be learning in their next class. But since finding out that she wasn't teaching this fall, she hadn't posted one thing.

Shaun was looking at her intently. "I can help you set up a new profile and fan page for Happily Ever Baking tonight, when we get to McKenna's."

"Shaun, don't. We don't know yet whether I'll get the loan or not."

"It doesn't hurt to get a jump on it now. Besides, you'll need to tell Gone Tiny about your bakery plans and where you'll be posting their pictures."

Lolly decided not to argue. If he wanted to waste time setting up stuff without any assurances, then whatever.

They took their place at the back of the line. After a while, a teenage boy wearing a Gone Tiny polo showed up with a spray bottle of disinfectant and wiped down the tables as customers got up and left.

"I'll be right back," Shaun said. "Hold my place in line."

She watched as Shaun walked over to the boy and chatted with him. At one point in the conversation, Shaun pointed to her and she waved.

Soon, Shaun returned to her side. "That's Trevor. His mom owns Gone Tiny. They live in a small town in California. On the weekends and breaks during the school year, they travel to other small towns and open up shop, just like I told you. His school is pretty lenient about him missing the first few days of the start of school. He's an A student."

"And?"

"He said it would be fine for you to take as many pictures

as you like. They're used to it. Their tiny house draws a lot of attention."

She wanted to kiss Shaun for getting permission for her. Instead, she squeezed his arm and said, "Thanks."

He took her purse from her and nudged her. "Go on and get to snapping those pictures."

"Bossy," she said. But he seemed desensitized to her pointing out his only major character flaw.

She took her phone and framed up Gone Tiny in the screen, taking several shots. When they got closer to the front, she took a picture of the menu and the food on display. She made audio notes on her phone about everything—from what the owner was wearing to what Lolly could see of the kitchen behind her.

"So do they live in the tiny house?" Lolly asked Shaun. She could see there were two lofts, one on either side.

"Sometimes. Mostly they stay with friends while they're working the small towns. Trevor said they have quite the friend network going. He's made a lot of friends his own age, too. The reason he was running late today."

When Trevor's mom, Priscilla, finally waited on them, Shaun explained everything to her. She was kind and had Lolly come in and help with a few customers, so she could get a look at the interior—a couple of ovens and a refrigerator on one side, and on the other side was an open-shelf pantry above a counter to prepare dough.

Lolly and Shaun ate their bear claws and drank their coffee at one of the picnic tables, while chatting with a couple of regular customers who lived an hour away. Lolly understood people in Alaska were used to driving long distances and didn't think twice about making a long run for a good pastry.

Shaun rose first. "We better get back on the road, don't you think?" He offered his hand to Lolly. She despised herself for relishing every second of skin contact as he helped her to stand. Yes, she was pretty pathetic.

Then Patricia crossed her mind, and Lolly dropped his

hand immediately. She had to be careful. If his mom knew she was falling for Shaun again, there would be hell to pay.

As soon as they were in the Jeep, Lolly pulled out her binder and turned to the blank pages she'd fortunately added in the back.

"What are you doing there, Lolls?" Shaun said as he pulled out of the parking lot onto the road.

"I want to get everything down while it's fresh in my mind." The space he'd left in the itinerary for notes just wasn't big enough. She listed what was special about Gone Tiny, from the unique small structure to the tasty bear claws, which Priscilla said were her number one seller.

"What's the name of the next place? The one in Anchorage? I know they close early," Shaun said.

"Yes, the Baked Raven." She made a face at the name. Alaska was known for its raven population. She just hoped they didn't have baked raven pie on the menu. "They close at two."

"Which is why we're going there next."

He handed her his phone. "Can you plug in the address?"

"Passcode, please?" she asked.

He hesitated.

"Shaun?" She waited a second. "I promise not to tell anyone."

"I knew I should've changed it," he mumbled.

She decided not to push him on it. Some things were private. "Do you want to pull over and put the code in yourself?"

"No. I'm counting on you to be the navigator for the trip, which includes plugging in all the addresses as we need them."

"Well, then?"

"Zero-six-eighteen-zero-seven-fifteen." He stared straight ahead as he spoke, as if each number was killing him to say it.

She typed in the number, not sure why he'd been so

reluctant. Like she would ever remember a list of numbers like that.

But . . . then it hit her. "Your birthday and my birthday?" she whispered, feeling confused and maybe a little dizzy.

He looked like he wanted to jump from the moving vehicle . . . while she had a million questions. Did he recently change his passcode to their birthdays or had he used their birthdays together for a long time, since he got this phone? She examined the phone, front and back, trying to figure out how old it was.

"What time will we get there?" he asked as if to change the subject.

"Oh. Give me a second to plug in the address." She did and gave him the approximation. Then to ease the tension, she turned on the radio, but they were out of range to get any station.

"There are CDs in the glove box," he said.

She opened it and found a couple of country CDs and a mixtape. She scanned the titles, handwritten on the outside. All of them were favorites from their high school days. She mostly listened to Christian music now, but country music had been popular with their crowd then, and just seeing the list of songs brought back a lot of memories.

"Wanting to re-create your glory days?" she asked with a laugh, trying to lighten the mood.

"Yeah. Exactly." But then he glanced at her, and something about his eyes made her wonder if he had done this specifically for her . . . for this trip . . . for them to listen to . . . together.

Stop it, she scolded herself. *You're probably way off base*. She certainly wasn't going to ask. It would be too awkward to learn he'd made the CD for someone else, such as his ex-fiancée.

"I'll put this one in, if it's okay with you?"

He gave a curt nod, letting her know there would be no more conversation from him the rest of the way to Anchorage.

To occupy herself, and to keep from asking him fifty questions, and to keep from fretting over her current problems, and her future problems—like what was going to happen between her and Shaun, and what she was going to do if the new bakery didn't work—Lolly turned to a new sheet in her binder. She drew a table with columns and headed each with *Pastries, Hours, Prices, Miscellaneous, Etc.* and filled in Gone Tiny's info. By the end of the trip she'd have a clear understanding of how other bakeries worked. Later, she mused, she could put all this info into the computer and add the photos of each bakery.

But spreadsheets seemed more like something Shaun would suggest, and she wondered if he was rubbing off on her. She looked down at the last thing she'd written and realized it was his name! Quickly, she scribbled over it before he could see.

Shaun drove as if he were alone in the vehicle. He didn't act as if the songs from their high school years were bringing back a hundred memories—like they were for her. The first two songs were ones that they had danced to at their first homecoming. The next one, "Remember When," was the ballad playing during their first kiss. Memory Lane might as well have been the name of the road he was driving them down, so she redoubled her concentration on the itinerary, making notes, and adding a table like Gone Tiny's for each of the other bakeries he'd picked out for them to visit.

When she was done, she tried not to fidget. Or examine why her birthday was part of his passcode. But with each passing mile, it became harder and harder to keep from grilling him. Surely it meant something! Like . . . was he starting to care for her again?

But his silence said he was closed on the subject. If Lolly didn't do something soon to shut down her ever-growing feelings for him, she just might do something that would embarrass them both.

Chapter 15

SHAUN FELT COMPLETELY off-kilter. Taking her to Anchorage had been a horrible idea. Why had he spent so much time putting together this bakery tour? He already had too much on his plate as it was. And what about his convictions? When he'd come back to Sweet Home, he didn't want anything to do with any women, especially Lolly Crocker. Yet, it was so obvious now—to even his bonehead self—that he hadn't put her completely in the past. Yes, he'd told himself over and over again that he was done with Lolly, but he'd allowed a few remnants of her to remain. Until now, only he had known. Now she was onto him. What Lolly didn't know, thankfully, was that he had a dozen Lolly passwords scattered about in cyberspace. Things he remembered that no one else would. Such as his online banking password, *Lolly1014*, the date of their first kiss, a day he would remember until his last breath. They had both stayed after school—him for football practice, Lolly to help Ms. Newton bake something in the home ec kitchen. He offered Lolly a ride home in his old pickup truck. The whole ride he tried to get up the courage to ask her out. The way she kept looking at him and smiling, and then that song came on the radio, and he finally decided to risk looking like a fool and go for it. When he pulled in front of her house, she turned and gave him a look that made him feel like the strongest man in the world. He remembered it as if it had happened this morning.

"Thank you for the ride," she'd said kind of shyly.

"It was my pleasure." He was still trying to figure out the best way to ask her when she surprised him by scooting closer—and kissing him on the cheek. When she started to scoot away, he grabbed her hand. "I have something to ask you."

She grinned like she already knew. "Oh?"

"Will you go with me to homecoming?"

Next, she did the darnedest thing. She laid her hand on his cheek, gazed into his eyes, and leaned in to kiss him on the mouth. On the mouth! He was shocked, but he didn't let it throw him; he immediately wrapped his arms around her and kissed her back. It was the most wonderful moment of his life. Until, of course, when they'd danced at homecoming. And then every day after that, each day together better than the one before, as long as he could call Lolly *his*. It didn't take long for him to figure out he was lucky to have found the one he wanted to spend the rest of his life with. A forever kind of love. He didn't care that they were young. He didn't care when others would say, *You can't marry the first girl you ever loved*. It didn't matter. He and Lolly were always going to be together, and that was that.

But, of course, it wasn't. He glanced over at Lolly, but she seemed to be ignoring him.

What a mistake to make that mixtape! He had no excuse for picking *their* songs. He normally wasn't sentimental, so maybe he had just been sleep-deprived. He thought about popping out the CD and tossing it out the window. But if he did, Lolly would know how much this was affecting him— the songs, the memories, and the girl he'd loved with all his heart sitting next to him right now, torturing him. Instead, he let the music play on while those memories continued to flood him until he felt like gasping for air.

Seemingly an eternity later, he pulled up and parked in front of the Baked Raven, with less than ten minutes before they closed for the day.

"We'll have to make this fast," he said.

"I'm ready." Not meeting his eyes, she hopped out of the Jeep, and he did as well.

When they got inside, it looked as if the staff were cleaning up the sleek, modern space. Raven figurines sat on shelves for tourists to buy. Stuffed fabric ravens hung from the ceiling as if they were circling, looking for a spot to land. Only a few baked items were left in the case. Lolly started taking notes and Shaun spoke with the older woman who was clearly the manager or owner, as she was issuing orders to the others. He told her about Lolly's plan to open a bakery in *their* small town, and he asked if they could take pictures. He complimented the woman on the beautiful bakery and asked her if he could buy the rest of the pastries in the display case.

"Sure, take all the pictures you want. Keep in mind we're closing soon."

Lolly snapped away and asked the manager some questions while one of the younger men boxed the pastries, and then Shaun paid.

Lolly thanked the older woman and told her how welcoming the shop felt, before they headed out.

"Did you get what you need?" Shaun asked.

"No. What I need is for you to keep your wallet in your pocket. The bakery items are my responsibility."

He didn't want to argue with her. "I'll put it on your tab." Which meant he was still taking care of it all.

"Fine. I'll pay my tab in full when we get home."

Shaun smiled at her indignation and thought they could do some bartering. A few smoldering kisses for all the pastries she wanted.

At their next stop—the electronics store—Lolly stayed in the Jeep, making notes in her binder, while he went in to pick up his online order. After it was loaded and when he was behind the wheel again, she looked up from her work.

"Tortellini's next?" she asked rhetorically. "I already have it programmed into your phone."

Which only reminded him of how dumb it was to use her birthday in his passcode.

He started the Jeep without saying a word and drove to Tortellini's, three miles away. A woman was standing in the open doorway.

"Sorry we're late," Shaun said.

"I only just got here myself." She turned to Lolly. "I'm Olive Nightbranch. McKenna's told me a lot about you."

Lolly looked embarrassed. "It's nice to meet you."

"Come in and look around. I'll be so happy for you to take everything off my hands. The new owners are taking possession soon. The good news is they've already turned the power back on so you can see that all the appliances are working."

"Did McKenna tell you I don't have my financing yet?" said Lolly apologetically. "We may have made you come here today for nothing."

"McKenna seems confident that finalizing your loan is just a formality," Olive said. "I'll give you a really good deal. The new owners are bringing all their own equipment with them."

"We'll take a look," Shaun said. "Right, Lolly?"

"Sure." But her reply wasn't convincing.

Lolly examined the display cases first since they were in the dining area of the restaurant.

"We put our lemon ricotta cakes, cannoli, biscotti, and tiramisu in there. We had a lot of walk-in business for our desserts alone," Olive said as she turned on the lights in the cases before walking to a swinging door behind the counter.

Olive held the door open. "Come take a look in the kitchen. You're going to love the equipment."

Lolly passed through and Shaun followed. "Where do you want to start?"

"The ovens," Lolly said.

Olive gave her a bundle of papers stapled together. "I printed out all the info on the equipment. The top page has all the prices."

When Lolly looked at it, her eyes lit up. Shaun concluded that Olive must've given Lolly a heck of a deal.

Lolly shot him a look. "Help me check out the equipment."

"Take as much time as you need," Olive said. "Just holler if you have questions."

Shaun followed Lolly to the first oven. "So, is everything a steal?"

"Yeah. I wish I had the savings to take it all now." She opened the oven and peered inside at the racks. Next, she went to the huge range and turned on the burners. "Everything seems to be in working order." But that only made Lolly frown more.

"Don't worry," Shaun said. "I bet your loan will come through any day now." He'd call McKenna when he got a moment alone to see what the holdup was. "Let me take a look at that list. I'll mark things off as we go." Lolly handed it over, which allowed him to quickly calculate how much he'd need to pull out of savings. She wouldn't like it, but he wanted to give Lolly her dream professional kitchen now. Not later.

One by one they went over each piece of equipment. Shaun flexed his muscles a couple of times when Lolly wanted to see the back of three of the appliances. The refrigerators were plugged in, purring, and cold as a winter's day in Sweet Home. Olive had laid out cooking utensils, baking pans, and baking sheets in such good shape they looked like they'd hardly been used.

When they were done, Lolly went to Olive. "Everything looks in perfect condition."

"I'd still be in business if I could've sold my house in Arizona. But I couldn't make payments on my house, the lease for the restaurant, and pay rent on my apartment here. I had a dream to return to Anchorage. My dad was born and raised here, and we visited every summer when we were kids." Olive scanned the dining room. "But it just didn't work out."

Shaun thought it was foolish that Olive didn't sell her house first before moving to Alaska. But he realized he shouldn't be judging; he didn't know the whole situation.

Olive pointed at the door. "I'm headed back home. Back to teaching. Besides, the winters are brutal here!" So there was at least one thing about Anchorage she wouldn't mind putting in her rearview mirror.

"You're a teacher?" Lolly asked.

"Yes, mathematics and computer science. High school. I got my old job back."

"I'm a teacher, too." Lolly paused, her face dropping. "But my school has cut family and consumer science from the curriculum, which is the reason I'm opening a bakery."

"You won't regret it," Olive said, "even if it doesn't work out. Here, give me that price sheet. I want to make some adjustments . . . from one teacher to another."

Neither Shaun nor Lolly could believe it, since the prices were already rock-bottom.

"Do you have a number where we can reach you?" Shaun asked.

"At the top of the price sheet."

The three of them walked out together and Olive locked up. "I've really been missing my students. I can't wait to get home and get back to school."

"I completely understand," Lolly said. "Today's the first day of school back in Sweet Home, where we're from."

Olive looked as if she'd had an idea. "You know, you wouldn't have to give up teaching entirely if you opened a bakery. You can make the bakery your classroom. That's what I did. I did anything from one-day cooking classes to a series over six weeks." She glanced over at Shaun. "I didn't think of it until now, but wouldn't it be fun for you to have a just-for-men bread-baking class? Alaska is crawling with men!"

Lolly nodded. "That's a great idea. Having baking classes would be an extra source of income during the off-season, too."

Shaun only wished he'd come up with the idea. Not a men's-only class. He wasn't keen on the idea of Lolly teaching the lonely single men of Alaska how to bake bread; they might get the wrong idea and want to teach Lolly a thing or two.

The women shook hands and Olive said, "I hope to hear from you soon. It's been really nice meeting you and your husband."

"We're not—"

Shaun cut Lolly off by putting his arm around her and saying, "Come along, dear. We still have a couple of stops to make." He waved to Olive with his free hand. "It was great to meet you, too. We'll be in touch."

Surprisingly, Lolly walked away with him, but he noticed her mouth was hanging open.

Once they were outside, she pulled away and glared at him. "Why would you let her think we're married?"

"People are funny. I didn't want her to take the price sheet back and mark everything back up. Besides, we didn't want to waste any more of her time to explain, right?" He hated to admit it, but he liked casually wrapping his arm around Lolly. It wasn't just old times he was thinking about. He was thinking about the present, and how Lolly still fit against him like no other woman he'd ever known. "No harm done."

"I guess," Lolly said. "But what if someone saw? What if it got back to your mom?"

He couldn't help but shake his head. "We're in Anchorage. We're anonymous here. Besides, you care way too much about what other people think."

She gave him a pointed look. "That's because I care about others' feelings." Which implied he didn't.

"Look, you've got to quit putting others' feelings ahead of your own." To prove his point, he grabbed her hand and pulled her back to him—chest to chest. He stared at his target—her lips—for a long moment before bringing his gaze up to meet her eyes. Shaun was a patient man. He waited until her shock turned to permission, and then to impatience. He could tell she was longing to kiss him, too.

He leaned in and kissed her, taking his time, not caring a lick that they were standing in the middle of the sidewalk or whether someone they knew might drive by. He only cared he was kissing her again. But the problem now was he wasn't sure if he could ever be completely done with kissing Lolly Crocker.

"Why did you do that?" she asked, still looking dazed.

"To show you I don't care what other people think." He turned and walked toward the Jeep so she wouldn't see he wasn't telling the whole truth. He did care about what some people thought. Jesse, Luke, Hope, Donovan, and, of course, Mom was near the top of the list. Everyone knew Mom's view was skewed when it came to Lolly. Shaun just didn't understand it. If he could get over how Lolly had dumped him—get over it enough to kiss her!—then his mom should get over it, too.

Besides, it wasn't as if he wanted to *go steady* with Lolly again. Kiss her a thousand times more—*yes*. Hang out with her sometimes—*sure*. But nothing beyond that.

Lolly caught up to him as he opened the driver's-side door. "You told Olive we had other things we had to do, but the itinerary has us going to McKenna's now."

"It's a surprise." He reached into his pocket, pulled out an index card with two addresses on it, and handed it to Lolly before getting into the Jeep.

"What's this?" she asked.

"Plug the first address into my phone." He handed his cell to her.

"But where are we going?"

"Do you not understand what a surprise is?"

"I do, but I might be maxed out on surprises. You have to admit today didn't turn out one bit like I expected."

"Good." But he took pity on her. "We have time, so I thought you might like to check out a couple of the kitchen supply stores while we were in town. Especially now, since you know what supplies Olive is selling. You now have a good idea of what you might be missing to make your bakery a success."

Lolly shot him one of her brilliant smiles. "I don't have any extra cash, but I do love to window-shop."

"You can make a list. Maybe order everything online after your loan goes through."

"Shaun, I'm worried. What if Olive sells everything before I get my loan?"

"Put that worry aside for now. How do we get to the first store?"

Two hours and a long shopping list of kitchen tools later, they were both beat as they drove to McKenna's apartment.

"I'm too tired to eat." Lolly's eyes were closed and her head lay against the window.

He wanted to reach over and touch her, but he didn't. "I know we've had a lot of baked goods today, and we should have something green and healthy for dinner, but I'm in the mood for pizza. What if I order one and have it delivered?" He didn't wait for her to answer. "Unless you're in the mood to cook me a nice dinner for all the trouble you put me through today." He smiled; he'd really enjoyed himself today. He was pleased she allowed him to buy her a new set of measuring cups at the first kitchen store, and a really nice trio of spatulas at the next one. He'd never tire of her company . . . and that kiss.

"Pizza, yes," she said without opening her eyes. "Put it on my tab."

"Sure."

It didn't take long to get to McKenna's apartment. Her uncle, Montgomery St. James, had rented it for her when she first came to Alaska to work at his bank in Anchorage. Now she and Luke used it as a getaway from the homestead, when they wanted to catch a play or do some shopping in the city. McKenna had lent out the space to several people from Sweet Home. Now it was their turn, his and Lolly's.

Shaun turned the CD back on and sang with the hits all the way to McKenna's apartment. After they parked, he placed an order with a mom-and-pop pizza joint he'd been to with Jesse. "The pizza will be here in thirty-five minutes. I'm ready to relax. What about you?"

"Me, too, except I need to go over the numbers." Lolly looped her bag over her shoulder and got out of the Jeep. "I need to call Jilly to see how things are going. And to make sure she'll be able to take care of Thor tomorrow."

Shaun helped carry in her quilted duffel and they settled into McKenna's two-bedroom apartment. "Any suggestions for what we should watch on TV?" he asked as Lolly spread out her paperwork on the coffee table.

She grinned at him. "*The Great British Baking Show*? I know I've seen all the episodes a million times, but we *are* on a bakery shop hop."

"Sure." He fiddled with the remote for a minute until he asked, "Can you use my help with the paperwork?"

"Yeah. I would like that."

They sat on the floor and looked over the price list and the pictures Lolly had taken of the appliances and supplies. "I believe I could use everything Olive's selling. Ugh, I wish I knew whether I was going to get that loan. If only I could tell the future."

But he knew the future; he was going to make it happen for her. He wasn't going to berate himself over it. And he wasn't going to think about his big declaration to not get involved with any women from now on. Sometimes, a man just had to go with his gut. Besides, it wasn't like he was dating Lolly or something. He was just helping her make an old dream come true.

"I better call Jilly before the pizza gets here," she said as she stood and stretched.

"Sounds good." He watched Lolly go into the bedroom and made sure she shut the door . . . before pulling out his phone to make a call of his own.

ciousness. Apple pie à la mode. Brownies right out of the oven with a tall glass of milk. Ladyfingers with strawberries and cream . . . Yes, Jilly would find out. Her sister was a human lie detector, and she could always tell when Lolly was withholding something juicy.

Jilly laughed, as if she knew what Lolly was thinking. "Get home safely, Lollipop."

"Love you, Jilly Bean."

"Love you, too." They both hung up.

When Lolly returned to the living room, Shaun was at the counter, opening the lid to the pizza.

"It smells good, doesn't it?" he said.

"Pizza was a good idea; I need some comfort food after that news."

"You take the first slice and tell me what's going on at home."

It felt like déjà vu from pizzas past. While she laid a slice of thin, crispy pepperoni heaven on her plate and took it to the couch, she told him about Thor and the mishap with the clippers. She didn't mention anything about how he'd correctly assumed she still adored pepperoni pizza with extra cheese.

"I know this isn't going to make you feel much better, but I should remind you Thor's coat will grow back." Shaun sat on the couch, too, and took a bite.

"Yeah, but in the meantime, all the other dogs are going to laugh at him," Lolly said forlornly.

"I know what will make you feel better." He gestured toward the TV. "I've queued up *The Great British Baking Show.*"

"Thank you."

They each stretched out on their respective sides of the couch.

"You know, I've never watched this before," he said as it started.

"You're going to love it. I smile the whole time I'm watching it."

"Then yes, I will enjoy it."

She got the feeling he wasn't talking about the show, but that he would enjoy seeing her smile. She couldn't help the warmth that came to her cheeks.

After she ate a second slice and drank a large glass of water, she washed her hands. "I wish you would've told me we were going on a bakery shop hop. I would've brought sweatpants for my expanding waistline. I'm super full, but it sure was fun."

Shaun laughed and watched as she dug a sewing project from her bag. "What are you working on?"

"Adding embellishments to these pencil holders." She held up one of the fabric containers. "I used the scrap-and-rope technique to make these for Ella, Lacy, all the girls who took baking lessons from me over the summer. I just need to sew on a couple of charms and their name tags, then they'll be done."

"Those are cool."

"I thought they could use them now and then take them to college when they go. Piney said I could buy some of her quartz and polished stones at cost to weigh down the bottom. I think they're fun." She'd enjoyed making them. Cathartic, really.

"Clever. And beautiful. You are so talented." He glanced back over at her. "In so many ways." She would've sworn his eyes had drifted down to her lips.

She pulled her legs up and tucked them underneath her. "I can't take all the credit. The Sisterhood of the Quilt taught me how to make these a few years ago."

She turned her attention back to the TV momentarily, trying to stop thinking about Shaun in *that* way. But even her favorite show wasn't helping, because the man she'd like to kiss again was sitting at the other end of the couch.

Shaun stood. "I'll get the leftovers put away." She started to get up, too, but he stopped her. "You finish your project. I've got this."

Which gave her a bit of a reprieve. She pulled out a needle, thread, and a tag and began stitching Ella's name to her pencil holder.

By the time Shaun took his place back on the couch, Lolly was feeling a little more in control. She'd always enjoyed the creativity of sewing, but even more so, the therapeutic side. And she needed that now.

While her hands were occupied, and since she had to keep her eyes on what she was stitching, it was a good time to say thank you. "I have to say I really appreciate everything, Shaun. The bakery shop hop is the nicest thing anyone has ever done for me." That included when they were together in high school.

Back then, they seemed to mostly do things he liked to do. Which wasn't necessarily his fault. She'd wanted to please him, so she became interested in the things he liked. She kind of lost herself in their relationship, which was something she'd never examined before. Now that she was older and more mature, she knew what she liked and what she disliked. She guessed it was about striking the right balance. She hoped one day, when she was with her Mr. Right, that she would get it . . . *right*.

"I was happy to help out," Shaun said. "Besides, it got me out of town for a couple of days." He gave her a dazzling smile.

"Well, it means a lot to me, no matter your ulterior motives." The second she said it, she wished she'd chosen her words more carefully; the kiss from earlier came back to her in Technicolor, complete with all the *feels*—warm, gooey lovey-doveys. Something Patricia would not appreciate. But Patricia was not here, so Lolly decided to speak the truth. "You know you're a really good guy."

"I don't know about that." He seemed thoughtful for a moment, as if weighing everything he'd ever done. "I wasn't so nice to you when I first came back to town."

"Yeah, you almost ran me over."

"I'm glad I didn't."

"But I didn't blame you. You had every right to be mad at me."

"I think I was taking other stuff out on you, though."

"What other stuff?" She laid down her sewing and grabbed the remote to put the show on pause to give him her full attention.

"Tanya, my ex. I came back to Alaska mad at her, and I think I transferred some of that anger over to you."

"What happened with you two?" she asked, knowing she'd have to tread lightly to say the next bit. "The last I heard you were engaged." She had a feeling he needed to talk to someone about it, and who better than her, the first person to break his heart? And one of his oldest friends.

He stared at the frozen screen. "Now that I have a little distance from it, I see I was trying to make her into someone she wasn't. I was ready to get married, start a family, and live the life my parents had . . . you know, the fairy-tale ending."

A moment of pure jealousy came over Lolly. But she shoved her emotions aside. "How stupid of her not to take you up on that offer."

"In Tanya's defense, she wasn't at the right place. And now I know she wasn't the right person for me either. Did I tell you she's getting married soon?"

"So quickly?" Lolly asked. How could this woman get over a man like Shaun in such a short period of time? Lolly still wasn't over him and it'd been *years*.

"She's marrying her old boyfriend. When we started going out, I had the strong suspicion she wasn't over him and was just biding her time with me. But she said I was just imagining things, so I would tamp down that gnawing feeling something was wrong. Here's something weird. Apparently, I'm starting to forgive Tanya, because I really think her ex will make her happy. Which I certainly couldn't. We both should've chosen better in the first place. I think we were just wasting time."

"Or maybe both of you were growing into who you really were supposed to be?" Lolly offered. Because that's how she was starting to feel about herself. Maybe the door closing on her teaching career was the kick in the pants she needed to step out of her comfort zone . . . to clear the way to opening a bakery. She knew she was up to the task, a feeling that had snuck up on her. She guessed it all hinged on the loan now, because having her own bakery felt right.

"I never really thought about it as a growth experience." He looked thoughtful in that beautiful way he had of tilting his head when he was working out a problem. "Maybe I needed all that to happen to get me to the next phase in my life. I know it made it a whole lot easier to leave a job I loved and come home. Anyway, it was high time to come back and help Mom on the homestead. Jesse had carried the load by himself for far too long."

"You know what my mom always says? 'There is no wasted time.'" Which was something Lolly hadn't really considered until this moment.

"Candy sure loves dishing out those fortune-cookie sayings," Shaun said. "But that might be one I'm going to embrace."

"Do you want something more to drink?" Lolly stood. "I saw root beer in the refrigerator."

"Yeah, root beer sounds good. Thanks."

After she poured them both a glass, she left the drinks on the counter while she went around the room switching off lamps until the only source of light was the TV.

"What are you up to, Lolls?"

She rolled her eyes. "Don't worry. This isn't me making a move on you. I promise, your reputation is safe. I just like to watch the baking show like I'm at the movies, is all."

"No more sewing tonight?" he asked.

"No more sewing." She handed him his drink. He stilled her hand by wrapping his free hand around hers.

"It was a good day today, wasn't it?" he asked, with a surprisingly searching look.

"Yes. Really fun. It meant a lot to me." She went to her

side of the couch and settled in, knowing the feeling of his hand touching hers wouldn't go away anytime soon.

For the next hour, they both seemed to relax and get absorbed in the show's competition and camaraderie. When Shaun asked questions about the format, she explained the three different challenges and how she had a notebook full of ideas for baking projects because of the show.

When the episode ended, Shaun flipped on the lamp beside him before turning off the TV. "I need my beauty sleep. I have a long day of driving ahead of me."

"You could let me drive if you get tired," she offered.

"We'll see."

But she knew he was thinking about the time she'd put the Montanas' pickup in the ditch when it was snowy. "I'm an excellent driver." She laughed.

"Sure, Rain Man. Or would you rather be Rain Woman?"

She smiled at him. "'Night, Shaun."

"'Night, Lolly."

She went into her bedroom, which was McKenna's, and he took the guest bedroom. She was feeling so very close to the man she'd once been certain she would marry. But now, she supposed they were both prepping for their future spouses, or maybe for remaining single. She didn't know.

What she did know was that there was no wasted time.

SHAUN STOOD IN the guest bathroom, brushing his teeth and thinking how strange life was. The fact that he had just spent a great day and a relaxing evening with Lolly Crocker was something he could never have imagined would happen in his wildest dreams. But there it was. And he felt happy about it. Which was so out of character for the man he was when he returned home—upset about the breakup with Tanya and certain he would never be close to a woman again. Emotionally close anyway. But he felt close to Lolly, the biggest shock of all. Maybe Lolly was right. Maybe hard times were the things that made them grow. Medical journals say pain has a physical purpose. Maybe emotional pain had a purpose, too.

He slept quite soundly and woke early. He had coffee waiting when Lolly emerged from McKenna's room, wearing a flowery summer dress with a light sweater over it. "You look nice this morning." Actually, she looked nice to him all the time, whether she had on a T-shirt, shorts, and an apron, her face dusted with flour, or she was gussied up as she was right now.

She smiled and swayed from side to side as the dress's hem twirled around her legs. "Yeah, this dress is nice, isn't it? McKenna texted. Told me to raid the closet if I needed something to wear. She heard from Jilly that you hadn't told me we were going to be gone for two days." Lolly shot him a look as if her words were meant to scold. Then she shrugged as if all was forgiven. "I smell coffee."

"I was making you a to-go cup so we can get an early start. Can you wait to eat until we get to Nine Lives Bakery an hour away, or do you need a snack before then?"

"I'll have cold pizza with my vitamins."

He laughed. "Perfect breakfast food."

They straightened everything up, locked the door, and texted McKenna as directed, so she could alert the cleaning staff they had vacated.

While he drove, Lolly recited the details about Nine Lives Bakery. "A little off the beaten path, you'll find fresh pastries and rescue kittens and cats to cuddle and adopt. Come spend time with us to get to know our felines and our mission. Part of the proceeds go to help the humane society spay and neuter stray cats." She looked up from the itinerary he'd made for her and smiled at him. "This is fantastic—a socially responsible bakery. Do you know the one thing I'm gleaning from *all* the bakeries we've seen?"

"What's that?" he asked, unable to keep from smiling at her excitement.

"These bakeries have a theme, even the Baked Raven. I should brainstorm what my theme will be."

"I'm sure you'll come up with something great. I believe it should be something you love, something you're as passionate about as you are baking."

"Yes. That sounds right. I wonder if my bakery binder has any ideas," she said.

"That's a good place to start. But remember, you were a kid when you made your binder. Your interests may have changed." His interests had certainly transformed. When he was young, he assumed he would be a homesteader like his dad. But then Shaun found computers and programming, and he'd never looked back. From his peripheral vision, he caught Lolly ogling him. "Okay, cut it out. You are not allowed to put me on the menu."

"Hear me out," Lolly said, her cheeks flaming for a moment. "Maybe we could use the bakery to help Alaskan men find dates. That would be something unusual. Don't you think?"

"Jesse said Sweet Home already has a connection with a matchmaking service."

"Yes, Real Men of Alaska was here in the spring. I'm sure Piney or Hope has the owner's contact info."

"Jesse told me all about it and suggested I sign up the next time they do one of their events at the lodge."

"Yeah, a couple of love matches were made." But she looked pretty negative about it.

"So, you didn't find true love when they were here?" he asked, probably being more curious than he should be.

"No. I didn't really participate. I was newly single and had put myself on a man-free diet," she said with a chuckle.

Yeah, he was familiar with her breaking off engagements. But in this moment, he decided not to hold that against Lolly. Hadn't they decided last night that his broken engagement had been the catalyst to move him forward? He was growing into his future. He suspected her emotional upheavals had propelled Lolly into her future as well. Separate futures that started together in the past.

"And what about now?" he ventured. "Is the Real Men

of Alaska a viable option to find a mate?" He really wanted to know if she was still looking for someone. But he was darn proud of how he'd crafted the question to sound as if he were the one who was looking for a way to find someone new.

"So, you're interested?"

"Maybe," he replied, which wasn't anywhere close to the truth. And since she'd been direct, he should return the favor. "And you? Will you sign up with the Real Men of Alaska to find that special Alaskan *he-man* you've always dreamed of?" He hoped she'd say *no*, because he was already feeling jealous of this mystery guy out there somewhere, looking for a girl like Lolly.

She went quiet. He glanced over to see her hands in her lap, fidgeting with her fingers, which was one of her signature tells when she was nervous. "I don't know. Maybe. Who knows what the future holds? With all my blunders when it comes to love, I'm seriously considering staying single forever. Save other men from Love 'em and Leave 'em Lolly."

He hurt for her. *Physically hurt.* Which was absurd. When he first returned to town, hadn't he *wanted* Lolly to suffer?

He reached over and took her hand without looking at her. "Don't be so hard on yourself. Don't give up. You'll find someone. The perfect guy, who'll make you forget the past. I promise." He was just trying to be a good friend, but it was killing him to encourage her to keep herself on the market. He pulled his hand away even though he didn't want to.

They'd gotten pretty deep on this trip, though all he wanted was to keep things light between them. Yeah, he'd wanted to kiss her a time or two, also. But he never expected to feel so many emotions. To feel so *much*. To empathize with her. He was the first in a long line of men she'd loved and left. So why did he care so much about her happiness now?

"Thank you," she said. "You've cheered me up. Given me something to think about, too. Maybe there is someone out there for me."

Shaun jammed his emotions into the back corner. Everything in him wanted to yell at her that *he* was that guy—her *someone*. But he wouldn't. Couldn't. Never in a million years.

And not just because his mommy told him so either. It was that he wasn't prepared to get twice burned. He was too smart to do that. *Been there, done that*, the little voice in his head reminded him.

The Catsburg city limits sign came into view. He breathed a sigh of relief because soon they would be out of the Jeep and away from this conversation. Within minutes they were pulling up to Nine Lives Bakery, with the sign on the roof sporting its name along with three kittens with chef's hats on.

"You go on in," he said. "I've got to make a call."

She hesitated with her hand on the door handle but finally got out.

Shaun called his brother, Jesse.

"Is everything all right?" Jesse said. "Mom okay?"

"Yeah. Sure. Everyone's all right. I was just checking in with you." Shaun didn't know what he thought he could accomplish by talking to his brother. Jesse wouldn't be able to relate. He wasn't in turmoil over the women in his life. Tori was great and would never hurt Jesse. And Mom thought Jesse and Tori were perfect together.

"What's going on? Where are you?" Jesse asked.

"I'm in Catsburg." He should've thought this through before calling. He should've had something to say. Sometimes, though, he just needed to talk to his brother, the only other person in the world who might understand. But they'd lived very different lives.

"Why are you in Catsburg?" Jesse asked.

Shaun came clean. "I brought Lolly here to check out the little bakery that has rescue cats."

"Oh," Jesse said, as if he understood everything. "Are you okay? You don't sound like it."

"Not really. I drove her to Anchorage to look at some kitchen equipment from a restaurant that closed. We're checking out some bakeries on our way home."

"And now you're wondering why you did it?" Jesse filled in.

"Yeah, something like that. I've complicated things for myself," Shaun confessed.

"How complicated? What have you done?" Jesse was giving him that big-brother-to-little-brother are-you-in-trouble voice.

"I haven't *done* anything." Shaun wasn't going to tell him he'd kissed Lolly a couple of times. "We've just been talking. You know, deep stuff, the kind that no self-respecting man wants to talk about."

"I get it. It's the worst," Jesse said. "But that's what we do for our womenfolk."

"Lolly is not my woman," Shaun objected.

Jesse laughed. "Whatever you say, bro. Have you kissed her yet?"

Shaun rolled his eyes heavenward. Seriously, why had he called? "Maybe. A couple of times."

Jesse wasn't laughing now, as the other end of the phone went silent. For a moment, Shaun thought he might've lost the connection. "Listen, little brother. I don't want to tell you what to do, but don't mess around with Lolly unless you mean it. You and Lolly have a past. Don't yank her around. Don't use her. This isn't going to sound all that masculine, but you need to figure out where your heart is first, before anything else happens."

"What about having a little fun?" Shaun asked, but the statement tasted all wrong.

"You aren't built that way. Me either. Apparently, Dad was a one-woman guy, too. Don't become someone you're not because you got your heart stomped on before."

"You're certainly full of advice on this subject," Shaun said sarcastically.

"Hey, you're the one who called me. Besides, becoming wise is what happens when you marry the right woman. Do you hear me? Don't be stupid in the meantime, okay?" In the background, it sounded like someone was calling Jesse's name. "Hey, I gotta run. The producer wants me back on camera. You going to be all right?"

"I'll be fine." But Shaun wasn't all that certain.

"We'll talk soon. Love ya, bro," Jesse said.

"Yeah, me, too." They both hung up.

Shaun sat holding his phone for a full minute before getting out of the Jeep. *That hadn't helped at all.* But it had been good to hear Jesse's voice. He would have to talk to him again soon to make the final decisions about his and Tori's cabin. Shaun would be glad when the show finished shooting their first season and Jesse would be home for a while before starting season two.

Shaun walked up the steps and went inside the bakery. The owners had separated the building into two areas with plexiglass. On one side there were couches, recliners, and tables, pastry display cases, and bins full of stuffed cats of all kinds. This side also had real cats milling about or lounging here and there, seeking attention from the patrons. Behind the plexiglass, he could see two women and two men dressed in white, making the pastries for all the customers to see. He had wondered how the bakery stayed sanitary, but there was no way a cat could get into the kitchen without an employee allowing them through the double set of doors.

"Shaun," Lolly hollered. "Come meet Harry and his wife, Harriet; they own Nine Lives Bakery." She beamed at the owners.

After the introductions, the three bakers talked animatedly, while Shaun listened. When there was a break, Shaun asked about taking pictures. When the owners agreed, Lolly handed him her phone.

"Passcode," he said. Harry and Harriet stepped away to give them privacy.

Lolly leaned closer and whispered. "Three-one-four-one-five-nine."

Shocked, he turned to look at her. "You remembered." She never ceased to amaze him, and he couldn't stop himself from grinning like an idiot.

She smiled back. "You know I have a thing for pi."

He glanced down at the π tattoo on his wrist, and she held up her wrist for him to see her tattoo, too. "Yeah, I know you're a pie girl."

They stood there a long moment, staring at each other, before she said, "Go take some pictures for me."

He stayed on the cat side of the bakery taking photos, while Lolly went in to inspect the kitchen. He was glad for the separation, and at the same time, he wanted her near him again. Maybe he should've had plexiglass installed in the Jeep before they went on this excursion, a little separation for this trip.

He didn't realize he was staring at her until it registered that Lolly was looking back through the plexiglass at him. He covered by pointing to his watch. *We better go*, he mouthed, and she nodded.

They spent the next few minutes picking out baked goods, and Lolly found a stuffed cat for Thor. "I'm getting him a toy because he had to endure one of my mom's haircuts."

Back on the road, Lolly kept her head down, making notes, but talking the whole time about the highlights of the bakery. "That was great. Really unique," she said. "I still need to come up with a special theme for my place. After giving it some thought, I don't think my theme should be the Real Men of Alaska, though I'd like to partner with Kit to have a couples baking class at my place."

"I told you not to worry. I know you'll come up with something unique and special to you."

"Selling stuffed cats, real collars, and other cat paraphernalia is smart. Another income source. And one that isn't perishable. Brilliant."

He smiled and kept driving on. They hit two more bakeries—Hats Off to Baking, which sold pastries and hats of all shapes and sizes, and the Chew Choo Bakery, housed in an old red caboose—before they made their final stop of the day, the Bake Inn, which was also their B and B for the night.

The Bake Inn had a huge fluted pie tin attached to the roof, which from a distance, Shaun thought, looked like a flying saucer. But up close, it was a charming establishment with a large wraparound porch furnished with café tables and metal chairs. The owner, Mrs. Bees, was very welcoming and happy to chat, telling them a funny story about her late husband installing the giant pie pan on the roof. After he died, she'd started renting out the rooms as a way to make ends meet. "My kids want me to move to a warmer climate and be close to them. You see, they all moved to the Lower 48. But my George is buried here . . . so my heart is in Alaska."

Lolly audibly sighed. Shaun was afraid Mrs. Bees was going to make him tear up, too, if she didn't stop with all the mushy stuff.

Mrs. Bees gave Lolly the grand tour while two locals helped the other patrons. When they were done, they rejoined Shaun, who was just finishing a cup of coffee and a delicious banana nut muffin.

"This is fantastic," he said to Mrs. Bees. "Will you share the secret ingredient of your muffins?"

"Of course, dear. It's *love*. In every muffin tin."

He wasn't surprised.

"I know you reserved two rooms, but I'm modern enough not to mind if you two want to share," said Mrs. Bees without a hint of judgment.

"I told you we aren't married," Lolly said.

"Two rooms will be fine," Shaun added, wanting to nip this topic in the bud. Jesse was right when he'd said Shaun needed to get his own feelings figured out first. In the meantime, he had to avoid temptation at all costs, and sharing a room would be one step too far.

"All right, then," Mrs. Bees said, "if you're sure." She handed over the keys to their rooms. "After you're settled in, just down the street is Mac's Burgers, where you can find dinner. I'm going to close up now, so I guess I'll see you in the morning."

Lolly glanced at Shaun and then back at Mrs. Bees. "I would love it if you would let me help you in the morning. I told you I'm hoping to open a bakery, but I've never worked at one. It would be wonderful if you'd let me lend a hand."

Mrs. Bees smiled and all of her wrinkles smiled, too, making her look quite beautiful. "You are such a dear. Yes, I would love your help in the morning. I'm not fool enough to turn down an extra pair of hands."

"Oh, that would be great!" Lolly exclaimed. The two discussed what time Lolly should be up and how Mrs. Bees would give her a new hairnet so Lolly's *beautiful locks* wouldn't end up in the croissants.

"Hurry off and get some dinner. You'll have to be up early in the morning."

"Thank you, Mrs. Bees."

Shaun was thrilled for Lolly and proud of her for taking the initiative to make this happen. He was also darned proud of himself for coming up with this trip.

Together, they unloaded the car, got unpacked in their respective cozy rooms, then met downstairs to walk to Mac's. If Jesse hadn't warned him, Shaun would've liked to hold Lolly's hand as they walked to dinner. But he kept his hands to himself. He wouldn't touch her again until his head was on straight and he was certain what he wanted from her.

Lolly had brought her binder along to dinner, and he watched as she filled in her chart about the Bake Inn while they waited for their food. Because he'd had a muffin an hour ago, he spent most of his dinner watching Lolly speak animatedly about their day.

"Have you decided which bakery is your favorite?" Shaun asked.

"I can't answer that with one word. I loved the sleekness of the Baked Raven. The tiny house bakery was so smart. To be able to take her business down south for the winter made so much sense. She doesn't have to worry about the winter lull at all."

"You know, I could make you a tiny bakery," he offered, "to haul down to Texas or Georgia or wherever for the winter. Just say the word and I'll do it." He couldn't believe he was making promises without considering all the facts. First of all, Lolly could be married by the time he completed this tiny bakery he was promising. There was the expense, too—and how long could he put off finding or building his own cabin? And lastly, he didn't like the thought of Lolly being gone eight months of the year. She'd be on the road and he would be lonely in Alaska without her.

She reached over, laid her hand on his arm, and squeezed. "You are so sweet to offer."

Yeah, his grandmother had called him sweet. But Granny saying it never made him feel the way Lolly was making him feel right now. Like an invincible superhero.

"The tiny house was cute, novel actually, but I don't want to leave Sweet Home unless I have to. I worked so hard to get back; it would be a shame to leave." She looked up. "The thing is, I might still have to leave, you know."

His throat was tight. He wasn't sure if it was because she still had a hold on him, or if he was affected by the upheaval in her life. More than likely, it was guilt because he'd called his boss, trying to get Lolly a job and out of town as soon as possible. But since there had been no word, he felt sure nothing would come of it, which made him breathe easier. More than anything, he wanted to tell her not to worry, because he'd called Olive last night and put an offer in on the professional kitchen, but he had a feeling that it wouldn't go over so well with Lolly. He thought it would be better to get all the equipment hauled back to Sweet Home first, and put in the building, before she found out he'd paid for it. And when anyone asked him why—like his mom— he would tell them he felt responsible. He was the one who'd pushed Lolly into opening a bakery in Sweet Home. But most people wouldn't have to find out, as Lolly's loan would surely come through any day now.

The arrival of the check for the food saved Shaun from responding to Lolly's remark about leaving. His first instinct was to tell her not to go, to never leave Sweet Home. But that wasn't fair. He was starting to believe he himself might not be happy living in Sweet Home indefinitely, though that was the plan when he left Houston. But things were different now. For one, he missed programming more than he expected, and there wasn't a lot of programming happening on the homestead. Secondly, when Lolly married, it would be hard for him to see her with another man. Impossible, actually.

He pulled out his credit card and stood. "We better head back."

She slipped her binder back in her bag. "Yeah, I have to get to bed soon." She rubbed her hands together. "I can't wait to get in Mrs. Bees's kitchen."

He started to put his hand on Lolly's back to guide her along, but he was trying to do the right thing and not lead her on. He paid and they walked back to the B and B in silence. Mrs. Bees must've already gone up because there was a note on the door telling them to lock up and to turn off the lamp downstairs before going to bed.

Their rooms were at the top of the stairs, right next to each other. Shaun wanted to wait until Lolly was safe inside before he went into his own room. But she just stood there outside her door, staring at him. It looked like she was trying to telepathically send him a message, but he wasn't receiving the transmission.

He knew what he wanted, but he was going to stand firm. If only he hadn't called Jesse . . .

Lolly suddenly took three steps and stopped inches in front of him. Before Shaun could think about what was going on, she reached up and stroked his face. He felt trapped, happy to be hypnotized by her spell.

She slipped her hand around the back of his neck and pulled him down for a kiss. He told himself it was a thank-you kiss, but this kiss wasn't quick and chaste. She'd put a lot of feeling behind this kiss, at least that's what it felt like. He was working really hard not to enjoy how she'd taken the initiative. Finally, his resistance gave way. One second, he was just letting her kiss him, and in the next, he had her wrapped in his arms and was kissing her back.

The kiss went on longer than it should've. Finally, he had the presence of mind to pull away. He was breathing hard, and she was looking up at him as if he were the perfectly baked drizzle cake, ready to be devoured.

"Enough." He sounded like he'd swallowed a barrel of frogs. "You said it yourself; you have to get up early."

"Right. Right," she said stumbling back. He grasped her elbows to stop her from reaching the stairs. He quickly dropped his hands, not trusting them to keep from pulling her close again.

She motioned between them awkwardly, pointing at him, then her, and then back at him. "What just happened was simply because I was grateful for this amazing trip."

Which made him wonder what she'd do when he surprised her with the installed professional kitchen. "Yes. Sure. I know. No problem." He'd have to run down to the gas station and pick up throat lozenges for how hoarse he sounded. "Good night, Lolly. Sleep well." But he wouldn't sleep a wink.

"Good night, Shaun," she said shyly, which was cute as heck.

They both went into their separate rooms simultaneously and shut their respective doors behind them.

The wall between the two rooms was so thin he could hear her flop on her bed, which was apparently up against the wall, as he heard the headboard bang against it. To break the tension, he quietly knocked on his side of the wall. "Lolly?"

For a second, it was quiet on her side, until he heard the bed squeak, as if she were crawling closer to their shared wall. He pictured her laying her cheek on the wall, listening with her ear plastered against it. He put his hand against the wall, seeing if he could feel her there on the other side.

"What is it?" she said back to him.

"Keep it down in there, will you?" he teased. "I'm a light sleeper. I have to be bright-eyed and bushy-tailed in the morning while I watch my favorite pastry chef in action."

"Mrs. Bees?" she said with a giggle. "You dirty dog."

"Not Mrs. Bees, Lolls. *You.*"

"Don't worry about me," Lolly said. "I'll be as quiet as a tea towel. What I'm really worried about is you might snore and keep me awake."

"Nope. No snoring here," he said, laying his ear against the wall, too. "I had a really nice time with you today."

"I know," she said with laughter in her voice.

"Can we do it again sometime?"

She was silent for so long he was afraid she might not answer at all. He figured he'd gone too far but he wouldn't take it back now. Jesse's words came back to him, but Shaun felt like he could defend what he'd just done. How was he supposed to make a decision without having all the data? The only way to gather said data was to go on a proper date with Lolly Crocker. He pressed his ear harder against the wall until the answer finally came.

"Maybe. We'll see."

It wasn't a *no.* That kiss she'd laid on him in the hallway had been one for the books, and because of it, he felt encouraged that her *maybe* would change to a *yes.* He got ready for bed.

The next morning he made his way downstairs and

peeked into the kitchen, giving her a wave. Then he sat at a table in the small dining room, glad for some solitude to regroup. He needed time to think about how to handle the date they might be going on.

Mrs. Bees brought him coffee and unlocked the front door to open the bakery for the day. Lolly brought out trays of baked goods and arranged them in the display case. Next, she set a mini quiche in front of him. "Can I get you anything else?" she asked.

"I'm good."

Lolly went back to her place behind the counter as the first customer came in the door. She spent the morning bagging pastries and ringing up the purchases. During lulls, she and Mrs. Bees stood behind the counter and chatted while Shaun scrolled through his phone and finished up his coffee and quiche. Lolly seemed like she was having the time of her life and he didn't want to rush her.

At ten, she hugged Mrs. Bees and came toward him, freeing her "beautiful locks" from the hairnet. "I figured we better get on the road."

"You figured right."

After they visited the Bookshop Bakery and the Alaska Native Bakery, which sold all kinds of handmade items besides wonderful baked goods, they drove back to Sweet Home, the mood light and comfortable. He wondered if they should talk about last night—not the kiss, but the date he'd proposed. He didn't want to disrupt the contentment between them right now, so he remained silent on the subject. As they pulled into Sweet Home, he heard the chime of a text coming in. After he parked in front of Lolly's, he glanced at his phone and saw that Olive had accepted his offer. *Yes!* After he unloaded Lolly's things from the car, he'd head over to the bank and wire the money before closing time. Since Olive planned to leave by the end of next week, he'd have to figure out the logistics of getting the equipment moved, pronto.

He must've stared at his phone too long, because Lolly

had already retrieved her items from the back and was walking toward her little house. She waved. "Thanks for everything, Shaun. The trip gave me a lot to think about."

He didn't know if she meant the bakeries or his proposition through the wall last night. "My pleasure." He started the engine and headed toward the bank. But halfway up the street, out of the corner of his eye he spied the bakery binder; it was lying half under the seat. Instead of driving straight to the bank, he went around the block, coming to a stop in front of her house . . . and he couldn't believe what he was seeing.

His mother was standing on Lolly's porch, shaking her finger in her face and clearly giving her a piece of her mind.

Chapter 17

"I ASKED YOU to stay away from him." Patricia's tone was as hard as a granite mortar and pestle. Her glare would probably cause Lolly's face some permanent damage.

"Yes, you did tell me to stay away from him." *But this trip wasn't my idea.*

A car door slammed . . . the Jeep's door. Lolly hadn't noticed Shaun returning but was certainly glad when she saw him coming up the walkway. If not to rescue her, at least there would be a witness to her murder, which Patricia looked capable of committing at this moment.

"Mom? What are you doing here?" he asked without a hint of politeness.

"Getting to the bottom of things." Patricia kept her glare on Lolly, as if she couldn't look at her son in case Lolly made a run for it.

"Listen," Shaun said, "Lolly had nothing to do with me taking her to Anchorage. She was coerced." He frowned as if he had been coerced, too, which Lolly didn't doubt.

Patricia did face him then. "Coerced by whom?"

Thor had been barking at the door as if Patricia was Darth Vader's mother and had a death grip on Lolly, so Lolly took the opportunity to let her dog out. As soon as she cracked the door open, Thor tore out, changing focus the second he was outside. He ran for Shaun instead, who automatically handed Lolly her bakery binder, which he'd brought from his vehicle. Shaun picked up her poorly groomed pup and held him close.

Shaun was still silent about who was to blame for the Anchorage trip, and Lolly was beginning to wonder if he was using her dog as a shield against his mother. Finally, he said, "It was my idea." Lolly hoped Piney and the others would appreciate how Shaun had just fallen on his sword for them.

Patricia was now glaring at her son. "Maybe, but I expect Piney had something to do with this. Why would you get mixed up with Lolly again?" Lolly felt invisible. "Why not give Courtney a chance? She's been pining after you for ages."

Lolly held back a harrumph. Surely Patricia knew Courtney had a reputation for *pining* after every decent man within a two-hundred-mile radius. Courtney with her perfect features and perfect hair and perfect clothes. She had her pick of men and had no problem hitting on anyone with a Y chromosome.

Shaun rolled his eyes at his mom's suggestion and sighed heavily, which eased some of the Courtney-induced panic in Lolly's chest. He said, "I needed to pick up the sound system for Rick. I told you I wanted to get their place done so I could get back to working on Jesse and Tori's cabin."

Patricia's expression softened at the newlyweds' names, but only for a second. "If you were running an errand, why were you gone two days? And why take Lolly?"

Lolly mustered up every brave cell in her body to explain about the bakery shop hop.

"I—" Shaun started.

But Lolly cut him off. "I wanted to see a variety of bakeries in other small towns to get an idea of how they manage their businesses. I took advantage of Shaun. I twisted his arm, really. He wanted to head right back, but I begged him to take me where I wanted to go. I hope you'll for-give him."

Shaun looked surprised that she was throwing herself under the bus for him. "That's—"

Lolly cut in again. "Sorry I was selfish. I expect you needed him on the homestead, didn't you?" Though she knew he'd arranged for help. "I won't put him in that awkward posi-tion again."

Patricia cocked her head to the side as if she was trying to let the explanation roll to the other side of her brain. Shaun did that exact same gesture when he was trying to process something that seemed questionable. "Tell me this. Is there something going on between you two?"

"No," Shaun said convincingly. "Absolutely not."

Lolly's heart plummeted. She'd believed there was something going on, at least a spark. Those kisses. Every bonding gaze they'd shared. And what about the asking-her-out-through-the-wall thing last night? But now she was doubting everything, especially herself and how gullible she'd been.

Shaun was looking at her like he was waiting for her to back him up. Patricia was giving her a look, too. Lolly suc-cumbed. It was only right since she'd hurt Shaun in the first place. "Um, yeah, Shaun's correct. Nothing's going on. Nothing at all." She retrieved her dog from Shaun's loving arms, and Thor looked up at her with disbelieving eyes, as if this man was the love of his life and she had no right to interfere in their bromance.

She kissed Thor's head. "Let me put Thor in the back-yard, and then I'll pull a package of mini pecan pies from the freezer for you to have for your dessert tonight."

Patricia was staring at Shaun, and Shaun was staring at Lolly, or maybe at her dog; it was hard to tell. Lolly only knew she was close to crying. But still, she stared back at him.

"Where's your car?" Shaun asked his mother then. "How did you get here?" Lolly waited, as she wanted to know that, too.

"I parked at the Hungry Bear and walked over," Patricia said.

Shaun frowned at her, and rightly so. Apparently, Patricia had planned this surprise attack. "Lolly had nothing to do with this. I promise. You shouldn't have ambushed her."

Lolly had heard enough. "I'll be right back." She was shaking as she took Thor inside. She automatically grabbed her dog's spiky protective vest from the hook by the front door, slipped it onto him as she walked to the back, and let him out. She used all of her might to hold it together for one more minute. *Retrieve mini pecan pies from freezer. Deliver to Montanas. Close door. Fall apart.*

She went into the kitchen and pulled open the freezer door at the same time she heard the front door open and close. She prayed it wasn't Jilly or Candy. She couldn't handle explaining why the Montanas were standing on the front porch glaring at each other.

"Hey," Shaun said, startling her into hitting her head on the freezer shelf. "Oh, sorry!"

"Where's your mom?"

"I sent her home."

"And she let you stay?" That didn't seem plausible. "She must be slipping," Lolly said sarcastically.

"*Moms*," Shaun said with a tone. "They think they have the right to tell us how to run our lives." He hesitated a second before continuing. "Don't let my mom's surprise attack ruin what a good time we had together, okay?"

"Too late." Lolly pulled out the mini pecan pies and grabbed a bag of frozen lemon cookies, too, before shoving them both at him. "Here." She pointed toward the exit. "I'll see you around."

Shaun took the bite-sized pies and cookies but didn't leave. He set them on the counter, and in one smooth motion pulled her into his arms.

She gently collided with his chest with a *whoomph*. Being held tightly by him again, inhaling his scent, his breath caressing her cheek, felt so good! But she pushed him away;

it was the only thing she could do. "Nope." She was afraid to say more, afraid if she did, she really would cry this time.

He held up his hands in surrender. "What? What did I do?"

Frustrated, she exhaled, shook her head, and looked up at the heavens before answering. "You told your mom there was nothing going on between us."

"So?"

"I'm making sure to keep it that way. To keep you honest." Thor scratched at the back door and she turned around to let him in. Those few moments gave her a chance to regroup. Or at least try to. What she really wanted to do was to be in his arms again.

Thor ran to Shaun once more, but apparently the manly *dog whisperer* in her kitchen wasn't interested in cuddle time with her pooch. "Go lie down, boy." Thor did as he was told, but it was clear her dog was pouting.

"You have to understand," Shaun started, "I didn't mean what I said."

Lolly crossed her arms and waited.

"I'm still trying to figure out how to navigate my mother being in my life again. Being in my business, actually. I'm giving myself some time to figure it out, and I ask you to give me some leeway if I have to fib to my mom now and then. I'm not comfortable with it. It's just how it has to be until I can gently tell her to buzz off."

That made sense to Lolly, and Shaun must've seen her softening because he came closer, holding out his hands. Apparently, she didn't have any self-control whatsoever, because she put her hands in his and he squeezed in response.

"I meant what I said last night when I said I want us to go out."

"But I don't want to come between you and your mother."

"You're not coming between us. Mom and I are fine. We'll always be good. We love each other, and we both know it. She just doesn't realize I'm a grown man who makes his own decisions. She thinks of me as the broken-hearted boy who left town at eighteen."

"But why do you want to go out with me?" Lolly asked bravely. This had been the question burning in her mind since he'd asked her out through the wall last night.

"That's just another thing I'm trying to figure out. I can give you the short answer, if you'd like."

"Go ahead, then," she said, bracing herself in case it wasn't the answer she wanted. Like he was still attracted to her, or she was the "forbidden fruit."

He squeezed her hands again. "I want to go out with you because *I have to.*" His tone was serious, and his words made her heart take flight. "That's the best I can do. Will that work until I can give you an update?"

She stared at their linked hands. To make matters more confusing, he began stroking the top of her hands with his thumbs. "Okay," she whispered. This would surely be a monumental mistake—letting go and trusting everything would be okay. But she couldn't help trusting Shaun and couldn't stop herself from saying yes. She brought her gaze up to meet his and saw how sincere he was.

She wasn't surprised when he wrapped her in his arms, leaned down, and kissed her. She also wasn't surprised when she kissed him back just as fervently. It was wonderful kissing him. It was almost as if the past—and the present problems—didn't exist. *Almost.*

He stopped the kiss first by pulling back and touching his forehead to hers. "Thank you."

It wasn't every day a girl got that response from a kiss, but she'd take it.

After a long moment, he said, "I have to go." He straightened, standing tall. "I have time-sensitive business I must attend to."

"All right," she said. She knew there was more to say. Desperately, she wanted it all worked out now, one way or the other. But life didn't always conform to her deepest and desperate wishes. *Be patient*, she told herself. "Is there anything I can do about your mom? How can I make things better with her?" Besides give Patricia a complete brain wipe where Lolly was concerned.

He shook his head. "No. I believe this is more about me and her and doesn't really have anything to do with you."

But that couldn't be right. Lolly felt as if she'd hurt Patricia as much as she'd hurt Shaun when she broke up with him. Patricia had been invested in them as a couple. It was almost as if she knew she was going to become critically ill and wanted to make sure Shaun had a special someone to be there for him. That someone was supposed to be Lolly. But mama bears hold grudges, and Lolly just needed to figure out a way to earn Patricia's forgiveness. *The very definition of an impossible feat!*

But then Lolly had an idea. A crazy, wonderful idea.

She leaned up and gave Shaun a quick kiss. "You better go." He looked a little surprised when she picked up the baked goods, shoved them in his hands, and hurried him to the door. "I'll talk to you soon. Thanks again for the trip. It was wonderful, illuminating, more than I could've asked for." She didn't wait for him to respond but shut the door.

She rushed back to the kitchen and retrieved a notebook. With pen in hand, she sat at the table. She had three quilts to cut, piece, and quilt: one for Jesse and Tori, one for Luke and McKenna—and one for Shaun and his future bride. She didn't want to think about that because surely his wedding to someone else would destroy her. If she was still in Sweet Home, she'd be expected to attend and probably be forced to make the canapés and the wedding cake, too. But Lolly would just have to suck it up when the time came, even though her heart was breaking just thinking about it.

She looked back at the list of quilts and started brainstorming ideas, starting with activities Dale Montana, Shaun's dad, used to do with his boys. Next, she thought about things Jesse, Luke, and Shaun each liked. She drew three columns with their names as headings and started filling them in.

"This is going to be a lot of work," she said to Thor. Thor glanced up at her from his dog bed in the corner but immediately settled back down, as if he were depressed that Shaun had left. "A lot of work," she repeated. A really good idea came to her. She'd wrangle McKenna and Tori into helping make the quilts for their respective spouses. She could text Tori to see whether she'd be on board if Lolly sent her the design and the fabric. McKenna would be up for it, for sure. She was a sewing whiz. Lolly looked around the kitchen. "I guess I'll be responsible for Shaun's quilt." Thor barked at the sound of Shaun's name. What a silly animal. Well, even though Thor adored Shaun, he always gave Lolly unconditional love. Something she longed for in a human.

She tapped the plan with her pen, feeling good about it. But making the three quilts as a gift for Patricia might not change things one bit. Lolly sighed. She stood and looked out at where Shaun's Jeep had been, only now the street in front of her house was empty. Even if Shaun wanted to go out with her now, Lolly knew it wasn't for the long haul. She was on her own, and she'd better keep seeing it that way. Fantasizing about what could never be was a good way to get one's heart obliterated. It was best to be prepared for the inevitable. She'd be dumped this time; she knew she was due.

But while the future played out, Lolly had a plan in the here and now. Come hell or high water, Patricia would get her Montana Family Quilts.

Lolly was determined, but she was a realist, too, and decided to take inventory of her life. Baking for the locals, contract obligations with stores in surrounding towns, catering for Sparkle and Rick's upcoming wedding, and continuing to work toward her dream of opening a bakery . . . was a lot. Not to mention looking for a full-time teaching position even though it didn't sound appealing, because almost half of small businesses fail in the first few years! And now she was going to add three quilts for Patricia to her impossibly crowded schedule.

Normally, the Sisterhood of the Quilt would be involved, but Lolly didn't want to take the chance of Patricia finding out what she was up to. This could all go horribly wrong. Patricia might go postal on Lolly for taking on the project. But really, what did Lolly have to lose? Patricia didn't like her and might never forgive her. But Lolly would bravely forge ahead. She'd overheard Piney telling Miss Lisa that Patricia's strength wasn't completely back yet, and she just wasn't up to making quilts the way she once had. "At one time," Piney said, "Patricia could whip out a quilt lickety-split, but now she's as slow as a snail. I understand she's frustrated, but healing takes time. One day, she'll be running at full speed again."

"I'll just have to chance making Patricia mad," Lolly told Thor. Her baby got up and sauntered over to her to get a good scratching behind his ears. "Right, my little man?"

When Thor had had enough and headed back to his bed, Lolly washed her hands and started making her favorite chicken potpie recipe. She normally kept a few in the freezer, but she was all out now. She laid the cut-up chicken pieces—*chicken from McKenna and Luke's homestead*—on a foiled baking sheet to bake at four hundred degrees. Next, she made the crust. She made sure to add extra love while she was rolling out the dough. After she made the white sauce and took the cooked chicken off the bone, she put the potpie together and slid it into the preheated oven.

While it cooked, Lolly worked on sketching designs for the three Montana quilts. Similar but different. She had a second notebook beside her, so when an idea hit her out of left field for the new bakery, she wrote notes about it, too. *Yes, multitasking.* She couldn't wait to tell Shaun that she'd come up with the perfect theme for the shop. Quilting! She'd hire the local ladies to make items to sell—like quilted potholders, trivets, coasters, baby bibs, aprons—and maybe Tori would let her sell her Alaska Chic apron at the bakery, too. Lolly could even stock a small selection of full-size quilts. That way, the bakery would complement the quilt shop in A Stone's Throw Hardware & Haberdashery and the quilting retreats that were held at Home Sweet Home Lodge. She was so excited! This theme fit Lolly and it fit the town, too. It felt perfect! Now, if she could only get that loan.

Mom and Jilly came home as Lolly pulled the chicken potpie from the oven. "You two have a knack of showing up just when the food is ready."

Jilly smiled. "Yeah, Mom taught me that skill. It's the best way to get out of cooking around here."

Mom set her purse on a chair. "We'll clean up for you after we eat, okay, Lollipop?"

Jilly motioned to the paper and notebooks spread all over the table. "What's all this?"

Lolly set the potpie on the counter and quickly gathered her quilt plans, holding them to her chest. "It's nothing."

"It doesn't look like nothing," Jilly said.

"Just doodles."

"It's not nice to keep secrets," Candy said.

"Yeah," Jilly piled on. "Show us."

"It's not a secret. It's just stuff for the bakery. Possible items for sale."

"Things we can help make? You know I'd love to help," Candy said.

Lolly might have some problems with her mother, but she loved that her mom could be generous with her time and talents. "Yes, you can absolutely help . . . that is, if the loan comes through."

"In the meantime, I'll set the table." Mom kissed her cheek and then straightened the tablecloth.

"At least tell us how you got on in Anchorage," Jilly said.

Lolly kept quiet, watching while Mom retrieved plates from the cabinet. Jilly leaned into Lolly and whispered, "I expect full disclosure when we're alone. Especially why you stayed the second night."

"Grow up, Jilly," Lolly whispered back. "Nothing

happened. Except we're friends again. I think." And that, at least, was something.

"What are you two talking about over there?" Mom asked as she laid silverware next to the plates.

Jilly stuck her tongue out at Lolly and turned to their mother with an air of innocence on her face. "Lolly wants you to call Shaun and ask him if he'd like to come over for some potpie. Like right now. She made plenty."

"I did not say that!" Lolly couldn't believe her sister would do this . . . actually, it was exactly something Jilly would do to rile Lolly up. Her wild-child little sister, disrupting things. "Mom, please don't call Shaun. He was over here earlier, and he said he has some important business to attend to." Which seemed pretty mysterious. Lolly had to concede there was much she didn't know about this adult Shaun.

Jilly was looking at her as if she could read her mind. "You're doth protesting too much? No—Mom, what's that saying you're always using?"

"The lady doth protest too much," Mom said, laughing.

"Yes, that's it." Jilly was laughing, too.

The three of them sat around the kitchen table and Jilly said grace. While her sister and mom spoke about their respective days, Lolly only half listened.

When they were done eating, Lolly picked up Thor, needing an escape; their house was way too small for three women. "I'm taking Thor for a walk while you clean up." She didn't wait to see if they would come up with some reason for her to stay.

Before leaving the house, she grabbed her notebook with the newly designed quilts. Thor was happy to be getting out and about to greet the people of Sweet Home. He loved leading the way through town, and he seemed to smile at everyone they passed. Thor was kind of disappointed when she opened the door to the bank, but he perked up when he saw there were plenty of new people to greet inside.

"Hey, Lolly. Hey, mutt," Luke said as he came from behind his desk. "What can I do for you?"

"Do you know if McKenna's free? I have a quick request," Lolly said.

"Follow me," he said with a wink. "Her last appointment left a bit ago." He had always been friendly and nice, but since McKenna came into his life, he seemed happier than ever. Lolly and Thor followed him to McKenna's large office.

"You have two customers who would like to speak to you," Luke said to McKenna as he leaned in the doorway.

"Send them in." McKenna stood as Lolly and her dog came forward. Thor pulled at the leash to get to McKenna.

"Can I shut the door for some privacy?" Lolly asked.

"Sure." McKenna came around the desk and gave Thor a dog treat, something she'd kept in her top drawer since taking over the management of the bank. "If you're looking for Shaun, he's gone."

Shaun? Why had he been at the bank? Lolly wondered, but she put her curiosity aside. She had a big task to undertake, and she needed McKenna to help. "No. I'm not looking for Shaun."

"What can I do for you? If you're here about the loan, I haven't heard anything yet from Uncle Monty. He did send a note that he'll make the decision first thing on returning from his honeymoon with Peggy." McKenna smiled. "The wedding was gorgeous."

"I'm not here about the loan." *No news is good news.* That saying was one of Candy's favorites, too. "I wanted to talk to you about Patricia."

McKenna frowned as if she completely understood and pointed to a chair. "Sit."

Thor heeded the command and plopped his bum down on the tile. Lolly took the chair in front of the desk, while McKenna leaned against it.

"Tell me what's going on," McKenna said.

Lolly pulled the notebook from her quilted bag and showed McKenna the designs while she explained about Patricia and the three Montana quilts she wanted to complete.

"It's interesting you would bring this up," McKenna said.

"Why's that?"

"Just the other day, Patricia mentioned the Montana Family Quilts. She said if she didn't feel up to it soon, she was going to hire this woman in Fairbanks who's known for making memory quilts. She wants to put a checkmark by this item on her to-do list. Why not tell her what you're up to? She might thank you for taking the initiative."

"I suspect she won't." After hearing what McKenna said, Lolly was feeling more driven than ever to finish the Montana Family Quilts. "Did Patricia happen to mention specifically what designs she was looking for?" That would be a big help to Lolly.

"I asked. She said she didn't care, even if they were a simple patchwork. She just wanted them done so she could pass something special on to the boys. I thought about talking to Piney about involving the Sisterhood but decided to hold off until after the wedding." McKenna took a seat and held a pen at the ready. "So, tell me what you need from me. Anything. Just name it."

"I need help getting Mr. Montana's work shirts and jeans and the boys' old shirts from Patricia's closet without her knowing."

McKenna chortled. "That's a tall order." She pushed away from the desk and paced back and forth for a minute until she stopped suddenly and turned to Lolly. Thor gave a yip of excitement as if he knew McKenna was going to say something brilliant. "I think it can be done. We'll have to bring Hope under our dome of silence, though."

In the next ten minutes, they concocted a daring plan in which Hope would ask for Patricia's help out at the lodge. With any luck, Hope would say yes and not tell anyone.

"Listen, I'd like to be the one to piece Luke's quilt together. Do you mind?"

Lolly laughed. "I was hoping you would offer."

"Good," McKenna said. "How about if we send fabric, shirts, whatever, to Tori for her to make Jesse's quilt? Split three ways, we'll get these quilts done in a jiffy."

"Thank you. You're the best." Now the task didn't seem so overwhelming. Lolly only needed to make one quilt, Shaun's. But the thought hit her again. The quilt would be for him and his future wife. And her happy heart sank. She willed herself to snap out of it and not let the thought of another woman being in Shaun's life disrupt her momentum.

When she said good-bye and she and Thor left the bank, Lolly was feeling pretty good about her decision. She let the fantasy reel run in her head of Patricia hugging the quilts, hugging her, and telling her all was forgiven.

But that feeling didn't last. The next day, when she walked into the Hungry Bear, it felt like all bets were off.

Chapter 18

AS SOON AS Lolly saw who was standing in the aisle of the Hungry Bear, she tugged on Thor's leash so they could turn around and hightail it back home. But, too late, Patricia had seen her. She barreled toward Lolly with the determination of a Spartan. Thor hid behind Lolly.

"Shaun says I should leave you alone," Patricia said.

Which was funny since Patricia had told Lolly she should leave Shaun alone. She guessed it was a Montana family trait, telling people who they could and couldn't see.

Patricia continued. "But I believe you and I have an understanding, right?"

What could Lolly say? *Yes and no?* Lolly wanted to obey Patricia, but at the same time she really wanted to go on that date Shaun insisted they have.

Patricia huffed. "Don't let me down, Lolly." Then she walked away.

This was not how Lolly wanted things to go with Shaun's mom. It was a catch-22. Either Patricia was going to be upset with her . . . or Shaun was. Discouraged, she went into the store and picked up the items she needed for the next round of baking.

As soon as she got home, a text from McKenna arrived: Come to the bank. Lolly quickly put her purchases away, grabbed the quilt-project notebook, and headed back out the door. She assumed the summons had to do with the Montana Family Quilts caper. But she was wrong.

McKenna eyed the notebook as Lolly walked into her office. "I didn't bring you here to plot how we're going to break into Patricia's cabin. I brought you here to discuss the loan for your bakery. Brace yourself." McKenna had an unreadable expression on her face. "Uncle Monty didn't approve the loan."

"Oh." Lolly always knew it was a long shot, but she was still surprisingly disappointed. "It's okay. I didn't expect him to go along with it." She would just have to put her dream away, shove the binder to the far reaches of her closet, and get back on the job hunt in earnest. The idea of opening a bakery was so outrageous she never should've let herself get excited in the first place. But she couldn't help this lump in her throat. It felt like her heart was breaking. And the wasted trip to Anchorage! She'd have to call Olive and tell her she couldn't buy the professional kitchen from her after all.

"Wait, wait!" McKenna had her hands up. "Stop looking like that, because I wasn't done." She broke into a big grin. "It's all going to be fine. Uncle Monty didn't approve the loan because he thinks the amount you asked for is too small. Instead, he's decided to invest in the bakery. He said it was better to just grant the money to you. He mentioned taxes as one reason. Also, it would cost the bank more to process the loan than what it would make back in interest. The catch is he would like to own a two percent stake in the business, but between you and me, that's negotiable. He just loves investing in Sweet Home."

"A . . . grant?" Lolly felt shell-shocked.

"Uncle Monty has a few stipulations, but we can go over those later."

"Wh-what stipulations?"

"He wants you to sign a three-year lease on the building and agree to keep the bakery open for all three years."

"And if I fail to do so?" Lolly only asked because, according to Google, one in five bakeries fails in the first few years.

"If you shut down before three years are up, the original grant turns into a loan with interest and the total will have to be repaid within one year." McKenna didn't seem shook up at all about the terms. "Uncle Monty wants to see the bakery succeed. He thought this would be an incentive to help you do just that."

To Lolly, it felt like pressure—no, a *threat*. But when McKenna and Tori's uncle was in town for their weddings, he seemed to be a kind, friendly person. Of course, doing a business deal with him was a whole other pan of biscuits.

"I need some time to think this through." Lolly needed to speak to Rick, who knew so much about business. She'd like to speak with Shaun about it, too. After all, it was his idea to open a bakery. But she knew exactly what Shaun would say: *Just do it. You've dreamed of owning a bakery your whole life. If you didn't want it, why did you put so much time and effort into your bakery notebook?* All kinds of emotions were brewing inside Lolly. Fear. Excitement. Circumspection. What if the bakery didn't work out? Monty wanted her to sign a three-year contract. Lolly didn't know what the next three minutes held, let alone three years!

"Take all the time you need . . . as long as it's less than seventy-two hours."

This was so much to take in. "Three days? Why three?"

McKenna laughed. "Uncle Monty knows you have a lot of work ahead of you to get the place open in time." She winked; apparently, she was picking up habits from her husband.

"In time for *what*?" Lolly was now filled with dread.

"The Pine Cone Fall Festival," McKenna said, smiling.

"Why does it have to be open by *then*?"

"Oh, didn't I tell you? A camera crew from WHPP is coming to the festival. They've agreed to feature local businesses and are interested in Tori's clothing company, A Stone's Throw Hardware & Haberdashery, Home Sweet Home Lodge, and your bakery. Basically, we want to show the world what Sweet Home has to offer." McKenna paused. "It's one of the stipulations in Uncle Monty's contract. You should read it over carefully." She passed her a stack of papers fastened at the top with an extra-large clip.

"Do you know any good lawyers?" Lolly asked sarcastically; she didn't have the funds to pay for one anyway.

Apparently, McKenna didn't pick up on the tone. "I bet Luke can hook you up with someone inexpensive. He has all kinds of contacts in Anchorage. I'm going to email you a copy of the contract now, too."

"Thanks." But she hoped asking Rick to read the contract would be good enough. If not, she'd probably have to ask "Uncle Monty" to give her a loan for legal fees, too!

Lolly's heart had become set on having her own bakery. There were just so many unknowns, it was overwhelming. But Sweet Home would be the perfect place to own a business. She had her family, the Sisterhood of the Quilt, and all the folks of Sweet Home to lean on for help. Shaun would be a big help, too. Actually, he'd already done a lot by being the bakery's lead cheerleader.

"Thanks," Lolly said. "I'll get back to you."

When she arrived home, she went into her room, shut the door, and called Rick right away.

"Can you email me a copy of the contract so I can take a look at it?" he asked cheerfully.

"Are you sure you'll have time to review it, especially with all you have going on?" Lolly thought about the wedding preparations, little Ava, and all of life's turmoil that had come his way recently.

"No problem, Lolly. I'm happy to do it. Besides, Sparkle and I are officially setting a new wedding date, which we haven't decided on yet. We need some time to get adjusted to having a little girl. So you can hold off thinking about the wedding for now. But not too long, only for a few months, okay?"

"Okay." Lolly was relieved that Rick sounded so good. "Let me know as soon as you've set a date, and I'll start planning again." The delay was a blessing, Lolly thought a little guiltily; she could put more time into the bakery, *and* the quilt for Shaun.

"How about we get together tomorrow?" Rick said. "Come prepared to ask questions. Also, think about any items you'd like to counter."

"Why would I counter on a grant?"

"Just think of any *asks*, anything extra you might want. He can always say no, but maybe he'll say yes."

"Okay. McKenna said I have to give him an answer within three days," Lolly said. "Apparently, Mr. St. James has already arranged for some Anchorage newspeople to come to town to do a story on Sweet Home's new businesses."

"Yes, Tori contacted me, too. The chamber of commerce and Tori's uncle Monty are trying to have Sweet Home gain traction as an emerging tourist site. I'll get back to you about what time we can meet up tomorrow. But in the meantime, I'll be sure to look over the contract and see if there's anything we need clarified."

She hated putting him out. "Are you sure you don't mind?"

"No problem. If it's okay with you, I'll have Donovan take a look at the contract, too."

"I'm sending you the contract now." A second later, she heard his computer ding.

"Got it," Rick said. "Don't worry. We'll make this happen for you."

"Okay. Thank you so much." But she was worried about the three-year commitment. She was worried there wouldn't be enough business. She was worried about what people were going to say, especially her mother, who always had opinions about Lolly's decisions. She was worried about the quilting project she planned to do at the same time. She was worried Patricia was going to be even more upset with her for doing said project. And finally, she was worried about Shaun. About the upcoming date. Especially about what would happen after the date was over. What condition would her heart be in then?

"Stop it," she said to herself, making Thor perk up.

"Not you, little man. Just me and my racing mind." Right now, she needed to read the contract. And think about what Rick said . . . What would be her *ask*?

LOLLY HAD JUST pulled two pans of brownies from the oven. She loved having these on hand for when she was anxious—*medicinal brownies*, she jokingly called them, because the gooey chocolate magically soothed her frazzled nerves. She seemed to need them more and more these days, especially when she thought about Shaun. As she set the pans on the cooling racks, her phone buzzed. She leaned over and saw the call was from McKenna. Lolly slipped off her potholders and answered.

"Are you ready to do this thing?" McKenna's voice was filled with excitement.

"What?" Lolly asked.

"The great Montana quilt caper," McKenna said.

"Now?" Lolly looked longingly at the brownies, but she knew it was too soon to carve a big one for herself.

"I just got off the phone with Patricia," McKenna said. "She says she's on her way to the lodge to sew with a few members of the Sisterhood of the Quilt. Apparently, Hope wanted her there. Good ol' Hope! I think this is our chance."

"Let me take Thor out first and then I'll be on my way out to the homestead." Shaun passed through her thoughts, and she wondered what he was up to today. Quickly she pushed him out of her mind. She didn't have the mental bandwidth to worry about him *and* burglary. Besides, the quilt caper was all about Patricia, not Shaun.

"Drop by the bank. I'm just locking up. Luke said he'll go to the lodge to keep an eye on Patricia. He'll text me if she leaves unexpectedly."

"You told Luke?" Lolly asked accusingly.

"Of course. I tell my husband everything. *Almost everything.*" She laughed. "He's standing right here. You should be grateful I'm married to him. He's the one who confirmed the location of the box of clothes we're going to use for the quilts."

"Okay. I'll be right there."

Lolly's nerves were zipping out of control as she took Thor out. "Promise you'll be good while I'm gone, little man."

He didn't answer but did his business by one of the bushes before running back to her. She let him in and grabbed her purse. "I'll be back soon." She prayed they didn't get caught rummaging through Patricia's things.

When Lolly picked McKenna up at the bank, she had a gleam in her eye. "You seem much more excited about breaking into Patricia's house than you should," observed Lolly.

McKenna pulled a key from her purse and held it up. "Not breaking in. I'm family, remember? I have total access."

"Well, that's something." Lolly wasn't family, wasn't anything to Patricia, except maybe bits of eggshell in the batter of her life.

"Don't worry," McKenna said. "We'll be in and out with no one the wiser."

Lolly prayed that was true. And this was just the first hurdle! The final one would be seeing if Patricia hated her even more for butting into her business.

Sure enough, when Lolly pulled up to the homestead, there were no other cars around and she relaxed a little. Maybe they would get away without being caught.

They got out and walked up to the door. Things seemed too quiet. "Where's Checkers?" Lolly asked because there wasn't any barking.

"Probably with Shaun. Or maybe Patricia took her to the lodge to play with Boomer."

"That's probably it."

McKenna unlocked the door and they went inside. "Here's the deal. I'll watch the door while you get the box."

"Where is it? Patricia's room?" Which only made sense, since it was mainly her husband's clothes they were after.

McKenna shook her head. "It's in Shaun's closet. Luke checked last night when we were here for dinner." She smiled broadly. "Dinner and reconnaissance."

"Okay." Lolly hadn't been in Shaun's room since high school. The house rule was the boys' doors always remained open, so she and Shaun barely spent any time in there. But she did know where it was.

When she stepped into his room, it was a surprise to see it had been transformed from a teenage boy's room into a makeshift sewing studio. A sewing machine sat on a small table in the corner, a kitchen chair slid underneath the tabletop. A stack of fabric sat beside the machine. But the extra-long twin bed was the same. The dresser was the same. His poster collection—*Legend of Zelda*, the band Lonestar, Steve Jobs and Steve Wozniak from the early days—was gone from the walls, but Lolly could picture each one still there.

Lolly went a little light-headed. If she hadn't broken up with Shaun, she wouldn't be nervous at all about being here; she would be one of the family, like McKenna.

As Lolly opened the closet door, she heard barking. Then the back door banged. She instinctively hopped inside the closet and closed the door to hide. She could hear a male voice—*Shaun!*—say, "Hey." She moved some coats and pressed her head against the wall facing the living room so she could listen.

"McKenna?" Shaun said, sounding surprised. "What are you doing here?"

"Uhhh," McKenna said loudly. Lolly wished they'd come up with an excuse in case someone dropped in. "Just picking up a few things for Luke." McKenna sounded proud of herself.

Something was poking Lolly in the head. She gently pushed it back, but her action started an avalanche of boxes falling from above. *Shoot, shoot, shoot!* She wondered if she could crawl out of here and slip out the back door before being found.

She heard footsteps and McKenna saying, "I'm sure it's just the cabin settling. No need to look in there."

Before Lolly could make any kind of evasive move—like find the opening to Narnia or dig her way to China—the closet door was slung open.

Shaun took a step back and put his hands on his hips. "Lolly, what the heck are you doing in there?"

"Um," Lolly said.

McKenna stepped around him and helped Lolly out, which made the rest of the small boxes spill into the room. "Come on, kid. We've been found out. You might as well come clean."

Lolly gave her a look, trying to convey a sarcastic *Thank you for throwing me to the wolves*. Or in this case just one wolf.

"Sit," Shaun ordered, "and tell me what's going on."

Lolly sat on the edge of the bed, feeling awkward. "I had this idea. I know your mom is anxious to create quilts from your dad's favorite clothes, and maybe something that belonged to you boys, too." She stared down at her hands as if they were the most interesting things in the world. "Quilts for you, Jesse, and Luke."

"Yeah, so?" he said. "She's mentioned it a couple hundred times."

"Well, I thought I could make them for her. As a gift. So she wouldn't have to worry anymore about getting them done." She pointed to McKenna. "She's offered to make Luke's."

McKenna gave a reaffirming nod. "I talked to Tori last night and she's excited to make Jesse's."

Shaun studied Lolly for a long moment. "I doubt getting the quilts done will sway my mother's opinion of you. You know how stubborn she is."

McKenna jumped in. "Do you mean Patricia is still upset with Lolly because she broke up with you in *high school*? Piney says—"

Shaun cut her off. "Can you give us a minute alone, McKenna?"

She nodded and left the room. Shaun shut the door behind her, breaking the rules and closing them in, all cozy-like.

Irrationally, Lolly felt giddy with the close proximity, but Shaun's fierce gaze brought her back to reality. "I know you're right about your mom. But that's not why I'm making the quilts." She wondered how she could say this without making him feel guilty about being gone while Patricia was sick. "It's just that I want to help her. She confided in me that it weighed heavily on her mind, the thought that the worst might happen before the quilts were done." She watched his face and could see the wheels turning. "You've probably noticed your mom isn't back to her full strength yet." Actually, it was amazing how well Patricia was doing, considering she'd been near death's door only six months ago. While Patricia was ill, she'd been somewhat friendly to Lolly and grateful for the comfort food she brought. But now Patricia seemed to have loads of energy, especially when it came to yelling at Lolly. "I thought I could make the quilts to take the worry from your mom's mind. Get something done for her she really wants done. No strings attached. No quid pro quo." She stopped for a second. "That's not exactly true. I would get something out of it. It would be a blessing to me to ease her mind."

Shaun looked a little stunned, then he seemed to snap out of it. "What can I do to help? I know I missed most of the rough patches with Mom. Though Jesse and I were in constant communication." He exhaled. "I came to visit, but I know it's not the same as being here at her side."

"It would be a big help if you could assist me in picking out her favorite pieces."

"Sure. I'd be happy to. But I can't do it right now—I need to see to the animals. Just tell me when and where and I'll be there."

"Tonight? I need to get started ASAP. I want to get Tori's stuff in the mail to her right away." Lolly didn't want to put it off, not even for a second, but she figured his help would be valuable. "Only if you're free."

"It's a date," he said.

There was that word again, *date*. He had a way of throwing it around as if the word didn't conjure up all kinds of intimate images—holding hands, gazing into each other's eyes, kissing. Her danged heart kept hoping for more. But she and Shaun weren't getting back together, no matter the kisses he'd given her, or that he'd asked her out. As anticipation morphed into anxiety, she needed a brownie to make her feel better, but there weren't any in sight.

McKenna knocked on the door. "Is everything all right in there?"

Shaun pulled Lolly to a standing position and gave her a quick kiss. Up this close, she could see flecks of light blue paint in his hair and on his arms. If he hadn't rendered her speechless with the kiss, she would've asked him what he'd been up to.

Shaun tucked a lock of her hair behind her ear. "Thank you for what you're doing for my mom." Which made her heart decelerate and stutter to a disappointing crawl. He then hollered over his shoulder, "Come on in."

McKenna eyed them suspiciously. "Better hurry and get what you need, Lolly. We don't know who might show up next."

Lolly turned to him and said, "Where's your Jeep? It wasn't out front when we pulled in."

"I've been staying at Jesse's cabin over the hill. I walked over here to check on the livestock." He laughed. "I never imagined I'd find you hiding in my old closet."

"I wasn't hiding, exactly," she said with a bit of indignation. "I was looking for the box McKenna said was in here."

"In the back," McKenna said, moving the other boxes out of the way.

"Here, let me get that." Shaun carried the box marked *Dale's Clothes* out to Lolly's car, while Lolly stacked the fallen boxes back in the closet.

"I think he has a crush on you," McKenna said when Shaun was out of the house.

"Don't be silly," Lolly said.

"Actually, I'm sure of it." She acted like she was privy to some secret.

Lolly wasn't going to probe for answers. "Shaun is just happy the quilts are going to get made. All of this is for his mom."

McKenna gave an exaggerated nod. "Riiighhht."

"Stop it. I'm not listening to you anymore." Yes, ignoring McKenna was the best thing to do. Shaun didn't have a crush on Lolly. He only kissed her because she was doing something nice for his mother.

But he was coming over tonight! That would give her a chance to tell him all about the loan. She could do it now, but he'd wonder why her cheeks were so red. Which was totally his fault. If he hadn't kissed her, she wouldn't be burning up.

"Oh, crud," Lolly said, remembering Jilly and her mom.

"What?" McKenna asked.

"Nothing." Lolly would have to find somewhere else for her and Shaun to go through his dad's clothes and the boys' old T-shirts. Someplace where they could spread out and not be bothered by her mom and Jilly. Anywhere else. Alone.

But as soon as she had the thought, a text came in from Rick: Meet me tonight at the lodge to discuss the contract. 7 pm? Frustrated, Lolly hesitated with her thumbs over the screen until she finally texted back: I'll be there. The bakery had been Shaun's idea, but now the bakery was keeping her from Shaun!

"McKenna, are you ready to go?"

"Luke said he'll pick me up here. You go on and we'll talk later."

Lolly peeked out the window but didn't see Shaun. He was probably checking on the livestock, like he said. She wouldn't be able to tell him in person she was canceling on him tonight. Instead, she sent him a text and hurried to her car.

As she drove down the driveway away from the homestead, all the emotions of being in Shaun's room, being in Shaun's room with him—alone!—had been a thrill but also made her feel a little panicked. She knew her heart was investing too much in this *friendship* with Shaun, her little heart hoping for so much more than he was offering. A date wasn't a promise for the future; it was only a placeholder while he figured out his own feelings. Her feelings, on the other hand, were becoming crystal clear. But her growing feelings weren't based in fact, only fantasy and hope. Nothing concrete. She realized then that she had a death grip on the steering wheel. She loosened her hold, deciding she should just worry about what was real, here, in the present.

The contract. The bakery. Would it really happen? Or would she once again be at a loss for what to do next?

Chapter 19

SHAUN WAS PRETTY ticked off as he crossed the homestead's yard to where the Highland cows were penned. With no explanation, Lolly had canceled their date tonight. Tanya used to cancel on him all the time. Now Lolly was doing it, too. All she said was they'd have to pick out clothes for the quilts another time. He felt deeply unappreciated, maybe a little hurt, and was kicking himself for all he'd been doing for her.

He turned on the water and filled the trough. "You know how I spent my day?" Shaun said to the cows. "I painted her dang bakery kitchen. And out of the goodness of my heart, too. We won't even talk about the time and money it took for me and Luke to pick up the kitchen appliances in Anchorage and bring them back." The cows, though, weren't fazed by his confession. As repayment, Shaun had promised to take Luke and McKenna out to dinner. He'd almost said he and Lolly could double-date with them. Thank goodness he stopped himself in the nick of time as Luke would've given him all kinds of razzing.

Somehow, Shaun had gotten ahead of himself. He and Lolly weren't a couple. They hadn't even gone on a date. If they were in Houston, he'd ask her to a movie or something.

But it wasn't so easy here. It felt like dating in a display window with the good folks of Sweet Home watching their every move.

As he put fresh hay in for the Highland cattle, he thought about how pure luck had been on his side when he was in the hardware store at the exact moment Donovan was describing for Luke the paint Lolly wanted for her professional kitchen, if her loan went through. *Light calming blue*, Donovan said. Apparently, Lolly had read somewhere that light blue in a commercial kitchen can improve overall productivity.

Shaun had wasted no time purchasing the "light calming blue" paint and put it to good use. Donovan gave him a look as if he understood—Shaun *had it bad*. Then, while Shaun was taping up the room, Luke had shown up in his old painting clothes and with his own paint roller, ready to work. Now the kitchen looked amazing, freshly painted with all the equipment moved in and polished within an inch of its life, courtesy of Shaun's elbow grease. It was going to be some surprise when Lolly saw her professional kitchen was done. If he knew what color she wanted for the rest of the place, he'd probably have started on that, too. He thought it would be nice if Lolly's bakery was all fixed up before she saw it.

But now he was disappointed she'd canceled their evening plans. He'd really been looking forward to it. And here he'd spent time today getting work done just for her.

But how could she know? He hadn't told her a thing, figuring she'd put him off. He stewed at his own grumpiness.

A second text came in. *Probably more bad news from her.* But the text was from Rick: Can you come to the lodge tonight? 7 pm?

He probably wanted to discuss the repairs and upgrades for his and Sparkle's house. Sure, Shaun texted back. He had nothing better to do.

He finished the chores, went back to Jesse's to take a

shower, and then drove to the lodge. He was surprised to see Lolly's car parked in the circular driveway. It didn't make any sense. And then he got a little ticked. She was probably here to do something or other for the Sisterhood of the Quilt. They were always asking favors of her, and she was always obliging them. What about obliging *him*? The worst part was that he had no idea how she felt about him, and it was uncomfortable to be so insecure. But that's what Lolly did to him—and he didn't like it.

Suddenly his hard feelings toward her evaporated. Lolly was the warmest, nicest person he'd ever known! But he was glad she'd be in the quilting studio, a place she loved so much. Plus, the added bonus of her in the studio meant he wouldn't have to see her this evening, especially since his feelings about her were so jumbled.

When he got inside, however, he was astonished to see Lolly sitting in the expansive living room with Rick and Donovan. For a moment, he wondered if this was some kind of intervention. If it was, it could only be because he'd been doing way too much *for* Lolly . . . and *with* Lolly.

Rick came over and patted him on the back. "Don't worry. You're not here for the hot seat. We're here to discuss Lolly's contract for the bakery. Have you had a chance to read it yet?"

"The . . . contract? What contract?" He turned on Lolly. "The loan's been approved? Why didn't you tell me?"

Lolly straightened up a bit. "I-I was going to tell you all about it . . . tonight. You know . . ." She gave him a look that said she was embarrassed that she had to mention their plan to meet up tonight.

"Yeah. Okay," Shaun said, as he took one of the wing-back chairs, while Rick handed them each a sheet of paper.

"This is the agenda for our discussion. I thought it would be helpful to take notes," Rick said as Shaun looked over the sheet.

"The first thing we need to discuss is the three-year stipulation."

Rick went over the requirement that the business had to be open continuously for three years, the penalty for closing before then, and the percentage of the business Monty wanted. "I believe the three years are doable."

Lolly shook her head. "Twenty percent of bakeries fail. What if mine is one of them?"

"I have a plan," Rick said. "The first part of the plan is to start a cut-and-run fund."

Shaun's logical brain could see why Rick was suggesting it, especially to the hesitant Lolly; but to Shaun, starting an escape fund seemed like a defeatist's attitude. He thought if Lolly started a business, she should be *all in*. No safety net. But he kept quiet.

"What you need to do," Rick said, "is open an account in which you deposit a percentage of sales. Normally, I would tell you to invest all your money back into the business—especially when just starting out—but in this case, you might want to have this fund to take some of the pressure off, if closing the bakery becomes imperative. Which brings me to my next point."

"Can I ask a question?" Lolly said. "What do I do if the bakery is doing okay but I get a teaching job out of the area and I have to leave?"

Rick nodded. "We're on the same wavelength. Well, sort of." He pulled over the rolling whiteboard normally used for brainstorming craft projects and wrote *Cut-and-Run Fund*. Underneath it, he wrote *Staff*. "I think it's important to start lining up staff immediately. While you're hiring, you need to think about who could manage the place in your absence, like if you're on vacation—or if you get a job elsewhere—so the bakery can keep going."

Lolly was writing something on the yellow pad balanced on her lap. "Okay," she said, "That's a good idea."

"It's just another safety net for you," Rick said. "You have to be comfortable signing the contract and running the business."

Donovan jumped in. "Lolly brought up a good point. We don't want Lolly to leave, but if she has to, do other people run the place indefinitely?"

Rick turned back to the whiteboard and wrote *Sell*. "You could always put the bakery up for sale if you have to move away semi-permanently. To manage that, I promise to help you find a buyer. Donovan will use his connections to help, too, won't you, Don?"

"Sure. With the way Sweet Home is growing, I expect it wouldn't be too hard," Donovan said.

Lolly put her hand to her throat. "But what about this deadline to get the bakery up and running? I don't know if it's humanly possible."

"What deadline?" Shaun asked, frustrated again.

Donovan fielded this question. "Monty has arranged for a TV news crew to do a story on the exciting growth of businesses in Sweet Home. They're featuring the lodge and the hardware store."

"And Tori's clothing company," Rick added.

Lolly frowned. "Monty wants the bakery up and running so it can be included, too."

"By when?" Shaun asked.

"By the beginning of the Pine Cone Fall Festival," Lolly said, sounding hopeless.

He could take some of her sadness away if he were willing to tell her what he'd been up to. But now wasn't the time or the place. He wasn't sure how Lolly would handle it. She might think he had been high-handed with her again.

"Getting the bakery up and running in time is doable," Rick declared. He shot Shaun a knowing glance. Shaun would have to talk to Donovan about blabbing to his friends! "As we know, everyone in Sweet Home likes to pitch in and help. If we can't get enough volunteers, maybe hiring help could be your ask, *Lolly.*"

"I wouldn't worry about volunteers," Shaun said. "We'll be able to rustle up plenty. But it would be great if Monty provided a fresh coat of paint to the outside of the building and a sign out front for the bakery. Some flower boxes for the summer months would be nice, too."

"That's a great idea," Rick said.

"Wait a minute," Lolly interjected. "I've actually given this a lot of thought. Yes, painting the outside and having a sign are good ideas, but I was going to ask Monty to pay for the lumber I'll need for built-ins."

"They can all be *asks*," Rick said. "They're all reasonable, because they will increase the value of the building."

Lolly stood up, holding in her hand something made of fabric. "I guess this is as good a time as any to tell you. I've decided on a theme for the bakery. It's *quilting*, which complements some of the other businesses in town, like the quilt shop within the hardware store, which has always been a tourist draw. But now that the lodge is holding quilting retreats, the bakery can complement it as well. When people stop by for coffee and a treat, I'll have posters up to advertise the other businesses. I'd also like the shop to sell quilt-related items." She held the fabric, which turned out to be an apron, to her chest. "Like this. Tori made it for me and it would be great to sell these in the bakery. I thought the Sisterhood of the Quilt might like to make things to sell in the shop, too. Piney could hang a couple of quilts in her windows. And any new businesses could do the same. I've been thinking Sweet Home could become known as the Paducah of the North."

"Wow!" Shaun burst out. "You have been busy since our trip." He immediately felt stupid for being so excited. Rick and Donovan were giving him knowing looks. He modulated his voice. "Everyone knows that Lolly and I went to Anchorage and checked out bakeries along the way."

"Yes, we heard," Donovan said. "Piney—and Patricia—had a lot to say on the subject of you two going off together."

"It was a business trip," Lolly said defensively. She sat down and Shaun could see she was as embarrassed as he was, since her cheeks looked a little seared.

Rick and Donovan exchanged glances but remained silent.

Shaun decided to change the subject. "You said something about Monty's percentage. What is he asking?"

"Two percent," Rick said. "I suggest Lolly say she can't go any higher than one percent, and then settle for one and a half. It doesn't hurt to negotiate, and if he says no, it's not that big of a deal." He wrote *1 1/2 %* on the whiteboard. "The rent breakdown is more than fair. Monty is only asking one-quarter of the going rent the first year, one-half the second year, and full rent the third year."

"Yes, that's very generous of Mr. St. James," Lolly said.

"If it's okay with you, I'll put your asks and adjustments in an email to McKenna. You don't mind me acting as your business manager, do you?"

Lolly looked so grateful that Shaun was worried she might burst into tears. "I don't know how to thank you for everything." Lolly turned to Donovan. "I really appreciate you taking a look at the contract and being here as well."

"It's my pleasure." Donovan stood. "I should run. I promised Ella I'd take her to get ice cream. You know, father-daughter time."

"Have fun," said Shaun, and Donovan gave a wave as he left. Shaun wondered if he'd ever be able to say he was off to spend time with a kid of his own. Probably not, at the rate he was going. But then he looked at Lolly . . . and she was looking back. Maybe she was thinking about her chances of being a parent, too.

Rick ran a hand through his hair. "Listen, while I have you two, I need to ask a favor."

"Anything. Just ask," Lolly said.

Rick continued. "Since Ava came into my life, Sparkle and I haven't had much alone time. Piney suggested I ask you two to babysit one evening so I can take Sparkle out to dinner. I know it's a lot to ask."

"Not at all. I'll be happy to babysit," Lolly said. She gestured toward the whiteboard. "I owe you. Besides, I love watching kids."

Shaun remembered Lolly's babysitting days fondly. In a selfish way, of course. Back then, he and Lolly would have an intense make-out session after the kids were down for the night.

Rick turned to Shaun. "Piney said you used to help Lolly when she watched the kids around town, when you two were kids yourself. I could tell Ava really likes you from when we were at Lolly's for the cake testing."

"Sure, I'll help," Shaun said. But he wasn't certain it was a good idea to be in such a tempting situation with Lolly again. He slapped a neutral expression on his face. "Just let me know when."

"I was thinking tomorrow. Sparkle likes this restaurant in Homer. It's a long drive, but she deserves something special after what I've put her through."

Lolly stepped forward and patted Rick's arm. "Don't worry. I've got this. Take all the time you need. Do you mind if I bring Thor with me? I know how much Ava likes him."

Shaun didn't like how Lolly seemed to be counting him out. He said quickly, "Yes, take all the time you need." Then an idea came to him. "Do you think Ava would like to have a sleepover-campout at Jesse and Tori's cabin? You know, since the plumbers still have the water off at your new place and there's not a lot of room in your small cabin at Donovan and Hope's. Ava could help me feed the animals; that would be fun for her, right?"

"A sleepover sounds like fun," said Rick, "and I appreciate the offer, but I think we should come back, even though it'll be late. I want to be there when Ava wakes up in the morning. The social worker said it's so important to be consistently present."

"Yes, of course," Lolly said, looking a little embarrassed, maybe at Shaun's mention of a sleepover.

"I totally get it," Shaun said. "Instead, we can have a pretend campout in the living room. We'll roast hotdogs in the fireplace and make s'mores. I'll grab a tent from Mom's house for Ava to play in. I bet Thor will like the tent, too. What do you say, Lolly?"

She hesitated for a second before saying, "Sure. We'll make it fun for her. I'll bring the supplies for s'mores. We always have extra around the house."

Rick looked satisfied and grateful. "Thank you both. Piney knew what she was doing when she said you two were the best babysitters."

But what Shaun couldn't understand was why Piney didn't offer *herself* to babysit Ava. He'd seen she was a natural when it came to the little girl. Whether Piney liked Rick or not, she'd been awfully sweet to Ava.

Shaun suddenly realized he had a couple of things to get done at Jesse's before they had their indoor campout. Like hook up the range. With Lolly in residence, there was bound to be some baking done. His mouth was watering just thinking about it. Knowing her, she'd get him and Ava involved, too, making them wear aprons and mix up batter. Suddenly, he was really looking forward to tomorrow. Even more so, to tomorrow night after Ava went to sleep.

They said good night to Rick and walked out together. Shaun stopped her before she got into her car. "Hey."

She turned to look at him, the full moon making her lovely features clear. "Hey."

"You're really going to have a bakery! I'm so happy for you, Lolls. Great job picking out your theme. I love all your ideas." He was getting excited, too. Shaun had decided to make the finished kitchen a surprise for Lolly. But now he wanted to do more, like finish up the *whole* inside before he gave her the big reveal.

She looked at her watch. "It's probably too late to call Olive tonight, isn't it?"

Shaun didn't want her talking to Olive because it would ruin his plan. "Yes. Try her in the morning." He would text Olive and tell her not to pick up when Lolly called. He hoped the older woman wouldn't give him away. "Listen, I was thinking . . . what if you came out to Jesse's cabin tomorrow after church? It would give us some privacy to go through my dad's clothes before Ava comes out to the homestead."

"You're right. I was thinking it wasn't something we could do just anywhere. Especially not at my house, with Jilly and Mom always in and out. Jesse's cabin is a good choice. But what about your mom? Doesn't she stop by every now and then?"

He shook his head. "Not since I told her to quit it. I explained she should get used to not popping in unannounced because Jesse and Tori would get sick of it pretty quickly. She hasn't dropped by since."

"But she might see my car coming down the driveway, headed for their cabin."

"Didn't you know a driveway has been added from Cemetery Road? Now there are two ways to get to their cabin. It's something I suggested to Jesse for extra privacy—they could come and go as they please without anyone knowing—and Jesse agreed. Dewey Winkle finished the road last week. You can't miss it. It's the second turnoff on the right, past the cemetery."

"I guess that covers it, then."

"We'll figure out the clothes for the quilt, and you can help me install the oven." He couldn't help but grin at her.

"Oh, I get it now. You want free labor. Will I be doing some painting, too?"

"I thought about asking you to paint their bedroom, but I don't think the paint fumes would be good for little Ava."

She grinned back. "But I suspect you'll keep me busy with something."

Oh, he thought of a hundred ways he could keep her busy, but none of them had to do with finishing up the cabin.

"Stop looking at me like that," she said, blushing.

"I was only thinking you could put that new oven to good use. Maybe make some goodies for us, plus some to put in Jesse's and Tori's freezer."

"That's a great idea. It'll be a nice welcome-home present. When will they be back?"

"He said the shoot was planned for four months, but it kind of depends on how production goes and whether there are delays. In any case I'll have their house done way before then." After that, Shaun would start on his own. "I'll see you tomorrow." He was tempted to give her a quick kiss, but there was no telling who might be looking out the windows of the lodge, or if Rick might catch them as he walked back to his cabin. It was for the best. Shaun needed to cool things down between them anyway. After all, he hadn't made any decisions about Lolly yet. He probably shouldn't have asked her to spend the day with him at Jesse's secluded cabin. And then playing house with Lolly as they watched little Ava for the evening? Shaun had lost his mind! The way he'd been acting, he wouldn't be coming to his senses anytime soon.

AS PINEY WALKED up the church aisle toward the exit, she was feeling quite proud of herself. Early this morning, she'd gotten a text from Courtney, who said her blind date with Benjamin last night had gone wonderfully. Of course, Piney couldn't take all the credit; she'd called Kit, the matchmaker, to find Courtney a businessman, one who lived in Anchorage. Maybe Courtney and Benjamin would get married. But if not, at least Courtney's focus would be off Shaun while the universe worked its magic.

Piney was also proud of what a good job she'd done of fixing it so Lolly and Shaun would be babysitting Ava tonight . . . a couple . . . alone at Jesse's cabin! Yes, Piney was quite pleased. What a win for her and the universe. And, well, for Shaun and Lolly, too. Except Pastor Joe's sermon nagged uncomfortably at Piney. Had he been directing the scripture specifically at her? *Not my will, but Yours, be done.* She should shrug it off. This wasn't the first time she felt singled out at church. The sermons often seemed aimed specifically at her. Once, Miss Lisa had asked Piney why she bothered to go to church since she talked so much about the power of the universe. Piney didn't understand the confusion; she was sure God had His hand in everything—the cosmos, the universe, the wind, the rain, and all.

Patricia passed her, looking unhappy; Shaun must've mentioned Lolly to her this morning. It was a shame mother and son weren't getting along. But, then, Piney and Sparkle had been having trouble, too, ever since Rick brought Ava to Sweet Home. Piney didn't know why Sparkle was so aggravated with her; she had only been speaking her mind. She caught up to Patricia and touched her shoulder. "May I speak with you for a minute?"

"Yes. What do you need?" Patricia seemed to be trying to calm herself with deep breathing.

"I'm wondering how you're feeling today. You look a little tense. Have you been drinking your special tea every morning?" Piney asked.

"The tea is lovely. But it can't fix my mood right now. I'm irritated. I saw Shaun talking to Lolly outside the lodge last night. This morning when I asked him what they were talking about, he clammed up. Do you know what's going on with those two?"

Piney put her arm around Patricia and began walking her to the Hungry Bear, thinking one of Lolly's cookies would be just the thing to settle her down. But she wouldn't say that just yet. "You should leave them to their own devices."

"Are you telling me to butt out?" Patricia said accusingly.

"I think you would be happier if you did. Shaun might be happier, too. You should trust that the universe knows what she's doing," Piney said. *Wait.* Those last words hit home and Piney stopped, bringing Patricia to a stop as well. "Ohhh."

"What's wrong?" Patricia asked.

"I just heard my own advice." Piney frowned, looking

off into the distance, knowing she hadn't been trusting the universe at all when it came to her own family. "I've always felt it was my right, actually my responsibility, to guide Sparkle in the correct direction and steer her out of harm's way." She looked back at Patricia. "I thought Rick's story about how Ava came about sounded fishy. But I was also worried that if it was true, other children might come forward in the future, and I asked Sparkle if she knew what she was getting into. But what I was really trying to do was guide her away from him. Rick reminds me so much of Sparkle's father. Not in his looks but how he acts. So carefree and charming to everyone. I've always suspected that Rick would eventually run off like Sparkle's father did, and we'd never hear from him again."

"Rick would never do that!" Patricia said adamantly. "He's a good man, a straight arrow, and has certainly proved himself to the whole community. He didn't hesitate at all when it came to Ava. He stepped up. As straight arrows do."

"I know. At least I know it now. I can see he's very genuine and nothing like Sparkle's father." Piney had been hard on Rick but was strangely proud of him now. "I see that Rick is actually perfect for Sparkle. She loves him so much, I shouldn't have interfered. He's devoted to Sparkle and seems to be a wonderful father."

"I know you care for Ava," Patricia said. "You have a way with that little girl."

"Maybe," Piney said. "She *is* a sweet little thing." But it was time to get back to Patricia's problem. "What do you say? Can you give Shaun room to breathe and quit worrying about Lolly? Let him make his own decisions? You and Dale did an amazing job raising those boys, and Shaun's a fine man now. It's time to let go, for both of us, you and me. Cut the apron strings. We could work on this together. Let our grown children soar. What do you say?"

"I'll think about it."

"Now that you're *thinking* about it, there's something I need to tell you."

Patricia looked wary. "What?"

"Shaun and Lolly are babysitting Ava tonight at Jesse's cabin." Piney watched for her reaction but didn't see anger, only resignation. "Are you going to be okay with it?"

"I guess I have to be," Patricia said with a sigh.

"Good girl," Piney said.

Patricia gave a sad chuckle. "I'm hardly a girl."

Piney patted her back. "Come to the store for a cookie? I have to relieve Uki at the cash register. Gotta take care of the after-church crowd."

"No. I'm heading home to rest." Patricia gave her a hug. "I'll see you later." She walked across the street to her SUV.

Piney couldn't help but turn back to look for Sparkle. She spotted the three of them coming out of the church—Rick holding Ava in one arm and clasping Sparkle's hand with his free hand—looking more relaxed than they had been lately. Maybe pushing the wedding date a couple of months had given them some relief. Plus, it gave Ava more time to adjust to her new life. At first, Piney had wondered if Ava would be the beginning of the end for Rick and Sparkle. But now, Piney could see that Ava might be the perfect addition to the start of Rick and Sparkle's life together. Maybe she should tell them so.

Ava reminded Piney of Sparkle at that age—shy of most folks. But Piney had one of her feelings—strong feelings—that Ava would outgrow her shyness and become a bright light in Sweet Home. Which forced Piney to admit, with some pleasure, that Ava had a bit of her dad in her. They certainly looked like father and daughter. And she felt like Ava could be a leader of the community one day.

Piney hurried over to Sparkle and Rick, determined to try to undo the awkwardness she'd created between them. "Would you come over to the Hungry Bear for noonday meal? Bill is bringing smoked ribs and I thought I'd take one of Lolly's pies from the freezer to throw in the oven." The pies Piney had ordered from Lolly had been selling fast, and she hadn't even had one yet.

"I don't think so," Sparkle said.

But at the same time, Rick said, "We'd love to." He looked at his daughter. "What do you think, little one? Do you want to have lunch with your gran?"

At *gran*, the last piece of Piney's hard feelings toward Rick cracked and fell away. She liked the sound of *gran*. It made her feel all soft inside. *Gran*. She was Ava's gran.

"Is that okay with you?" Rick asked. "Or do you have another name you'd like Ava to call you?"

Sparkle rolled her eyes. "When I was little, she always made me call her *Piney*."

Piney reached up and wiped a smudge from Ava's face. "But this is a different time, a different age. I like *gran*. Very much. What do you say, Ava, do you want to call me Gran?"

Ava stuck her thumb in her mouth, leaned her head against Rick's shoulder, and nodded yes.

"Then it's settled. I'm Gran. So will you come to the diner right now and we'll have lunch? As soon as I take care of the rush of customers first." Piney should've invited them sooner; she should've accepted Rick's situation sooner, too. Now she worried Sparkle would say no on principle alone. "And, Ava, if you like, I can start teaching you how to sew."

Ava's eyes lit up, though she still had her head pressed against her father.

Rick brought Sparkle's hand up to his lips and kissed it. "I think that sounds wonderful."

"It's settled, then," Piney said. "I'm going to teach you to sew just like I taught your new mama."

Sparkle looked shocked.

"You remember, don't you?" Piney said, trying to engage her daughter. "I punched holes in paper plates and you stitched them together by using a big needle threaded with yarn? You loved that." Sparkle didn't answer, so she turned to Rick. "If that's all right with you."

Rick smiled. "That sounds nice. I'd love it if Ava could

sew as well as Sparkle one day. I'm so impressed by all the beautiful quilts that Sparkle makes."

Piney put her arms out to Ava and the little girl didn't hesitate to climb right into them. "Let's go to the Hungry Bear and you can help me work the cash register while your mama and papa get lunch set up for us. Does that sound like fun?"

Piney expected her to nod like she normally did, but Ava pulled her thumb out of her mouth and said, "*Yes.*"

Rick and Sparkle looked at each other in amazement while Piney just turned back toward the Hungry Bear with her new granddaughter in her arms. No time like the present to start training Ava how to run the store . . . just like she had done for Sparkle.

Chapter 20

AFTER CHURCH, LOLLY ran home to pick up Thor. While she was there, she left a note for Jilly to explain that she and Thor were babysitting Ava, with strict instructions not to tell Mom that Shaun would be babysitting with her. Lolly was in and out of the house before her sister and mother made it back from church. She drove to Jesse's cabin, using the new driveway as Shaun had directed. Patricia's clothes box was in her trunk, where Shaun had placed it. She hadn't dared to take it out at home, lest her mother or Jilly ask her what was in there.

Yes, it was insane to take on another project, but Lolly was hell-bent on making headway today—getting the clothes sorted, distributing fabric to McKenna and Tori, and starting on Shaun's quilt. This urgency had to do in part with the bakery. There was this little hope inside her that the bakery would take off and be such a success that she wouldn't have time for anything else. Hadn't everybody said new businesses required at least five years of nonstop attention before you could take even a couple of days off? She'd read that somewhere. Anyway, she was anxious to get Shaun's quilt done.

And anxious to see Shaun himself. She should've gotten

her fill of him last night, but that's not how she was about Shaun . . . either back then or now. He'd texted this morning before church to let her know he would provide provisions for their indoor wiener roast, and the ingredients for Peach Puzzle, saying he hoped she'd make this upside-down peach cobbler for them as well. It was always one of my favorites, he wrote. As though she'd ever forget. She was really looking forward to this date that wasn't quite a date.

From a distance, she could see Shaun come out on the porch as she made her way up the driveway. Either she had excellent eyesight or she had perfect radar for him. When she pulled up in front of Jesse's cabin, Shaun was already in the yard, walking toward her car. He motioned for her to pop the trunk.

She figured he was in a rush, as he had the box of clothes out of the trunk before she and Thor even got out of the car.

"What's the hurry?" she asked. Thor went running after him.

"I want to make sure we have plenty of time to get these sorted before Rick drops Ava off."

That made sense. Lolly followed him inside the cabin and was wowed by the modern open plan and sleek kitchen. Thor took up residence on the big dog bed Shaun must've put there for Checkers. "Not your typical homestead cabin in Alaska."

"It was Jesse's idea. After the obstacles Tori had to overcome living alone on Monty's homestead, Jesse wanted to pamper her a bit."

"It's beautiful. You've done a great job." Lolly went into the kitchen to inspect the six-burner, two-oven range. "I thought you needed my help installing the stove." She ran her hand lovingly over the stovetop, wishing she could have something this nice at home. She immediately corrected herself; as Mom often said, it wasn't wise to get too big for your britches, because in the end, you had to wear them. Lolly was grateful she was receiving the grant to buy Olive's used kitchen equipment—although she was still waiting for Olive to text her back.

"Nah. It was no big deal to hook the range up," he said. "Listen, I was wondering—if it's not too much trouble—maybe you could make my mom a memory quilt, too, from my dad's things? I know she misses him every day." Shaun frowned, as if he'd added the ingredients of a recipe in the wrong order. "No, scratch that. Instead of making *my quilt*, like she wants, make one for her instead. I don't need a wedding quilt, at least that's what my mom sometimes calls them. Besides, I don't have plans to marry . . . *ever*." Ouch, that hurt. His ex had certainly done a number on him. But Lolly shouldn't forget that she'd done a number on Shaun, too.

"Well, I hope to get married someday," she said without thinking. "I'd like to have a family of my own. Some kiddos to bake and sew for, you know?" She felt shocked by her admission. These were things she hadn't allowed herself to dwell on, let alone say out loud. Love 'em and Leave 'em Lolly was the reigning queen of broken engagements, and she didn't deserve to dream about having a husband and family of her own.

"Was that why you got engaged so many times?" he asked, looking as serious as a mid-winter blizzard. The blunt question caught her by surprise.

"I guess so. But as I told you before, no one ever seemed quite right." Her cheeks went hot and she wished she could keep from blushing. She'd told Shaun that those other guys weren't *him*. "Let's change the subject."

"Agreed," he said. "But what do you think about my idea? Making a quilt for Mom instead of me?"

"Yes, I'll make your mom a memory quilt." To Lolly, there was no question both he and Patricia were going to get memory quilts of their own. Patricia to remember Dale, and Shaun to share with his future wife. "Let's get to sorting to see what we have here."

Lolly spread out a sheet she'd brought to put on the

beautiful hardwood floor. Thor came over and lay in the middle of it. They laughed. "I guess he wants to help."

"I guess so."

She pulled one of Dale's checkered shirts from the box. He'd worn this one Thanksgiving when Lolly had made the turkey and the pumpkin pies. "Which quilt should this go in?"

"Dad loved that shirt. His dress shirt, he called it."

"I know," Lolly said. "Good memories."

"Put it in Jesse's pile. I remember Dad wore that to Jesse's high school graduation." He stepped over to the box and looked inside. One by one, Shaun pulled out items and made decisions about where they would go.

"Dad's favorite work shirt," he said, holding up a worn chambray shirt.

"Which pile gets it?"

"Mom's," he said without hesitation.

"Good choice. But you're only picking stuff for Jesse and Luke and your mom. You need items for your quilt, too," Lolly told him. "Whether you like it or not, you're getting a quilt from the Montana Family Quilts project, too."

"Well, okay. But I know you're already booked to the gills."

"Here's something you may not know. Rick and Sparkle have pushed their wedding out until New Year's Day, so that's one less worry for right now. All I have is the crunch to prep the bakery for now. So I'm good. I really want to be the one to make your mom's quilt and"—she felt embarrassed to continue but she did anyway—"I don't mind making your quilt either. I promise to make it as easy and simple as possible, so you won't feel guilty about overworking me."

He grinned at her. "I promise not to feel too guilty you're making me a quilt, Lolls. Here." Shaun tossed a Sweet Home High football jersey, number eighty-eight, to her. He needn't have told her who it had belonged to. "You can put that in my pile, Lollipop. I can't believe Mom kept that old thing."

Lolly couldn't admit that it was *she* who had kept the jersey and had only dug it out last night before putting it in the box in the trunk of the car. It had been time for her to give the jersey up. *Give him up.* She smelled the jersey before putting it in Shaun's pile. It smelled of Downy and sunshine, as if Shaun had just walked onto the football field before a game.

"Did you just sniff my shirt?"

"Um, yeah," she said, owning it. "I wanted to make sure it had been washed thoroughly." She knew it had been—she had washed it last night.

As they sorted the clothes, Shaun shared stories of where the family was when an item was worn or something notable that had happened while one of them was wearing the garment. With others, he just smiled in recognition and didn't say anything at all.

"I really appreciate your help," Lolly said as Shaun handed her the last item. "You made the job so much easier."

"But now what?" he asked. "You have all these piles of clothes."

"Can you fetch my notebook from that gorgeous dining room table?" she asked.

He brought the notebook to her, and she flipped to the pages where she'd sketched out three quilts. "Here," she said. "When I thought I was going to make all three, I came up with three different designs. But now I'll only need to make two. Why don't you pick which one you want for yourself? I'll do something more feminine for your mom." Lolly thought maybe a Daisy quilt would be nice—Patricia had once said daisies made her smile. But she knew in her heart Patricia would love the Chevron quilt, a classic design. Lolly could put daisies on the tag on the back, though.

"You said you were going to make mine with simple blocks. I'm a simple kind of guy. Just make some big squares. Don't put a lot of effort into it."

Shaun was the opposite of a simple guy, at least in her eyes. He was multilayered and complex—keeping her at arm's length one minute and kissing her the next. But it was more than that. He was the last man who would want her to stay in Sweet Home. Yet, he had facilitated—no, *championed*—her getting the bakery. His actions didn't always make sense to her, and at the same time, he was perfect. He was kind to dogs and children. Intelligent. Fun. And she loved him more than ever. Yes, she finally had to own that, too.

From the moment she knew she would be making Shaun's quilt, she'd been racking her brain. Suddenly, an idea came to her. She'd make him a two-sided quilt. On one side, she would fashion a large pi symbol in the center with the value of pi in numbers bordering the outer edge of the quilt. The other side would have a computer monitor, keyboard, and mouse. Shaun's Pi-Computer quilt. Something totally unique for him. A quilt that he might remember her by in the future. She took the notebook and began sketching her ideas.

"What are you doing there?" he asked.

"Never mind what I'm doing. Do you have something to put Tori's and McKenna's fabric into? Two plastic bags or something?"

Thor got up and followed him. "Will garbage bags do?" he asked as he reached under the kitchen sink.

"That will be fine."

"We got those sorted quicker than I thought. What are we going to do now?" Shaun brought her the white kitchen bags.

"I have two pairs of scissors in my tote. Do you mind bringing them over here?"

"Why two pairs?" he asked, seeming suspicious.

She laughed. "Because I can't do everything by myself."

After bagging McKenna's and Tori's project fabrics, Lolly showed Shaun how to cut the remaining clothes on the seams. Then she gave him a homemade cardboard template so he could start cutting out pieces of fabric for Patricia's Chevron quilt. They both took an end of the dining table and got to work cutting.

"I'm impressed by how handy you are with those scissors," she remarked, so happy to get help.

"In first grade, I got double pluses for scissor technique," he said.

"Congratulations!" She chuckled.

"Seriously, though, Mom would sometimes have me help her with her quilts. A little rotary cutting here and there. Mostly, she had me snipping threads at the end."

"Multitalented," Lolly said. "And good to know. I hate cutting away all the threads after the quilting has been done. That will be your job, too."

"Are you going to make me work on my own quilt, then? Jesse and Luke don't have to work on theirs."

"We don't know what Tori and McKenna will make them do."

"Fair point." Shaun picked up the next piece of clothing and began cutting.

When the fabric had been cut and stacked, Lolly looked at her phone. "I think I have time to start sewing on some of these. Do you mind getting my sewing machine from the trunk of my car while I take Thor out?"

He grabbed her keys off the counter. "I'll be right back."

Thor wanted to go with Shaun, but Lolly picked him up and went out the back door. On their short stroll, she considered where to start and decided to work on the chevrons first. Ten minutes later, Lolly was set up and sewing away on her machine. Shaun chatted with her about the evening's activities as he fixed them sandwiches and orange juice. After they ate, he went to work transforming the living room into a campground a child would love, except for the tent, which he left for later.

"What else can I do to help?" he asked.

She opened her mouth, but she didn't get to answer, as Shaun's phone rang.

He frowned at the phone for a long moment, but finally picked up. "What can I do for you, Mom?"

"DO YOU HAVE a minute?" Mom asked. "I know Lolly's with you."

Shaun wasn't surprised his mom was checking up on him, but he was surprised at her tone. She didn't sound angry and disappointed as she usually did when Lolly's name was mentioned. "Yes, Lolly's here." He held Lolly's gaze while he said it. She looked half-panicked. He might as well tell his mom the rest of it. "The two of us are going to watch Ava for Rick and Sparkle tonight."

"Yes, Piney told me."

Shaun rolled his eyes. "Of course she did." Was Piney trying to cause trouble by stirring the pot? "What can I do for you, Mom? You must've called for a reason."

"I wondered if you could come over to the house for a few minutes . . . so we can talk." Mom never sounded as hesitant as she did right now.

Fear rose in him. "Are you feeling all right?"

"I'm fine. I thought, well, maybe you and I needed to get some things straight is all." If she'd been demanding, he would've told her no. But since she sounded calm, he said, "Yes, I have some time. I can run over right now." He hung up and looked helplessly at Lolly.

"Is everything okay?" Lolly asked. "How mad is she that I'm here?"

He shook his head, trying to make sense of it. "It's weird. She doesn't seem upset at all. You don't mind being here by yourself for a little while, do you?"

"Not at all. Besides, I'm not alone. Thor is here with me, and"—Lolly waved her arm over the table—"as you can see, I have plenty to do. I might even put your Peach Puzzle together and get it baked while you're gone."

He'd done a good job today of not kissing Lolly or leading her on, but as he walked past her to the door, he automatically leaned down and kissed the top of her head. She smelled like sunshine and happiness. *What the heck did I just do?* he demanded of himself. *It felt like second nature*, he defended. *It shouldn't. It really shouldn't*, he argued back, *and sunshine and happiness, dude, really?* He just wasn't the kind to wax poetic. "I'll be back soon."

He walked out of the cabin and headed over the hill to his mom's house. He'd been thinking of the homestead as *Mom's house* since he'd moved into Jesse's cabin. If Shaun didn't get a move on and buy a place of his own, he'd be back in his childhood bedroom as soon as Jesse returned with his bride.

When he summited the hill, he saw Mom waiting outside. He wasn't looking forward to this talk, but it was certainly overdue. He should've set her straight from the beginning.

When he stepped onto the back porch, he kissed her cheek before taking a chair. Checkers stuck her head under his hand, and Shaun obliged, scratching her behind her ears. "What's this all about?"

"I wanted to talk to you about Lolly." Mom seemed very chill for such a hot subject.

"Listen, Mom. Go easy on Lolly. From day one, she's been defending you and telling me to give you a break." He thought he needed to get the first word in before she let him have it. "And recently, I found out that her breaking up with me back in high school was never even her idea."

"If it wasn't her idea, whose idea was it, then?" his mom asked.

"Take a guess. You know Candy has always had a hold on Lolly, plus she's given her this overwhelming fear of commitment. Lolly has always been obedient to her mother . . . and to others. It must be exhausting for her to do what everyone else wants her to do." He took his mom's hand. "I've moved past what happened and I want to get along with Lolly. You know I love you. And I respect you. But I have to live my own life. I've been doing a pretty good job of taking care of myself, haven't I? I think so."

She patted his hand. "Shaun, I brought you here to tell you I'm going to butt out. You know I loved Lolly; it was just very hard to see her break your heart the way she did. You were miserable, and you couldn't get out of Sweet Home fast enough. Dad and I missed you, and we blamed her."

Shaun clutched his mom's hand. "I'm sorry I wasn't here when Dad died."

"I could've used you here, but I understand. You had your job and your life in Houston. And Tanya."

He sat back. "Now that I've had some time to think, the whole Tanya thing was a mistake. When I proposed, it was because I thought I should move on to the next phase of my life. Get married, have kids. I wanted what you and Dad had. I wanted that great love and everything that goes with it."

"And Tanya wasn't that girl?"

"No. Even in the beginning, I knew things weren't quite right. She didn't want the same things I did, like a house. She wanted to live in a downtown loft and schmooze with the upper echelon of Houston. Tanya made it sound shiny and fun, and it might've been fine for a while, but I knew I never wanted that in the long run. Not even a little bit." He gestured to the expanse of the homestead around them. "I wanted open spaces for our kids to run. I'm glad I'm finally home."

"But . . ." Mom prompted.

"But I miss my job. I was challenged every day by it. My brain needs that stimulation. I just haven't found anything to take the place of it here in Sweet Home."

"*Yet.* You haven't found anything yet," Mom finished for him. "Do you want Lolly to be a part of this life you envision for yourself?"

Shaun rubbed his forehead, hoping an answer would come. It didn't. "I'm not sure what I'm doing when it comes to her."

His mom gave him a knowing smile. "You never did, son. From day one, she's had a hold over you."

"When I came back to Alaska, I didn't want anything to do with Lolly . . . or any woman, for that matter."

"But now you do?"

"I don't know. It's what I've been trying to figure out. I can't exactly put my finger on it. My latest theory is that maybe I've been trying to save Lolly because she's going through a rough patch. But that's probably not true either, since most of the time she seems to have her act together better than I do." They were both quiet for a moment, as if they needed time to let that sink in. "It's my turn now: What are your plans as they pertain to Lolly? Are you going to be nice to her?"

"I'll be civil, but I'm not sure things can be how they once were. I'm still a little wary. But I have to admit, while I was sick she cooked and baked for me more times than I can count. I probably owe her an apology."

"I think so."

"My problem is, I'm afraid she'll break your heart again. Have you heard what they call her?"

"Yeah, she told me."

"Love 'em and Leave 'em Lolly."

"I hope you'll never call her that." For a second, Shaun considered telling his mom what Lolly was doing at this very moment—working on a quilt for her. Lolly was thoughtful and giving, even when her own life was a disaster. But he kept silent, knowing Lolly wouldn't want him to say anything. She'd want to share the news of the Montana Family Quilts project herself.

Patricia continued. "I told you I'd butt out. You're a big boy now—a man, actually—and you don't need your mom to tell you who you can and cannot date."

"We're not really dating. I'm not sure what we are. Friends? I don't know. Yeah, friends." *Really?* He didn't ache to kiss his friends the way he ached for Lolly. "But thank you for saying you'll let me manage my own life." He leaned over and hugged his mom. "You know you're the best, right?"

"I try. So, tell me what your plans are." Patricia smiled.

"First and foremost, I've enjoyed staying at Jesse's. I hope that doesn't offend you, but I need my own space."

"I know you do," Mom said. "I'm not offended. Your dad and I were so proud of you and all you have accomplished. You did it on your own."

"It wasn't completely on my own. You and Dad gave me a great upbringing, such a good start that it was inevitable, right?"

"Maybe so."

"I need to build a house of my own, or buy one. It would be nice if I could find a programming job I can do remotely. I really miss coding. But the most important thing is that you know I'm not abandoning you again. I'll still be here to work on the homestead. There's a lot of hours in the day and I'll be here for you, no matter what."

Patricia stood. "Compared to last year, I'm feeling much better. I expect I'll be back to my old self by the first snow-fall." She nodded at the hill he'd come over. "You better get back to Jesse's. What time will Ava be there?"

He looked at his watch. "Soon. Yes, I better head back." He pulled his mom in for a hug, and he was happy to feel the strength she'd regained in her tight hug back. "I love you, Mom."

"I love you, too, son."

WHEN SHAUN LEFT for his mom's cabin, Lolly popped up and nervously paced the floor, wondering what Patricia was saying to him. Probably something about calling the cops on Lolly and having her forcibly removed from Jesse's cabin.

Lolly picked up her phone and called her best friend, Paige, but the call went straight to voice mail. She left a message, "Call me as soon as you can."

While she had her phone, she pulled up "Be Alright" and hit the play button. Within the first few notes, her panic lifted and she felt better. She sang along loudly as Thor snoozed away in the dog bed in the corner. A minute into the song, Lolly felt calm enough to start on the Peach Puzzle. It was an easy recipe and she quickly had it ready to go. Since Shaun still wasn't back by the time the dessert went in the oven, she returned to sewing Patricia's quilt, while listening to the rest of the songs on the album, feeling okay inside and happy with the progress she was making on the quilt.

A while later, she heard the front door open. "Hey, I'm back. Wow, it smells good in here."

"Yeah, the Peach Puzzle is in the oven. Is your mom doing okay?" Lolly cared about Patricia's health, and at the same time, she wanted to know why Shaun had to suddenly go see her.

"She's doing all right." Shaun didn't seem in a talkative mood. "What can I help with next? Keep me busy."

The lightheartedness of earlier was gone, and there was nothing Lolly could do about it. Clearly, his mom had reiterated her position: Stay away from Lolly or else. Lolly wondered if it had been a mistake to work here at Jesse's. She was almost certain it was a bad idea to have them babysit together, even though she'd been looking forward to it. She glanced at her watch. It was too late to change the arrangements.

"I can give you something to do, but Rick and Sparkle will be here any minute with Ava." The timer went off and she moved the Peach Puzzle from the oven to the cooling rack. "Can you set a timer for thirty minutes? That's when I'll turn it over."

He pulled out his phone and a moment later, he said, "All done."

"Great—next thing. Come here." Lolly dug in her bag and found the six-inch plexiglass template she'd brought with her. She handed it to Shaun. "Can you trace around your dad's shirts and cut out the squares? They'll be for your quilt, okay?"

"Yeah, I can do that." Shaun laid out the first shirt and got to work. Soon, he seemed lost in his own thoughts. Lolly stopped herself from asking more questions. Maybe after Ava went to bed, he would open up and tell her what was going on.

Fifteen minutes later, Lolly heard a car pull up the gravel driveway.

"Rick and Sparkle are here," Shaun said, looking out the window.

Lolly quickly slid her finished quilt blocks and other fabric into the empty clothes box from earlier.

"Come on in," Shaun said, opening the door wide. Ava hid behind her new parents and didn't come out until Thor trotted over to greet her. Shyly, she reached out to him and he licked her hand.

"Thor is very happy you're here. So are we," Shaun said. "I've brought a pop-up tent for us to have our campout in the living room. A little later, I'll need your help to set it up, okay?"

Lolly picked up Thor's ball and rolled it past him, and he ran after it. As she hoped, Thor grabbed the ball with his mouth and brought it to Ava. "Thor wants you to throw the ball for him, Ava. Tell him to drop the ball. Say *drop*."

"Drop," Ava murmured.

Thor just wagged his tail at her.

"A little louder," Lolly said, "like this: *drop*," and her dog dropped the ball. "Roll it on the floor and he'll go after it." She went over to show Ava how to play fetch with Thor, while Rick gave Shaun Ava's backpack and Sparkle handed him a list of phone numbers and instructions.

Ava seemed to be having a good time. *All babysitters should have a helper like Thor*, thought Lolly.

Rick and Sparkle gave Ava hugs and kisses, reminding her they would be back after she went to sleep. She regarded them for only a moment before tossing the ball again, and the chase was on. They waved good-bye and Lolly and Shaun were alone with Ava.

When Thor retired to his water bowl to get a drink, Shaun coaxed Ava into setting up the tent with him, praising her for being such a good helper. "Lolly, can you bring the hot dogs and sticks over, while I add some blankets and pillows to the tent?"

"Yes. I'm hungry. What about you, Ava?" The girl nodded. "Want to help me in the kitchen?"

Ava came over and climbed on the step stool Shaun must've brought over. Shaun was thoughtful that way, always going the extra mile.

Lolly helped Ava fill a small tray with a stack of buns. On a bigger tray, she put the hot dogs, condiments, and sliced cucumbers, baby carrots, and celery sticks to dip into ranch dressing. Together they took their trays to the raised hearth in front of the fireplace. Shaun had made a small fire, Lolly noted appreciatively, so Ava would be safe.

Dinner was a huge success, except the first time Ava tried to put a hot dog on the stick, it fell and Thor quickly went for it, but Shaun snatched it up before the dog could eat it. After their main course, they sang silly songs around the campfire; Shaun turned "Mary Had a Little Lamb" into "Mary Had a Little Cow," which made Ava laugh. S'mores was a messy affair, but it was worth it to see Ava's delight. While Shaun took Thor out for an after-dinner break, Lolly guided Ava into the bathroom to wash up and dress for bed in her cute kitty pajamas. Ava then helped Lolly scoop out a portion of Peach Puzzle for each of them before Lolly carried the tray over to the fire.

When Shaun came back, he sat beside them and ate his final dessert. He couldn't stop grinning at Lolly as he ate bite after bite until his bowl was clean. He pointed to Ava's backpack. "Your dad said you brought some books. Would you like to get them out and we'll read them in the tent?"

Obediently, Ava pulled her backpack into the tent and dug out four books, all about cats, and Thor followed her in and lay down beside her. As Lolly settled in on the other side of Ava, and Shaun took his place next to Thor, she imagined them as happy sardines. Shaun picked up the first book and began to read in funny voices, making Ava laugh and laugh.

Lolly couldn't help but stare at him as he entertained Ava; *Shaun will make an excellent father one day.* His life partner would be a lucky woman, and their kids would be happy to have such a great dad.

"Here," he said, handing a book to Lolly. "Your turn."

"But I can't do voices," Lolly argued.

He looked at her with encouraging eyes. "Don't worry about it."

Lolly looked at the cover—*Kitty Cat's Marvelous Bakery.* She leaned up to smile at him before flipping to the first page. Kitty Cat's best friend was a mouse who stood on a little stool at the counter to help the customers.

"That's like me in the kitchen," Ava said, pointing to the mouse.

"Yes, it is," Lolly answered before returning to the story. Many of Kitty Cat's friends came into the bakery: a butterfly, a moose who had to duck his head to make it through the door, a monkey who paid for his pastries with bananas. Kitty Cat thanked the monkey, thinking of the banana bread she would make tomorrow. Lastly, a wise owl came into the bakery as Kitty Cat was closing for the day. Owl was the last customer, as she was only just waking up while the others were heading home to sleep. The last page in the book showed Kitty Cat putting her chef's hat on a rack, then climbing into bed and dreaming of what she was going to bake in the morning.

Ava listened intently as Lolly read, and Lolly gave her plenty of time to study the pictures on each page before turning to the next one. About halfway through, Ava laid her little head on Lolly's shoulder. The weight of her head and her warm little body cuddled up next to Lolly felt wonderful. How lovely to have a child there beside her. She ached for children of her own and wondered about the future. Her uncertain future. Her biological clock wasn't just ticking, it was clanging a metal spoon against a pie pan, making all kinds of racket, signaling that the time to start a family was *now*. Shaun was probably right; she suspected it was this—a family of her own—that had her accepting the proposals from her three ex-fiancés. Though each of those men might have made fine fathers and acceptable husbands, she'd crushed those lovely men, just like she'd crushed Shaun. She leaned over and looked at him, knowing her gut would never tell her to end it with him. He held her gaze for a long moment, and she knew she had to say something. "That was a great book."

"I thought you might like it." He picked up the next book and read, in a quiet voice this time. Ava's eyes were drooping and she gave two big yawns. By the time he finished this one, Ava was asleep and Thor was snoring softly, his head tucked under her arm. Shaun rolled on his side and, reaching over, took Lolly's hand. They lay like that for a while, Shaun stroking her fingers with his, until Lolly whispered, "We should leave her to sleep. Let's go make some peanut butter chocolate chip cookies. Sparkle said Ava loves peanut butter." Shaun nodded and they both slowly crept out of the tent.

But Shaun took her hand again as she turned to go to the kitchen. "The cookies can wait a minute. Sit with me on the couch for a bit?"

"Okay." She wasn't clear where Shaun stood, but there was no doubt she'd fallen completely in love with him again. Actually, she'd never stopped loving him. But holding his hand gave her hope . . . hope they were going to be a couple again.

"Is it a good idea?" she asked, but he was already pulling her into his arms and kissing her. The good feelings from this evening, and the days leading up to this moment, had her giving in, kissing him back . . . had her believing he loved her, too.

He stopped for a moment but didn't pull away; instead he gazed into her eyes, pushed her hair behind her ears, and said, "You've been kind of wonderful today. To Ava. To my mom for volunteering to make her quilts. To me. How do you do it?"

"Do what?"

"Just be so good all the time." He didn't give her a chance to answer, as he was kissing her again. She thought she'd died and gone to heaven. And hoped the moment would never end.

But uncertainty began to niggle at her and she pulled away. "Shaun, we have to talk."

"I'd rather keep doing what we've been doing." He leaned in to kiss her again, but she stepped back.

"You know I like being with you, but I have to know."

"Know what?" he asked, frowning.

"I have to know where this is going."

He turned away and ran a hand through his hair. "I don't know, Lolly. I enjoy being with you?" It came out as a question, as if he wasn't quite sure where he landed.

For her, that feeling of heaven was gone and reality was back. She might be confused about a lot of things, but at least she knew that she loved him. With all her heart. Shaun, on the other hand, was caught in some kind of conflict and didn't really know what he wanted. From her perspective, it felt a little like he was taking advantage of her, which was a position she never wanted to be in. While in college, she saw this happening to her friends all the time and she'd promised herself then that she'd never allow herself to get into a situation like this. But here she was! "You need to figure out what you want." She started to add that she'd wait for him to do just that, but self-preservation had her remaining quiet. She was proud of herself for taking a stand, even if she hated putting Shaun on the spot. He looked none too happy about it either.

Suddenly there was a buzz coming from his pocket. He

pulled out his phone as if it were his savior. "I have to take this."

It was probably his mom, calling to check up on him again. *Figures.*

"Hey, Brian, what's going on?" Shaun turned to her and mouthed, *My boss.* He turned away and nodded at whatever Brian was saying. "Uh-huh." He went to his messenger bag by the door, pulled out his laptop, and booted it up. He took it to the counter and sat at the last barstool at the end.

Lolly stood there, wishing Shaun would hang up and talk to her . . . tell her what he wanted. Instead, he kept talking to Brian, while she felt abandoned. No, let down. But maybe it was for the best. Who knew what might've happened if they had carried on as they were doing? For certain, her heart would've believed they were on the path to forever. She probably would've been picking out the dress for walking down the aisle and choosing names for their brood of children. Little Montanas to cook and bake for.

Shaun continued his phone conversation. "What about the backup? Hold on. Let me get on the server."

Though her lips were still tingling from that amazing kiss, she couldn't stand there all night looking like a doofus. She peeked in the tent and saw Ava was still sleeping. Next, she went into the kitchen, wishing Shaun were free to help her make the cookies. She washed her hands and pulled out the ingredients, forcing herself away from letting her wild imagination run wild any longer. *Down, girl*, she told her heart. The man at the computer right now wasn't her man. And he hadn't been in a long, long time.

"Okay, I'll call you back." Shaun hung up and laid his phone by his laptop, clicking and typing away and not looking up. "The plant is having a critical error. The woman I trained to replace me was in a car accident and is in the hospital undergoing surgery right now. Brian needs me to fix the bug for them." He looked up then. "I hope you understand."

"Of course I do." But her heart was sulking, where it had been happily pounding away only minutes before. As if she were alone in her kitchen, she silently creamed the butter and sugar by hand, added eggs, and sifted flour and baking powder, while Shaun typed and texted with his brows furrowed. Yet Lolly could see he was thrilled to be in his element, just as she was in hers, and though their evening together had been cut short, she was surprisingly happy for him, because he was doing what he loved. There was no denying it.

When Rick and Sparkle showed up hours later, Shaun only waved, still absorbed in his computer. Lolly quietly gushed over Ava to her parents, who both smiled proudly. Then she handed Sparkle the backpack and a Rubbermaid container filled with peanut butter chocolate chip cookies for Ava to have tomorrow, while Rick retrieved his daughter from the tent. Both he and Sparkle looked refreshed from having alone time together.

"Thank you both so much," Sparkle said. "We needed time alone to talk."

"Yes," Rick said. "We really appreciate you both."

"It was our pleasure," assured Lolly.

"Any time you need us," Shaun said, looking up briefly from his computer, "we're happy to watch her."

After Rick and Sparkle left, Lolly cleaned up the kitchen, packed the pop-up tent, and loaded her car. She wanted to put her arms around Shaun and kiss him goodbye. Instead, she stood at the door and called, "See you later." Without moving from his spot, Shaun waved to her. She went home feeling sad and kind of cheated.

The next morning, Shaun left Alaska for Houston.

Chapter 21

LOLLY FELT DISTRAUGHT as she walked to the bank, even though she should be elated; she was on her way to pick up the keys to the bakery. *Her bakery!* But she'd gotten a one-two punch first thing this morning. Olive had finally texted her, saying the kitchen equipment had already been sold. Next there was a call from Jilly, who had been out jogging when Shaun stopped her on his way out of town, asking her to relay the message that he was off to Houston. His excuse for not telling Lolly himself: no time to stop and text. Lolly couldn't help but recall one of Mom's favorite sayings: And the hits keep on coming.

Another text dinged and she rushed to look at it. But it was only one of Aberdeen's new connections ordering six loaves of poppyseed bread for delivery next Saturday, early. Lolly would need to pay Aberdeen a percentage of the business she was generating. She also needed to quit expecting every text to be from Shaun.

When she arrived at the bank, she slapped a smile on her face and knocked at McKenna's office door.

"Are you all right?" Apparently, McKenna wasn't fooled by Lolly's less-than-genuine expression.

There was no way Lolly was going to mention anything

about Shaun. Everyone already thought something had been going on between them. But apparently, there hadn't been. Not really. There was something on which she could blame her mood, however. "Truthfully, McKenna, I'm not okay. Tortellini's equipment has already been sold."

"Oh, really?" McKenna turned around and shuffled a few papers on her desk. "That's a shame. Did you make a decision about the contract?"

"Yes." Lolly pulled it from her bag. "It's all signed." If she was going to be ready by the Pine Cone Fall Festival, she would have to order equipment today. Hopefully, it would arrive in time. But with the way things were going, she doubted it. As excited as she'd been over the weekend, today the bakery felt doomed before it even got started.

"Here, I'll trade you." McKenna took the contract and handed over the keys. "I'll make sure the grant money is transferred into your account. Uncle Monty had me take care of a couple of things already. The electrical and plumbing have been inspected and are in good condition. Aberdeen told me Dewey Winkle is a fantastic artist and has offered to paint a sign for you, if you like. I wish I had some champagne for us to celebrate." But Lolly wasn't in a clinking-glasses mood. "Don't hesitate to call if you have any questions." Why did McKenna seem so jumpy?

"Thanks. See you later." Before Lolly was even out of the bank, the long list of what had to be done was roiling through her brain, enough to give her a migraine. She considered stopping at A Stone's Throw Hardware & Haberdashery to check if they had the light blue paint she'd asked about, but she decided to see the building first. She knew from peeking in the windows with Shaun that she had her work cut out for her.

She hurried toward her—*her*—storefront and jumped when another text came in. It was only Jilly, wondering how she was doing. But there was no time to answer her now. Lolly unlocked the door and stepped inside—only to stop abruptly, shocked at what she saw. It was almost too much to take in. The wainscotting had been painted Lolly's perfect light blue, while the walls above it were a light cream and the crown molding and baseboards white. The whole place looked fresh and inviting, modern with a touch of traditional. Three display cases were positioned just the way she had drawn them in her bakery binder. And if Lolly wasn't mistaken, they looked a lot like the ones Olive had been selling. The hardwood floor was waxed and polished. The windows were clean. An old-fashioned cash register that looked exactly like Olive's was sitting on the checkout counter. Tortellini's tables and chairs were all set up, too. "What in the world . . ."

She rushed across the room and pushed through the swinging doors to get to the kitchen. It had been painted in the same calming light blue as the wainscotting. All the cooking utensils were hanging from the chrome shelves, which looked exactly like the ones from Tortellini's. The gleaming stove, refrigerators, and ovens were in the perfect spots, exactly how she'd drawn them in her notebook. Only one person knew her bakery notes as intimately as she did, especially since he'd studied each page while on their road trip. He'd probably taken pictures of the layout when she was in the bathroom or on the phone with Jilly in the bedroom of McKenna's apartment.

She turned around and marched out of the building, locked it, and stomped her way back to the bank. McKenna was outside, casually leaning against the wall.

"Hey, stranger," she said, smirking as if this were some kind of joke.

"How did Tortellini's equipment get in the building?"

"You'd have to ask Shaun."

"Who paid for the equipment?"

"You'd have to ask Shaun."

"Cleaned up and painted?" The only things left to do were to fill the shelves with ingredients, paint the outside, and hang a sign. Perhaps fill the bakery with gift shop items for the patrons to buy, too.

McKenna pushed away from the wall, turned Lolly around, and started walking them along. "Let's get a coffee at the Hungry Bear and I'll tell you everything I know."

"What about the bank?"

"I told Luke that you and I were going for coffee."

"I'm angry with you," Lolly said.

"That's okay. I can take it."

Lolly was furious that Shaun wasn't here so she could yell at him. He didn't have any right to do these things for her. He'd done too much! Even if it were okay with *Lolly*, when Patricia found out, she would lose it! And then blame *her!* Shaun hadn't thought this through. What gave him the right to make all kinds of decisions without her approval?

The last thought made her stop, though, which brought McKenna to a halt, too, right in front of the Hungry Bear. *Shaun hadn't made* any *decisions*. He'd used her bakery binder as a step-by-step guide, doing all the things Lolly planned to do herself, if she ever had the opportunity. She pulled open the door to the Hungry Bear and waited until McKenna walked in. Lolly followed, saying in as calm a voice as she could muster, "We're here. Start talking. Tell me when Shaun got the equipment."

"I don't know, I think a day or so after you two got back from your adventure. Not to sell my husband down the river or anything, but Luke helped him haul the equipment and install it. Go get us a booth. I'll bring over the coffee." McKenna poured two cups and brought them to the booth. As soon as she was seated, Lolly hit her with more questions.

"Who painted the place?"

"Shaun and Luke."

"So, Donovan tattled to Shaun about what paint colors I wanted."

"*Tattled* is kind of a harsh word. I think you're the one who told Donovan about the paint, so that one is all on you."

"You're enjoying this, aren't you?" Lolly felt so many emotions she didn't know what to do with them.

"Yep," McKenna answered, smiling broadly.

"Am I to assume Shaun solely paid for the equipment?" Lolly said.

McKenna shrugged. "That I can't say. I'm not allowed to share transactional information from one bank customer to another. You know, for legal reasons and all."

"Great," Lolly said. Well, she'd just have to write Shaun a check when he returned home. But the thought that had been haunting her since Jilly called this morning was . . . *What if Shaun didn't consider Sweet Home his home anymore?* What if he'd gone *home* to Houston to stay?

"Give Shaun a call," McKenna said.

"I will." But Lolly didn't know what to say. She took her phone out and looked at it. She was too angry to speak to him right now. She set her phone on the table facedown. Why hadn't Shaun texted *her*? He was the one who had disappeared. He should be the one to contact her now. "I expect he's on a plane somewhere over the Lower 48."

"What?"

Lolly rolled her eyes. "Wow, at this point, I can't believe I know something you don't already know." Which made her feel like the laughingstock of Sweet Home for all Shaun had done for her without telling her. "Shaun's on his way to Houston, or at least that's what he told Jilly on his way out of town. His old boss called last night and needs him, apparently."

"For how long?" McKenna asked.

"Your guess is as good as mine."

Piney sauntered up to the booth. "Scooch over, McKenna." As soon as she was seated, she patted the table. "The Sisterhood of the Quilt is all in and will start showing up today to help with whatever you want. I hear you're going to have a quilting theme for your bakery. I like it. I like it a lot." She pulled a notepad from her pocket. "Tell me what you need, and I'll make sure you get it. But first, drink your coffee before it gets cold." Piney looked at McKenna. "Make sure to pay for that before you leave."

"Aye-aye," McKenna said with a salute. "Well, Lolly sure was surprised by all that's been done."

Piney reached across the table and patted Lolly's hand. "Don't worry about a thing, Lollipop. We'll have the place in tiptop shape before the grand opening. You know the Sisterhood of the Quilt can *quilt* that place up from head to toe."

Lolly pulled her hand away and took a sip of coffee, which wasn't easy, as her hands were shaking. If only Shaun were here. He would make her feel calm and confident—after she gave him a piece of her mind for sneaking around behind her back. She wasn't completely sure she could trust him anymore, after all he'd done.

But it was all for me. Of course she could trust him. And now he was gone.

Well, maybe it was good he was gone. With him away, she could concentrate on the bakery . . . instead of on him. Or, on worrying and wondering when he was going to pull her into his arms and kiss her again.

Her phone dinged with another text. Lord, she was being sorely tested. It was probably just Jilly again, or someone else, but it wouldn't be Shaun.

After the follow-up ding, McKenna chuckled. "Aren't you going to check that?"

"No. I'll look at it later." Lolly took another sip of coffee.

McKenna grabbed the phone from the table and looked at it. "It's from Shaun. He says—"

"Give it to me." Lolly yanked the phone away from her. She flipped the phone over and read the first line of the notification. Sorry I didn't text before I left town. Boss . . . She had to enter her passcode to read the rest. Boss really needs me in Texas to fill in for a while. In Seattle, boarding now. That was all. He could've said something more. But no, he'd left her dangling, which was nothing new. He'd been stringing her along now for quite some time. And she'd been happy to be strung, because it was Shaun, after all. Her Shaun.

But he wasn't *her* Shaun. He'd been clear that he wasn't *clear* about anything when it came to her. Lolly wished now she'd protected her heart more, instead of falling in love with him again. Even more in love than before.

"Aren't you going to text him back?" McKenna asked.

Not with everyone around, Lolly thought, but didn't say it. "Maybe later. I really should get to work on the bakery. Besides getting everything ready there, I have orders to fill." Plus, finish Patricia's quilt, and Shaun's quilt, too.

Lolly scooted out of the booth and stood. "I'll see you later. Thanks for the coffee."

Piney waggled her notepad. "What do you want me to put on my list?"

"There's so much to do." Lolly had copied the list from her bakery binder into her phone, as she was adding to it continuously. She pulled out her phone now. "Can you arrange for the Sisterhood of the Quilt to help me move all my ingredients to the bakery first thing?" That big bread order was due soon. "I'll place an order from the Hungry Bear after I make the list for next week's baking schedule." She scanned her to-do list. "Let's see . . . I need to switch over the electricity and water into my business's name. The outside of the building needs to be painted. Can you help me find the right person or persons? Jilly and Mom came up with a cute logo for the shop." Lolly reached into her bag and pulled out the printed design, which sported a happy bowl, a whisk, and a cupcake. "Can you get that to Dewey so he can add it to the sign?" She needed to buy software to keep track of inventory and to set up a point-of-sale system. "Also, I need someone to source cleaning supplies, hair nets, gloves, and other items like that. Scratch that. What would be more helpful is a list of supply distributors."

"Yes, you'll need a distributor for all kinds of things for your business." Piney held up the new logo. "What about napkins with your name and logo on them?"

"That's a great idea." Something else to add to the to-do

list. Just thinking about everything that needed to get done was making Lolly feel overwhelmed.

Piney took her hand and squeezed. "This is all doable, Lollipop. You have me and the others to count on. Don't you worry one bit."

"Thank you. That means so much. I better go." But instead of heading back to the bakery, Lolly headed home to get Thor. She needed him with her while she figured out what was top priority at the bakery.

She didn't trust herself to respond to Shaun just yet. Her emotions were raw. The rawest of all was the hurt from thinking he didn't care enough about her to tell her he was leaving.

She suddenly wondered how Patricia was taking it, the fact that Shaun was gone. What if Shaun hadn't told his mom that he was leaving either?

She pulled out her phone and texted Jilly. Can you let Patricia know about Shaun?

Jilly wrote back. No need. He mentioned he'd said goodbye to her after he fed the animals.

Of course. He'd never skip out on his mama. Lolly was sure he'd made arrangements for someone to help out on the homestead, too, as he'd done when they were on their shop-hop adventure. He was very organized, and she sure could use his help right now.

For the rest of the day, Lolly made notes, answered questions from the quilters who stopped by, and made a schedule of how to get the shop open and functioning before the Pine Cone Fall Festival. She wouldn't even think about the TV interview or being on camera because she couldn't squeeze one more worry in right now.

After everyone cleared out for the day, she and Thor headed home, though her dog kept looking around expectantly, as if Shaun might show up any minute. "It's just you and me, little man." Once she was home, she grabbed a cheese stick and an apple from the fridge and headed to her room, where she set up her sewing machine on the small table she and Jilly shared as a desk. Lolly hadn't even considered trying to keep the Montana Family Quilts project from her sister, with whom she was sharing the room. Jilly would surely give her some ribbing, teasing her that she must have a huge crush on Shaun to do so much for his mom. Lolly immediately went to work, piecing the top, deciding to worry about the ribbing when the time came.

A few hours later, Jilly peeked her head into the room. "Are you going out to the lodge tonight? The Sisterhood of the Quilt wants you to parcel out tasks."

"Just give me a minute to splash some water on my face, okay?" Lolly figured there would be no rest from here on out. She quickly shoved the newly finished quilt top out of sight and into one of her cloth shopping bags to take with her.

When they went outside, Lolly headed to her car.

"I thought we'd ride together," Jilly said.

"I may need to stay late." That is, if she could get Hope alone to tell her what she needed her to do. Which was to put Patricia's quilt on the longarm and start quilting it.

"All right. I'll see you there."

At the lodge, things went as Lolly expected. Piney took charge and made a signup sheet for everyone who wanted to help get the bakery going. There were two more signup sheets: one for making quilted items for the shop—decorations as well as items for sale—and the other for people interested in working at the bakery. It warmed Lolly's heart to think that the women of Sweet Home, for whom she cared so much, could make extra money by participating in her bakery venture. Lolly looked at the list of potential employees. Her favorite high school students—Ella, Lacy, Annette, Uki, and Ruthie—had all added their names to that list. Below them was a name that could've knocked her over with a feather . . . *Patricia*.

Lolly's head snapped up and she looked around the room to find Shaun's mom. There she was looking back at Lolly with the same eyes Shaun had. Patricia tilted her head and gave a tiny shrug. Lolly gave her a small wave back, trying not to make a big deal out of it. But it was a big deal! Questions bounced around in her head. Was this the beginning of a truce with Patricia? Did Shaun make this happen before he left? Was there another shoe about to drop?

Patricia ended her conversation with Aberdeen and made her way over to Lolly. "I saw only teenagers had signed up so far and thought you might need an adult to keep them in line." If anyone could keep kids in line, Patricia was certainly the one to do it.

"Thank you. That's very kind." Lolly wanted to say more. Wanted to hug her. But Patricia only nodded and walked over to Miss Lisa, who was laying out several different color combinations for patchwork curtains. Lolly wished she could tell someone what had just happened; she wished Shaun was here.

McKenna came over and muttered, "I need to talk to you." The whole room stopped talking and seemed to lean closer to hear whatever news McKenna had. But she took Lolly's arm and dragged her out into the hall.

"What's up?"

"I told Hope you need to schedule time on the longarm." McKenna winked at her. "By yourself."

"You certainly do take the initiative, don't you?"

"I assumed you needed to reserve some time without everyone finding out. Sorry." But she didn't look sorry at all. "Also, I thought you and I could get together and piece our quilts. I assume you still have piecing to do?"

"I've finished Patricia's top," Lolly whispered, "but I need to piece Shaun's."

"Good. It'll be fun to get in some sewing time together. How about at the bakery, after you're done working there tomorrow?"

Lolly guffawed. "It feels like the work will never be done. But come by when you close the bank, and we'll set up our sewing machines."

They slipped back into the bustling sewing studio, where everyone was working on Lolly's bakery. She had decided to have separate quilt blocks on the wall above the display case with bakery items printed underneath to give the place a cohesive quilty feel. Jilly and Mom took ownership of that project and they were turning out nicely. Lolly hadn't been sure the shop would come together in time, but her family and the Sisterhood of the Quilt were really putting their hearts into making it happen, which only made Lolly love them more.

Eventually, the group broke up and went home, until only Lolly and Hope remained. Lolly wondered how long it would take her to longarm Patricia's quilt.

"I thought I'd stick around and help you set up," Hope said, taking Patricia's quilt top from Lolly's bag. "You're very sweet to work on this quilt for Patricia, especially since you're so busy."

Lolly felt her cheeks flush. "I'm happy to do it."

Ella wandered in and helped her mom put it on the machine. "Ms. Crocker, can I do the longarming? I've gotten pretty good. Mom, tell her."

Hope smiled proudly at her daughter. "She seems to have a knack for it."

Lolly was overwhelmed with gratitude. She wasn't good about accepting help, but it was something she'd been getting used to since returning to the amazing community that was Sweet Home. "Sure. If you want to, Ella."

Lolly explained the all-over floral design that she thought would contrast nicely with the chevrons, and Ella got started with Hope looking over her shoulder.

Lolly pulled out Shaun's quilt fabric and began cutting out the rest of the quilt pieces for her pi and computer designs, feeling lighter than she had before. She was still upset that Shaun was gone. But quilting was therapy, something her mom had often said. In this case, it was even more. With nearly every piece of clothing or fabric, a pleasant memory came back to her. Instead of tamping it down as she usually did, she opened her heart to the recollections . . . and how each one made her smile.

"Lolly?" Hope looked at her watch. "It's getting late. Piney said she'll have a crew at the bakery first thing in the morning, remember?"

Reluctantly, Lolly put her scissors and rotary cutter away, along with the fabric. "Yes. Thanks. I'd lost track of time." She glanced over at Ella, who was still working on the quilt. "You're doing a marvelous job! Thank you! But it's a school night. I don't want your teachers mad at me because you didn't get enough sleep."

Ella glanced over at her mom. "I'll quit in five minutes, promise."

"Okay." Hope helped Lolly gather her things and take them out to the car.

"It's been a good day. You and Ella have helped so much."

"It was my pleasure. And Ella's pleasure, too." Hope waved as Lolly exited the lodge's circular driveway.

The next morning Lolly was setting up the kitchen at the bakery when Hope came through the swinging door with a dark plastic bag.

"All done," Hope said.

"You didn't." Lolly hurried over to see.

"I couldn't sleep so I finished it up. I thought you could do the binding tonight."

Lolly took the finished quilt in one arm and hugged Hope tightly with the other. "How can I ever thank you?"

Hope got a mischievous look on her face. "You know that Christmas stollen you brought to the wine tasting last year? I'd like two of them for our family, when you start the holiday baking."

"Done," Lolly said, knowing she was the luckiest person in the world to live in Sweet Home, Alaska, and have such wonderful friends—wonderful friends who quilted!

As promised, when the bank closed, McKenna came to the bakery and hung around while the other quilters cleared out for the day. When they were gone, she brought her sewing machine and fabric in. The two of them chatted and sewed and Lolly made great strides on Shaun's quilt before McKenna packed up and hurried home to her hubby.

That night, before Lolly started working on the binding for Patricia's Chevron quilt, she put a pan of cinnamon raisin bars in the oven. Then she went to her room, put on *The Great British Baking Show*, and handstitched the binding.

THE FIRST THING Lolly did when she woke up was to text Patricia: Can you come early to the bakery? She knew Patricia was an early riser and wasn't surprised when she received a text seconds later. Sure. 7:30?

Lolly was so nervous about seeing Shaun's mom she could barely put the cinnamon raisin bars in a container for her. Before bed last night, she'd wrapped the quilt in tissue paper and made a bow out of scraps of fabric for an old-fashioned but festive look.

Lolly hurried to the bakery and unlocked the door, hoping no one would bother them. She set the gifts—the quilt and cinnamon raisin bars—on a table and paced. She was starting to regret what she'd done, beginning with going into Patricia's house and taking the clothes she'd set aside for memory quilts. Lolly had doubted herself many times in the last few days, but not as much as she was doubting herself now.

The door opened and in walked Patricia. "What do you need? Do you have the work schedule figured out? I'm pretty flexible as long as I can get a few chores done in the morning before work. Dewey, thankfully, has mostly taken over caring for the animals."

Lolly bit her lip and then decided to get it over with. "I did something I'm worried you aren't going to approve of."

Patricia's face had been neutral when she came in the door, but now she frowned. "What did you do?" It wasn't a question really, more like an accusation.

Lolly walked over to the wrapped quilt sitting on the table and gave it a little shove in Patricia's direction. "Here." She felt like her face was contorting as she searched for the right words. "Just know I did it because I care about you. I promise it wasn't to make you mad."

Patricia's frown deepened as she walked over to the package and tore it open. "What—?" She was definitely surprised. "What is this?" Lolly couldn't tell if she was shocked in a good way or a bad way. And Lolly didn't answer her question; instead she let Patricia figure it out for herself. "How did you know about the memory qui—?" Patricia stopped and nodded. "Oh, I remember now. I told you that day, when I was so sick, and you brought me bone-broth soup."

"Yes," Lolly said in a whisper.

"I don't understand. Are you trying to get on my good side? You know I already told Shaun I was butting out of his business, including whatever you and he are getting up to."

"Oh—oh, no, he didn't tell me. But that's not why I did it. I just wanted to help you. I figured all the baked goods in the world couldn't equal what those quilts would mean to you."

"Quilts?"

"Oh, yeah." Lolly had to tell her the rest. "McKenna is making Luke's quilt and Tori is making Jesse's."

"And Shaun's quilt? I assume you're making his?" She didn't sound angry, only reconciled to the thought.

"Yes. I'm making Shaun's so it will be done, and you won't have to worry about it any longer." The next part was going to be hard to say, but Lolly was going to say it anyway. "It's for Shaun and whomever he marries." In other words, Lolly was telling Patricia—and herself—that she wasn't expecting to be in the picture. For a moment, she wondered how long it would take for him to find someone new in Houston.

Patricia nodded, seeming to accept what Lolly was saying. "You know, for a long time, I loved you as a daughter."

"I know. Before I messed everything up." Lolly wanted to tell her how much she had loved her, too, how she'd learned so much from her just by being around her. How to be a good wife. A good friend and confidante. A good mother. Lolly loved her own mother, but she wasn't the nurturer that Patricia was.

"Shaun told me it was Candy who put you up to breaking it off with him," Patricia said.

Lolly didn't reply; it felt disloyal to her mother.

"But I have to know . . . did Candy tell you to break it off with the other men you've been engaged to, or was it just Shaun she didn't want you to marry?"

Now Lolly had to defend her mother. "Mom loved Shaun; she still does. She wanted me to have fun at college and date a lot only because she never got to. She somehow convinced me I was too young to be serious about Shaun and shouldn't let myself be tied down at the same age she was." Lolly cleared her throat, which was filling with emotion. "About the other engagements, that was all me. Actually, my gut, if I'm being honest. Each time, after getting engaged, my stomach would start hurting, and wouldn't let up until I broke it off." *Love 'em and Leave 'em Lolly at her finest.*

Patricia stared at her for a long moment before continuing. "And with Shaun. Has your stomach ever hurt because of him?"

"No. But I've never been engaged to Shaun." There was so much more Lolly could say. She could tell Patricia that she'd never stopped loving Shaun, but what good would that do? Lolly could tell her about her fear of becoming like her father. That it would make no difference what she did; her genetics would surely always have her breaking the heart of the one who loved her. But she thought there was really only one thing Patricia wanted to know. "There's nothing going on with Shaun and me. Nothing much anyway. We're just . . . friends." Actually, Shaun had disappeared without a word, so Lolly had to assume she'd been nothing more than a convenience for Shaun, a girl to kiss in the land that was short of women.

Patricia nodded. "I see." But Lolly felt so confused she didn't exactly know what she was seeing.

Patricia ran her hand over the quilt lovingly. "The quilt is beautiful. Lolly, I can't tell you how much this means to me. Come here, sweetheart." She pulled Lolly into her arms and hugged her, a real hug, like only Patricia could give. She kissed Lolly's head and held her tighter.

Lolly choked back a sob. "I've missed you," she said into Patricia's shoulder. "I was so scared when you were sick. You don't know how much you've meant to me." As a teenager who couldn't understand her own mother, Lolly looked to Patricia to guide her into young adulthood with love and compassion and some straight talk.

"You mean so much to me, too. I'm sorry I was angry. I should've known it was your mother's fault."

Lolly pulled back a little and wiped her eyes with her hand. "No, I'm to blame. I didn't stand up to her when I should've. Mom was coming from a place of hurt and only wanted me to have a better life than she'd had."

Patricia pulled a package of tissues from her purse. "Here. You're right about your mom. She had a tough go of it, and I admire how well you girls have turned out. She did it all on her own."

Sweet Home had been there to help them. And Patricia had been extra help for Lolly when she'd needed her.

"Do you think you can forgive me for hurting Shaun?" Lolly asked earnestly.

"It's me that needs to ask for forgiveness. I never should've blamed you. I felt like Shaun abandoned us when he left for Texas with his heart broken, and I guess it was easier to be angry at you than at him. But you had no control over what he did. Will you forgive me for being angry and bossy and for trying to come between you and Shaun?"

Lolly was in shock and had to blow her nose before answering. "Of course I forgive you. You're my second mom."

Patricia was teary-eyed, too, and took a tissue for herself. "Let's spread out this quilt and let me get a good look at it." They each took a corner and Patricia examined the fabrics. "It's incredible. I love it so much. Did you know I love chevrons?"

"Yes, I knew." Lolly tilted her head toward the container she'd moved to a chair. "You love cinnamon raisin bars, too."

"You do know me well," Patricia said, gathering the quilt in her arms and hugging it. "I'm sorry I didn't come to my senses sooner." She gave Lolly a meaningful look. "What can I do to get you and Shaun back together?"

Lolly felt her cheeks flush. "I don't think there's anything you can do. He said he needs to figure out how he feels."

It felt strange to say that out loud because it was like she was only hearing it for the first time. Her attitude shifted, too, and she was mad at Shaun Montana. By golly, if a man loved her, he should know it, and not have to balance the pros and cons of the relationship in a spreadsheet, or whiteboard his feelings for her before deciding whether to be with her or not.

Without warning, a realization hit Lolly, rocking the foundation she'd stood on her whole life. She, Lolly Ann Crocker, had to start living for herself and stop waiting on tenterhooks for Shaun to make up his mind. Yes, she loved Shaun, but somewhere along the way, she'd forgotten to love herself.

"What's wrong?" Patricia asked.

"Nothing's wrong. I just figured something out. Something I should have been doing all along."

"Good." Patricia gave her a look as if she'd been reading Lolly's mind and she approved. Patricia liked women who were strong and decisive, and that was exactly the woman Lolly was going to be from here on out.

Chapter 22

FOR THREE WEEKS, Shaun had been working intensively, stopping only for short breaks and to sleep. He'd assumed he and Lolly would stay in constant contact, but from the start, her replies to his messages were distant texts—Sorry. So busy. We'll catch up later. He was getting worried. Hadn't their time together meant anything to her? What about the kisses they'd shared?

He sent long emails about the job, good and bad. He told Lolly about seeing Tanya, how they'd had coffee at Starbucks, and he'd wished her well in her new marriage. He asked question after question about the bakery and about Lolly's grand opening, even after his mom told him it was a great success. When the news crew came to town, Shaun expected Lolly to let him know how it went, but it was his mom who told him Lolly had done a wonderful job of representing the town, that she was a natural in front of the camera. Shaun was starting to feel desperate. Though Brian was thrilled with his work, Shaun's budding relationship with Lolly had somehow gone off the rails. She hadn't even acknowledged his last email or the three voice mails he'd left on her cell. Finally, he called Patricia.

"Mom, is something going on with Lolly?"

"Oh, I don't know. She's so busy. We all are. I'm the afternoon manager, which gives me time in the morning to work on the homestead." Shaun was shocked by this news and wasn't sure what to say.

"You aren't overdoing it, are you?" he finally asked. "Dewey's supposed to be doing the heavy lifting."

"Oh, I'm fine. Lolly said I can work around how I'm feeling. Besides, Dewey has been a great help. Don't worry about me."

He hated to spoil the surprise, but he had to know if Lolly had finished the Montana Family Quilt for his mother. "Did Lolly say anything about working on a quilt?"

"Oh, didn't I tell you? Lolly made me the most beautiful Chevron quilt. It includes fabric from your dad's clothes, and yours and Jesse's, and Luke's, too. It was so sweet of her to take time out of her busy life to make it for me. Did you know I've been wanting to make all you boys a quilt like that for years?"

His mom sure had turned around where Lolly was concerned. "Yes, I knew. Did Lolly say anything about a quilt for me?"

"Sorry, honey, I've got to run. Candy and Jilly are waiting on me. We're off to a Sisterhood of the Quilt meeting. When Lolly opened the bakery, we'd only made curtains, but she decided we needed to quilt up the bakery some more. Tonight, we're finishing up quilted tablecloths." There was a pause. "Oh, Candy just honked again. I really do have to go now. I love you!" She hung up before he could say good-bye.

It was after ten in Houston, but Shaun called Brian anyway. "Hey, boss. Sorry to call so late," he said, when Brian picked up.

"What's going on? Another problem?" Brian asked.

"No. I'm just wondering when I can get back to Alaska. Any word on when Lucinda will be able to come back to work?"

"It's funny you ask. I spoke to her this evening. She's

feeling better, but the accident really shook up her family and she wants to go part time. Spend more time at home with her husband and kids."

Shaun had the sinking feeling Brian was about to ask him to stay another six months or a year to train someone to take his spot. Maybe longer; he and Lucinda had been working together for years. "Oh, well, that's good that she's feeling better but, um, what does this mean for me?"

"I can't lose you," Brian said. "It's out of the question."

But Shaun couldn't stay in Houston. His new life—and old life, for that matter—was in Alaska.

Brian continued. "What would you say to returning to your position full time?"

"I don't think—"

Brian cut him off. "Return full time but work remotely from wherever you want. Just come back to Houston a few times a year for face time with the team and the exec committee. What do you say?"

It seemed like a dream come true! Shaun had missed his job so much. "I'll need a couple of days to think about it." What he meant was, he had to see what Lolly thought about it first. For him it was a no-brainer. He could bring her along when he made his trips to Houston, so they wouldn't be separated. Surely the folks of Sweet Home could take her place at the bakery. He looked forward to showing her around Houston. He bet she'd love the yearly International Quilt Festival. His next thought was about his mom. He'd have to find full-time help on the homestead. But Dewey seemed keen to take on as much work as Shaun could throw at him. He wondered if he could hire Dewey on a permanent basis.

Brian gave a laugh of relief, as if Shaun had already agreed. "Take all the time you need . . . as long as you say yes. We need you. Heck, I need you for my sanity alone."

"We'll talk tomorrow. Thanks. Good night." Shaun hung up and packed up his laptop. Time to head back to the hotel.

When he got there it was only a little after seven in Sweet Home.

He called Lolly first—as always, the call went to voice mail. "I really need to speak to you, Lolly. Please call me!" Next, he reached Dewey Winkle about not just continuing on but expanding his hours at the homestead. Dewey's answer was a resounding yes.

He waited all evening for Lolly to call him back. But when she hadn't called by midnight, her time—three a.m. in Houston—he went to bed. He'd just have to wait until he got home to talk to her. He fell asleep, feeling sure she would be excited for him to work remotely so they could continue seeing each other.

But he had a dream in which he got home and discovered Lolly had gotten married. He argued and argued that it had been a bad idea for her to marry old Mr. Brewster, but Lolly just kept saying she had no choice. Shaun woke up in a cold sweat, her words from the dream haunting him. *I moved on, Shaun. Maybe you should, too.*

LOLLY HAD FALLEN into a sort of rhythm for the last two weeks. She spent a lot more time working side by side with her mom in the bakery. Mom had a real flair for the gift shop side of the bakery, and Lolly had given her free rein to organize it however she thought best. Somewhere along the way, Lolly had forgiven her mom for always telling her what to do. Mostly, Lolly realized that she didn't have to always do as her mother said, which was so freeing. She felt like their relationship had turned into one of friendship.

Lolly was proud of herself for not spending her time worrying about Shaun. Or at least for stopping herself from spinning out of control when he popped into her mind. Even while working on his quilt, sewing each piece together, she had purposefully distanced herself from the man who would get the quilt. She told herself she was making the quilt for a stranger, with whom she had no connection. That was how she'd spent many of her evenings—not allowing herself to answer his texts, emails, and calls. Which freed up more time. In his texts and voice mails, he hadn't said a thing about the two of *them*—as in being a couple. She'd hoped by now he might've come to his senses and would tell her that he loved her. But nary a word. Last night she'd put the binding on his Pi-Computer quilt. She was done. Another checkmark. Another reason why she shouldn't factor Shaun into her decisions anymore.

Besides, Shaun seemed to really be settling in, since all he wrote about was work. It was starting to feel as if Shaun had no intention of coming back to Alaska. Which was actually the answer to the question she'd asked him before he'd hightailed it out of town.

But focusing on this new life of hers wasn't easy. Shaun seemed to be everywhere she looked. He'd bought practically everything in her entire bakery. He'd painted the walls. He'd taken her on the lovely shop hop, which helped her hone her theme. And then there was Shaun's mother, who was here every day, helping out in so many ways.

Every morning, Lolly rose at three thirty and hurried to the bakery to start the ovens and get the first bakes going. Now that the last Montana quilt was done, or at least her portion of the project, she'd have more time to think of recipes to add to the menu, maybe even time to make herself a quilt. There were scraps left from Patricia's stash of clothes, and part of her yearned to make her own Montana quilt. But no, she wouldn't. She wouldn't undo the good work she'd done on herself since Shaun had left town.

She planned to give Shaun's quilt to Patricia when she came in a little before noon. It was a bit after ten now. The last of the morning crowd had left and Lolly sat down with her coffee and a cream cheese Danish. She adored cream cheese, whether in a sweet bake or in a savory. She picked up the Danish and admired the lamination and what she believed was the perfect filling-to-dough ratio before taking the first bite. But her phone rang, interrupting her well-deserved break. She didn't recognize the area code.

"Hello. Happily Ever Baking." She expected the call to be from a store looking to get on her regular delivery schedule. Which had grown, thanks to Aberdeen's efforts to build the wholesale business, plus her willingness to deliver to the out-of-town businesses. For her efforts, Lolly gave her a nice cut on every pastry and loaf she sold.

"I'm looking for Lolly Crocker, the family and consumer science teacher. Is she there?" the caller asked.

"Speaking?" Lolly said tentatively. *Was* she a teacher anymore?

"Good. I'm Rhonda Pettigrew, principal of Evermore High in Evermore, Montana."

Lolly racked her brain but didn't remember applying for a job in Montana. Oregon and Idaho, yes, but not Montana.

"I'm so glad to have found you." Rhonda gave a throaty laugh of relief. "My friend Georgia, superintendent of Houston ISD, didn't have your résumé, but I was able to check your credentials on LinkedIn."

"Georgia from Houston?" Lolly said, once again racking her brain. She didn't know a Georgia. But *Houston* . . . ?

"Oh, yes, Georgia and I went to school together. One of her husband's former employees recommended you highly."

Lolly got a horrible sinking feeling. The only person she knew in Houston was Shaun, the love of her life.

But suddenly it all made sense. Maybe Shaun did want to come back to Alaska. No, *of course* he did! He wanted to be near his mom. But the only way he could think to do that was to get Lolly out of town.

Lolly cleared her throat and made sure all her emotion was packed away so it wouldn't come out in her voice. "By any chance, was the former employee Shaun Montana?"

"Why, yes! I do believe that's his name."

Lolly felt crushed, but she didn't have time to nurse her broken heart right now. "I'd love to hear more about the job. And possible next steps." Her hand shook as she tried to take a sip of coffee, but she ultimately had to put the mug down.

Rhonda told her all about the high school, the classes she'd be teaching, and their delightful small town. "Can you come check us out? That way we can both be sure you'll be a good fit for us and us for you."

"Of course," Lolly said, "there's nothing holding me here." *What about the bakery?* said the little voice in Lolly's head. Well, Patricia and Aberdeen could run it. Or she could pay back Montgomery St. James. The most important thing was for Lolly to get out of town. It was the least she could do for Shaun. Maybe this final act of kindness would make up for what she'd done to him in the past.

"How soon would you be able to come? This week? The sooner the better, I say," Rhonda said. "The kids are not enjoying me as their substitute teacher. *Poor dears.* I'm horrible at all things homemaking."

"How about day after tomorrow?" Lolly answered automatically. She seemed to be having an out-of-body experience. For the next few minutes, they discussed the logistics of travel and accommodations."

Rhonda finished by saying, "I'm so excited to meet you."

"Likewise." They said their good-byes and hung up.

Lolly sat, immobilized. Everything she'd wanted had come to pass. She'd wished for a bakery and her wish had come true—thanks in large part to Shaun, who had encouraged her and supported her in a hundred different ways. When she lost her job, she'd prayed for a new teaching position, and now the opportunity had arrived. Apparently, Shaun was responsible for that, too.

Thor came and put his paws on her thigh, as if he recognized she was about to spiral out of control. She picked him up and held him close. "I suppose we're moving to Montana, little man."

The dream of being with Shaun was well and truly gone. She couldn't reconcile everything that had happened between them, though. How close they'd become. The laughs they'd shared. The kisses! And why had he insisted they go on a date? And tell her he was trying to figure things out? It was to close the book on her, apparently.

She sat there until Mr. Brewster came in to get an apple fritter and coffee to go. As he left, Lolly's cell phone rang. Shaun, *naturally*. She made no move to answer it. A minute later, she heard the chime of a voice mail. She wouldn't listen to it. She knew what it said. She deleted it and for good measure blocked his number. She even deleted him from her contacts. She couldn't bear to hear how tickled he was to have orchestrated a job for her in Evermore. What a weird twist of fate to leave the Montana family behind to start a new life in Montana.

Fifteen minutes before the lunch crowd would start arriving, Patricia came through the door. "Is everything all right?" she asked immediately. "It looks like something's worrying you."

"Oh. No. I'm fine." Lolly plastered a smile on her face. "It's just, I hope you can hold down the fort for a couple of days."

"Why?" Patricia asked suspiciously. "Where are you going?"

"Nowhere. I'm just taking a couple days off." Lolly felt caught in the lie, especially the way Patricia was eyeing her. "I just need a little break." To change the subject, she pulled the sack out from under the counter and held it out to Patricia. "I finished the last quilt." She couldn't bring herself to say Shaun's name.

Patricia pushed it back. "Why don't you give it to him when he gets home?"

Just then, Piney came through the door, saving Lolly from answering. "Lollipop, is my order ready?"

"Yes. All ready." Lolly put the sack in Patricia's arms and went to the kitchen to collect the Hungry Bear order.

While she was in the kitchen, she took a moment to wipe her eyes, wash her hands, and fasten her pretend happy face securely in place before going back out.

But she was fairly certain *pretend happy* would be all she could manage from here on out. She would never be truly happy again.

SHAUN WAS CONCERNED before he picked up the phone. Mom never called before eight in the evening, even when he'd lived in Houston before. This past week she'd gotten into the habit of calling him on her way home from her shift at the bakery. "Are you feeling okay?" he said, getting right to the point. He needed to know if something was wrong.

"I'm fine. Don't be such a mother hen," his mother said.

"But you never—"

"It's Lolly."

His heart skipped a beat, maybe a whole row of them.

His mom continued. "Have you heard from her lately?"

"Not recently." Dread, or something more sinister than dread, overtook him. He'd let Lolly's silence go on for too long. He should've made her respond, somehow. He should've gone home to see her, make her talk to him, face-to-face. But he wasn't going to share that with his mom. "What's wrong with Lolly?" He braced himself.

His mother paused. "I don't know. Something's off."

"Off, how?"

"When I got into work today, she didn't look right. Even though she's been burning the candle at both ends, she was always energized about the bakery."

"But now?"

"She finished your quilt, but when she gave it to me today she didn't even show it off to me. All quilters want to show off their work to other quilters." Mom paused. "But the lunch rush was just starting. I suppose that could be why. By the way, your quilt is a real work of art. You're going to love it. It's really beautiful. But . . ." she trailed off.

"But what?"

"Lolly made me take the quilt. She didn't seem to want to give it to you herself."

"That's strange. We picked out the fabric for it together. She seemed excited about working on it." It meant so much to him that Lolly was making his memory quilt. "Mom, listen, I've got to let you go." He'd call her later, after he'd booked his flight. He was going home.

"But wait—"

"I'll call you later." He hung up and opened a new tab on his computer.

Immediately a text came in on his phone. Don't hang up on your mother again. What I wanted to say is Lolly is taking a few days off. It doesn't sound like something she would do.

Shaun texted back. I agree. Sorry for hanging up. I really will call you in a bit.

THIRTY-SIX HOURS LATER, he retrieved his car from long-term parking and headed away from Anchorage's Ted Stevens Airport. He couldn't wait to get home. He'd been quietly panicking since talking to his mother, and he knew whatever was going on with Lolly was his fault. He'd strung her along. Why had he told her he needed to figure things out? There was nothing to figure out. His choice was simple. What he should've done was to set aside his pride . . . or fear.

He had never stopped loving her. Lolly was as important to his existence as the air he breathed. He was stupid for not realizing that sooner. The side of Shaun that had hesitated was the scared teenager afraid of getting his heart broken again. When Lolly told him why she'd done it, he should've pulled her into his arms right then, forgiven her, and vowed to never let her go. He'd missed out on time they could've had together—wasted time—and he wasn't going to make that mistake again.

He turned the radio on but got only static. He leaned over and pulled Lolly's mixtape from the glove box and slid it into the CD player. As he listened, he allowed himself to believe everything was going to be all right. That they were going to be together. If for no other reason than he wanted it more than anything in the world.

When he got to Sweet Home, he didn't drive directly to the homestead but stopped at the bakery. He didn't believe for a second Lolly could stay away from her beloved bakery.

When he walked into Happily Ever Baking, he almost didn't recognize the place. There were quilt decorations everywhere and several display carousels with quilt-themed items for sale. It was the epitome of coziness, from the patchwork curtains to the quilt-block runners hanging above the chalkboard menus. Two teenagers, Ella and Lacy, stood at the counter, chatting. Ella stopped and smiled at him, looking just like her mom. "What can I get for you, Shaun?"

"Is Lolly in the kitchen?"

"Ms. Crocker isn't here."

Disappointed, he turned to leave, but Ella said, "But your mom's here. Do you want me to get her?"

"Yeah, that would be great."

But Patricia came out then, wiping her hands on a towel. "Why don't you two go work on the dirty dishes for me?"

Immediately the teenagers left them alone.

"Is Lolly at her house?" Shaun asked.

"This morning I talked to Jilly, who found out from Piney, who had gotten a call from Paige, who told her what Lolly had been up to."

"Just tell me," said Shaun impatiently.

"Lolly's gone."

"Gone where?" The panic that had eased when he pulled into town was back in full force.

"To Montana. Apparently, she has a teaching job lined up. She's gone for the final interview, but Jilly says it's only a formality." His mom laid a hand on his shoulder. "I'm sorry, son, but it sounds like she's leaving for good."

"What? How did this happen?" He pulled out his phone, hoping there was a call or text from Lolly. But the only texts were from Brian. *Probably work related.* The first text was indeed about work. The second text, though, was about Lolly: Good news! Georgia found a job for your friend. It sounds like it's A GO.

"Shaun? What are you thinking? You've got that crazy look in your eyes."

Shaun pulled out his phone and called Brian. "Hey, it's me. Is your wife there? It's an emergency. About my friend." Shaun had better bring it down a notch with the man who'd offered him the chance to work remotely. "I would really appreciate it, Brian, if I could speak with Georgia."

"Sure. Then I need to speak with you about Sector Three."

A moment later, Georgia came on the line. "Hello?"

Shaun got right to it. "This is Shaun. I need to know the name of the school that is hiring my friend Lolly." Though *friend* didn't come close to covering how he felt toward her. "Where is it, if you don't mind?"

"Rhonda is thrilled that Lolly's joining their teaching staff. The school is Evermore High, the only high school in Evermore, Montana."

"Thanks. You've been a big help. Tell Brian I'll call him in a bit." But only after he booked a flight. Shaun said good-bye and hung up before turning back to his mom. "Did Jilly say when Lolly was getting home?"

"Maybe the day after tomorrow. Jilly said she wanted to find a place to live before coming back. I'm so sorry, Shaun."

"There's nothing to be sorry for. This is all on me. Just wish me luck."

"What are you going to do?"

"I'm going to bring her back." But Shaun knew he had to

do more. Win her heart. Do whatever it took to have her in his life.

"Then you're going to need this." Mom slipped her ring off her finger, the one with the single diamond. "You can't show up empty-handed."

He sometimes forgot how smart his mom was. Shaun seldom felt like crying, but at this moment his eyes misted over. "You never take off your engagement ring. Dad told me that once."

She reached up and touched his face. "It's okay, honey. If Dad were here right now, he'd be okay with it. He'd want you to have the ring he bought for me. Your father was a big believer in true love."

Shaun hugged his mother and then, taking her face in his hands, kissed her on each cheek. "You are amazing, Mom. I don't tell you that enough."

She was smiling and had tears in her eyes, too. Happy tears. "It's easy to be *amazing* when I have such wonderful boys." She patted him on the arm. "Now get going."

TWENTY HOURS LATER, Shaun pulled into Evermore after what felt like a never-ending series of flights. The clerk at the car rental moved at a snail's pace, not understanding the urgency Shaun felt. It was Saturday, so it wouldn't do any good to look for Lolly at the high school.

Shaun pulled the car to the side of the road and called Jilly. "I'm in Evermore, Montana, and I'm worried about Lolly. She hasn't answered my calls in days. Please, Jilly, tell me where she is."

"Why would I do that?" Jilly always had an edge to her, but this was worse than her usual.

"Because I love her." His words had rolled out automatically, but shocked him. Shocked Jilly, too, if her gasp was any indication. "I'd like to tell her in person, if I can. Will you tell me where she is?"

"Maybe. What are your intentions toward my sister?"

"So you know her location?"

"That depends on what you tell me."

"I've brought a ring, if that helps to sway you. I wanted her to know first, before everyone else in Sweet Home has the information."

"She's at 875 Deer Park Place. At least that's what it says on my phone."

"You track your sister?"

"Only recently. I've been worried about her since she lost her job."

He exhaled. "You're a good sister." Hopefully, he'd be able to call her sister-in-law soon.

"Are you going to tell her I'm really a softy under my black eyeliner and black nail polish?"

"Not a chance."

"Thanks, Shaun. I think you'll make a good brother-in-law."

"Now let me go find her."

Shaun plugged the address into his phone and saw that Lolly was five minutes away. He couldn't believe all his dreams were about to come true. After traveling so far, he was almost there.

Chapter 23

EVERMORE WAS A sweet small town with a Main Street of businesses and a few residential streets on either side of Main. Not much going on. Larger than Sweet Home but very similar. Lolly shouldn't have much trouble adjusting to it. Or that's what she was telling herself. Jilly wouldn't be here. Her mom wouldn't be here. The Sisterhood of the Quilt wouldn't be here. Patricia wouldn't be here. The students she'd grown to love, her Sweet Home High students, wouldn't be here. But most importantly, Shaun wouldn't be here.

Shaun would have Sweet Home all to himself. Without her in town, he could find someone new to share the quilt that she'd made for him. Everyone thought Courtney and Shaun would make a good couple. The thought made Lolly ache. She tried to shake off the dark cloud that had descended but she couldn't.

The Realtor had given her a list of apartments, houses, and condos to look at, along with the code to get into each place so she could take a self-guided tour of the possibilities. She'd seen three so far that were perfectly adequate, but not one had spoken to her heart. She wished Jilly was here with her. When Lolly relocated to Oregon, Jilly and Paige both flew in to help her find an apartment. They'd had a wonderful girls' weekend and found the perfect place. Now, though, Lolly was all alone. She turned off the ignition and sat staring out at the fourplex housing, the next apartment on her list.

I wish Shaun was here. She had to stop thinking like that, she told herself sternly, or she'd sabotage the new life she was starting for herself. It was because she loved Shaun that she was moving to Montana, to give him the space he wanted. She only wished he had told her straight out that they couldn't be together.

Well, he had—in the beginning.

But then he'd kissed her.

And finally, he'd said he needed time to figure it out.

Which she now knew meant he needed time to figure out how to tell her he didn't want her in his life.

She'd been such a dope. The second she'd gotten laid off, she should've left town. To where, she didn't know. Maybe to Texas to hide out at the ranch with Paige and her new husband, Holt. Instead she'd caused a huge mess that ended with getting her heart broken . . . again.

She took in what could be her new home. The fourplex wasn't bad. Well-kept. The landscaping was nice, with bushes all around. In the distance, she could see a lake, which would make a nice view, if the apartment faced that way. As she reached for the door handle, her phone dinged with a text. It was from Jilly and it contained only one word. Sorry.

That was strange. What did Jilly have to be sorry for? Was Thor okay? Or had Mom taken the clippers to him again? Still sitting in her car, Lolly quickly called her sister. "What's going on? Is Thor all right?"

"Thor is fine. Say hi to your mommy." Thor barked.

"So what's the *sorry* text for?" Lolly asked. "Is it about Mom? Did you divulge something you shouldn't have?"

"Maybe," Jilly prevaricated. "But not to Mom."

Lolly saw a car pull in behind her. "What did you divulge? Just spit it out."

"Um, your location?" Jilly's voice squeaked like when she was a little girl caught sneaking into the cookie dough Lolly had chilling in the refrigerator.

Lolly's eyebrows pulled together as she saw a man get out of the car behind her. It took less than a millisecond to realize who it was. "Jillian Beatrice Crocker! How could you?"

"Oops, gotta run," Jilly said. She hung up. Seething, Lolly stared at her phone and—

There was a knock on her window.

Damn it, now she had to deal with Shaun. She rolled the window down partway but didn't look up at him. "What are you doing here?" Maybe Jilly told him some kind of lie, like she was dying or something, to induce him to come after her. "Did Jilly put you up to this? Because I'm fine. Really."

"Jilly didn't put me up to anything." He opened the driver's-side door as if to invite her to get out.

Lolly stayed behind the wheel. "Well, I guess a *thank-you* is in order." She *should* feel grateful he'd found a job for her, but currently, she was more upset than anything else.

"Get out of the car and talk to me." He sounded angry, which rankled her. "And for heaven's sake, look at me."

"Shaun, stop bossing me around." She was the one in the right here. "You have no cause to be angry with me. I'm out of your hair, like you wanted." If only he'd been honest with her. "I'm the one who gets to be angry here. And you're responsible."

"Responsible for what?" he said, much gentler this time. He squatted down to be at her eye level. "I'm sorry I was acting bossy. I'm only concerned."

She glanced at him for a second and was surprised that he seemed sincere. "Fine. Why are you concerned?"

"I needed to tell you something. It's urgent. I came all the way from Texas to Alaska, only to find out you were gone." He sighed heavily. "Please get out of the car."

"I will, but only because you asked nicely." She stepped from the car but pulled away when he tried to touch her arm. "You could've told me the truth, Shaun. I'm no longer your teenage girlfriend. You didn't need to go about it the long way."

"What truth? I have no idea what you're talking about." Clearly exasperated, Shaun ran a hand through his hair. "I'm exhausted from trailing you all over North America, Lolly. But I'm here. So can you just tell me plainly what you have to say, so I can get to what I need to tell *you*?"

"You're being so obtuse. I'm talking about this job! You got me this job here in Evermore. You had your boss's wife on the hunt to find me a position. Congratulations on succeeding. Now I'll be out of your life. *For*evermore, get it?" Her voice had gone from loud and angry to almost a croak at the end. Oxygen seemed to be in short supply. Her eyes were burning with the tears she was holding back. Or trying to hold back. Her stomach hurt and her chest ached. He was so close, but she couldn't have him. Why was he torturing her like this? He'd wanted her gone, yet here he was five inches away. She turned her face so he wouldn't see her cry.

He grabbed her upper arms and spun her so they were face-to-face. "Good grief, woman. You've only got half the story. *Yes*, I did ask Brian to talk to his wife, the superintendent, about a job for you. But at the time, I thought I was doing you a favor." He stopped, seeming to frown at his own words. "Okay, that's not completely true."

"Well, it doesn't matter. In the end, you got what you wanted," Lolly said, refusing to look into his eyes. She chose to focus on the freckle on his temple instead.

"Let me finish. This was when I first arrived in Sweet Home. I wanted to get you out of town because I knew I wasn't strong enough to be around you without falling, totally and completely, in love with you again." He huffed like a dragon who had run out of fire. "That's the honest-to-God truth, Lolly. Just so you know, no man likes to admit that he's weak because of a woman." He was still frowning, but Lolly's heart had lifted, feeling hopeful for the first time since she'd heard about the job in Evermore.

Shaun continued. "When Brian didn't get back to me, I figured there were no jobs—and there was no reason to tell you what I'd done . . ."

She looked at him then—and *dang his gray eyes*, they were so caring. His caring was one of the reasons she loved him so much. "So this wasn't a recent deal? You asked your boss a long time ago?"

"Yes. Of course."

"But you admitted you were conflicted about us. You said you needed time to figure things out. When the principal from Evermore High called, I assumed it meant you'd made up your mind."

"You assumed wrong." He took her hands in his before gazing into her eyes again. "I *was* conflicted, but it had more to do with my pride, and the resolutions I'd made about never falling for you again. Which turned out to be a bunch of bull I'd been telling myself. Fooling myself, really. Lolly, I've never stopped loving you. Yes, I was angry with you, but it was just a way to cope. When you told me why you broke up with me in high school, I understood; I knew how it was between you and your mom. I've been kicking myself that I didn't pull you into my arms while we were standing there in the church hallway, because our life together could've started at that moment, instead of waiting until now. But here we are."

"You've never stopped loving me?" Her brain—or was it her heart?—had gotten stuck on those words. "Does that mean you love me now?"

He dug around in his pocket and pulled something out. "This isn't exactly what I imagined when I dreamed about this moment, but here goes."

She couldn't believe it, but right there on the pavement, he got down on one knee and lifted a ring up to her. "Lolly Ann Crocker, you are the love of my life. Always have been, always will be. Will you make me the happiest man in the universe and marry me?"

Tears were streaming down her face, which she hadn't

noticed before because she was in shock. She never expected her day to go like this. She'd been proposed to by more than her fair share of men. But none of them came close to being this man, *her man*, Shaun Montana. She touched his face. "You're the love of my life, too. Always have been, always will be."

"Does that mean you're saying yes?"

"Yes, I'm saying yes."

He stood and pulled her into his arms, and kissed her, first lightly, then deeper. The tectonic plates beneath them must've moved because her world shifted from out of whack to back in place . . . for the first time since she was eighteen. Shaun loved her and she loved him. All was right with the world . . . no, perfect, in fact.

Finally, he pulled away but kept his arms around her waist, as if he couldn't bear to let her go. "On the way here, I had a lot of time to think. I should've come after you when you went away to college. But I was young and stupid. You have to know I'm never letting you get away again. Wherever you go, I go. If you want to stay here in Evermore, I'm staying, too." When she started to interrupt, he held up his hand. "But if you stay, just go in with your eyes open. Your students are going to have a heyday with your name. Mrs. Montana who lives in Montana." He grinned at her, that grin she loved so much. "But the decision is totally up to you. I only want to be with you, no matter where you choose." He wiped away her tears with his thumbs and kissed her tenderly.

Now she was grinning like a goof, but she was so happy, she could hardly stand it. "I couldn't be Mrs. Montana who lives in Montana."

"Does that mean you're not taking my name?" he asked hesitantly. "I'd be okay with it." But he seemed a little hurt.

"No, you silly man. Don't you know that since our first date, I've been practicing writing *Lolly Montana* in all of my notebooks?" Many, many years before she had the right to do so. "What I'd really like to do is for us to go home.

Home to Sweet Home, to all of our family and friends. But I'll need to speak with Evermore High's principal first." Lolly didn't want to leave Rhonda in the lurch. She'd have to explain about Shaun, their past, and how hard she'd worked to get back to her hometown. She was determined to help Rhonda find her replacement. Surely there were other family and consumer science teachers who had been cut from their positions and were looking for a job. Lolly would ask her other teacher friends in Oregon if they knew of anyone, and check with schools who had dropped their home ec program. She had a brilliant idea. "Shaun, would you mind calling your boss's wife again to see if she might know of another family and consumer science teacher looking for a job?"

"Anything for you, Lolly." He hugged her again. "Are you looking forward to getting home to your bakery?" He seemed so proud of her.

"Yes, to my bakery." She laid her head on his shoulder and placed her hand over his heart. "And to be with you. You realize I have a lot to say to you about the bakery, too, don't you?"

"Good things, I hope." He grinned, but he looked a little guilty, too.

"We'll talk about it on the way home."

"Okay. But about going home"—he kissed her again—"what if we fly to Vegas first and get hitched? I don't want to wait one second longer for us to start our lives together."

Love surged up in Lolly for the one man who was meant for her—true back in the day and just as true now. "I can't wait to be married to you either. I say *yes* to Las Vegas. Then home to start our happily-ever-after in Alaska . . . after all."

Acknowledgments

MY UNDYING GRATITUDE goes to Tracy Bernstein, the best editor ever. Thank you for always pushing me to be better. I am honored to call you friend. Thank you also to Liz Sellers and the whole team at Berkley for making my books become the most that they can be. You all are the best!

Thanks also to Kathleen Baldwin for being my sister in writing. A big shoutout to Kate Jackson for your support, which means everything to me.

Thank you to all my readers for making all of this possible. You are the reason I write!

Last, but not least, a big thank-you goes to PhD, Cagney, Mitchell, Annie, and Jamie. And to Scout, the best dog ever. You make up all the light in my life. I love you.

Keep reading for an excerpt from

One
Snowy
Night

available now from Berkley Romance!

THIRTY-FOUR-YEAR-OLD HOPE McKNIGHT tried *not* to watch the clock, which hung on the dingy blue wall of her minuscule living room. But it was impossible to keep from glancing at it every other second. She turned and gazed out the frost-covered window into the pitch-black of night and shivered before peeking at the clock again.

Ten thirty.

Ella should've been home from the football game an hour ago. Calling and texting her daughter's cell phone hadn't eased Hope's worry, as Ella hadn't responded.

Hope always agonized over Ella's safety when it snowed, even when it was only a dusting. Sweet Home was remote, with winding roads leading in and out of the town, population 573—Alaska Native people, transplants, and multigenerational Alaskans like herself—and Hope knew better than anyone how treacherous the roads could be. Plus there was a deeper threat hanging over their little house. For the past two Friday nights, her sixteen-year-old daughter had staggered in the front door, clearly drunk. Hope felt defeated . . . and guilty. Lecturing Ella from birth about the pitfalls of alcohol—even being the head of the local chapter of Mothers Against Drunk Driving—hadn't prevented her daughter from getting caught up in Alaska's number one pastime.

Is Ella doomed to repeat my mistakes?

Hope tried to shove the thought from her mind, but she couldn't stop feeling—down to her bones—that Ella's drinking was inherently her fault.

Hope glanced at the car keys hanging on the hook by the front door. At least there was that: Ella wouldn't be driving. But that didn't mean she wasn't getting a ride home with another inebriated teen.

To stop fretting, Hope pushed herself off the couch to rearrange the furniture in her living room, anything to occupy her mind. At one time she'd thought about getting a degree in interior design, but that was before. And because her living room was tiny, the rearranging took no time at all. She needed something else to keep from going crazy with worry. She strode to the closet and pulled out a rucksack. "I'll start packing without her," she said to the empty house. Every year they took several snow camping trips in the thick forests surrounding Sweet Home, where Hope could test Ella's survival skills.

Hope's gaze traveled to the clock once again. Yes, according to the experts, only five percent of what people worried about actually happened. But Hope knew that danger lurked around every corner, ready to ruin lives. She was living proof of how a good life could turn awful in an instant. And how, once things went bad, there was no way to turn back time and recapture the joy she once had. When her parents named her Hope, they'd made a grievous error . . . because she had none. She hadn't been prepared for what life had thrown at her. Her *job one* now? To prepare Ella for what lay ahead, good or bad.

She went to Ella's room and unearthed her daughter's backpack from beneath a pile of clothes. As an exhausted and overworked single parent, she'd thrown in the towel about Ella keeping her room picked up. In the vast scheme of things, an untidy room wasn't important. Having the skills to make it alone was. Knowing how to survive in the wild was key, too. Their camping trip would only be two days—Saturday and Sunday—the first days Hope had had off since September.

She dug past the second layer of clothes on the floor but couldn't find Ella's wool socks. Just as she was going to look in her daughter's closet, Hope's phone rang. She raced for the other room and caught it on the tail end of the second ring, knowing it had to be Ella.

"Where are you?"

But Hope was wrong. It was Piney Douglas, the closest thing she had to a mother now. Not that she didn't love Piney, but Hope's heart sank. *Where are you, Ella?*

"Where am I?" Piney chuckled. "I'm in my drafty apartment above the Hungry Bear"—the grocery store–diner where Hope worked. "Where else would I be?"

"I thought you were Ella." Hope could've added that Piney might've been anywhere, even the cabin next door to Hope, where Piney's boyfriend, Bill Morningstar, lived. Bill was known throughout Sweet Home for making Alaskan quilts.

Piney clucked. "Ella's fine. I'd know if something was wrong."

Hope sighed, thinking of Piney's crystals, tarot cards, tea-leaf readings, and other psychic stuff. Bill thought Piney's belief in the spirit world was complete rubbish and didn't seem to think twice about voicing his opinion. But Hope had to admit that at times Piney had an uncanny ability to know what was up with Ella, and thus decided that Piney was an intuitive. Piney maintained that she was more in touch with the universe than regular folks because she was born on the summer solstice. She certainly looked like Mother Earth—her gray hair curled at her shoulders, her Bohemian skirts flowing about her, and her wise smiling face, as if she were privy to the world's inner secrets. A self-proclaimed hippie, Piney had arrived in Alaska in the seventies, searching for the truth, traveling and sleeping in her converted blue school bus, way ahead of the current tiny home movement. Piney and her thirty-four-year-old daughter, Sparkle, had lived in that blue bus until just a few weeks ago, when two suits from Juneau had arrived, asking to purchase the bus for the state capitol as part of a pioneer sculpture. Piney took the money, telling everyone she'd outgrown the bus. But Hope knew money was tight since Sparkle's emergency appendectomy. It was perfect timing, too, as the apartment above the Hungry Bear had been vacated the week before.

"Keep your chin up, buttercup," Piney said. "Don't let your negative thinking carry you away. Besides, I'm calling to see if you know whether the rumor is true."

Once again, Hope glanced at the clock. *Ten forty.* Maybe she should call the Alaska State Troopers to find Ella. "What rumor?"

"Mr. Brewster heard at the bank that Donovan Stone is coming home."

It felt like a lightning strike. Hope couldn't breathe. Couldn't think either. "Donovan? Here?" *What am I going to do?* She hadn't seen him in seventeen years, not since his grandmother's funeral . . . where he'd told Hope he never wanted to see her again. And he hadn't.

The front door creaked. For a second, Piney's call kept Hope from being able to move. But as Ella tripped on the threshold, Hope yelled into her phone, "Gotta go." She lunged for her daughter, breaking her fall and keeping Ella's head from hitting the corner of the side table.

Ella's response was to laugh as she went down. "You should see your face!"

Hope didn't think it was funny. "Where have you been?" She kicked the door shut with her foot. Winter was just getting started, and the baseboard heaters were expensive to run.

Ella stopped laughing. "Chill, Mom. I was just out with friends." Her words were slurred, and her breath smelled of cheap wine.

A smell that brought back awful memories.

"Who drove you home tonight?" Hope hadn't heard a vehicle. "Were they drinking, too?"

"I walked home from Lacy's."

"The trail through the forest?" Hope glanced out the window to the black sky beyond. "Did you have your flashlight with you?"

"I was fine," Ella said. "I didn't need my flashlight. I know my way."

But Alaska was dangerous!

Sweet Home wasn't Anchorage, but someone could've kidnapped Ella and Hope would've never seen her again. Or Ella could've fallen into the river. Or she could've encountered a late-to-hibernate bear!

Hope got to her feet and helped Ella to her feet, too. "We're going to talk about this tomorrow. I know you're sad about Grandpa's passing—"

Ella swayed from side to side. "Don't bring Grandpa into this. He has nothing to do with *anything*." She wobbled into her room.

Hope followed and caught the door before Ella slammed it shut. Hope's heart was heavy, so very heavy, as she watched her teenage daughter stagger across her room and fall into bed. Hope plodded over to Ella and pulled off her boots. "I think your drinking has everything to do with Grandpa's death."

Death was such a harsh word, but it had been harsh for Hope to see her dad lying in that casket, felled by a heart attack. There hadn't been time for her to fall apart, though. Hope had to keep it together for Ella. Remain strong. Even when she felt her life coming apart at the seams. Sometimes it was best to focus on the small things.

Hope laid a hand on her daughter's arm. "I couldn't find your warm socks." She congratulated herself for coming up with something so benign.

Ella rolled her eyes. "Please don't start lecturing. They're at the bottom of my closet. I'll pack in the morning, all right? And yes, you've told me a hundred times to take care of my feet, especially during winter." She rolled away, burying her face in her pillow, which muffled her voice so she sounded a bit like Charlie Brown's teacher. *"It can mean the difference between having a good time and losing toes."*

Hope wasn't deterred, only determined. Determined not to waste these two days off from her job at the Hungry Bear. Determined to teach Ella how to start a fire with wet wood and no matches. Mostly, she was determined to get Ella out of the funk she'd slipped into. They both were still reeling from the loss. She'd love to coddle her daughter, but that would be a disservice. "Listen, the world is harsh. It's my job to teach you survival skills." Things Hope had been forced to learn on her own, when she had to grow up all at once.

Ella sighed heavily, as if having a mother were the most annoying thing. "You've told me a million times: 'We're all alone in this world. I better be prepared to fend for myself.'"

"It's nice to know you've been listening. I'll see you in the morning." Hope started to leave, but Ella grabbed her hand.

"Stay. Tell me a story." Ella had switched gears again, from cranky teenager to affable angel. She'd always loved stories.

"Which one do you want to hear? The one where I stared down a bear?"

"No. I want to hear about Aunt Izzie."

Have people been talking? Has someone said something to Ella about Donovan returning to town? "You haven't asked about Izzie in a long time."

"I know. I want to hear about her now." Ella reached over the side of the bed and pulled a ribbon from between the mattress and box spring. "I found this ribbon to tie on the Memory Tree."

Hope reached out and ran her fingers over the ribbon. "We can do that on our camping trip, okay?"

"Sure," Ella said.

Hope had started the Memory Tree after Izzie died. It was the same mountain hemlock where Donovan, on Izzie's eleventh birthday, had carved her name—*Isabella!*—declaring that the tree was now hers. She'd been thrilled. After Izzie's death, Hope had started visiting the tree, bringing trinkets, things Izzie might've liked, to decorate it. Over the years, the two of them had continued the tradition, as Ella had enjoyed finding new treasures for Aunt Izzie.

"Go ahead." Ella closed her eyes, as if ready for a bedtime story.

Hope understood. Only the two of them were left. When Ella was little, Hope had started telling her stories about Izzie. It was one of the ways Hope kept her sister alive, and a way for Ella to know her namesake. Hope's mother had hated that she'd named her child Isabella after her dead sister, telling her it was cruel, making Mom despise Hope more.

Izzie was always a clear image in Hope's mind and she never tired of talking about her. "Izzie was just a little thing with a big personality. Even though she was six years younger than me, she tried to act like we were the same age and wanted to do everything I did. Because your grandmother worked nights in the ER, I babysat her a lot. It was fun. I taught her so much, from how to say her ABCs to how to tie her shoes. When we'd go with Mom to the Sisterhood of the Quilt stitch-ins, Izzie and I would set our sewing machines side by side and make all sorts of things from the fabric the Sisterhood would give us. Like matching pillowcases for the bedroom we shared, and blankets for Izzie's stuffed animals. We used to play Barbies together, bake cookies, and I really didn't mind if she tagged along with me and my friends." *Most of the time, anyway.* Donovan and his brother, Beau, were great about letting Izzie hang out with them, too.

"I know that stuff already. What happened to Aunt Izzie?" Ella said.

"You know what happened," Hope answered. "She died."

"You've never told me *how*." The whine in Ella's voice almost stopped Hope. But for the first time, it felt like the right moment. Sharing the sobering story would be one more way for Hope to atone for what she'd done to Izzie and their family. Tonight, especially tonight, Ella needed to hear it.

But it was hard to lay open the gaping wound of what had ruined Hope's life. How *she* herself had ruined it. How it'd been no one's fault but her own. "This isn't easy for me, Ella." She took a fortifying breath. "I really need you to pay attention and take everything I'm going to say to heart. Okay?"

Ella sighed. "You're being dramatic."

"No, I'm not. I'm going to tell you how it is. How it *was*." She started at the beginning of that awful night. "It was New Year's Eve. I was at a party, celebrating with my friends."

Hope left out the part about Donovan, how they'd fought that night. How her friends had encouraged her to dull her anger and disappointment with alcohol after he'd dropped the bomb that he was going to stay in Alaska for college, not go to Boston like they'd planned. Maturity and years of adulting had Hope seeing things differently. She understood now why he couldn't turn down a full ride, when every penny counted at his dad's house. Yes, Hope would leave out Donovan when telling Ella the story, but she wouldn't shy away from her guilt in the tragedy. "I had a few sips of wine from one of those red Solo cups."

"So what? A few sips won't kill you, Mom," her inebriated daughter countered. "I drank more than that tonight and I'm fine."

"Yeah, sure, you're fine. I should've videoed your swan dive through the front door a few minutes ago. Even a few sips of alcohol can impair your reflexes." *When you need them the most.* It had been that way for Hope. She'd been lucky when they tested her blood alcohol level and it was under the legal limit.

Hope moved closer. "Scooch over so I can tell you the rest." She sat beside Ella on her twin bed. "While I was still at the party, my mom called from the hospital, telling me to pick up Izzie from a sleepover, because she was complaining of a stomachache."

"I bet you didn't want to leave your friends," Ella said.

Guilt covered Hope, wrapped around her like a familiar, well-worn robe, the tie in the middle squeezing her stomach until it hurt.

It was true. Her senior year, she'd begun resenting how much of her time wasn't her own, how she had to drop everything to take care of Izzie. Izzie wanted her to play like they used to, but Hope only wanted to spend time alone with Donovan. After being best friends their whole lives, Donovan had finally stopped serial dating every girl at Sweet Home High and saw Hope as more than a pal. If Hope had known sooner that going out with Jesse Montana—tight end on the football team and good friend of Donovan's—would wake Donovan up, Hope would have accepted Jesse's offer a few years earlier. Apparently, Donovan didn't have a clue that Hope had loved him since the first day he'd moved in next door.

"Mom? Mom! You're doing what you always do when you talk about Aunt Izzie," Ella said.

"What?"

"Zoning out. Get back to the story."

It wasn't just a story to Hope. She'd lived it. And now she had to make her daughter understand how life could go wrong in an instant. She dropped into lecture mode. "My mom always told me not to drink, to stay away from alcohol. Working the night shift in the ER, she saw the disastrous outcomes of drinking and driving—mangled bodies, loss of life." It hurt to say those words, but Hope was doing penance. "At the time, I didn't think it was a problem to have a few sips. I didn't know I was going to be driving right after. But I was the one with the car keys and I shouldn't have drunk at all." Also, Hope never understood those who couldn't have fun without knocking back a few. Donovan was one of them. She'd loved him, but she didn't like that he drank so much, and so often.

"So . . . you picked up Aunt Izzie . . ." Ella had missed the point completely.

Hope sighed, feeling defeated, but plowed on anyway. "The point is, I should've listened to my mother and stayed away from alcohol."

Ella rolled her eyes. "Enough with the sermon, already. What happened next?"

"I yelled at Izzie for being a nuisance. For faking being sick." Hope had railed on her little sister, telling her that she'd ruined her night. Hope would never forget how Donovan had reached over and laid his hand on hers. *Don't take it out on Izzie. I know you're mad at me.*

"Then?"

This was the hardest part, recounting those horrible details. "There was a snowplow in the other lane."

"Was it snowing hard?" her daughter asked.

"Not when I'd left home, but by the time I left the party, visibility was horrible, nearly a whiteout." Donovan had offered to drive, but Hope wouldn't let him. He'd had too much to drink. Sixteen-year-old Beau was three sheets to the wind, too. It was left to Hope to get them all home safely.

"But you've driven in snow your whole life. What's the big deal?" her daughter prompted.

"There was a moose. He charged into the road in front of the snowplow." Hope took a deep breath to get the next words out. "The snowplow hit the moose and sent it flying toward my side of the road. I hit it. The moose flipped backward and crushed the back of my car." If only she'd had better reflexes to swerve and miss the bull. The biggest *if only* of her life.

Hope didn't remember too much after that, only what the snowplow driver had told her and the state trooper at the hospital. She'd often wondered if she could've saved her sister if only she'd been prepared—stopped the bleeding, kept Izzie from going into shock. It was one of the reasons Hope was adamant about teaching her daughter survival skills, beyond hunting and fishing, although those things were very important, too. Alaska was wild and anything could happen.

"I don't know why Donovan and I were brought to the hospital first."

"Who's Donovan?" her daughter asked.

"Nobody," Hope said quickly. "I was dazed from the accident and only had a broken arm." Donovan had just cuts and bruises. "Even though I confessed right away to my mom that I'd had some wine, she didn't yell at me but was only relieved I was okay." Beau arrived in the next ambulance and was pronounced dead on arrival. "When Izzie was wheeled in on the stretcher, she looked so small and broken. She only lived an hour before dying." Hope would never forget seeing her mother collapse with grief beside Izzie's hospital bed. "And that's why I'm head of MADD in our area," Hope finished, though the story was far from complete. She left out the part where her mother never forgave her. How her parents split up over Izzie's death, motivating her father to move to the North Slope. How it was her mother who brought MADD to their borough, and then on her deathbed insisted that Hope take over.

Hope had been looking off into space but glanced down at her daughter now.

Ella's mouth was open, making her look completely stunned. "You were driving the car? *You* killed Aunt Izzie?"

It was an icy knife to the heart, but it was true. Hope nodded bravely. "Yes. I'm responsible for my sister's death."

"That sucks . . ." Ella shook her head. "I can't imagine. How did your mom take it?"

"Badly."

"You would've grounded me forever. Whatever happened to your mom? You and Grandpa never talked about her."

Hope definitely wasn't ready to get into that. "She got sick—cancer—and died a few years later." Mom had been livid when Hope got up the courage two months after the accident to tell her that she was pregnant. *It's a slap in the face*, her mom had said. *Haven't you hurt this family enough?* When baby Ella was born, Mom pretended her granddaughter didn't exist. After her death, Dad had moved back to Sweet Home, continuing to work on the North Slope and commuting home on his weeks off, which eased Hope's load of raising a child alone. But now he was gone, too.

Ella looked stricken, then turned to face the wall. "Mom?"

"Yes?"

"What if you die, too?" Ella's voice was strained.

Hope understood. They didn't have anyone now, now that Dad was gone.

She wanted to tell her: *There are worse things than death*. Like being disowned at seventeen by your own mother and being forced from the house, alone and pregnant. Whenever she thought about that dark time, Hope tried counting her blessings. She owed Piney so much: for supporting her emotionally, for giving her a job and letting her stay with them in the bus until Mom died and Dad moved back to Sweet Home.

But all she said was, "You know how hard I try to be prepared for every contingency." Hope wanted to reiterate how important it was that Ella be prepared, too . . . for accidents and to go it alone. If Hope had been prepared seventeen years ago, she might've handled her mother's rejection better, instead of letting grief and depression nearly consume her.

Maybe it was time to tell Ella more of the truth. How Donovan and Beau had been in the car that night. How her mother couldn't stand to look at Hope after she'd killed her sister. Maybe the truth would scare Ella *straight*.

But Ella had fallen asleep.

Hope brushed her daughter's dark blond hair from her face. The same color hair as Ella's father, a father she'd never known. Hope had been sure she'd never have to tell Ella about Donovan. There was no reason to. But apparently, Donovan was returning home.

Hope turned off the light and left Ella's room, feeling drained. She'd spent the last seventeen years feeling tired. Exhausted to the bone.

She didn't have the energy to finish packing for their camping trip tonight or to worry about Donovan coming to town. She shuffled to her ten-by-ten-foot bedroom. She didn't turn on the lights but slipped off her slippers and jeans before climbing into bed, leaving on her turtleneck and kuspuk, a kind of loose Alaska Native hoodie. She threw her coat over the bed, too. Anything to keep warm tonight.

Before she fell asleep, Hope knew her eleven-year-old sister—*dead eleven-year-old sister*—would come to her in her dreams. Izzie had visited her on and off for the last seventeen years. But since Hope's daughter had started drinking, Izzie had visited nearly every night. Her sister was always sparkling, almost glowing. Hope didn't shy away from her sister's pop-ins, as they comforted her in ways the town's platitudes never had. Her sister would be wearing the same red moose flannel pajamas she'd worn on the night Hope had picked her up from the sleepover. But instead of covered in blood, the pajamas would be clean and new. Hope never told anyone about the dreams, which seemed so real.

For dreams they must be.

The first time Izzie had visited Hope was two days after she'd died. Her sister hadn't been chatty then but sat cross-legged on the floor beside Hope's bed, something she'd done a million times in real life. But this time, she stared off into the distance, looking lost. When Hope called out to her, Izzie had shaken her head, as if she didn't want to talk.

But these days, Hope couldn't get her to shut up. Eleven-year-old Izzie, still in her little-girl body and her moose pajamas, spoke as a woman who'd lived a lifetime and had plenty of advice to give. Hope welcomed seeing her sister. It was hard to imagine that Izzie would've been twenty-eight a few months ago. If only Hope hadn't killed her.

Hope closed her eyes, and before she'd really drifted off to sleep, Izzie appeared, sitting at the foot of Hope's bed.

"Piney certainly threw you for a loop." Izzie had a twinkle in her eye, as if she were having fun, stirring up trouble. "Didn't you ever suspect Donovan might come back after his grandfather died?"

"I suppose." Since Charles Stone had moved away seventeen years ago, the news of his death took nearly a month to reach Sweet Home.

Izzie reached out as if to pat the quilt covering Hope's legs but withdrew her hand before touching it. "Do you think he's coming back to reopen the hardware store and lodge?"

A Stone's Throw Hardware & Haberdashery had been everything to this town when Hope was growing up. Her dad had worked there on weekends sometimes. And the lodge, well, Hope loved going to Home Sweet Home Lodge with her mom and Izzie, when the Sisterhood of the Quilt gathered for their monthly get-togethers. But that had been then.

Hope shook her head. "No. He wouldn't reopen his grandparents' businesses. He's probably just coming to Sweet Home to sign papers at the bank, probably get a real estate agent, too . . . if I had to guess."

Izzie slipped off the bed and put her hands on her hips. "Are you finally going to fess up to my namesake—my niece—and tell that child that Donovan is her father?"

Hope shivered. She couldn't imagine telling anyone the truth. Though all of Sweet Home must have a clue.

"No. I'm not going to tell Ella about Donovan. I told you before. Ella thinks her father was an oil worker who lived in the Yukon, that he died in a work-related accident before she was born."

"Are you at least going to tell Donovan that my niece belongs to him?"

"No!" Hope couldn't. Donovan had been crystal clear at his grandmother's funeral. *I never want to see you again.* There had been such vehemence in his voice.

Her last act of love was to respect his wishes. Besides, she didn't want him to hate her more than he already did.

"Donovan might be coming to Sweet Home, but the fact is, my know-it-all little sister, I don't plan to see him at all."

Ready to find
your next great read?

Let us help.

Visit prh.com/nextread